D0954257

"I have decided that I will marry you. . . ." Arabella turned to face Justin, looking at him squarely in his gray eyes.

"Not an ounce of preamble," Justin said, as he picked up Arabella's hand to study her fingers. "Not even a small warning or the barest signal that you were going to blast me out of the water. Would you believe me if I told you that you have just made me the happiest man alive? No, I can see that you won't believe me. Actually, I wouldn't either."

"This has nothing to do with happiness, sir. Why are you looking at my fingers? You're playing with them. They are just fingers. Why?"

"You have lovely fingers. Graceful hands, quite unlike mine. No happiness for us, ma'am?"

"You know very well why we must wed. I am willing to do my part. Are you willing to do yours?"

"Part. An interesting word. There will be many parts for us, ma'am, if we marry. Are you willing to accept me as a man and not just a poor fellow who happens to live in the same house with you?"

"What do you mean exactly?"

He raised her hand to his mouth and kissed each one of her fingers. "A preamble, ma'am."

UNFORGETTABLE ROMANCES FROM CATHERINE COULTER

☐ **LORD HARRY** When Henrietta Rolland discovers that a notorious rake, Jason Cavander, is responsible for her brother's death at Waterloo, she sets out to avenge her dead brother. Henrietta disguises herself as the fictitious Lord Harry Monteith, hoping to fool Cavander and challenge him to a duel. But the time comes when all pretenses are stripped away, as Henrietta and Jason experience how powerful true love can be.   (405919—$5.99)

☐ **THE DUKE** Ian Carmichael, Duke of Portmaine, is the new master of Penderleigh Castle, home of the Robertsons, in Scotland. He's already an English duke and has just been named the Scottish earl of Penderleigh. One look at the duke is enough to set Brandy Robertson's—the old earl's granddaughter—heart aflutter. The problem is the duke is already engaged and if that's not bad enough, someone wants to kill him. One of the embitted Robertsons?   (406176—$6.99)

*Prices slightly higher in Canada

Buy them at your local bookstore or use this convenient coupon for ordering.

PENGUIN USA
P.O. Box 999 — Dept. #17109
Bergenfield, New Jersey 07621

Please send me the books I have checked above.
I am enclosing $_____ (please add $2.00 to cover postage and handling). Send check or money order (no cash or C.O.D.'s) or charge by Mastercard or VISA (with a $15.00 minimum). Prices and numbers are subject to change without notice.

Card #_____ Exp. Date _____
Signature_____
Name_____
Address_____
City _____ State _____ Zip Code _____

For faster service when ordering by credit card call **1-800-253-6476**

Allow a minimum of 4-6 weeks for delivery. This offer is subject to change without notice.

The
HEIR

Catherine
Coulter

A TOPAZ BOOK

TOPAZ
Published by the Penguin Group
Penguin Books USA Inc., 375 Hudson Street,
New York, New York 10014, U.S.A.
Penguin Books Ltd, 27 Wrights Lane,
London W8 5TZ, England
Penguin Books Australia Ltd, Ringwood,
Victoria, Australia
Penguin Books Canada Ltd, 10 Alcorn Avenue,
Toronto, Ontario, Canada M4V 3B2
Penguin Books (N.Z.) Ltd, 182-190 Wairau Road,
Auckland 10, New Zealand

Penguin Books Ltd, Registered Offices:
Harmondsworth, Middlesex, England

Published by Topaz, an imprint of Dutton Signet, a division of Penguin Books
USA Inc. Originally published in somewhat different version in a Signet edition
under the title *Lord Deverill's Heir*.

First Topaz Printing, October, 1996
10 9 8 7

Copyright © Catherine Coulter, 1980, 1996
All rights reserved

Cover art by Gregg Gulbronson

 REGISTERED TRADEMARK—MARCA REGISTRADA

Printed in the United States of America

Without limiting the rights under copyright reserved above, no part of this
publication may be reproduced, stored in or introduced into a retrieval system, or
transmitted, in any form, or by any means (electronic, mechanical, photocopying,
recording, or otherwise), without the prior written permission of both the
copyright owner and the above publisher of this book.

BOOKS ARE AVAILABLE AT QUANTITY DISCOUNTS WHEN USED TO PROMOTE
PRODUCTS OR SERVICES. FOR INFORMATION PLEASE WRITE TO PREMIUM MARKETING
DIVISION, PENGUIN BOOKS USA INC., 375 HUDSON STREET, NEW YORK,
NEW YORK 10014.

If you purchased this book without a cover you should be aware that this book is
stolen property. It was reported as "unsold and destroyed" to the publisher and
neither the author nor the publisher has received any payment for this "stripped
book."

To Anton,
the second time around

1

Magdalaine

Magdalaine lay within herself again, waiting, waiting for the opium to shroud the ravaging pain in her body. She could scarce make out the high vaulted ceiling and the dark oak-paneled walls in the dim winter-afternoon light.

At last the pain is lessening, soon I will be freed from the terrible gnawing that comes from my very soul. Please, let the opium last until the end. God, why did he wait so long to give me the opium? He wanted me to fight, that's why, but finally he realized I didn't want to fight, I didn't want to live.

Was he still beside her? She didn't know. She really didn't care. He had been with her for so very long. He had spoken softly to her, tried to help her, but he hadn't given her the opium until she had screamed at him to let her go, bowing in on herself, ravaged both within and without. Now, she was free from the pain, at last.

My little Elsbeth, my poor baby. But yesterday you toddled to my outstretched arms. Oh, my child, so soon, so very soon you will forget your mama. If only I could hold you to me one more time. Dear God, you will forget me, strangers will take your love, and he will be there, not I. God, if only I could have killed him.

But he will live and I will rot in the damned Deverill family cemetery alone and forgotten.

Silent tears slid from the corners of Magdalaine's dark almond eyes and coursed unchecked down her cheeks, for there were no wrinkles or aged hollows to impede their downward flow. They rested briefly against the raised fullness of her lips before she licked away their salty wetness. She felt the soft touch of material against her lips. Who held it there? It was he, she knew that. But she didn't acknowledge him. It was too late for that. She turned inward again. There seemed so much to regret, so very little to give meaning to her short life.

Come, Magdalaine, savor the small triumphs, the fleeting moments of pleasure. Remember the victories. Why can I not? It is ridiculous to be so helpless, so alone. A cry. It is Elsbeth. Please, Josette, take her from the crib, hold her close. Flow my love into her small body. Comfort her, protect her, for I cannot.

The piercing, angry child's cries stopped. Magdalaine calmed. She tilted her head back onto the lacy pillow and focused her gaze at the darkened oak beams overhead. Elsbeth and Josette were just above her in the nursery. They were so very close to her, just minutes away. Such a short time ago she could have raced up the stairs, her step light and sure, at the sound of her baby's cries.

No, not a short time ago . . . centuries ago. You will only know my tomb, my little one. Only a carved plaque with your mother's name. I will be but cold gray stone and a simple name to you. Aged, lifeless stone pressing down upon me, shrouding me forever.

Magdalaine shifted her weakened eyes to the large gilt-framed painting of Evesham Abbey, hung above the mantelpiece so proudly by the last Earl of Strafford. As if in a trance, her eyes unwavering, Magdalaine stared at the painting. It was as if she was

standing in the green undulating park that surrounded
the red brick house. The magnificent lime trees that
lined the graveled drive shaded the bright sun from her
eyes and the hedges of yew and holly were so vividly
alive that she felt she could reach out and touch them
and feel the very texture of their leaves. She remembered seeing them for the first time so clearly, so very
clearly. Now she wished she had never seen them, had
never come to this cursed house, had never married this
man, this man who was supposed to have saved her,
but of course, that was impossible. But she had married
him and come to this house and now she would pay
for it.

She couldn't seem to look away from the painting.
How very English were the gables and chimney stacks
that rose up the walls and towered beyond the slate
roof. Forty gables; she had counted them. And just beyond the house were the old abbey ruins, crumbling
with eloquent dignity for nearly four hundred years.
Time had etched inexorably into the mortared walls,
tumbling countless stone hulks into characterless
heaps. But still huge walls stood upright, reaching high
into the sky. But one day they would crumble and fall,
too. And all because a king had wanted to divorce his
queen and marry his leman. But she loved the ruins.
Each stone was filled with a past so dark and mysterious that she had at first been afraid to draw near to
them. One of those stones would be hauled to the Strafford cemetery to mark the earth where she would lie.

Magdalaine's opium-clouded mind drew her eyes
away, to the wall opposite the bed, to seek out the
bizarre carved oak panel—*The Dance of Death*, it was
called. A grotesque skeleton, a blunted sword held high
in its bony grip, held dominion over an eerie host of
demonic figures, the gaping hollow of its mouth chant-
ing soundless words.

I am so very cold. Why does not someone build up

the fire? If only I could burrow down into the covers. I'll be colder soon but I won't realize it for I'll be dead.

Once again Magdalaine's eyes swept the room, more slowly now, for an uncontrollable lassitude was dragging her down deeper and deeper. Soon there would be no return journey upward. A slow smile spread its way over her face, creasing her smooth cheeks. It was a precise smile, even a triumphant smile.

I have won a final victory over you, my lord husband. I will defeat you with my death.

The smile froze on her lips forming a ludicrous jagged line. An infant's cry rent the silence.

The bedroom door burst open. "Await me outside. I wish to speak to my wife."

The doctor straightened slowly. A tall man himself, he drew up to his full height, but the Earl of Strafford seemed to dominate the room. His tone was abrupt, his breathing hard and sharp. The doctor did not release the countess's wrist from between his long fingers. He said evenly, "I am sorry, my lord, but that will not be possible."

"Dammit, Branyon, do as I tell you. I want to be alone with my wife. I have questions for her and it is time she answered them. Leave us alone, man. It is my right."

As the earl strode toward the bed, the doctor saw that his regular features were distorted into a mask of fear and rage. The two together—it was strange and inexplicable, but it was so.

The doctor gently lowered the countess's hand under the covers at her side. The simple movement gave him time to control his anger at the man he'd hated since the moment he had seen how he had treated his gentle wife. He said quietly, "I am sorry, my lord, but her ladyship is beyond words. She is gone, my lord, but a few minutes ago. She did not suffer at the end. Her passing was painless."

"No! Dammit, no!" The earl rushed at the doctor to fling him away.

The doctor quickly stepped aside. He stood silently as the earl gazed mutely down at his wife's calm pale face, as he took her hand and shook it. Dr. Branyon placed his hand firmly upon the earl's arm. "The countess is dead, my lord. There is naught either of us can do for her now. As I said, her passing was without suffering."

The earl stood motionless by the bedside for a long while. Finally he turned and said more to himself than to the doctor, "It is unfortunate. I did not get to her in time. I have lost. Damnation. Those lying French bastards. It is not fair." Without again looking at his dead wife, the earl turned abruptly and left the room, his boots ringing sharp and loud on the oak floor.

2

Ann

EVESHAM ABBEY, 1792

Four people stood around the writhing naked woman on the sweat-soaked sheets. The doctor had thrown his coat to a tabletop many hours before, his full white shirt was now loose about his neck and wrists. Fine lines of fatigue drew his mouth taut, and beads of perspiration stood out on his smooth forehead. He was a young man, but the young girl on the bed was younger, barely eighteen. And her life was in his hands.

The bleary-eyed midwife and housekeeper kept silent vigil at the foot of the bed, their hands dangling helplessly at their sides.

It was ghastly hot, so stifling that the woman in her ceaseless misery had thrown off the cover, uncaring that her swollen body was exposed to these people. She was beyond thinking, almost beyond the searing pain that receded quickly, only to explode with greater ferocity within her belly, tearing hoarse screams from her parched throat.

She lay now gasping for breath, her senses momentarily returned to her, as the agonizing pain waited for its next inevitable onslaught on her body. She gazed up at the doctor, her large blue eyes glazed with fear and suffering.

He leaned over her and wiped rivulets of sweat from her brow. He put a glass to her lips. "Drink the water,

Lady Ann. That's it. No, not so fast. I will hold it for you as long as you wish. Drink slowly."

When she had drunk her fill, he said quietly, "Lady Ann, you must try harder. You must bear down with all your strength when I tell you to. Do you understand me?"

She licked her tongue over her cracked lips and whimpered, a helpless sound, but she was helpless, held captive of her body and the forces that no one could stop. She wanted desperately to detach herself from her gross child-filled body. She sought his steady dark eyes and wished herself a part of him. So intense was her longing that he felt that part of her that was the laughing, gentle girl burn into the very depth of his being. His voice faltered as he knelt beside her and clasped her limp fingers in his hands. "Lady Ann, please, you cannot, you must not give up. Please, help yourself, help me. I know you can do it. You are strong. You want to live. You will do it, you must do it. You will birth your babe."

A horrible shriek tore from her throat and she was lost to him, consumed back within her body as the vicious contractions tore through her belly.

He quickly eased his hand inside her, felt the baby's head, and shouted at her, "Push! Now, bear down!" He hesitated only the briefest moment, then splayed his fingers over her belly, and pushed downward with all his strength.

Her scream and the baby's cry came together, burning into the very depths of him.

The doctor walked softly into the earl's library and stood wearily in the dim-curtained room. "You've a girl, my lord. I congratulate you. She is in your image. Your wife is very weak but she will live."

He stood there, so tired, he wondered why he didn't fall over, waiting for the earl to speak. The earl brushed careless fingers over his immaculate waist-coat, eyed the blood-flecked white shirt of the doctor with distaste, and said indifferently, "A girl, eh, Branyon? Ah, well, it is but her first. She still has many years of youth to bear me sons. I fancy I will have my son within the next year. Aye, ladies love babies. She'll want another very soon. This weakness, it's non-sense. She'll forget about this by the end of the week, if the babe survives, of course. Many do not. Elsbeth did, but perhaps this one won't. Who knows?"

Angry bile rose in the doctor's throat. Hadn't the man heard his wife's screams? They'd been endless. The face of every servant in this huge mansion was leached of color. Surely the earl, her husband, had heard her. Surely he had been at least a bit concerned about her.

The doctor would never forget her suffering. He wanted to kill this man, not for making her pregnant, but for not caring if she survived or didn't. It was one and the same to him, the bastard. Yes, he wanted to kill him. Very much. Maybe shoot him cleanly between the eyes. However, he couldn't. He managed to control himself, saying in his detached professional voice, al-though he really wanted to shout it, "I'm afraid that it will not be possible, my lord." He paused, seeing the earl's face darken. It was a handsome face, a strong in-telligent face, and Dr. Branyon hated that face as much as he hated the man. Ah, but he was delighting in this news he had for this damned man. "You see, my lord, Lady Ann very nearly lost her life birthing your daugh-ter. When I said she will live, I meant it was very close. She nearly bled her life away." He paused a moment, relishing the words even before he spoke them. He said finally, "She will be unable to bear you further chil-dren."

The earl roared to his feet, shouting, "The devil you say, Branyon! Why, the girl is but eighteen years of age! Her mother assured me that her hips were wide, that she would be an excellent breeder. I even spanned her belly myself and although she is small, her pelvic bones were beyond my reach. Her mother has borne six children, four of them boys. Damnation, I selected her because of her youth and her mother's assurances. I will not tolerate this. You must be wrong."

Her parents had let this man touch their daughter? Let him put his hands on her belly? Jesus, it made him sick. "Unfortunately, my lord, the lady's years make very little difference, nor do the width of her hips. She will bear no more children, either boy or girl." *God, how I hate this man. I am the keeper of life, yet I want to kill him. My poor Ann . . . you are nothing to him, just as Magdalaine was nothing. And now he has another daughter to ignore, perhaps even to send away. At least you will not have to suffer him again.*

The earl turned abruptly away from the doctor and cursed long and fluently. He did not hear the doctor leave the library to return to the upstairs bedchamber, to keep vigil over his wife.

3

Arabella

Sir Ralph Wigston peered over his spectacles as he droned on with his duly practiced, and, hopefully, elegant phrases of condolence. He had painstakingly committed the brief message from the Ministry to memory, believing that he owed the mental effort required not only to the earl's lovely widow, but also to the Earl of Strafford himself.

The late earl had been a splendid man, renowned for his powerful intelligence, his uncanny ability to read the enemy's mind and act immediately upon his intuition to his majesty's advantage. He willingly took risks where other men would have wavered and backed away. He had been bold, dauntless, and had died as befitted such a fine leader of men, in battle, leading, shouting orders and encouragement. Proud he was, very proud and unbending, and a determined autocrat, demanding unswerving obedience, but, of course, that was as it should be. He was a man to trust, a man to revere, a man to follow with unquestioned loyalty. His men had worshiped him. He would be missed sorely.

But now the Earl of Strafford was dead, and Sir Ralph had to continue his passionate performance for his widow, who looked particularly beautiful in her black mourning gown. He did not wish to be accused of according the late Earl of Strafford less than his very best. Nor his beloved widow.

He cleared his throat, for this was more difficult. "We do, however, regret to inform you, my dear Lady Ann, that the earl's remains have not as yet been recovered from the conflagration that ensued."

"Are you not then being premature with your visit, Sir Ralph? Is it not very possible that my father still lives?"

The words were spoken with a cold flatness, and underlying them, Sir Ralph sensed a flicker of hope, almost a challenge to his authority and position. He carefully stored away his few remaining phrases and bent his myopic gaze upon the Earl of Strafford's daughter, Lady Arabella. She didn't resemble her mother at all. She was the very image of her father, with her inky black hair and light gray eyes. He cleared his throat. "My dear young lady, let me hasten to inform you that I would most certainly not be executing this most unhappy mission were your father's demise not a proven fact." He had spoken too harshly, and hurried to soften his tone. "I am truly sorry, Lady Ann, Lady Arabella, but there were trustworthy witnesses whose word cannot be gainsaid. Exhaustive searches were done. Countless men were interviewed." He wouldn't talk about all the charred remains that had been duly examined. "There is no doubt that the earl died in the fire. It was an overwhelming fire. There was no chance of survival. Please, do not entertain the idea that there is a chance he still lives, for it is quite impossible."

"I see." Again that cold, emotionless voice. Sir Ralph disposed of his remaining phrases neatly and quickly. "The Prince Regent wishes me to assure you, Lady Ann, that there is no question of the speedy disposition of the earl's estate, in view of the reliability of the witnesses. I will, if you wish it, notify your solicitor of this tragic circumstance."

"No!" the earl's daughter bounded from her chair, her hands clenched in front of her.

Sir Ralph stiffened, frowning at the earl's daughter. What was she about? What was all this nonsense? Did not her mother, this lovely fragile lady, have any control over her?

Lady Ann said, her voice far too gentle for Sir Ralph's liking, "My dear Arabella, surely it would be best if Sir Ralph did contact your father's solicitor. After all, there is so very much for us to do already."

"No, Mother." Arabella turned cold gray eyes to Sir Ralph's flushed face. The earl's eyes, there was no doubt about that. And that coldness of hers, just like the late earl's. Yes, this damned impertinent girl probably also had her late father's arrogance, not that Sir Ralph would ever say that the late earl did not deserve every whit of arrogance he chose to exhibit.

"We appreciate your kindness, Sir Ralph, but it is for us—my mother and me—to make whatever arrangements are now necessary. Please extend our gratitude to the Prince Regent. His words would touch the coldest of hearts."

Now, what did that mean? Sir Ralph did not appreciate irony. It annoyed him. He disliked having to decipher it, having to puzzle over it only to discover that no irony at all had ever been intended. But what had come to him loud and quite clear was that the damned girl was dismissing him. Him! To give himself time so he wouldn't box the girl's ears, Sir Ralph slowly pulled off his spectacles and raised his ample bulk equally as slowly from the chair.

Arabella rose also, and to Sir Ralph's chagrin, her cold gray eyes were on a level with his. She had winter eyes, he thought, as cold and harsh as her father's. He wondered if they ever warmed, as he had once seen her father's warm when he had touched a very lovely young courtesan's exquisite white shoulder. He shouldn't remember something like that, particularly in the widow's presence. He would forget it, now.

The daughter extended a slender hand. Her voice was clipped, yet even the most ardent of sticklers would have found no fault with her. "Thank you, Sir Ralph. As you can see, the news has been quite a shock to my mother. If you will forgive us, I really must see to her needs now. I will have Russell show you out."

He found himself reacting to her just as he would have to her father. He moved quickly. He spoke in his most conciliatory voice. "Yes, yes, of course. My dear Lady Ann, if there is anything I can do, anything to relieve you of the burdens that now afflict you, do not hesitate to call upon me. I will be here instantly to assist you." And he was thinking, *just as long as this bitch of a daughter isn't with you.* He preferred his women gentle, soft-spoken, and obedient. Like Lady Ann. But then, he wondered, why had the earl kept a mistress in London, a mistress in Brussels, and frequented brothels in Portugal, from all Sir Ralph had heard. Ah, but a fragile creature like Lady Ann surely wouldn't be expected to service such a demanding man, as the late earl surely was. As for the daughter, he would admit that she was beautiful, ah, but so cold, so forthright, so unconciliatory.

The countess had averted her face and did not rise. Only a slight nodding of her fair head acknowledged his words. By all that was holy, she was exquisite. He really didn't want to leave her, but he had no choice, not with that dragon of a daughter looking at him as if she'd like to chop him into small pieces with a knife she doubtless carried at her waist.

"Good-bye, Sir Ralph," Arabella said, her voice as wintry as her father's eyes.

Again, he thought regretfully that he would have liked to clasp the small trembling hands of the countess in his own, to assure her that he would protect her, comfort her, share her grief, not that the late Earl of Strafford had afforded him all that attention, the earl having paid very little attention to anyone he did not deem worthy of killing the French. He was not, however, in a position to carry out his wishes. He looked unwillingly away from the beautiful countess into the set, unsmiling face of the late earl's daughter.

As the parlor door closed with a snap behind him, he was again struck with the thought that the earl's daughter was molded in his very image. Their physical likeness was striking—the same ink-black hair and dark arched brows set above haughty, arrogant gray eyes. But it was not simply their physical similarities. How very alike in temperament they were. Proud, autocratic, and most damnably capable. Even though Sir Ralph was displeased at being dismissed by an eighteen-year-old girl, he felt it rather a pity that the girl could not have been born a boy. From what he had just witnessed, she could have most ably filled her father's position.

The Countess of Strafford raised wide blue eyes to her daughter's fine-featured face. "Really, my dearest, were you not a bit harsh with poor Sir Ralph? You must know he meant well. He was trying to spare both of us unnecessary pain."

"My father need not be dead now," Arabella said in a cold flat voice. "Such a stupid waste. Stupid, stupid war to appease the ridiculous greed of stupid men. Dear God, could there be anything more unjust?" She flung away her mother's open arms and pounded her fists against the paneled wall.

My poor foolish child. You will not let me comfort you, for you are too much like him. You grieve for a man whose very existence made mine an endless misery. Is there no part of me in you? Poor Arabella, to shed tears is not to be despicable and weak.

"Arabella, where are you going?" The countess rose quickly and hurried after her daughter.

"To see Brammersley, father's solicitor. Surely you know who he is, Mother. He has tried to flirt with you every time Father has been out of England, the inept buffoon. Damnation, I detest dealing with him, but Father trusted him, more's the pity. Speaking of buffoons, I do not believe the Ministry sent Sir Ralph. Goodness, I thought he would try to seduce you right here."

"Seduce me? Sir Ralph? That paunchy old man?"

"Yes, Mama," Arabella said with great patience. "Are you blind?"

"I noticed nothing amiss with Sir Ralph's presentation. He was quite proper. But, dearest, surely you are in no fit condition to go out now. Surely you would wish a cup of tea? Perhaps a rest in your bedchamber? Perhaps, although it is a bit far-fetched, you might even like to talk to me, Arabella?"

"I am not tired or weak or lily-livered," Arabella said over her shoulder. "I always talk to you, Mother. We speak at least three or four times every day." But she didn't slow. She was consumed with bitter, raging anger and boundless, helpless energy. She was suddenly pulled from her own pain at the sight of her mother's pale, pinched face. "Oh, God, I am such a beast." She dashed a hand across her forehead. She would not cry. She would not. Her father would send a lightning bolt down to dash her to the dirt if she cried. "Mother, you will be all right without me, will you not? Please, it is something I must do. I could not bear that Father not be given a proper service before there is any disposition of his estates. I will make the arrangements to leave London. We must return to Evesham Abbey, I will see to it, I must see to it. You do understand, do you not?"

The countess held the stormy gray eyes in a steady

gaze and said slowly, with only a hint of sadness, "Yes, my love, I understand. I shall be quite all right. Go now, Arabella, and do what you must."

The countess felt immeasurably older than her thirty-six years. It was with an effort of will that she dragged herself to the front bow window and sank down into a winged chair. Thick gray fog swirled about the house, twining itself about tree branches and obscuring the green grass in the small park opposite the house.

She saw John Coachman holding the skittish horses. And there was Arabella crossing the flagstone in her long, sure stride, looking dismal in her black gown and cloak. Arabella would arrange everything and no one would know that her determined, implacable energy cloaked a despairing grief.

Perhaps it is better that she will not even seek comfort from me. For then I, too, would have to feign sorrow. She cannot even see that his death means only the end of my imprisonment. Her furious energy will burn out her grief. It is just as well. Dear Elsbeth, innocent elfin child. Like me, you are now to be freed. I must write you, for now you belong at Evesham Abbey. Now you may return to your home, to Magdalaine's home. Such a short time you lived, Magdalaine. But your daughter will know my care. I will take care of her, Magdalaine, I promise you that. Thank you, God. He is gone. Forever.

The countess rose from her chair with such a spurt of activity that her blond curls trembled about her face. She threw back her head and walked purposefully to a small writing desk in the corner of the parlor. It was a curiously odd gesture, one of confidence, reborn as if by instinct after eighteen years. With crisp, almost cheerful movements, she dipped the quill into the ink pot and plied her hand to a sheet of elegant stationery.

4

EVESHAM ABBEY, 1810

Lucifer's massive hooves sent loose gravel pitching from the lime tree-bordered drive. The rhythmic, powerful beat brought little comfort to his rider.

Arabella turned in the saddle and looked back toward her home. Evesham Abbey stood proudly in the hazy morning light, its sun-baked red brick walls extending upward to innumerable chimney stacks and gables. There were forty gables in all; she had counted them. As a child of eight she had eagerly announced this arithmetic feat to her father, received a startled look, a hearty laugh, and a powerful hug that had left her small, sturdy ribs bruised until Michaelmas Day.

So many years ago. And now there was nothing. Nothing at all, except those forty gables. And they would remain until well after she was dead.

They had buried an empty coffin in the marbled family vault. After the women, save for Arabella, had left the cemetery, four of her father's farmers heaved a huge stone slab over the coffin and the local smithy set about his painstaking job of chipping and hewing out fragments of stone, leaving in the indentations the earl's name and titles and the years that marked his life. The empty coffin rested beside Magdalaine's, the earl's first wife. It chilled Arabella to see the empty

cavern to the other side of her father's coffin, destined
for her mother.

She had stood in quiet command, stiff and cold as
the marble wall behind her, until finally the smithy's
ringing hammer and chisel ceased their monotonous
echoing.

Arabella guided Lucifer off the graveled drive onto a
narrow footpath that wound through the home wood to
the small fishpond that nestled like an exquisite circular gem set amidst the green oak and maple forest. The
day was too warm for the heavy velvet riding habit.
The morning sun baked through the stark black material, plastering her chemise to her skin. Only a splash of
white about her neck broke the somberness of her
dress. Even the soft lawn ruffles about her throat made
her skin itch.

Arabella slid off Lucifer's muscular back and tethered him to a low sturdy yew tree. She hadn't bothered
with a saddle. She remembered clearly how her father
had drawn her aside one day when she was no more
than twelve years old, and told her he didn't want to
take a chance on losing her, not when she was the best
rider for her size in the county. Side saddles were death
traps. He would not allow her to hunt in a side saddle.
She could pose on one while an artist painted her, but
that was all. She would ride astride or she would ride
bareback.

She lifted her skirts from the wet morning grass and
walked slowly about the edge of the still water to the
far side, careful not to tread on the long, silken water
reeds. They were beautiful, those reeds. The thought of
trampling them was anathema to her.

What a blessed relief to escape from all those black-
garbed visitors, with their long, unsmiling faces, nodding and bowing and reciting in low, doleful voices
their mechanical phrases of sympathy. She marveled at
how graciously her mother moved among them in her

black rustling widow's weeds, all in the latest style, of course, seemingly tireless, her charm and smile perhaps a bit brittle, but there and well in place. Lady Ann always knew exactly what was expected and executed every duty to perfection. Only Suzanne Talgarth, Arabella's best friend from her earliest childhood, had pulled her aside, said nothing at all, and hugged her close.

Arabella paused a moment to listen to the baleful croaking of a lone frog, hidden from her view in the thick reeds. As she bent down with a graceful swish of her black skirts, she chanced to spot a patch of black, quite at variance with the myriad shades of green, in a cluster of reeds but a few feet away from her. She forgot the frog, and with a frown furrowing her brow, moved slowly and quietly forward.

She carefully parted a throng of reeds and found herself staring down at a sleeping man, stretched out his full length on his back, his arms pillowed behind his head. He wore no coat, only black breeches, black top boots, and a white frilled lawn shirt that was loose and open about his neck. She looked more closely at his face, calm and expressionless in sleep, and started back with a swallowed cry of surprise. It was as though she were looking at herself in a mirror, so alike were their features. His curling raven hair was cut close above his smooth brow. Distinctive black brows flared upward in a proud arch, then sloped gently toward the temples. His mouth was full, as was hers, and his high cheekbones accentuated his straight Roman nose. His chin was firm, stubborn. She was certain that his nostrils flared when he was angry. She had dimples. She wondered when he smiled if he had dimples, too. No, he looked too stern a man to have something so whimsical. Naturally, the dimples did not suit her either. She had never even entertained the notion that she was beautiful, but looking at him, she thought he was the most beautiful man she had ever seen.

"You cannot be real," she whispered, still staring down at the man, wondering, yet knowing who he must be. Then as the reason for his presence hit her, she cursed. "You damned bastard!" She was yelling now, so furious she was shaking with it. "You miserable scrap of filth! Wake up and get off my land before I shoot you! I might still whip you to within an inch of your miserable life!" She stopped then because she didn't have her pistol with her. It didn't matter. She still had her riding crop. She brought it up.

The man's heavily fringed black lashes parted slowly, and she found herself gazing into her own upward-tilted gray eyes. His were just a bit darker than hers, as were her father's. Dear God, but he was beautiful, more so than her father.

"My word," the man said slowly, his voice as smooth as a stone at the bottom of a creek. He did not move, but narrowed his eyes against the glare of the sun to take in the flushed and furious face above him.

"I declare, it is a *lady* I see. Look at those white hands, never done a day's work in her life. Yes, doubtless it is a lady. But where, I wonder, is the tavern wench who spoke such foul curses at me? She wants to shoot me? She wants to whip me? Certainly, this is a dramatic situation better suited for Drury Lane."

He spoke well, like a gentleman. No matter. She continued to search his face, unmoved. There was a deep cleft in his chin that she did not have, and he was tanned, with a pirate's dark face. She had always hated pirates. No, she wouldn't let this man anger her. She asked, her voice as arrogant as her father's had ever been, "Just who the devil are you?"

Still he did not shift his position, just lay there, stretched out at her feet, as indolent as a lizard on a sunny rock. But he was grinning at her now, showing strong white teeth. She saw then that his gray eyes were flecked with pale gold lights. It was an odd distraction. Neither she nor her father had that. She was glad. She decided it looked common, those pale gold lights.

"Do you always talk like a slut off the back streets?" he asked in a calm easy voice, bringing himself up to rest on his elbows. Those eyes of his were deep and clear, and there was an intelligence in them that she recognized and hated.

"The way I choose to talk to an insolent ruffian lazing about on Deverill land cannot be questioned by the likes of you." She brought her riding crop up from her side and slapped the leather thongs lightly against her black-gloved hand.

"Ah, am I now to be whipped?"

"It is very possible. I asked you a question, but your reason for not answering now occurs to me." She stared at him thoughtfully and felt a sickening tightness in her chest. But she'd been taught to face even the most unpleasant things straight on, with no shying away. "You are obviously a bastard—my father's bastard. You cannot be so blind as not to notice the great similarity between our features, and I am the very image of my father." She averted her face, unwilling to let him see her pain. Tears burned her eyes. Yes, she was the image of her father, but not the right sex. Poor father, he had not the good fortune to beget a son in wedlock. But he'd gotten a bastard son. She turned wintry eyes back to his face and said bleakly, "I wonder if there are others like you. If there are, I only pray that they do not all resemble him as closely as you do. I always wished for a brother, for now, you see, my father's line will die out. I am only a female and thus not acceptable. I have never believed it fair."

"Perhaps it isn't fair, but it is the way things are. As for a bastard of your father's so closely resembling him, it would seem unlikely to me. But you appear to be in a better position to know of such matters than I. What, however, does seem likely is that if the earl sired children out of wedlock, they would have the good sense not to show their faces here." He spoke with calm matter-of-factness, sensing her hurt. He rose unhurriedly to his feet to face her. He didn't want to frighten her. He didn't want her to feel threatened by him. That would happen soon enough.

"But you are here." She was forced to look up as she spoke. "Damn you to hell, you are even of his size. Dear God, how can you come here at such a time? Have you no sense of honor, no sense of decency? My father is dead and yet here you are, acting as if you belong here."

"You question my honor. I wish you would not do that. I do have some, so it is said of me."

She felt a terrible urge to slash his face with her riding crop. He stepped toward her, looming over her head, blocking the sun. Her nostrils flared and her eyes darkened, mirroring her violent intent.

"Don't do it, my dear," he said, his voice as quiet and gentle as a summer rain.

"I am not your dear," she said, so angry with him, with herself, she backed away from him. Her eyes narrowed and she said with cold cruelty lacing her words, "You need not tell me your purpose for being here. I am a fool not to have guessed sooner. My father's bastard, come for the reading of his will. You have no more honor than that croaking toad over there. Do you think to be acknowledged, to be given some of my father's money?" She was shaking with anger, shaking with frustration, for he was the larger, larger than even her father, and she wasn't a man and thus couldn't beat him into the dirt. Ah, and she wanted to. She wanted to pound him. She wanted to grind him beneath her heel. She sensed his indifference to her as he leaned down, brushed twigs and grass blades from his breeches, and picked up his coat. She hated him for his indifference.

"Yes," he said slowly, as he rose, "I am here for the reading of the earl's will."

"God, you are damnable, unspeakable!"

"What venom from such a lovely mouth," he said mildly as he shrugged into his coat. "Tell me, gentle lady, has no man yet taken you in hand? Perhaps taken that lovely throat between his hands and forced you to pay attention to his words? No, I can see that you have run wild, that you have been allowed to do just as you please with no regard to others and what they may be thinking or feeling." He took a step toward her. "Perhaps I could be convinced to bring you to some sort of obedience. You do want taming. Perhaps I could even bring myself to thrash you."

Joy filled her. He had threatened her. He was as vulgar and common as she had first believed. She said almost jovially, "Come here, you bastard, and let me show you what a lady can do." She took a sudden step to her right, waving her hand at him, taunting him, motioning for him to come to her.

But he didn't move. His left eyebrow shot up a good inch, making the arch more arrogant, just as her father's eyebrows had done, particularly when he had spoken in that cold indifferent way to his wife, to Arabella's mother. No, she wouldn't think about that. Surely when her father had done that, her mother had done something to provoke it. Yes, certainly. It had happened rarely. It had been nothing.

"If I am a bastard, then you must be the ill-begotten daughter of a fishmonger. As to my coming near to you, why, I can think of little else that would give me lesser pleasure. You think to strike me with the riding crop? I recommend that you think carefully before you raise that crop to me. I am larger than you and I am a man. I do caution you to exercise caution."

"I have thought through everything very carefully. You are a coward."

"You are very lucky that you are female," he said finally, and then he laughed, fully and richly, and she saw that he had dimples, as deep as hers, in each cheek.

"Yes," he said, looking at her up and down, insulting her with that male assessing look, and knowing it. "One would almost think that you wished me to wrest that riding crop from you and give you a sound thrashing. Are you one of those females who enjoy rough play?"

"You try it and I will see you in Hell." It dawned on her with something of a shock that she no longer held the reins of control. She knew a moment of uncertainty about herself. Because she could not bear to feel the weaker, her anger twisted and knotted inside her. She clutched the riding crop in her hand so tightly that a stab of pain shot up her fingers.

No, she wouldn't let him have control. She forced herself to loosen her grip on the riding crop. "Get off my land," she said, her voice as autocratic as her father's had been when military men had come to Evesham Abbey to speak to him on war matters.

"Your land? Though you have the manners and tongue of an ill-bred, spoiled young man, you surely cannot mean to lay claim to the earl's title? No, you cannot do that."

He unwittingly struck at the festering wound deep within her, laying it open, raw and ugly. She was filled with the despair of failure, with the old hatred of herself for not being born a boy, her father's heir, her father's pride. A curse lay leaden on her tongue. She whipped back her head, drew upon a reserve of strength unique to herself, and said with dignity that took him off his guard, for it sat strangely upon the shoulders of one so young, "I suppose it is now my mother's land. Unfortunately, my father did not have a son, as I said earlier, nor did his younger brother, Thomas. It grieves me as it must have grieved him, for his title must become extinct. My father was not blessed in the sex of his offspring."

Admirable, he thought. Dear God, she was beautiful, now more beautiful than she had been five minutes before. Aloud he said easily, "Don't reproach yourself for being a woman. Surely you cannot imagine that the fault somehow lies within you. Your father was more proud of you than he would have been of a dozen sons." He felt a stirring of compassion for her, for the leap of hope in her gray eyes, eyes so much like his. He didn't like it.

Lady Arabella, daughter of the late Earl of Strafford was back again, her voice filled with contempt. "You could hardly know what my father felt. He would not have recognized you. If you ever saw him, it was only at a distance. If he did sire you, he would have never allowed you to come near Evesham Abbey, near his wife, near me, his daughter. My father was honorable. He was faithful to his wife. He held honor dear."

He wanted to tell her that what she'd said hadn't made a lot of sense, but he said only, "As you will."

Arabella stiffened rigid as an oak sapling. He was dismissing her? She sensed in him a habit of command, the easy use of authority, the confidence of a man used to being obeyed, but surely that couldn't be right. He was probably exactly what he looked like—a pirate and a rogue, a man who lived by his wits, a man who cared little for anyone, in short, her father's bastard.

She said calmly, "I bid you good-bye. I only hope that your sense of honor will prohibit your presence at Evesham Abbey. It would cause my mother great pain were you to intrude upon her grief. If you have any decency at all, you will stay away." Would he think she was begging him? God, surely not. She shouted, "Stay away! I order you to stay away from my home!"

She turned from him abruptly and strode with the
long strides of a man away from him. She paused, and
turned back to him. "As a bastard, you should speak to
my father's solicitor. Perhaps he left something for
you, a token, perhaps. Had I been he, I wouldn't have
left you anything." She turned on her heel again and
walked quickly away. She tasted victory; she had taken
control from him at the end. She had that, at least.

He stood in thoughtful silence, staring after her.
"No," he said quietly, lightly tapping his gloves against
his open hand, "my presence won't cause your mother
pain. But you will suffer, Lady Arabella. You are perhaps more arrogant than your father, though that is a
very close call. You are damnably proud, but still, I am
sorry for it."

There was only silence save for the gentle rustling of
the thin-armed water reeds.

5

Lady Ann sat between her daughter and Elsbeth, her stepdaughter, her shoulders hunched slightly forward and her ivory hands clasped tightly in her lap. The heavy black veils hung about her face, obscuring the smooth plaits of blond hair and weighing down her back so that she could no longer sit board-straight. She was hot and wished only that it were evening so she could be alone in the curtain-drawn coolness of her bedchamber, out of the wretched black clothing that shrouded her from head to toe.

George Brammersley, solicitor to her late husband, had arrived only yesterday in one of the earl's crested carriages; now he arranged himself with his usual show of dignity behind the great oak library desk. Lady Ann watched as he dallied, first polishing the small circles of his glasses, then settling them with practiced ease on the bridge of his vein-lined hawk nose. He slowly spread a sheaf of papers before him on the top of the desk, arranging them first one way and then another. His rheumy old eyes studiously avoided the three women. Lady Ann longed for a brush to smooth down the unruly wisps of gray frazzled hair that stood about his scalp at odd angles. He was a very old friend of her late husband's. She had always felt sorry for him. Now, she wished she could spare him, but she knew she wouldn't be able to.

She could feel a mounting intensity in Arabella's

body, now too thin since she had not eaten much of anything since they had been informed of her father's death. Lady Ann knew that Arabella wouldn't hold herself in check much longer. She knew, too, that her daughter viewed the reading of her father's will as the irrevocable recognition of his death. There could be no more questions, no more doubts, no more hope.

She knew that soon Arabella's control would crack under the strain of Mr. Brammersley's delay. She sought for words to whisper to her daughter. Not comforting words, for Arabella would never accept those from anyone. Just words that were commonplace, words that would mayhap distract her, words that would send her mind for just a brief moment in another direction.

Lady Ann was too late. Arabella sprang from her seat and strode to the desk. She leaned toward Mr. Brammersley, her hands splayed on the desk, hands covered with black mittens.

She whispered with ferocious calm, "I do not wish you to delay further, sir. I do not know your reason for tarrying in this ridiculous manner, but I will not have it. My mother grows weary, if you have not sense enough in your head to see it. Read my father's will now, else I shall relieve you of the responsibility and do it myself."

The red veins on Mr. Brammersley's nose seemed to stand out even more and seemed to grow like a fine-webbed network to his wizened cheeks. He sucked in his breath, outraged, and looked toward Lady Ann. She nodded to him wearily. He assumed a dignified position, thrusting his receding chin out over his shirt points, cleared his throat, and said, "My dear Lady Arabella, if you will please return to your seat, we will begin the reading."

"A miracle has visited us," Arabella said, not masking the contempt in her voice. "Get on with it, sir." She

returned to her chair. Lady Ann didn't have the energy
to reprimand her. She felt a flutter of apprehensive
movement at her right, and turned a gentle smile
to Elsbeth. Taking a small hand in hers, Lady Ann
squeezed it. Shy Elsbeth, as different from her half-
sister as was a sword from a pen, not that Elsbeth could
write all that well. That made Lady Ann smile behind
her black veils. Odd the thoughts one had at the most
inappropriate moments.

George Brammersley grabbed an impressive document, smoothed down the first page and said, "It is an
unhappy occasion that brings us together this day. The
untimely demise of John Latham Everhard Deverill,
sixth Earl of Strafford, has touched us all—his family,
his friends, those in his employ, and above all, his
country. His courageous sacrifice of his life, so self-
lessly and gallantly offered to preserve the rights of
Englishmen . . ."

There was a flutter of movement, and Arabella felt a
light brush of air on the back of her neck. She realized
the library door had opened then closed. She didn't
care. Nothing mattered now. Maybe it was a magistrate
come to remove George Brammersley, thank the good
Lord. No, not now. Now, at least, Brammersley was
getting on with it. There was a sudden new crispness to
his voice, but she didn't care. At last he was doing as
she had bade him to.

Lady Ann shifted gracefully in her chair and gazed
from the corner of her eye toward the library door. She
turned back, drew a determined breath, and straightened, her face straight forward, now looking neither to
her left nor to her right.

". . . and to the faithful Deverill butler, Josiah Crupper, I bequeath the sum of five hundred pounds, with
the hope that he will remain with the family until such
time as . . ."

He droned on and on, mentioning, it seemed to

Arabella, the name of every servant in her father's employ, both past, present, and future. How she itched for all of it to be over and done with.

Mr. Brammersley paused in his reading, raised thoughtful eyes to Elsbeth, and allowed a tight smile to crease the corners of his mouth. His voice softened and he read more slowly, speaking very clearly and precisely, "To my daughter Elsbeth Maria, born of my first wife, Magdalaine Henriette de Trécassis, I bequeath the sum of ten thousand pounds for her sole and private use."

Well done of you, Father, thought Arabella. She turned at the gasp of surprise from her half-sister and saw her lovely dark almond eyes widen with disbelief, then with barely suppressed excitement. Ah, yes, it was very well done. Arabella had no idea why Elsbeth hadn't been raised with her. She'd always trusted her father implicitly, and when he'd said simply that Elsbeth didn't want to be here, that she preferred living with her aunt, she had believed him. And now he had left her a rich young lady. She was pleased.

Mr. Brammersley chewed furiously at his lower lip, guiltily aware that he had violated a professional trust. But the final statement the earl had written about his gentle eldest daughter had seemed so malevolent, so unnecessarily cruel, that he could not bring himself to say the words. What had the earl meant in any case— "that she, unlike her whore of a mother and the rapacious de Trécassis family, will honestly and freely bestow this promised sum on her future husband." Yes, what had the earl meant? No, he wouldn't read that, not here, not now, not ever.

Arabella pulled her attention back to Mr. Brammersley and waited, impatiently tapping her fingers on the arm of her chair. She assumed that now would come her father's instructions for holding his estates in trust for her until her twenty-first birthday. She hoped her mother would be named her primary trustee. But she knew a profound sadness. There was no male relative to assume the title.

George Brammersley looked down resolutely at the finely written script in his hands. Dash it all, he had to get it over and done with. He read, "My final wishes I have weighed with careful deliberation for the past several years. The conditions that I attach to them are binding and absolute. The seventh Earl of Strafford, Justin Everhard Morley Deverill, grandnephew of the fifth Earl of Strafford, through his brother, Timothy Popham Morley, is my heir, and I bequeath to him my entire worldly fortune, whose primary assets include Evesham Abbey, its land and rents . . ."

The room spun. Arabella stared at Brammersley, his words hanging about her, but yet she couldn't take them in, couldn't make sense of them. The *seventh* Earl of Strafford? Some sort of grandnephew of her grandfather? No one had ever told her that any such grandnephew existed. God, there must be some sort of mistake. This man wasn't even here. Surely there was no such male. Suddenly there was a stirring in her memory of the opening and closing of the library door. Almost reluctantly she turned in her chair and met the cool gray eyes of the man she had seen only that morning by the fishpond. Her absolute astonishment held her silent and still. He wasn't a bastard, the wretched bastard wasn't an actual bastard. He was real. It was all she could think of, all that made any sense to her. He merely nodded to her politely, nothing in his calm expression to betray that he had even met her.

"Arabella, Arabella." Lady Ann gently shook her daughter's sleeve. "Come, my dear, you must listen carefully now. Please, Arabella, you must pay attention. I'm sorry, but you must, dearest."

Arabella turned back in her chair, gazed with dumb shock at her mother and then at the solicitor, whose lined cheeks had taken on a sudden purplish hue. He read in a faltering voice, "The following stipulations are binding to both my heir and to my daughter, Arabella Elaine." He looked like he would have an apoplectic fit, but then he managed to right himself. He drew a deep breath, and said, "It has always been my fondest wish that my daughter, through her body, would continue the proud heritage of the Deverill line. To encourage her in my wishes, I stipulate that she must wed her second cousin, the seventh Earl of Strafford, within two months of my death in order to retain her wealth and position. Should she refuse to follow my wishes within this stated time, she is to forfeit any and all monetary claims to the Deverill estates. If the seventh Earl of Strafford disinclines to wed with his second cousin, Arabella Elaine, he will take claim only to the earldom and Evesham Abbey, as all other lands, rents, residences, etc., are unentailed and mine to bestow as I deem fit. In this event, my daughter Arabella Elaine shall take possession of my entire worldly estates, excepting any entailed property, upon her twenty-first birthday."

"NO!"

Arabella jumped to her feet. Her face was ashen. She shook her head back and forth. "No, no, it must be a mistake. My father would never have done such a thing to me. Never would he consider such a thing, never. You are lying, sir, and it is not well done of you! Damn you, tell me you are lying!"

"Arabella, be seated." Lady Ann spoke with unaccustomed authority. Arabella turned stricken eyes to her, then slowly sank back into her chair.

"Lady Arabella," Mr. Brammersley said, no smile for her as there had been for Elsbeth, "your esteemed father's instructions, as I have detailed them, are binding. I wish to add that the earl left a sealed envelope for you. I assure you that no one save your father is aware of the contents." He rose as he spoke, and skirted the large desk. Arabella automatically extended her hand to grab the letter. She jumped up from her chair, nearly tripping on her long black skirts, to gaze at the now thankfully blurred sea of faces around the room. Clutching the envelope to her chest, she whirled about, toppling her chair to its side on the carpet, and sped to the door. Long fingers closed about her arm as she wrenched at the bronze knob.

"Your behavior is that of a spoiled child," the new earl said to her, his voice colder than a fish on ice. "I will not tolerate such speech, such lack of control from you. It is offensive and shows that your father did not sufficiently discipline you."

She looked up at him with blank misery, read the disapproval in his gray eyes—her gray eyes, damn him—and felt as if all the demons in hell were breaking loose within her. This man was disapproving of her? This man had the gall to tell her that she was offensive? She wanted to bite his hand, but she didn't. "Take your hands off me, you damnable bastard! God, how I hate you. Why are you here and alive and he is gone?"

She jerked violently away from him, and as his grip did not loosen from her sleeve, she felt the material rip. She looked down stupidly at the gaping tear, nearly howled in fury, for she had no more words, and flung from the library, slamming the door behind her.

A delicate Dresden shepherdess trembled, then toppled from its longtime place on the mantelpiece, and shattered onto the marble hearth.

Arabella rushed to her bedchamber, unaware and uncaring of the shocked silence she had left in the library. She kicked the door shut behind her. She ground the key into the lock, cursing it even as she forced it before it finally clicked into place. She stood for a moment, panting heavily, trying to gain some sort of understanding, to gain any meaning from what had just happened. All she could think of was that her father had died and after his death, he had betrayed her. He had planned all along to betray her, to force her to wed this stranger, this man who looked like her.

She could not accept it. She looked within herself, but there was nothing there but emptiness and the rawness of her pain. She stooped, grasped a brocade-covered stool by a spindly leg, and hurled it with all her strength against the wall. It thudded and dropped, now two-legged, to the carpet. Suddenly she felt drained of all anger. She stared down at the stool blankly. What an incredibly stupid thing to do. She stared down at the crumpled envelope she held fisted in her hand.

Her father's letter. He would explain that it was all a mistake. He would explain that everything that Brammersley had read he had changed. He loved her. He wouldn't give her over to a stranger. She walked to her small writing desk, seated herself, and with steady fingers gently drew out a white sheet of paper. She felt a tightening in her throat at the sight of her father's bold handwriting. She formed her letters in exactly the same economical manner, with the same flamboyant strokes, for he had taught her. So many years ago. A lifetime ago and now he was dead.

She shook her head and began to read.

My dearest child,

That you are reading this letter means that I am now gone from you. If I know my Arabella, you are in a rage. You believe I have betrayed you. No doubt your grief at my death is distorted by anger and misunderstanding of my instructions. As I pen this letter to you,

you and your mother prepare to go to London for your first Season.

Arabella stared at the paper, suspended in surprise. Why, he had written his will but five or six months ago. She gazed back at the letter and read rapidly.

I myself prepare to leave for the Peninsula to assume the command of an area that is noted for the brutality and bloodiness of its conflicts. If I am fortunate enough to return from this assignment, you will not be reading this letter, for I will tell you of my wishes in person. I ramble. Forgive me, daughter. You have by now met your second cousin and my heir, Justin Deverill, or, more appropriately, I should write *Captain* Justin Deverill, for he is a brave and intelligent military man himself. Either rightly or wrongly, I kept you from meeting him, indeed, even knowing of his existence, until you reached a marriageable age. Do not blame your mother for not telling you that there was a male heir to the earldom, for I forbade her expressly to do so. Evesham Abbey is *your* home and I could not bring myself to inform you that there was someone who could possibly usurp your position. Forgive me for what I believe to be a necessary deception.

As to your second cousin, I have been in close contact with him for some five years now, critically following his career, to determine in my own mind if he were indeed the man I wished to sire my grandsons. I assume that you have found the physical resemblance between you to be striking. I conclude that you cannot think him ill-looking, for to do so would be to insult your own fine features. He is much like you and me, Arabella; fiercely loyal, proud, and possessed of the Deverill stubbornness, the Deverill strength. I beg you do as I have instructed. Evesham Abbey is your home. If you do not wed your second cousin, you will forfeit your birthright. I don't want this to happen, but I know you, know that you will see my fondest wish as a command that is meant to crush you and deprive you of what is rightfully yours. It is a command, Arabella, but I do it for you and for myself.

You have much to think about. If you decide to follow my wishes, you will have given my life meaning. Never forget that as you struggle with your conscience. Never forget as well that I have loved you more than any other human being in the world.

Adieu, my dearest daughter.

Late-afternoon sunlight sent shafts of dazzling gold from between the low clouds to blend with the forty stalwart red brick gables, coloring them a deep titian. Arabella walked swiftly across the green lawn, unmindful of the gay parterre with its crisscrossed walks hedged by yew and holly, and the yellow daffodils that clustered about the middle in colorful profusion. Nor did she pay any attention to the great massive green cedar set in the middle of the west lawn, said to have been planted by Charles II.

She walked to the south of the old abbey ruins, where the ground rose gently. She turned off the wide path into the neatly plotted Deverill cemetery. She made her way through the straight rows of Deverills from generations past to the very center of the cemetery to where her father had erected his own Italian marble vault. The archangel Gabriel hovered overhead, his white stone wings spread protectively over the heavy oaked Gothic doors.

Arabella tugged open the wrought handles and slipped into the dimly lighted chamber. She sank wearily down to the cold stone floor beside the earl's empty coffin. Her long slender fingers, with infinite sadness, slowly traced out each individual letter of his name.

Dusk was shadowing the season-faded names on the

gravestones when the earl eased open the vault doors and stepped quietly inside. His eyes widened to adjust to the dim light, and he made out Arabella curled up like a small child, asleep, her feet tucked up beneath her skirts and her arm resting gently atop her father's coffin. She looked vulnerable. She looked utterly helpless. He hated it, hated what he must do, hated now what he had promised to do five years before.

He moved to her side and dropped to his knees. His eyes followed the unremitting black of her gown to where it cut a severe line at her throat, casting a dark shadow over her pale cheeks. She whimpered in her sleep, her hand fisting for an instant, then easing again. Pins had worked themselves loose and her dark hair fell in thick waves over her forehead and across her shoulders, hair the blackness of his own. He saw that she didn't have a cleft in her chin as he did. Her father hadn't had a cleft either. He wondered if she had dimples. He had always hated his until he had seen her father's dimples, rarely, of course, since he was a man who was usually in command, unsmiling. But when he did smile and laugh, those dimples dug deeply in his cheeks and it changed him utterly. The dimples humbled a man, made him more human, gave him a charming indulgence when he laughed.

It seemed a pity to awaken her. Even as he gently shook her shoulder, he knew that when she opened her eyes and saw that he had awakened her, all thoughts of compassion he felt for her would flee in an instant of time. He couldn't begin to imagine what she would say to him. It wouldn't be conciliatory, that, at least, he knew.

She awoke slowly, with another soft whimper, as if loath to quit a sleep that kept her from what was real, from what she would have to face. She opened her heavy black-fringed lids and looked straight into clear gray eyes. The dim light and her drowsiness clouded her sight as she gasped, "Father!"

It needed but this, he thought. He cleared his throat and said slowly, very slowly, so as not to shock her more, "No, Arabella, it is not your father. It is I, Justin, come to fetch you back to the abbey. The light is very dim in here. Your mistake is natural. I am sorry to have frightened you."

Arabella flung out her arms, nearly unbalancing him, and scrambled to her feet. She stared down at him. "No one said you could come in here. You don't belong here. I should have locked the vault against you. How dare you make me believe you were my father?" She felt fury at herself for showing him her pain. "You did not frighten me. You haven't that power."

The earl rose slowly to his feet, looking for control, for patience. He looked searchingly down at her, and saw the furiously pounding pulse in the hollow of her throat. "We seem to meet in the most peculiar places. First the fishpond and now the cemetery. Come, Arabella, it is chilly and dark in here. Let us return to the abbey. It is a long walk, but it is just as well, for I believe we have much to say to each other." He sounded calm, bored, really, and wanting nothing more than to walk away from her, to never speak to her again, to never have to look upon her face again.

"We have nothing to say to each other, *Captain* Deverill. Oh yes, my father wrote what a great military man you were. I imagine he provided you with a rank and position that suited your ambitions? I imagine that he protected you, saw to it that you advanced?"

He wanted to smack her. Instead he said easily, "No, he didn't, actually."

"Naturally I don't believe you. Now, I suppose I have no choice but to see you at the dinner table." She turned and walked away from him, out of the crypt, into the early evening. It was very nearly dark.

"Arabella—"

She didn't even turn to face him, just said over her shoulder, with complete indifference, "I am not Arabella to you. I don't wish you to address me, thus you have no need of a name for me."

"I assure you that I am right this moment considering many names for you. However, in the name of conciliation, I will call you cousin if you like. We can work that out later. For now, you will act like a lady. You will walk beside me. You will converse with me. Don't push me on this."

He waited a moment, but she remained quiet. She wasn't looking at him, but rather down at her slipper, whose ribbon had become untied. She went down on her knees and retied the ribbon. Her hands weren't steady. It took her too long to do it. When she rose, she still didn't look at him. She turned to walk away.

As he had done in the library, he grabbed her arm to stop her. "I don't wish to tear your other sleeve. Listen to me now. I am willing to make allowances for your behavior because of your bereavement, but stupid childishness, this churlish conduct, I will not tolerate."

Unconsciously she moved her hand to the rent sleeve and rubbed her arm. She had acted the fool, but no more, because, quite simply, it gained her nothing. He released her.

"Yes," she said finally, "it is chilly here. I will walk with you, Captain Deverill. It seems I have no choice. Say what you will say. Speak of the weather. Speak of the atrocities on the Peninsula. Speak of whatever pleases you to speak of. I really don't care. None of it makes any difference."

"I will say only that everything I do will eventually make a very big difference to you, cousin."

6

Her hands were fists at her sides.

He said only, "Don't."

Her breathing was fast and jerky, but her hands smoothed out at her sides. Then he simply kept pace with her, out of the vault, pulling the doors closed behind them. They walked in silence through the cemetery until they gained the yew-lined path. Arabella looked at his strong profile, still distinct in the fading light. She didn't mean to speak to him but she couldn't seem to hold the words back. "You knew of this arrangement, did you not? Even this morning, you knew."

"Yes, of course I knew. The earl approached me some years ago. I must say that he was very thorough in his examination of my character and prospects. I believe he even interviewed my mistresses, my friends, and my enemies as well. He left no stone unturned to strip me down to the bone."

"And if my father had not died, he would have presented you to me as my future husband?"

"Yes." He stopped a moment and looked down at her. "Your father always spoke of you in such glowing terms, I expected a veritable sweet-voiced angel to greet me. I expected to feel exalted in your presence, to be overwhelmed in the warmth of your spirit. I expected my soul to glow in your brightness. He told me you were smarter than most men, that you could figure and calculate more quickly than he could, that he had taught you chess and you had bested him within two years. He told me you were as brave as he had found out that I was. In short, he told me that we would suit each other perfectly.

"However, after meeting you, cousin, I now understand what I didn't understand before. He only wanted me to meet you at the very last minute, so to speak, when we were of marriageable age. He had an excellent point. He knew you very well."

"Marriageable age," she said, looking straight ahead, saying the words slowly, thoughtfully. Then she looked up at him. "I would not marry you if you were the last toad on earth."

"I suppose a toad is better than a bastard," he said, and sighed. All of this was absurd and not at all to the point. She was staring at him now more in dawning shock. "Marriageable age is what my father wrote in his letter to me. I think it a strange coincidence, sir, that you use the very same words."

"Not so strange. Your father and I spoke of you often. I did not read your letter. Your father wrote it to you only, not to anyone else. Surely you must realize that your father and I discussed the matter at great length."

"You are saying then, that you would be willing to follow my father's instructions?"

"You aren't stupid, cousin—"

"I am not your bloody cousin, don't call me that."

"What shall I call you then?"

"I will call you sir. You may call me ma'am."

"Very well, ma'am. As I was saying, you aren't particularly stupid. You must see that marriage with you would be to my great advantage. I have money, don't mistake me on that. Don't take me for a fortune hunter. Rest assured, if your father had scented anything of the villain in me, he would have kicked me as far away from you as possible. No, I have money, but not nearly enough to maintain Evesham Abbey and now that I am the Earl of Strafford, it is my responsibility. It is my duty not to let this pile of stone fall into rubble on my watch. Wedding you saves Evesham Abbey and, I daresay, it also saves you. Did you not carefully attend to the details of your father's will?"

"You mean that you wish to wed me for the wealth I would bring to you?" Her voice was flat, deadened. He didn't hear the wistful catch.

He shrugged his broad shoulders and nodded. "It is certainly a powerful motive, and not one to dismiss out of hand. But of course, you would gain also by such an alliance." He saw her hands fisted at her sides again and it angered him. He was being honest with her, just as her father had been. Very well, he wouldn't go gently with her. She didn't deserve it.

"If you don't wed me, ma'am, I'm afraid that you will find yourself quite penniless. As I imagine that the term 'penniless' has little or no meaning to you, let me tell you quite frankly that in spite of all the young lady's accomplishments I am certain you possess, you would not survive in our proud and just land for more than a sennight." He paused and looked down at her with cool appraisal. "Though with your looks and figure—once you are not so thin—and with some luck thrown in, you could perhaps become a rich man's mistress."

She laughed, actually laughed at him. "You and your man's observations. They are paltry. But I suppose you have nothing else. You know, sir, I didn't like you when I saw you sleeping near the fishpond. I liked you even less when you grabbed my arm in the library and ripped my gown. At this precise moment in time, I think if I had a knife I would stick it between your ribs. My father was mistaken in you. You're a bastard in every way that it counts. You sicken me. Go to hell."

A cynical note entered his level voice. "You disap-

point me, ma'am. Your language was much more colorful this morning. Though you may heartily dislike
me, though I may sicken you, though you wish me to
go to hell, I speak the truth. If you do not wed me, you
will leave Evesham Abbey in two months' time. If you
believe I will allow you to remain as a poor relation,
you are mistaken. I will personally boot you out. After
all, you have not given me a single reason to let you remain on my property. And it is my property, ma'am.
As of this morning, as of the reading of your father's
will. I am master here and you are nothing at all."

Arabella suddenly felt quite sick. Her stomach was
tied into knots, and bile rose in her throat. Her well-
ordered, quite satisfactory world as the favored daughter of the Earl of Strafford had crumbled, like the old
abbey ruins. He was right about one thing—she had
nothing left, nothing at all. He was the master and she
was nothing. She fell to her knees in the soft grass
lining the drive and retched. Since she had eaten very
little during the day, the spasms were dry heaves, making her quake and shudder.

The earl drew up in astonishment, looked within
himself, and saw a good deal lacking. He cursed himself in far more descriptive language than had ever
made its way into Arabella's vocabulary. He had mis-
takenly read her disdainful bravado as vain, prideful
arrogance. Her father's death, his own unexpected en-
try into her life, the terms of the earl's will—all had
been a great shock to her. He had blundered, he had
ridden her too hard. God, but she was young and
wretchedly confused. She had to feel betrayed by the
one person on earth she loved and trusted the most—
her father.

He steadied her, closing his long fingers protectively
about her heaving shoulders. He gently pulled black
masses of hair that hung loosely about her face. She
seemed unaware of him. When she stopped retching,

he drew a handkerchief from his waistcoat pocket and handed it silently to her. She clutched it in her hand, and without looking up, wiped her mouth.

"Arabella—"

"Ma'am."

He had to smile. "Ma'am, then. Can you rise if I assist you? It is nearly dark now and your mother will be quite worried. I promised her that I would bring you back to her unscathed. You are only a bit scathed."

How calmly he speaks, as if we had stopped to admire the daffodils. Unscathed? She felt scathed from the inside out. Come on, Arabella, stand up. See how dark it becomes; he cannot see the shame etched in your eyes. He can see nothing that is really you, nothing.

She drew a deep breath and with an effort of will locked her knees to support her weight.

The earl slipped his hands beneath her elbows and held her upright, her back to him.

She tried to pull free of him but he had a good grip. "I don't need you." The naked pain in her voice sliced through the still evening air. Her hands clenched into fists, and in a swift, totally unexpected movement, she whirled about in his arms and smashed at his chest with all the mindless fury of a trapped animal.

He dropped his arms and sucked in his breath, more from sheer surprise than from any pain she caused him. "That was a good blow. Thank God you didn't go lower."

She ran from him, thick masses of hair streaming out about her shoulders and down her back.

Sharp gravel bits dug into the thin soles of her kid slippers, sending stabs of pain up her legs. Blind, unreasoning panic blurred her vision, yet she ran on as if death itself pursued her. A gently rising slope rose before her, but her mind did not tell her legs to adjust for the abrupt unevenness. She went hurtling forward, clutching frantically at the empty air to balance herself. Instinct brought her arms in front of her face to cushion the impact as she sprawled facedown onto the drive. Gravel cut into her arms, tearing her gown, digging into her flesh. She cried out just once. The pain from her body seared through to her mind, unleashing the unshed tears for her father. They coursed down her cheeks, burning tears that had not touched her face since her father, with grim resolution, had put his pistol to her pony's head, and pulled the trigger. Years of stoic discipline, of scorn for such despicable weakness, were stripped from her.

The earl loomed above her within an instant of her headlong plunge. It is becoming quite a habit with me, he thought almost inconsequentially as he knelt down beside her. Her gown was grimy and rent with small jagged tears; blood welled up and spread, blending into and encrusting the black material. He knew with an uncanny sense that the deep rending sobs were not from her fall; nor, he guessed, did tears come easily to her. He did not attempt to speak to her or soothe her. Rather, with a sigh, he grasped her about her waist, hauled her upright, and swung her into his arms.

She went rigid and he thought wearily that she would lash out at him again. He tightened his grip and strode on, not looking down at her.

It did not occur to Arabella to fight him. She had tensed with shock at the touch of a man's hands. No one save her father had ever before held her. She felt the strength of his arms, and for a fleeting instant sensed an inner strength in him, a calm self-assurance that heightened the stark emptiness deep within her.

The earl halted a moment at the edge of the front lawn, staring thoughtfully ahead at the bright candlelit mullioned windows.

"Is there a staircase to your room through the west entrance?"

He felt her nod against his shoulder.

As the earl turned to skirt the front doors, they were suddenly flung wide and Lady Ann waved to him. She looked frantic.

"Justin, thank God. You have found her. We've been distraught with worry. Bring her here, quickly, quickly."

He leaned his face close to Arabella's and said, "I'm sorry, ma'am, but there seems to be no hope for it. I would have spared you if I could have. But she is your mother. I would never disobey a mother. I'm sorry for it, but there it is."

She said nothing at all, but she was as still as a board in his arms. He called out, "Yes, Ann, I have found her. I'll bring her to you."

Lady Ann did not shriek or fall into hysterics. Her blue eyes fastened with disbelief on her daughter's ravaged face. She saw the tear streaks trailing through the dirt and blood down her white cheeks. "Dear God," she managed, then fell silent.

The earl felt Arabella clutch at his coat as if she wanted somehow to disappear inside of him. He sensed her deep shame and said quickly, "She isn't hurt, Ann, merely cut up a trifle from an accidental fall. It is nothing more than that. Is. Dr. Branyon still about? I think it wise that he see her."

Arabella gathered remnants of pride and struggled in the earl's arms to face her mother. "I do not wish to see Dr. Branyon. Mother, I am perfectly fine. It is as he said, I simply took a stupid fall and hurt myself just a bit. If you will please let me down, sir."

"Yes, ma'am." He dropped her to the ground.

She staggered against him and would have fallen had he not slipped his arm around her waist. She had dignity, she simply had to dredge it up. She raised her chin, placed her hand calmly upon his arm, and walked stiffly beside him into the house.

* * *

Dr. Paul Branyon straightened over a now clean Arabella and said with his charming smile, "Well, my little Bella, though you were a rare mess to be sure, I can find nothing in particular wrong with you that your bath did not cure. You will be a trifle sore here and there for a couple of days, but nothing of consequence. I do, though, insist that you have a good night's sleep."

This evening the lurking twinkle always present in Dr. Branyon's brown eyes didn't draw a smile from her. She adored him, always had, for he had been a part of her life since she was born. Still, he had seen her fail, even though he didn't realize it. She hated herself. She also felt sore from the top of her still-damp head to her bruised feet. She eyed him as he carefully measured out several drops from a small vial into a glass of water. Like her father, Arabella hated sickness, the earl having convinced her over the years that weak persons used various illnesses to gain attention. Succumbing to common complaints showed lack of character. "I will not take that laudanum, for that is what it is, isn't it, sir?"

"Yes, just a bit, my dear."

"No. Give it to Mrs. Tucker. I know she uses it in her tea. She says it makes her feet relaxed."

"Always giving orders," Dr. Branyon said, smiling at her. "You do it well, but it doesn't matter this time. I do not wish to have your mother shred me into pieces, and that is what would happen if I don't take thorough care of you. Isn't it, Ann?"

Lady Ann stepped forward. She said with a firmness that Arabella found unnerving, "Be quiet, Arabella. It has been an extraordinarily trying day. There is much change and much for you to think about. I will not have you bleary-eyed and in a snit all for want of a good night's sleep. Drink the water."

Arabella could not believe it had been her own dear mother speaking to her all hard and calm like that.

"Mother? Is that truly you speaking? It isn't right, Mother. You never raise your voice, you always fade away. You never fight or argue. It isn't what I'm used to. I don't understand any of this."

"Perhaps you will, in time," Lady Ann said, her voice just a bit sharp, but there was amusement there as well. "Come, Arabella. You have far more need of this than do Mrs. Tucker's feet. Drink your medicine. Do it now or you will have to deal with both Paul and me."

Arabella, still stunned by her mother's unlikely behavior, downed the entire glass without pause. Lady Ann could scarce restrain a chuckle. Had she been so weak then? Had she but to be firm and Arabella would obey her? "I will send Gracie to you now, my love. Just ring if there is anything you need." Lady Ann bent swiftly over her daughter and kissed her lightly on the cheek. She said softly, "Forgive me for not telling you of Justin's existence. I have grown more and more concerned about your not knowing, yet it was a promise I made to your father. I did try to get him to change his mind, but he never changed his mind about anything, once he'd made it up, you know that."

"Didn't he? About anything, Mama? Surely Papa wasn't that certain of himself all the time, was he?" Then she sighed in the face of her mother's silence. Perhaps he had been. She had always prayed that she would have her father's strength of will. But look at where his strength of will had brought her. She had two months to marry a man who looked like her, who looked like her brother and her father as well, was more arrogant and cold than her father at his most displeased, and she hated him.

What to do?

"Good night, little Bella." Dr. Branyon smiled and

patted her cheek. His hand was firm and strong. She remembered his hands from her earliest years.

She was asleep before they were out of her bedchamber, their heads close together, their talk too quiet for her to hear.

Dr. Branyon couldn't prevent his chuckle. "I now believe I have seen everything," he said, grinning down at Lady Ann. "You telling Arabella what to do? By all that's holy, that was Arabella obeying? It boggles the mind. Perhaps you have become a witch. If I look about closely will I find a black cat who is your familiar?"

She remained silent, and he knew she was thinking. He knew that look, he knew her every look. "You have stolen the indomitable will from your daughter. Never before have I observed you having the last word. It pleased me, Ann."

Lady Ann sighed. "You are right. I was a Milquetoast, wasn't I?"

"Well, no, not that, exactly. It's just that the earl and Arabella—they seemed somehow to smother you with their vitality, their boundless energy. And both of them autocrats, no denying that. I could never quite feel Lady Ann's personality in Evesham Abbey."

"They are terribly alike. Sometimes, Paul, I wonder what I did all those years, what I thought." She frowned a moment and gazed almost unwillingly down at the huge Deverill family ring on her third finger. Somehow it did not seem to weigh so heavily as usual on her hand. She drew a deep breath and looked up with absolute trust into a face whose every expression she had memorized long ago. "Many times I have felt that I am the child and Arabella, the fond, yet dominating mother. I have felt sometimes very out of place with her, as if she regarded me with a sort of affectionate condescension. You know, of course, how the earl felt." She found, surprisingly, that she spoke without bitterness.

Dr. Branyon fought down the familiar surge of anger that had gnawed at his belly so many times during the past years. "Yes, I know." She didn't see his jaw tighten or his eyes darken, but he knew that even if she had, it wouldn't have surprised or dismayed her.

Lady Ann stopped in the middle of the entrance hall and looked dispassionately about her. There were grand Renaissance screens, with two archways divided by fluted pilasters and enriched with elaborate paneling of splendid craftsmanship. All the trappings of war were displayed on and about the walls—hand breast-plates and morions, buff leather jerkins, matchlocks, and many other articles of equipment worn or used by the foemen of the civil wars. Faded Flemish tapestries depicting scenes of battle shimmered in soft glowing patterns. Ancient flambeaux sent spiraling threads of blue-black smoke upward to the blackened beamed ceiling.

"It is really quite strange, you know," she said aloud, "but I have always hated Evesham Abbey, though I cannot deny its incredible beauty. The history of England still lives in this hall, yet I have no pride in it, no flights of fancy over its grandeur. You said, dear friend, that I am drawing upon Arabella's strength. I will tell you that if she were forced to leave Evesham Abbey, I would dread to think of what would happen to her." Lady Ann waved her hand out about her. "Every panel, every armament, shield, every nook and cranny of this house is a part of her. Much of her indomitable will, as you call it, is tied up with this house. So, you see, I must be firm with her, try to make her understand that her father didn't betray her, that he did what he could so that she would remain here."

"So you believe she should marry the new Earl of Strafford as her father demanded?"

"Oh yes, Paul, she must marry Justin."

7

He hadn't quite expected this. He looked down at her, wishing for just an instant that he could touch the soft blond hair over her ears. He cleared his throat instead and said, "Judging from the events of the day, I would say that you have your work cut out for you."

"Arabella cried," Lady Ann said. "I could not believe it, but she did. Did her rage at Justin bring it out of her? Or were they finally tears for her father? She never cries, you know. I don't know about this time, but it seems a good sign."

She turned then, nodded to the footman who held open the door, and walked into the Velvet Room.

"Justin, Elsbeth," she said, giving them both her smile, which was soft and warm and quite beautiful. "I trust we have not kept you waiting overlong."

"No, dear ma'am," Elsbeth said. She walked to her stepmother and asked in her shy voice, "Is Arabella all right, ma'am?"

Dr. Branyon said, "She was sound asleep by the time we left her bedchamber. On the morrow she will be quite restored to her usual self."

"That could be a pity," the earl said to no one in particular. "Are you certain, sir? Could she not perhaps have a relapse into common sense and sound reason? Perhaps even a bit of amiability? I shan't repine if she only chooses to dip her finger into just a cup of benevolence."

Lady Ann held down the chuckle, gave him a frown, and said, "Are you and his lordship becoming acquainted, my dear?"

She saw that Justin started in surprise. It was the new title, she realized. He would have to become used to it.

"Oh, no, not as yet, Lady Ann. His lordship had to change his clothes, you see. He was really quite dirty from arguing with Arabella. He had been with me but a moment before you and Dr. Branyon arrived, but he does seem nice. He called me ma'am, at first, but I told him that since we're cousins, he's to call me Elsbeth."

"I like the sound of ma'am," the earl said. "But if you prefer that I call you Elsbeth, I shall have to ask Lady Ann's permission."

"Ma'am?" Lady Ann said, cocking her head to one side. "I think it dreadful myself. It makes a lady sound old. Do call her Elsbeth, Justin."

"Thank you. Would you like to sit on that very small crimson velvet and gold chair, Elsbeth? I don't dare try it, it might collapse."

Lady Ann sat in front of the ornate tea service. "Do you take cream in your tea, Justin? Sugar? We must accustom ourselves."

"Just as it comes from the pot, Ann," he said.

"No frills, hmm, my lord?" Dr. Branyon said, raising his own teacup to the earl in salute.

"On the Peninsula there was little milk unless we could catch a wandering goat. As for sugar and lemon, they were unheard of. One becomes very basic when one has to."

Dr. Branyon liked the new earl. He wasn't pompous and utterly cruel like the former earl. He was a large man, much like his late relative, and carried his size with loose-limbed grace. Though his bronzed face looked more suited to rugged adventuring, his elegant fitted evening clothes were not at all out of place on him. He looked to be as much at ease in the drawing room as he would be on the battlefield. The earl sensed eyes upon him and turned to Dr. Branyon, an inquiring smile spreading over his face. It softened his features.

Dr. Branyon was beginning to think that Ann was quite correct in her hope. The earl might be just the right husband for Arabella. At least he wouldn't let Arabella walk all over him. On the other hand, she might shoot him if he believed, as had the late earl, that a woman's only use was to bear sons. Or if he believed, as had the late earl, that a gentleman was free to betray his wife whenever it pleased him to do so.

The earl shifted his attention to Lady Ann. "I compliment you, Ann, on your furnishing of this room. The Velvet Room, I believe it is called?"

"Thank you for the praise, but it isn't deserved. This room hasn't been touched in years. The velvet has lasted beautifully, has it not? The earl's first wife, Magdalaine, recovered all the furnishings. I believe the crimson velvet and the gold make a very rich effect. And with those white columns throughout the chamber, I sometimes feel as though I should be awaiting the king. Well, perhaps not George, for he is quite mad, poor man."

The earl sipped his tea. It was rich and dark, just the way he liked it. He said to Elsbeth, "Do you plan to make your home at Evesham Abbey?"

Elsbeth's teacup clattered into its saucer. "Oh goodness, no, my lord. That is, well, I do think it most *kind* of your lordship to perhaps not mind if I did stay, but now I can afford to have quite different plans." She beamed at him. "I still have to pinch myself to believe it's true. But it is, Lady Ann has assured me again and again that it is, that I did not misunderstand. It isn't a mistake. Perhaps my father did care just a bit for me after all. Lady Ann assures me that he did. I never believed that he did, but he proved it in the end, didn't he?"

There didn't seem to be a ready answer to that. The ten-thousand-pound legacy from her father. "Yes," the earl said finally, "he obviously did care for you. What do you intend to do with your fortune, Elsbeth? Travel to Paris? Buy a villa in Rome?"

"I haven't yet decided, my lord." She shot a look toward Lady Ann, who said immediately, "We are just beginning to speak of possibilities, Justin. But I think that Elsbeth would greatly enjoy a prolonged stay in London. I would, of course, accompany her." She paused a moment and met his gray eyes squarely. "After you and Arabella are wed, we shall firmly settle our plans. We will not remain here in your way."

The earl's left eyebrow flared upward to his temple, an identical habit that Arabella had inherited from her father. It shook Ann a moment. They looked so much alike. She could but pray that they wouldn't come to think of each other as brother and sister. He said nothing to Ann's outrageous statement, but she knew he wanted to.

After Crupper had cleared away the tea tray, Dr. Branyon moved closer to Lady Ann, and said quietly, "Don't rush your fences, my dear. I do wonder though what the earl wanted to say to you. It was difficult but he held his tongue. That is excellent and perhaps bodes well for the future."

"Nonsense. Justin knows quite well what is at stake. He will do his best to drag Arabella to the altar, just you mark my words."

"If she does not care for him I don't know what we will do."

"We will simply watch and wait, Paul. I do not believe Justin is stupid or clumsy. We will see. Actually, we have no choice but to wait and see."

Dr. Branyon looked toward Elsbeth, who was painstakingly making conversation with the earl. "You didn't tell me that you were leaving with Elsbeth."

Lady Ann felt a sudden quickening deep inside her. She blinked, looking away from him. A long-buried memory rose in her mind, and she said unexpectedly, "Do you remember, Paul, when I was birthing Arabella? I have never told you, but I know that you were with me for all of those long agonizing hours. I know that you never left me. I remember your voice urging me, always urging me, even when I wanted to die. I know that you saved my life."

He would never forget the horror of those long hours, his fear that she would die, his ultimate fury at the earl for his damned indifference. "No," he said slowly, "I did not think you would remember. The pain was so intense that I believed your mind wouldn't allow you to remember." She was being polite, he realized, making certain that he knew he was still welcome here, that he would always be welcome. He rose suddenly, wanting only to leave. He didn't believe he could stand kindness from her. "It grows late, Ann, and I should stop by and check on Mr. Crocker's stomach pains. It's a thirty-minute ride. The old man will probably be cursing the air blue by the time I get there. He calls me boy, at my age."

He doesn't want those memories, Lady Ann thought, staring up at him. It was a horrible time for me, but he was my physician, nothing more, and I have made him uncomfortable. She rose to stand beside him. She found an easy smile for him, but it was difficult. "Do come by tomorrow, Paul, if for no other reason than to pronounce Arabella fit again. I do hope that you will since I don't wish to hear her argue with you."

"Of course."

Lady Ann placed her hand upon his arm and again felt a surge of pleasure course through her. She said shyly, "It would give me—give us great pleasure if you would stay to dinner. I will have cook prepare capon, your favorite, with almond sauce and those small white onions." Her husband had hated capon. She determined to have it at least once a week now.

You do not owe me your gratitude, he wanted to shout at her. "As you wish, Ann," he said instead. Through long years of practice, he kept other thoughts to himself. He patted her hand as he would a patient's who had just followed his instructions perfectly. "Tomorrow, then, my dear."

Lady Ann stood silently at the door of the Velvet Room until Dr. Branyon had accompanied Crupper out of her hearing. She realized in that instant that she felt warm all over. Yet the evening wasn't warm. The fire was banked. It was ridiculous. Goodness, she had a grown daughter.

She turned an absurdly youthful face to find the earl's eyes on her, his look too intent for her comfort. Because she was not a young, inexperienced girl, she was able to smile at him, as if nothing at all in the world was on her mind and say, "Elsbeth, if you do not retire to your bed soon, I shall have to fetch some matchsticks to keep your eyes propped open. Come, love, say good night to Justin and come with me."

Elsbeth yawned, then clapped her hand over her mouth.

"Have I been such a boring companion, Elsbeth? Don't spare me the truth, I can deal with it. After all, I have already dealt with far worse from your sister."

"Oh, of course not, my lord. Not boring at all, I swear it to you, my lord."

"Justin."

"Yes, Justin, but that is difficult, my lord. You are a lord while I am not much of anything. You are very kind to let me call you by your name."

Damnation, her candor would smite the coldest of hearts, except for her father's. Justin wondered if the late earl had even known his eldest daughter, if he would have recognized her if he'd passed her in his own house. "You may call me other names as well. I'm certain your sister will. She will show no restraint at all."

"Oh, no, my lord, that's not true. Arabella is perfect. It is I who am terribly gauche. I never know the right thing to do. I would love to be like Arabella. She's so confident, so sure of herself. Yes, forgive me. It's just that I'm very tired and that's why I yawned in your face. It has nothing to do with you, my lord, er, Justin."

Lady Ann rescued her stepdaughter. "Pay no attention to his lordship, my dear, he's teasing you. As for Arabella, she is herself and I am glad you aren't like her. One of each of you is just right. Now, off to your bed." She clasped Elsbeth's hand and leaned close. "We have much to discuss tomorrow, my love. Sleep well."

Elsbeth's dark almond eyes glowed. "Oh yes, Lady Ann, to be sure. I shall sleep like a log." She turned and sketched her best curtsy to the earl, then nearly ran from the Crimson Room.

"You should have been a diplomat, Ann," the earl said when they were alone.

"Ah, that mission seems to be reserved for you, brave, courageous men," she said, still thinking about Paul Branyon, so many years of memories coursing through her mind.

"True, but I cannot image that it will always be so."

"What will not always be so?"

"You weren't attending. It is no matter. Ah, Dr. Branyon seems a charming man. Most devoted to the Deverill family."

He saw too much, she thought, merely nodding, saying nothing. He wasn't like her husband, cold and distant, telling her what to do, many times paying no attention to her at all when she happened to be in a room he entered.

The earl tucked away her reaction and changed the

subject. "I knew your husband for over five years, Ann. I find it quite strange that he never once mentioned that he had another daughter. She is a charming girl, but—" He paused.

"But what, Justin? Go ahead, say it."

"If that is what you want. She is starved for love, for attention. She doesn't have an ounce of guile in her, which could prove dangerous if she is not careful."

"You're right, of course. The earl, her father, did not allow her to live with us. She was but a small frightened child when he packed her off to Kent to make her home with his older sister, Caroline. I have maintained a constant correspondence with the child all these years, but of course it cannot be the same thing. I am certain that Caroline did her best by Elsbeth, but as you said, she is starved for love." Lady Ann drew a deep breath. "I fully intend to remedy all the past ills Elsbeth has suffered."

"But why did the earl treat her so?"

"I've often wondered that. I finally decided it must be because he loved Arabella so very much, he did not want to share her or himself. There was, quite simply, no one else for him." Lady Ann added, "And for some reason that I could never discover, he bore some sort of grudge toward the de Trécassis family. That was his first wife's family. The earl was never a very forgiving man, you know."

"Does it not seem rather curious to you, then, that he bequeathed her ten thousand pounds?"

"Yes, I was shocked. Perhaps he regretted what he had done, but I am not at all certain that is true. I fear that we shall never know his reasons for doing so. Ah, Justin, do forgive me for being so very blunt about you and Arabella. Dr. Branyon wasn't pleased with me. He said you held your tongue, but it was difficult for you."

"Just a bit difficult." The earl rubbed his chin, looking into the orange embers in the fireplace. "Let us just say that you did not leave me a great deal of latitude on the subject. Though I made up my mind several years ago that I would marry Arabella, it still comes as a shock to be thrust so baldly into the cauldron. You know, Ann, that I shall try to do my best by her."

"If I had believed otherwise, my dear Justin, I would have fought the entire proposition with the ferociousness of a mother lion. Although I felt a great deal of doubt about the earl's deception, I thought his decision to be the best solution. You know, it was all I could do to keep quiet while George Brammersley dallied about before you arrived. I spoke briefly to Arabella this evening. If naught else, I believe she begins to understand her father's motives as well as my silence over the matter. Still, it is difficult for her. It will be difficult for her for a long time, I fear."

"You are a remarkable woman, Ann."

"You are kind, but that isn't true. Over the years I have become a very realistic woman, nothing more. Years of life do that to one, you know. Perhaps it was wrong of the earl to wish to protect Arabella. You know how he felt."

"Yes. If Arabella had known that there was an heir to the earldom, she would have been distressed."

"An understatement."

"Yes, her father thought and thought and worried. I remember him telling me that he couldn't allow her to feel dispossessed."

"Well, now it's over. We will see what happens. Oh, Justin, what do you think of your new home?"

He laughed. "I feel daunted by such magnificence. I have never before in my life had more servants than I had relatives. Only this evening I noticed the truly vast number of gables and chimney stacks."

Lady Ann chuckled as a memory rose in her mind. "You must ask Arabella the exact number of gables. When she was only eight years old she came rushing into the library and proudly announced to her father that there were exactly forty gables on Evesham Abbey. She was such a sturdy little girl, her hair always a tumbled mess and her knees invariably scratched. Oh, I don't know but even then she was so full of life, so inquisitive. Do forgive me, Justin. I do not mean to bore you. I cannot imagine why I thought of this. It was a long time ago."

The earl said brusquely, "That doesn't matter. Anything you could tell me about Arabella could doubtless be of assistance. I do not believe that this marriage business is going to be an easy thing."

"You are right about that. Now, if you really wish to hear this, very well. Back to Arabella's forty gables. A short time later, her father sent her to Cornwall to visit her great-aunt Grenhilde. No sooner had she left than he commissioned carpenters and bricklayers to add another gable to the abbey. When Arabella returned and bounded into his arms, he held her away and said in the most stern voice you could imagine, 'Well, my fine daughter, it seems that I will have to hire a special mathematics tutor for you! *Forty* gables indeed. You have disappointed me gravely, Arabella.' She said not a word, slipped out of his arms, and was not to be seen for two hours. Her father was beginning to grow quite anxious, nearly to the point of berating himself, when the little scamp comes running in to him, completely filthy and utterly frazzled. She stood right in front of him, her little legs planted firmly apart, grubby hands on her hips, frowning, and said in the most scathing voice, 'How dare you serve me such a trick, Father? I forbid you to deny it. I have brought your bricklayer to be my witness that before there were indeed forty gables.' As I remember, from that day on the earl ceased to pine about not having a son. He kept Arabella with him constantly. Even in the hunt, he bundled her in front of him on his huge black stallion, and they would go tearing off at a speed that made my hair stand on end."

The earl grinned, then threw back his head and roared with laughter. "So are there forty or forty-one gables, Ann?"

"Under Arabella's instructions, the earl had the forty-first gable removed. Such a little commander she was. Actually, she still is. It is part of her, Justin. It is something you will have to become accustomed to."

The earl rose, stretched, and leaned against the mantelpiece, hands thrust into his pockets. "You're right. I wonder if I will let her order me about? I never knew my mother, for she died birthing me, so there has never been a woman to order me to do this and that. I don't believe I would allow her to do it, Ann. But we will see."

Lady Ann turned in her chair, her black silk skirts rustling softly. "This forthright side of her—I believe it part of her charm. Poor George Brammersley, though, I fear her treatment of him sent the poor man to his room with a fierce headache."

"Yes, well, just think of the shock to her, hearing her father's conditions in his will." He thought about his first meeting with Arabella earlier that morning, but said nothing of it. Perhaps that had been the greater shock.

"Well, this is progress indeed, Justin. Already you defend her high spirits."

"High spirits, you say? Too pallid a description for your daughter's dramatics. No, I should say rather that she has energy and resolution and, in addition, the sensibilities of a deaf goat."

What was there to say to that?

8

Arabella came down the great front stairs of Evesham Abbey the following morning feeling flattened. It wasn't something she was used to. She hated it. Her situation, which she'd thought about it from every angle she could dredge up during the hours since she'd awakened at dawn, wasn't enviable. She either had to leave Evesham Abbey or marry the new earl. And, naturally, it was really quite simple. She knew in the deepest part of her that she could not leave her home. As for the new earl, she didn't like him, didn't want him around, didn't want to speak to him, actually, didn't even want him to exist, but she knew she would have to marry him.

So be it.

She walked through the large entrance hall, under the great arch, to a narrow corridor that led to the small breakfast parlor. Only she and her father ever breakfasted so early, and she looked forward now to being alone with her favorite strawberry jam and toast.

"Lady Arabella."

Arabella turned, her hand on the doorknob of the breakfast parlor, to see Mrs. Tucker balancing a large pot of coffee near one dimpled elbow and a rack of toast near the other.

"Good morning, Mrs. Tucker. You are looking well. I am glad you've prepared my breakfast as usual.

Please don't forget the strawberry jam. It will be a lovely day, don't you agree?"

"Yes, yes, of course, Lady Arabella, I am quite well and lovely. Well, the day will be lovely, that is." Mrs. Tucker's two chins wobbled a bit above her ruched white collar. She twitched her nose to keep her spectacles from sliding off. "You are feeling better this morning? I must say that I don't like those scratches on your poor little cheek. The cheek on your face, naturally. As for your dear little chin, it is scuffed up like your knees were when you were a little girl, but naturally it is still a dear chin."

"I'm fine, Mrs. Tucker, truly, chin and all." She smiled at the housekeeper. She couldn't help it. Mrs. Tucker had been in her mother's life before Arabella had even come into the world. She was also used to the way she spoke. The local vicar, however, was not. His eyes glazed over when Mrs. Tucker managed to corner him.

Arabella pushed the door open and stepped aside to allow Mrs. Tucker into the breakfast parlor first. She didn't want her to spill that coffee or drop that toast. Arabella would kill for some coffee.

She turned to follow her through the open doorway, looked up, and froze where she stood, so surprised her normally agile tongue was lead in her mouth. The new earl sat at the head of the table, in her father's chair, platters of scrambled eggs, bacon, and a haunch of rare beef arrayed in front of him and on both sides of him, his eyes upon a London newspaper. He glanced up at the sound of a sharp intake of breath, saw that Arabella had turned into a stone at the unwelcome sight of him and rose. He said politely, "Thank you, Mrs. Tucker, that will be all for now. Please compliment Cook on the beef. It is cooked—or rather left uncooked—to perfection."

"Yes, my lord." Mrs. Tucker achieved a fairly

creditable curtsy, fluttered her sausage fingers about her netted cap, and retreated from the room, patting Arabella's shoulder as she passed her. Arabella called after her, "Please don't forget my strawberry jam."

"Will you join me, Lady Arabella? May I call you that yet?"

"No."

"Very well, ma'am. Would you care to sit here?" He pulled out a chair beside his own at the table. "No, from the look on your face, I daresay you would rather take your breakfast and eat in the stable. Anywhere but near me. However, I would appreciate it if you remained. I believe there are some subjects that are of immediate interest to both of us, as loathsome as these subjects might be to you."

She sat down. She had no choice. She wanted to be churlish, but there wasn't any benefit in it, as far as she could see. She would have to marry him.

She might as well speak to him. She would have to sooner or later. "Do you always eat breakfast so early? It is very early, you know, earlier than most people would even deem early. Perhaps you usually eat later in the morning? Perhaps this is just a very special day that sees you up and about so very early?"

"Sorry, ma'am, but I am always early. Do sit down. My beef is getting cold." He grinned, noting her riding habit, and said, "Not only do I eat early, I always like to ride early as well. Just after my breakfast. It would seem, ma'am, that you are in the same habit. Does that, perhaps, presage good things for the future? For us, I mean."

No way around it. "Probably so," she said. She accepted his assistance into her chair and began to dish eggs and bacon onto her plate before he had again eased back into his place. Her strawberry jam sat beside her plate. But how did Mrs.Tucker know where she would be sitting? Ah, he'd told her, naturally. She began to spread the jam on her toast.

"Don't you think it would be a mite more polite if you were to contain your enthusiasm for eating until your host was seated?"

Her hand tightened involuntarily about the handle of her spreading knife. Host? Surely the fork would slide easily into his heart. No, he didn't deserve for her to kill him for that bit of gloating. No, stabbing him in the arm would be the appropriate thing. "You really aren't the host, sir," she said finally. "You just happen to be the lucky male who was born of the right parents at the right time. Nothing more, nothing less."

"As were you, ma'am."

"But I don't claim to be the hostess. I am merely the poor sacrifice, tossed onto the marital altar by my own esteemed father."

He was, he supposed, pleased to hear some wit from her rather than curses rained down upon his head. "In that case," he said, seeing her fork halfway between her plate and her mouth, "wait a moment while I take a bite of my toast. There, now continue with your eggs. Ah, you do like that jam, don't you? Is it special?"

"Very. Cook began making it when I was a child. I used to sneak into the kitchen and she would spread it on scones, on cucumber biscuits, on anything in sight."

He ate a thick slice of the rare beef, picked up his paper, and lowered his head.

"Would you please pass the coffee?"

The earl looked up from the newspaper.

"If, of course, a host does such things."

"Certainly, ma'am. I begin to believe that a host does everything to keep the ship afloat. Now, I wonder if you will also consider me the master? Here you are."

The master? Curse his gray eyes, that were also her gray eyes. She said, "Ah, and a page or two of the newspaper, if you please."

"Of course, ma'am. I understand that it isn't really the done thing for ladies to read newspapers, other than the court pages and the society pages, but, after all, you are Lady Arabella of Evesham Abbey. As your gracious host, it would be impolite of me to give you guidance. Is there any particular page you would prefer?"

"Since I would not wish to deprive you, you may give me a page that you have already read."

"Here you are, ma'am." As she twitched the pages from his outstretched hand, he noticed angry scratches on the back of her left hand. And there was that scruffed-up chin of hers and the long scratches on her cheek. He wondered what other damage there was beneath her clothes. And there was a thought. He could easily imagine that her breasts were really quite lovely, and a handful. His hand cupped around his coffee cup inadvertently. As for the rest of her, he swallowed his coffee and choked. She just stared at him with vague disinterest until he stopped coughing.

"If you had turned blue in the face, I promise I would have done something," she said, her voice as bland as the yellow draperies on the windows.

"Thank you. I am fine now. I was just thinking rather disconcerting thoughts. I hope you are feeling better this morning? Here, have some more eggs. You need to gain flesh."

"My papa always said that a woman should never gain flesh. He said it was displeasing."

"Displeasing to whom?"

"Why, to gentlemen, I would think."

"And should gentlemen gain flesh?"

"I believe," she said very clearly, "that gentlemen can do whatever pleases them without fear of much or any retribution. What lady, after all, is going to tell her husband that she dislikes his heavy jowls or his paunch when he is the one who doles out the money?"

"That is an excellent point. However, I will allow it.

You may eat. Then, if you've eaten enough in my estimation, I will give you your allowance."

She gave it up, tossed up her newspaper and let it fall to the carpet.

"Yes, I'm relieved you appear quite recovered this morning, but not surprised. Dr. Branyon assured me last evening that you would be restored to your *usual self* today. Since that made all present roll their eyes, I imagined that your usual self is something of a treat for everyone."

"I'm not a treat—no, no, you meant that as a trial and I'm not a trial to anyone. Well, maybe to you, but surely that's understandable. I don't like you. I wish you weren't here. Rather, I know you have to be here since you're the new earl, but I don't have to like it. Damn you."

Her fork trembled in her hand, but she quickly raised it to her mouth.

"You said a lot there. Much of which I would say myself about you, but I am a gentleman. I am polite. I am the host. I must be polite. Would you care to ride with me, ma'am? After you've finished your breakfast, of course. I am nearly done myself. I would appreciate a tour of the property. If you can bring yourself to do it."

She wanted to refuse him. She wanted him to ride out and get lost and maybe have his horse toss him into the fishpond, but it didn't make any sense since the fishpond was only a couple of feet deep. "I will take you about," she said. "I am not illogical."

He raised a black eyebrow to that, in just the same fashion that she did, as her father had done. *Her father.* She felt her throat close. Damnable pain. She welcomed it but she hated it, too, because it stripped her and laid her raw.

He saw it, knew she would hate it if she knew he'd seen it, and said, "Excellent. Which horse do you ride, ma'am? I shall send word to the stables."

"The earl's horse," she said without thought, still sunk in misery.

He didn't like her sunk like this, thus he said, "Oh? Do you not think it will be a trifle uncomfortable riding pillion? Not, of course, that I would necessarily mind sharing my horse with you, at least until you've gained more flesh. Then perhaps the poor beast would not be too pleased carting about the both of us."

That did the trick. She looked at him as if she would like to wrap the tablecloth about his head and smother him. He grinned at her.

"You did that on purpose. You know I did not mean your bloody horse. I meant the earl's, that is, my father's—"

"You mean Lucifer."

"You knew that I did all along."

"You have my permission to ride Lucifer."

"I shoot very well," she said, shoving back her chair in a motion reminiscent of her display in the library the afternoon before.

"I would appreciate it, ma'am, if you would contrive to take better care of my furniture."

She couldn't find words to demolish him. It was because she was tired. It was because she'd so recently felt flattened. She could only stare at him, hoping he could see the killer light in her eyes.

He rose and came to her. "Come, my dear ma'am. Don't you think we've flayed each other sufficiently this morning? I, for one, would not particularly care to have my breakfast disagree with me." At her continued silence—actually, she was grinding her teeth—he added with a smile, "I will make Lucifer a gift to you. Soon we shall rename him the countess's horse."

"Ah, that is bald speaking."

"Naturally, I'm a bald man." She snorted, he was sure he heard it. The preamble to a laugh. Her grief for her father would lessen, slowly, but it would lessen, and he could help her if she would allow it. Odd that he did not believe her a shrew, a harridan, and a termagant all rolled into one this morning. He thought he had died and gone to Hell after meeting her the previous day. She had rubbed him rawer than a pair of new boots. He hadn't believed it possible that a man could exist with such a woman. Today, though, was different. Today he nearly made her laugh. Today he had seen the quickness of her mind. He had actually heard her utter witticisms. He drew out his watch and consulted it. "Coming, ma'am?"

"Yes," she said slowly, eyeing that cleft in his chin. "I am coming."

Dr. Branyon didn't move a muscle when Lady Ann lifted her skirts to step over a tiny blossoming rosebush. Beautiful ankles, but then again he believed every inch of her was beautiful. She wasn't wearing a bonnet and her thick blond hair shone like minted gold beneath the bright midday sun. She held a handful of cut roses in her right hand. It seemed to him that her face glowed with a new health and vitality. He wasn't prejudiced about this, he knew it.

As Lady Ann was carefully stepping over a rosebush, she was wondering where in heaven's name Paul could be. It was growing quite late, and he had not even sent a message. She clasped her daffodils and roses more securely and looked up, a tiny frown puckering her forehead. She saw him standing but a few feet away from her, looking at her. Just looking. How long had he been there, just looking at her? Why was he just looking at her like that? She flushed red to the roots of her hair. No, that was silly. She was thirty-six years old. She shouldn't be flushing all because he was staring at her, just standing there, saying nothing, just staring at her.

This was ridiculous. She nearly yelled, "Paul, how-ever did you find me?"

"Crupper is very observant. I've been here but a mo-ment. Less than a moment, actually." It had been a bit longer, but who cared?

"Oh, that's all right then, perhaps." So he hadn't been staring at her. Well, piffle. She wished she could curse as fluently and raucously as Arabella, but she couldn't. Every time she tried, she pictured her own mother's face, and turned white. Her dear mama had made her eat soap every time she had even whispered the mildest of curses.

What was she to say now that wouldn't embarrass him? She could but try. "I thought that perhaps you were too busy with your patients to come to us today." Surely that was innocent enough.

"Only the imminent birth of triplets would have pre-vented me. May I carry those murderous-looking cut-ters for you, my dear?"

"Yes, thank you, Paul." She handed him the flower cutters and found that the mundane action brought back some perspective. The good Lord knew she needed it. Yes, everything between them was back into focus, and he was again her old friend of many years. *Her old friend.* How depressing that sounded to her. Still, she could not recall having ever found his dark brown corduroy suit so terribly smart. His eyes were very nearly the same color, filled with a sharp cutting intelligence and with humor, and oddly, they seemed all the brighter today.

Dr. Branyon matched his stride to her shorter one as they walked through the ornamented parterre back to the front lawn. "How is our Arabella getting on?"

"Do you mean her physical health or her relationship with Justin?"

He chuckled, smiling down at her. "Well, knowing my little Bella, she is again as healthy as that black beast she persists in riding. Justin, ah, now there's the rub. I do believe he will handle her very well. He isn't stupid. I imagine he's quite excellent at strategy."

"I don't know about his strategy, but they did ride together this morning. I have no idea what went on between them. Neither said a word about it. I was also pleased that neither of them looked any the worse for it at luncheon."

"You mean that it didn't appear that they'd had a fistfight."

"Exactly. If Arabella wasn't as talkative as she usually is, well, she wasn't, at least, overtly rude to the earl. If I am not mistaken, I think the both of them are in the library poring over the Evesham Abbey accounts. Arabella knows as much as her father about running the estate. Poor child, I remember him drumming fact after fact into her young head. Dear Mr. Blackwater, the earl's agent, almost swallowed his tongue when Arabella issued her first orders to him at the advanced age of sixteen."

"What did he say? Do you remember?"

"As I recall, Arabella told me he gaped at her like a hooked trout. Arabella's father just gave the man a look. As you know, it normally took only a look to bring anyone into line. Except Arabella. I can still hear him yelling at her and she was yelling back. I used to quake in my slippers. But the two of them would come out of the estate room, grinning at each other like the very best of friends. He admired her as much as she did him, you know that."

"Oh yes, I know that. I got the look a couple of times. I don't remember hearing about that incident." He laughed this time, a deep rich sound that made the daffodils and roses tremble for a moment in Lady Ann's hand. Tremble? Goodness, she would be a halfwit by the end of the week if she didn't get a hold on herself.

"How do you think the earl will adjust to Bella's most unwomanish competence in a traditional man's domain? To boot, the chit is nearly eight years his junior."

"To tell the truth, Paul—and no, I am not being biased—he seemed to me to be rather pleased. I think he will come to admire her tremendously. Actually, I think he will exploit her shamelessly. I don't think he has any particular enthusiasm for estate accounting."

Dr. Branyon paused and dropped a hand on Lady Ann's shoulder, gripping it an instant. She stopped immediately and turned to face him. "I think you're right, Ann. Though I can easily picture some ferocious fights between them, they are perhaps better suited than most. Arabella needs a mate of great strength, else she would render the unfortunate's life miserable. As for Justin, I vow that, given an obliging, meek little spouse, he would become a household tyrant in very short order."

She'd rather hoped he would say something else. Well, he was right about Arabella and the new earl. She just prayed the two of them would see things in the same light. She wanted to sigh, but couldn't. She said lightly instead, "How very tidily you wrap up all my concerns." Had she really been concerned? She didn't think so, but she'd had to say something. She gaily plucked a daffodil from her bunch and with a mock curtsy pulled its stem through a buttonhole in his coat.

"And now I'm a dapper dog as well." He smiled tenderly down at her upturned face.

Lady Ann gulped. That look of his surely must be intended for something he was thinking. It couldn't be intended for her. It was too tender a look, too intimate, too close. Suddenly, she gave a guilty start. "Oh goodness, I forgot about Elsbeth. She will think I've given her not a thought, poor child. And I have, just not for the past fifteen minutes or so. And that is all your fault, sir. Come, let's find her. It is nearly teatime."

She didn't care a whit about tea or anything else, but she knew her duty, at least most of the time. Curse it.

He nodded, but then, without warning, he pulled up short in his tracks and gave a shout of laughter.

"Whatever is that for?"

"It just occurred to me, my dear Ann, that you will soon be the *Dowager* Countess of Strafford. You, a dowager. It boggles the imagination. You look like Arabella's sister, not her mother. Oh, how you're going to be teased and twitted and given such very complacent looks. Some of the old bats will be delighted. They'll doubtless try to convince themselves that you've gone all wrinkled and gray and gloat."

"Well, I am becoming quite matronly. Soon I just might have a gray hair. Goodness, do you suppose I'll pull it out? Do you suppose that by the time I'm of truly advanced years, I'll be bald?"

"You may tug and pull as you please. I promise now to buy you a number of wigs if you need one. Also, I will begin right now to assist you. Here is my arm to support you. When you can no longer walk without me, then I shall prescribe a cane."

She had no idea that her blue eyes were dancing as wildly as the wicked new waltz from Germany, but he did. He was enchanted. Oh God, he was more than enchanted. He was King Arthur. He was Merlin. He was everything in the world that could be enchanted and entranced and charmed and so in love that he could barely bring himself to breathe.

All he could do was watch her mouth as she said, all gaiety and lightness, "A cane. What a lovely thought. If anyone offended me, I could crack him on the head."

9

Elsbeth did not believe that Lady Ann had already lost interest in her. Nor did she believe that Lady Ann had gotten herself into an accident. Actually, she was not thinking about Lady Ann at all. Rather, she was staring off at nothing in particular, her small hand poised above her stitchery, her colorful creation for the moment forgotten. It was bluebells around a pond, or some such sort of water.

She was thinking about all the fun that awaited her in London. Balls, routs, even plays in Drury Lane. So much to do, so much to see. She had heard of the Pantheon Bazaar all of her life, where one could fine literally any color ribbon and myriad other gewgaws. And there was, of course, Almack's, that most holy of inner sanctums, where young girls spent untold hours dancing with charming, dashing young men. Her ten thousand pounds would ensure her foothold in London society. With Lady Ann, the widow of a peer and military hero, she could not imagine any door being closed to her. So excited was she at the prospect that her natural shyness and hesitancy in mixing in polite society lessened considerably.

She frowned, thinking suddenly of Josette. How she wished that her old servant would cease with her dark mutterings against every Deverill in sight and out of sight. After all, had not her father proven his love for her? Such a vast sum he had bequeathed to her. Elsbeth sighed. Josette was just getting old. Her wits were becoming clouded, too. Just this morning, Josette had called her Magdalaine.

Quite clearly she had said, "Come closer to the window, Magdalaine. How can I mend this flounce with you fidgeting about so?"

Elsbeth had chosen not to remind her faithful old servant that she was not her mother, Magdalaine. She had docilely moved to the window.

It was then that she had seen the earl and Arabella. "Oh, just look, Josette," she said, pointing as she moved closer to the window, "there come Arabella and the earl. Look at their stallions, how fast they're running." Indeed, the two great plunging stallions were cannoning across the drive onto the front lawn. "They are racing! There, Arabella has won. Oh my, just look how her horse is plunging and rearing. Oh, how exciting." Elsbeth shivered. Horses seemed quite unpredictable to her; they were nasty, jittery beasts, and not to be trusted. She hated them, but she would never admit it to Arabella.

Elsbeth heard Arabella's shout of victory and watcher her alight from her horse, unassisted. Ah, she was so graceful, her skirts whirling around her. Josette drew closer, narrowed her watery eyes against the glare of the morning sun, and muttered with heavy disapproval, "Just like her father she is, brash and conceited. Not a lady like you, my little pet. Leaping off her horse as if she were a man. And look at the new earl—encouraging her, that's what he's doing. Laughing at her antics. It sickens me and it will sicken him. Men do not like women to be strong and outspoken. He will give her orders soon enough, once they are married. And she will obey because she has no choice. Magdalaine had no choice. I know."

Elsbeth wasn't listening. She was thinking with a slight twinge of envy that she was older than Arabella, yet she felt so terribly—unfinished, as if God hadn't cared enough to give her due consideration, to wonder perhaps if she could be prettier, even wittier in her wit, which, in her view, was nil. Well, she was wittier than poor old Josette.

Elsbeth drew her thoughts back to the present. Her hands were still poised motionlessly above her stitchery. It was quite ridiculous, she decided, to be jealous of Arabella. After all, it was she, Elsbeth, who had the ten thousand pounds. All free and clear. She didn't have to do anything. It was hers, simply hers. If Arabella did not comply with her father's instructions, she would have nothing. Arabella would have to marry the new earl. Elsbeth shivered. She found the new earl almost as terrifying as the huge bay stallion he rode. He was so large, so overwhelming. He seemed to fill the room when he walked into it. She felt a sudden fearful tremor that caused her small hand to tremble. It was a delicious sort of fear that somehow caused her breathing to quicken. Oh dear, that wasn't right, was it? She grasped her needle firmly between her fingers and quickly set a stitch of bright yellow silk.

She did not look up until Lady Ann and Dr. Branyon came strolling into the Velvet Room, side by side, their heads close in quiet conversation. She sensed something about them that was somehow different, something that she did not quite understand. Not that it mattered. They were old. Perhaps they were talking about recipes for joint pains.

"Bravo, Elsbeth. You play Mozart beautifully." Dr. Branyon cheered and clapped loudly.

The earl was frankly surprised. Wasn't it unusual that such a painfully shy girl should play the pianoforte with such passion? Good God, what was Elsbeth? Underneath all that bland exterior was something wild and exciting.

Elsbeth rose from the piano stool and blushed pink with pleasure at the smiling faces. And they were smiling at her. Approving of her. It was true that she had played particularly well, losing herself upon several occasions in the thrilling tempo, the deep resounding chords. But had they really enjoyed it?

It was drawing near to ten o'clock in the evening and Lady Ann was on the point of excusing herself when the earl turned to Arabella and asked politely, "It is now your turn, ma'am. Won't you play for us?"

Arabella laughed until tears were swimming in her eyes. "Were I to play, sir, you would most certainly suffer for your gallantry. You would be praying for cotton to stuff in your ears. You would be praying that I would expire over the keys."

"Now, Arabella, that is not *quite* true," said Arabella's loving mother, who tried desperately not to be biased. She thought of all the torturous hours she had stood behind Arabella at the pianoforte, loving her even as she had gritted her teeth. But she had tried. But just look at the woeful result she had achieved.

"Oh, Mother, isn't it time to face up to the truth? Despite Mother's heroic efforts," she added over her shoulder to the earl, "I could never even execute a simple scale without falling over my fingers. I couldn't have recognized the key of a tune if my life had depended on it. Mother, come on, admit it, it is a dark day in her family's history. I am truly sorry, but there it is."

"But, Arabella, you do everything so very well," Elsbeth said, quite shocked that her perfect younger half-sister wasn't perfect in everything. "No, I can't believe that you do not play magnificently. You are being modest. Come, show his lordship how talented you are."

"Dear little goose," Arabella said fondly to her half-sister, "you have every scrap of talent in the Deverill family. I would much rather listen to you than have everyone howling at me with their hands over their ears. And trust me on this, Elsbeth, the earl would not hesitate to howl."

Elsbeth said hopefully, "Perhaps you play the harp?"

"Not a chance."

Lady Ann threw up her hands. "I am undone. All my efforts went to nothing. And the good Lord knows, I did try. Whatever is a mother to do now?"

"You're to love me and praise me in every other endeavor," Arabella said, as she rose quickly and hugged her mother. "Even if everyone else disagrees with you, you're to hold steady. All right, dearest?"

"I will, my love," Lady Ann said. "No matter how Justin complains about your win over him today in your horse race, I will tell him that you are perfect and there's an end to it. I will tell him not to whine or cry foul. I will tell him that your playing any instrument at all is a treat for him to enjoy until he cocks up his toes. Is that all right?"

"Tell him all those things, Mama. It is perfect. You are the most perfect of mothers."

After Lady Ann dispensed tea, Dr. Branyon asked the earl, "How did you find your first night spent at Evesham Abbey?"

The earl sat forward in his chair and clasped his hands between his knees. "It is strange that you should ask, sir, for I did spend a somewhat unusual night."

"You did that on purpose," Arabella said, wagging a finger at him. "You wanted attention and you got it through a display of drama. It was rather good, I must admit. Look at you, just like an actor, awaiting for his audience to accord him full attention. You have no shame."

"Behold one of my many talents, ma'am. No, seriously, I am inclined to think that it was all suggestion and my own imagination. In any case, all of you are familiar with that most unusual paneling in my bed-chamber—*The Dance of Death*."

"Oh, it's horrible," Elsbeth said, her teacup clattering onto its saucer. "I can remember seeing it when I was just a little girl. I believed the Devil was in that panel. He was waving something in his hand. Perhaps the Devil still is there."

"I'm not all that sure about the Devil," the earl said, "but it's very strange. I was looking at it closely before I went to bed, trying to determine its theme. I could discover no plausible explanation, and I was still dwelling upon it when I fell asleep." The earl paused a moment, then looked at Dr. Branyon. "That was my mistake. It was very late, well into the early hours of the morning, when I awoke suddenly, certain that I was not alone. I lit the candle at my bedside and lifted it to look about the room. I could see nothing save that hideous grinning skeleton on the paneling. I was beginning to feel particularly foolish when I heard a strange thudding sound near to the fireplace. I raised the candle but saw nothing. Then I swear I heard a high wailing cry, like that of a newborn infant. Before I could even react, there came, quite close to me, it seemed, another cry. Not a babe's, but a woman's cry—piercing and somehow incredibly anguished. Then there was nothing. I am still not certain in my own mind that I did not imagine it. But I will tell you, it was difficult getting back to sleep. When I did, thank God, there were no more dreams or visions or visits, whatever."

The earl looked around, somewhat apologetically, at the sea of startled faces.

Lady Ann said very gently in a soothing mother's voice, "You did not imagine it, Justin. You have made the acquaintance of Evesham Abbey's ghosts. What you have described happens on rare occasions, and only in the earl's bedchamber. The cry of the child.

The cry of the mother, so anguished, yet we don't know anything about her or her babe."

"You are not trying to stew up another nightmare for me, are you, Ann? Please, I will admit it. I'm weak. My heart was pounding. I broke out in a sweat. No more, if you please. I wish to hear that it was the boiled cabbage for dinner last night."

"We didn't have boiled cabbage last night for dinner. Get hold of yourself, sir, it's true," Arabella said, sitting forward in her chair. "My father heard just what you recounted at least a dozen times. It seems that well over two hundred years ago, before Evesham Abbey came into the Deverill family, a lord named Faber lived here. His reputation was that of a vicious cruel bully. He was also wild and somewhat unstable. The story goes that one stormy night a servant arrived at the cottage of the local midwife and ordered her to accompany him. She was afraid and refused, but he forced her. She was blindfolded and driven many miles. At last the carriage halted. She was dragged up a long flight of steps, through a large hall, up a straight staircase, and led to a bedchamber." Arabella, no mean actress herself, paused a moment, looking at all the faces and finally continued, her voice lower. "When the servant removed her blindfold, she saw a lady, huge with child, propped up in a great bed. A large, broodingly silent man stood by the fireplace. The lady began to scream, and the midwife forgot her fear and rushed forward to help her.

"After a long and difficult labor, the child was finally born. To the horror of the midwife, the man rushed forward and grabbed the babe and hurled it wailing into a roaring fire. The lady screamed and fell in a faint back on her pillow.

"The servant grabbed the midwife, tied the blindfold back on, and hurried her back to her cottage." Arabella was nearly panting. She gasped, "Oh goodness, I have gooseflesh on my arms and I have heard the story a good dozen times. But it always terrifies me, always."

"Good God," the earl said, just staring at her.

"There is a just ending, though," Lady Ann said. "It seems that the midwife remembered certain sounds, and even counted the number of stair steps. She was able to lead the magistrate to Evesham Abbey. Though the magistrate could find no conclusive proof of violence, and thus Lord Faber escaped lawful punishment, it did not end. It was reported that late one night, Lord Faber came bounding out of his bedchamber, his face contorted with sheer terror. He raced to the stables and threw himself upon one of his half-wild stallions. No one is certain what happened then, but the next morning Lord Faber was found under his horse, crushed to death, just beyond a small knoll behind the old abbey ruins. To this day, the drop is called Faber's Jump. I have only screwed up my courage once to visit that spot. I know it's haunted. There is so much madness there, I swear you can feel it seeping into you."

Elsbeth said, after she'd managed a delicate shudder, "Josette told me about Lord Faber, but I did not believe her. It seems my mother heard the mother and child one time. It is true, Lady Ann?"

"Yes, it is. At least it all happened a very long time ago," Lady Ann said. "Now, enough fodder for nightmares. Would anyone care for more tea?"

"A lady with nerves of iron," Dr. Branyon said. "I fear all of you will be hearing strange noises tonight, but not I. I will be sleeping soundly, no other thoughts in my brain than the delicious mutton Cook prepared for dinner this evening. Now, I must be on my way."

Lady Ann rose. "Well, I for one intend to do nothing save sleep." She turned to Elsbeth. "Come, love, you and I will both see Dr. Branyon out, then I will accompany you to your room. You are looking quite fagged."

Arabella watched them bid their good nights and

leave. She was suddenly alone with the nev earl. She thought to go to bed herself, but knew he would believe her running from him. Well, she wanted to run, but she couldn't bear to have him believe that she was running, that she was a coward. She eyed him as he rose and strolled to the sideboard. He stretched. He was a big man, well made, lean, really quite nice for a man. He turned, saw her staring at him, grinned briefly, then said in the most serious of voices, "A glass of sherry, ma'am?"

"Yes, thank you, sir." She tucked her knees up under her and balanced her chin on her hand. She had a very good hold on herself now. "You are certainly calm about all this. Were I you, I would sleep in the stable."

He handed her the glass, grinning down at her. "Believe me, I would gladly ask Dr. Branyon for a sleeping potion if I thought it would not lower me in your estimation. But it would lower me at least a bit, wouldn't it?"

"My father never asked for a sleeping potion. Perhaps he should have. It quite raises the hair on my neck every time I hear or recount that story. Now, as for you, that, sir, is quite the stupidest thing I've heard you say. Of course I have only known you for two days. Doubtless in the future there will be many more stupid things to come out of your mouth."

So she'd accept it. He felt a spurt of relief, but he said easily enough, "You call me stupid just because I try to butter you up? Don't deny it. Also, I find it invigorating that you speak of the future. Drink your sherry, ma'am, and stop frowning at me. That's a new frown, one manufactured just because I caught you in the truth."

"To your continued health, sir," she said, and tossed down the remainder of her sherry. "Maybe."

"When will you let me call you Arabella?"

She said, "It is far easier to keep you at arm's length

with ma'am. I think arm's length is a good distance for you. If I could but think of another appellation that would keep you further away from me I surely would use it."

"But I would prefer being much closer."

"I don't think so. You move quickly, sir, too quickly." Her voice had risen. She felt a spurt of panic, then knew that such a thing as panic was for lesser folk, those who weren't secure in themselves, those who were weak and feckless.

"I don't mind if you call me Justin."

"Sir suits you quite nicely. It grows very late. Good night."

"We're back to the beginning again," he said and managed a credible sigh. "You're fleeing me, ma'am. I will think you a coward." He set down his glass and walked toward her.

She showed no alarm whatsoever. "I don't believe you're executing a sound strategy. Come any closer and I will fire off my glass of sherry at you."

"Are you always so physical, ma'am?"

"Only when necessary," she said, her chin well up. "Keep your distance and you will remain intact."

To her, it was a challenge. To her surprise and perhaps a bit of chagrin, the earl backed away. He sat in a spindly chair that groaned under his weight. "So, now you will flee," he said, his voice all meditative and sad. "Now you will abandon me to my fate in the haunted bedchamber."

Now this wasn't something she'd expected. He was acting human. It was disconcerting. She said, her voice all grudging, "I suppose I cannot blame you after that terrifying experience. I have always felt uncomfortable in that room. Actually, I avoid it."

"How relieved I am to hear you say that. Is your bedchamber large enough for the both of us?"

"Oh dear, that really is too much," Arabella said, and dashed from the room.

"It's just the beginning, ma'am." He smiled, a confident smile. She was obstinate and headstrong. She was also an excellent rider, she had a brain in her head, and she could be amusing. Also, she knew how to run Evesham Abbey. She had talent and experience where he had none. Perhaps many men would have condemned her for that, but he found it a vast relief. Suddenly, he did not think that he would wish her to be any other way. He pictured her breasts. His hands curved. He was beginning to think that he had not made such a bad bargain after all. Surely he was a bounder.

10

The earl drummed long fingers impatiently on the most recent pages of the estate account book. Damn, he was not used to the endless rows of numbers to be tallied and retallied, all the details of what to do with this or that investment, or the juggling of rents of his tenants to secure the best income. He would just as soon that all the numbers would magically disappear and stay gone, just as had the ghost of Evesham Abbey a week ago after scaring him spitless that first night.

He sat back in his chair and dropped his pen on the open page. He had passed his adult years soldiering—a leader of men, not these damned numbers that seemed to dance from one column to another. Ah, Ciudad Rodrigo—there was a battle, and a decisive one. Yet, he thought, picking up the pen and tapping it on the open page, Napoleon still held Europe fast in his Corsican hands. England was suffering from the French blockade, and if rumor had it correctly, Napoleon was now casting greedy eyes to the east, to Russia.

And here he was, far from the thick of things, saddled with a damned title and a huge estate. With a frustrated grunt the earl shook his head and returned his concentration to the page of entries. What he needed was Arabella. The one afternoon she had spent with him explaining such things as rents, market prices, crops, and the like, she had spoken concisely and knowledgeably, and he had achieved at least some rudimentary

insights. Blackwater, his agent, had been far less help-
ful. The studious little man seemed to have difficulty in
focusing his fading wits on the new century.

Arabella. During the past week, she had been practically as nonexistent as his ghostly visitors. He guessed
that she was breakfasting very early in her room, to
avoid him. She rode out alone on Lucifer, and on many
days did not return until the sun was fading behind
Charles II's cedar in the front lawn.

Wisely, he left her alone. At least he thought he was
acting wisely. On many occasions it was Arabella who
maneuvered circumstances so as not to be alone with
him. He would have felt totally at sea had he not several times felt her gray eyes upon him while he was
speaking with someone else.

He started at a distant clap of thunder. Finally a diversion from his wretched task. He rose and walked to
the windows. Dark, mottled rain clouds hung low and
threateningly to the east. He hoped Arabella—rather,
ma'am—wouldn't be caught in the rain.

Layers of chill, heavy air swirled about Arabella. The
storm was closing fast. Yet she did not move from her
perch atop the highest outjutting gray stone in the old
abbey ruins. How strange it was that her father had always hated the ruins. Even as a child, he had forbidden her to go near them. This was the only instance
she could ever remember defying him. She'd loved the
ruins all her life. She smoothed her fingers over the
stone, remembering childhood adventures in the ruins.

She was no longer a child, and the ruins were just ruins. She sighed as a raindrop landed on her cheek and
dripped off her chin. What was she to do? Of course
she knew there was really no choice, but she wanted a
choice, a real choice that wouldn't leave her feeling re-
sentful and bitter.

She thought of Justin, picturing him in her mind. Her

twin, she thought, except for that dimple in his chin.
He had backed away, leaving her to herself, and she
liked him for that. Actually, she liked him for a lot of
things—his strength, his humor, his honor. She even
liked him when he acted like an ass. She even liked
him when he was mocking her or laughing at her or
treating her like she was a twit. As husbands went,
surely he wouldn't be so bad. He would be a handful,
but having lived with herself for eighteen years, she
knew all about handfuls. She smiled this time and a fat
raindrop fell right into her mouth. She laughed then,
rising reluctantly. She looked toward Evesham Abbey,
blurred now through the gathering darkness. It seemed
unlikely that Lady Ann and Elsbeth would venture
from Talgarth Hall with the storm brewing up so
quickly. She had watched them climb into the Strafford
carriage several hours before with only John Coachman in attendance. She wondered why the earl had not
accompanied them. She was glad that he hadn't. She
was glad she would have him to herself. She shook out
her skirts and began to run toward the abbey. She had
made her choice. She would marry him.

The earl stood, hands on his hips, under the protection
of the columned entrance. "Lady Arabella did not take
Lucifer?" he asked James, the head groom. Heavy rain
fell in sheets in front of them, and a chill wind billowed
the sleeves of the earl's white shirt.

"No, my lord."

"Very well, thank you, James, for coming to the
house. Fetch a cloak before you return to the stables.
It's going to get even colder."

Damnation. Did she find his company so damned
distasteful that she preferred catching a chill? In a very
short time his worry for her safety had worked its way
to anger. God, he would throttle her for being such an
idiot to remain out in such weather.

He was planning exactly how he would wring her neck when through the thick blanket of darkness and rain he made out the vague outline of someone running from the stables full tilt up the front lawn. The figure drew closer, and he saw it was Arabella, skirts held above her knees, racing toward him. She took the front steps two at a time and drew up panting in front of him.

She was a sodden mess. He looked her up and down and said in a voice of great disinterest, "Do you believe it wise to be out in such weather?"

"No, not at all. But these things happen, you know. It's not important." Then she had the gall to shrug.

"Just where the devil have you been?"

Arabella swept her soaked hair from her forehead, lifted a black arched eyebrow, and said, "I have been running in the rain. See, my hair and gown are wet. My slippers are soaked. Now, I believe I will go change my clothes."

He looked at that neck of hers and pictured his fingers tightening about it.

"Really, sir, you shouldn't be standing out here. It's cold and you just might take a chill. Just feel the wind."

Give him a crisis and he was the calmest of men. Give him a new situation and he would quickly adapt and show his experience. Give him troops and he would never lost his self-control. She swept past him into the front entrance hall. He stared after her, then yelled at the top of his lungs, "Ma'am, damn you, get back here! I have something to say to you. Damn you, don't you shrug at me or raise your damned eyebrows!"

She paused beneath the chandelier. He wished she had kept going because her gown clung to her like a second hide. He could clearly see her breasts and hips. He didn't like what it made him feel. He didn't want to be as hard as a stone when he was angry at her. At the moment, she didn't deserve him to desire her.

"Well, what do you have to say?"

She had the gall to tap the sodden toe of her left slipper against the marble floor. "Sir, are you suddenly dumb? I thought you had something to say."

"We shall dine in thirty minutes in the Velvet Room, ma'am," he said in a surprisingly calm voice. "I refuse to have my dinner delayed any longer."

She began up the stairs, pools of water forming at her feet, then turned to look down at him. "Now I understand. You're angry at me because you are too much the gentleman to eat your dinner without me. I'm sorry the time got away from me. I promise I will be down as quickly as I can change my clothes."

The earl wished there was something to kick in the huge entrance hall, but there were only two ornately carved massive chairs from the seventeenth century. They probably weighed more than he did.

He had downed only one snifter of brandy when Arabella came into the Velvet Room, wearing black silk, as usual, and looking as if she had napped the entire afternoon. She looked fresh and full of life. She also looked innocent and guileless. Ha, he knew better. He wished he hadn't seen her breasts and hips so clearly outlined through her wet gown. He wished he could keep this damned female in perspective. He would marry her, he had to marry her, but still, he didn't have to feel anything else about any of it.

He was immune to her, at least most of his body was. She didn't look particularly fashionable in that dreary black mourning gown. Ah, but that hair of hers. It hung down her back in damp waves, thick and glossy. A narrow black ribbon secured it back from her forehead. His palms itched to touch her hair, to wrap it around his hand over and over, to pull her slowly to him until her breasts were pressing against his chest.

This would never do. "Well, I can only hope that we won't have to call Dr. Branyon to prescribe for you."

He sounded annoyed, which was surely odd. Annoyed because he would be eating his dinner a bit late? She said, grinning at him because she was a girl who enjoyed fueling annoyance, particularly *his* annoyance, "I am blessed with my father's good health," she said, all good humor. She walked to where he stood by the fireplace. She didn't stop until she was less than a foot from him. What was she doing? Was she trying to goad the bear? The earl found himself a trifle daunted. No, he would never be daunted.

It was just that she wasn't behaving like she had all week. Rather than avoiding him, she was tracking him down to the very spot where he was standing. He turned away from her and walked toward the door. He would go to the dining room. That made sense since he had complained that she had delayed his dinner.

"Justin."

He whirled around and stared at her incredulously. Surely he had not heard her aright. Why was she behaving in this strange way? He said, "I am sir to you."

"Well, yes, you have been sir. I was wondering if you would mind if I used your given name now?"

"I have only known you for a bit more than a week. We haven't been sufficiently friendly or intimate to justify it. No, I will remain sir to you." Then, to his astonishment, he watched her run her tongue over her bottom lip. A very nice full bottom lip, he saw, now wet and shining from her tongue.

"I'm trying to become more friendly. Perhaps you would change your mind? Perhaps after dinner?"

He shook his head. "You cannot be Arabella Deverill," he said firmly. "Perhaps you are her twin sister, long kept in hiding in the attic, beneath one of those forty gables."

"No, she is still there, in her chains. Have you heard her howling? No, that's not possible. There hasn't been a full moon. She only howls at the full moon." She grinned at him shamelessly. "Now, sir, please come here and sit down. You and I have some serious matters to discuss."

"What serious matters?" he asked, not moving. "No, don't say anything. If there are serious matters between us it can only mean one thing. A woman does not woo a man. Besides, I will not speak to you about anything of importance until after I've had my dinner." He gave a ferocious pull on the bell cord.

"My father always said that a man's stomach was important to him. Not the most important—he would never tell me what that was—but nonetheless, I suppose I must agree that to be at your best, you must have a full belly."

He could but stare at her. He would marry her and bed her and then, at least, she wouldn't be so damnably innocent. "Ah, here you are, Crupper. Have the footmen bring out dinner in here this evening. Lady Arabella doesn't wish to travel all the way to the dining room."

A few minutes later, the earl looked down at the roast pork and fresh garden peas. "Just as Lady Arabella ordered, my lord," Crupper said. The smells were delicious.

"You ordered this?"

She nodded.

"I do not particularly care for roast pork, Crupper. Have you other dishes as well?"

"Of course there are other dishes," Arabella said. "Cook always prepares roast pork for me on Thursdays."

"Hell, leave the damned pork, Crupper, and forget the other dishes. This will do admirably."

His lordship's language was deteriorating alarmingly. Lady Arabella didn't seem to mind, so Crupper decided he wouldn't mind either. There were a lot of changes at Evesham Abbey. It was a trying time for everyone. If the earl wanted to curse, it was probably the best for everyone. It was better than him hurling something. As Crupper got older, it was more difficult to duck, and duck he had many times under the former earl's reign.

Crupper waited until he had very nearly bowed himself out of the Velvet Room before giving his message. "A footman arrived from Talgarth Hall, my lord. Lady Ann and Lady Elsbeth have decided to remain for dinner, not wishing to venture out in this weather."

So, Justin thought, he would be alone with her. For the first time. He wondered if she would try to bolt. No, not likely, particularly given the strange way she was acting since she'd come downstairs. He remembered to say, "Thank you, Crupper."

There was no conversation for ten minutes.

Finally, Arabella said, "Is the roast pork to your liking, sir?"

He was eating like a pig. He couldn't very well say that the damned pork irritated his stomach. "It's passable," he said, and took another big bite. Then he dropped his fork to his plate and sat back in his chair, his arms folded over his chest. He had given her the upper hand—rather she'd taken it and not given it up—and now she was in control, not he. He was obliged to laugh. He remembered thinking that she was admirable upon one occasion. He could not but admit to it again.

"Have you been rehearsing all week for this evening?"

"I don't know what you mean."

She did know, and he knew that she knew, but he said easily, "Well, you have avoided me, probably hidden under the stairs whenever I came too close. It's only reasonable that you've used your time this week to prepare your performance for this evening. Have you decided just how you would deal with me?"

He'd gotten her fair and square, but she wasn't ready to throw in her hand just yet. She slowly laid down her fork and leaned back in her chair, mimicking him, cocking her head to one side. "You know, sir, the cleft in your chin is really quite attractive. I wondered at first if I would ever find it anything beyond the ordinary, but I find that I have. You are quite handsome with it, sir."

"You will keep pushing? All right then, ma'am. Would you care to examine my attractive cleft more closely?" He paused just the barest moment, then added, "If you hadn't noticed, there is also a great deal more of me that I trust you will find equally attractive."

"I trust you will find the same true of me, sir."

"After seeing you in your drenched, very clinging gown, ma'am, I honestly can't imagine being disappointed. However, I am a man who prefers actual proof, not just speculation."

He wanted plain speaking, she'd give him plain speaking. She'd hit him on the head with plain speaking. "Oh, I see. You mean you want me to take my clothes off?"

"That would be an excellent start, but I doubt it is exactly the thing to do this evening. Come, ma'am, enough fencing about. Let's sit by the fire and discuss your serious matters."

He led her to a small sofa and sat himself very close to her. Probably too close, but that was just too bad.

She turned to face him, looking at him squarely in his gray eyes. "I have decided that I will marry you."

"Not an ounce of preamble," he said, as he picked up her hand and began to study her fingers. "Not even a small warning or the barest signal that you were going to blast me out of the water. Would you believe me if I told you that you have just made me the happiest man alive? No, I can see that you won't believe me. Actually I wouldn't either."

"This has nothing to do with happiness, sir. Why are you looking at my fingers? You're playing with them. They are just fingers. Why?"

"You have lovely fingers. At least in this, we are not

alike. Graceful hands you have, ma'am, quite unlike mine. No happiness for us, ma'am?"

"You know very well why we must wed. I am willing to do my part. Are you willing to do yours?"

"Parts. An interesting word. There will be many parts for us, ma'am, if we marry. Are you willing to accept me as a man and not just a poor fellow who happens to live in the same house with you?"

"What do you mean exactly?"

He raised her hand to his mouth and kissed each one of her fingers. "A preamble, ma'am." He pulled her closer and kissed her mouth. Not a deep kiss, just a light touching. Still, she jerked back. He looked long into those gray eyes of hers. He lightly touched his finger to her chin, then ran it along her jaw. "Never before been kissed, ma'am?"

She shook her head, all that lovely hair dry now, all glossy and blacker than a sinner's deeds. She was staring at him, at his mouth, then down at the hand he held, the fingers he'd kissed.

"There is a bit more. Perhaps you won't find that repellent either. But one shouldn't rush these things. Would you like to kiss me again?"

She nodded her head. "All right."

This time she came to him, her palms flat against his chest, but she wasn't pushing against him, no, she was just resting her hands there, one over his heart and he knew she could feel the quickened beat. He kissed her again, still lightly, not forcing her in any way. He touched his tongue to her lower lip, the one she'd licked. She jumped. He cupped her face between his large hands. Actually, he wanted to press her down on her back, pull up her skirts and look at her. He could only imagine how beautiful she would be. Then he wanted to kiss her, slide his hands up the insides of her thighs. He gently eased his tongue into her mouth.

She didn't jump this time. If he wasn't mistaken, and

indeed he wasn't, she was interested and becoming more interested by the moment. He began to stroke his hands through her hair, tangling his fingers, wrapping her hair about his hands, bringing her closer and closer until her breasts were against his chest and her hands, fluttering a moment, came around his back.

"These are parts," he said into her mouth. "The whole is when we will come together. Marry me soon, ma'am, or I just might expire from my need of you."

She raised her head. She seemed without words, which was a surprise, for since he'd known her—such a short time really—she'd always been brash, arrogant, ready to take on any comers, particularly him. She touched her fingertip to the deep cleft in his chin. She outlined it. She examined it. "A part," she said, leaned over and kissed his chin.

"I like all the parts I've seen thus far."

"Good."

"I like your coat, too, sir. Weston?"

It was her father's tailor.

"Yes," he said, and continued to stroke that soft hair of hers.

She leaned her forehead against his chin. She drew several deep breaths, saying finally, her voice scarcely above a whisper, "I've been so frightened—not scared frightened—but a new sort of frightened that has quite turned me tip over tail. I know I haven't treated you well, perhaps I have even been something of a shrew around you, at least before I decided to stay away from you.

"I've thought and thought, sir, and I think perhaps we can work a marriage out between us. A good marriage. I will try to do my part. What do you think?"

He laughed, kissed her, and pulled her against him. "I think that life will be very interesting from now on. Let's marry, ma'am. Let's do it soon. I will try to do all my parts as well."

"Perhaps we could celebrate our agreement? Perhaps you could kiss me again? I truly do not mind it at all."

The earl could practically taste her. He had her so close, so very close, her mouth just an instant away from his and this time he would teach her to open her mouth to him, and then he would—

"Well, hell," he said, and pushed her away just as the door opened and a laughing Lady Ann and Elsbeth came into the room, their cloaks glistening with raindrops, Crupper trailing behind them.

"It is pouring," Lady Ann said as she handed Crupper her wet cloak. "Perhaps we should have remained at Talgarth Hall, but both Elsbeth and I wanted to come home. Ah, you ate your dinner in here. But, goodness, the two of you ate so little. Why, you ate scarcely anything at—"

Lady Ann shut up. She stared at her daughter, then at Justin. It wasn't at all difficult to imagine what had been going on before her and Elsbeth's untimely entrance. Arabella's face was red. Her lovely hair had enjoyed a man's hands tangling through it.

The earl rose. His lust had died a quick death, thank God. "Lady Ann, Elsbeth," he said. "Welcome home. Perhaps you would care for some tea?"

Lady Ann wanted to laugh. It was only her daughter's embarrassment that kept her quiet. She saw that Elsbeth looked confused. She was staring at her half-sister, her mouth readying itself to open and ask questions. "Ah, my dear Elsbeth," Lady Ann said quickly, "I think we had best go to our bedchambers."

Elsbeth didn't look all that eager to leave. She looked eager to stay and talk. The earl said, "Yes, both of you are wet. We will see you in the morning."

"No," Lady Ann said, the laughter lurking in her voice, "I believe that Elsbeth and I will come down again and join you for tea. In about half an hour, Justin?"

He wanted to curse, but didn't. He wanted to take Arabella to the attic and show her more parts than she could as yet begin to imagine. Instead, he said on a sigh, "Yes, thirty minutes." He had never before imagined that Ann would do this to him. Ah, but she was enjoying herself immensely. As for the two of them, he didn't dare kiss Arabella any more during the next thirty minutes. He wouldn't be able to stand up if he did.

Upon their return to the Velvet Room, the earl placed crystal glasses of champagne in their hands and said, "Do wish us well, Ann, Elsbeth. Ma'am here has done me the honor of accepting my hand in marriage."

"Oh," Elsbeth said. "So that was why you looked so, well, not strange really, but not quite present, if you know what I mean. It's as if you wanted both me and Lady Ann to travel to the moon, immediately."

"Well, yes," the earl said. "But you see, it's the right thing to do when people agree to marry. They wish all their relatives would stay away."

"Very true," Lady Ann said. "And we will stay away, but not just yet." She laughed, then raised her glass to theirs. "To your health and happiness, my dears."

11

"Then we are all in agreement. We will be married Wednesday next. Do you agree, ma'am?" He was holding her hand, lightly squeezing her cool fingers.

"I agree, sir. But that is only six days away." She stopped then, looking away from him, toward nothing in particular as far as he could tell.

"What is it, ma'am?"

"I cannot very well wear a black wedding gown. What will I wear?"

He saw that her eyes were luminous with tears, and said quickly to Lady Ann, "She is right. What will she wear, Lady Ann?"

"You will wear a soft light gray silk, Bella, with pearls, I think. Yes, that will be fine."

"All right," Arabella said. She swallowed, then quickly rose.

"I am so very happy for you, Arabella," Elsbeth said. She lowered her voice and leaned toward Arabella's ear. She whispered, "Lady Ann assures me that the earl is kind, not that I don't know that for myself, but people are strange, don't you think? Who can ever really know another person? What is in their hearts? In their thoughts? But don't worry Arabella, he is certain to be kind. If he is not, why then, you can simply shoot him."

Arabella burst into laughter. How could she not? Her father surely would have enjoyed his first daughter. Why had he kept her away? She said to the earl, "I wonder, sir. Will you be kind to me? Or maybe even you're not yet certain? Do you think I should be prepared? Do you think I should clean my gun before the wedding? Have it handy just in case you suffer a lapse?"

"Give me a chance first, please, ma'am."

"I will consider it. Now, I would like to go riding. The sun is out and I wish to take full advantage of it."

The library doors opened, and Crupper, his back stiff with age and dignity, stepped into the room, cleared his throat, and announced, "My lord, Lady Ann, there is a young gentleman just arrived. A very foreign young gentleman. But he is a gentleman and not a merchant or a shop owner."

"Thank God for that," the earl said, the irony floating gently over Crupper's ancient head. "Just how foreign is he, Crupper?"

"It is awfully early in the morning for visitors," Lady Ann said, frowning toward the door.

"Who is this young gentleman, Crupper?" the earl asked again, standing now and walking behind the settee, lightly placing his hand on Arabella's shoulder.

"He informed me his name is Gervaise de Trécassis, my lord, cousin to Miss Elsbeth. He is French, my lord. He is very foreign indeed. He calls himself the Comte de Trécassis."

"Good heavens," Lady Ann said, jumping up. "I had believed all of Magdalaine's family dead in the revolution. Elsbeth, this gentleman must be your mama's nephew."

"A nephew, huh?" the earl said. "Then by all means, Crupper, show the comte in."

A few moments later a strikingly handsome young man preceded Crupper into the library. He wasn't a large man, barely of medium height and with a slender build, elegantly dressed in buff pantaloons and gleaming black hessians. His hair was black as night, his

eyes nearly as dark. The earl found himself looking
from the young man to Arabella, to judge her reaction
to him.

She was smiling at the comte, but actually, she believed he was a fop—surely that jewel-encrusted watch
fob was too pretentious and the several heavy rings he
wore made his hands appear nearly feminine. As for
his shirt points, they nearly touched his smooth-shaven
chin. Then she met his eyes—black eyes filled with intelligence and humor and surely a hint of mystery, a
pinch of wickedness—set beneath delicately arched
black brows and stylishly disarrayed black locks. He
looked both dashing and romantic. She wondered if
Lord Byron looked something like Elsbeth's cousin.
Lucky man if he did.

"The Comte de Trécassis," Crupper announced somewhat unnecessarily. The young gentleman, certainly not
much older than Elsbeth, looked at everyone, his smile
half apologetic, and yet, Arabella thought, he wasn't at
all apologetic, not really, he was as confident of himself
and his acceptance as was the earl, the man she hadn't
known a week ago, the man who would be her husband
within another week.

Lady Ann rose gracefully, shook out her skirts, and
extended her hand. "This is quite a surprise, my dear
comte. I had no idea that any of Magdalaine's family
still lived. Needless to say I am also pleased."

To her surprise, the comte clasped her fingers and
brushed his lips over her palm, in the French style,
which, she supposed, should be expected, since he was,
after all, French. "The pleasure is indeed mine, my
lady. I pray you will forgive my intrusion in your period of mourning, but news of the earl's death just
reached me. I wished to express my condolences in
person. I hope you do not mind?" He spoke with a soft,
lilting accent that made the three females in the room
most readily forgive any supposed intrusion.

"Not at all," Lady Ann said easily.

"You are the Earl of Strafford, my lord?" the comte asked Justin when he had released Lady Ann's hand. There was a brief moment of silent appraisal on the part of both gentlemen before the earl remarked with negligent politeness, "Yes, I am Strafford. Lady Ann informs us that you are nephew to the late earl's first wife."

The comte bowed.

"Oh goodness," Lady Ann said. "Where indeed are my manners? My dear comte, do allow me to present you to your cousin, Elsbeth, Magdalaine's daughter, and to my own daughter, Arabella."

Lady Ann was not at all surprised that the charming young man was greeted even by her normally standoff-ish daughter with a smile that would charm the color off Ann's roses. Elsbeth nodded, wordless. She drew back a moment, allowing Arabella to speak first.

"Although we are not related, comte," Arabella said, gazing at him with that open frankness of hers, "I do not take it amiss that you have come. I am pleased to meet you, sir."

The comte gave her an engaging smile. He did not kiss her palm, merely bowed to her. Lady Ann believed him very well bred indeed. He then turned to Elsbeth. "Ah, my dear little cousin, I count it my good fortune to at last meet the only remaining member of our es-teemed family. You are as beautiful as your mother, your smile as sweet, your eyes as gentle. My father has a painting of her, you see, and I have gazed upon it since I was a small boy."

Instead of taking her hand, the comte gently placed his hands upon her shoulders and lightly kissed her on each cheek. Elsbeth flushed scarlet, but she didn't draw back. She stared up at him with something akin to fas-cinated awe.

The comte stood back from Elsbeth, beamed at the

assembled company, and said, embracing them all with outflung arms, "You are so very kind to me, a stranger. Though my little cousin is my only blood relation, I think already you are like my family." He paused with an expectant look of charming inquiry.

The earl, clearly seeing his duty from all three eager female faces, said a trifle too coolly, Arabella thought, "Monsieur, allow me to ask you to remain at Evesham Abbey for a time, if, that is, you have no other pressing engagements. Of course if you do—"

"I was going shooting with friends in Scotland," the comte said quickly, splaying his hands in the French manner that quite made the earl want to hit him. "But I assure you, my lord, that remaining here would give me the greatest pleasure. And such very lovely pleasure."

From that moment on, the earl thought that Gervaise de Trécassis should be shot.

"Excellent, comte," Arabella said.

"Ah, please call be Gervaise. Unfortunately, my title is only that—a title that has only emptiness. You see before you a simple émigré, torn from his home by that damnable Corsican upstart."

"How horrid for you," Elsbeth said, and there were indeed tears in her eyes.

Oh good Lord, the earl thought. He wanted to puke.

"Yes, but I have survived. I will continue to survive and retake what is rightfully mine after that Corsican is defeated or dead. You have the soul of an angel, my dear Elsbeth, to feel so for me. How like your mother you are. My aunt Magdalaine was a goddess, a lovely gentle goddess."

It was difficult, but the earl managed to keep his snort behind his teeth. However, his black eyebrows shot up at the caressing tone in the young man's voice. He thought he read an almost imperceptible calculating gleam in those flashing black eyes as they rested on

Elsbeth, and thought cynically about Elsbeth's ten thousand pounds. The comte was certainly dressed like a rich young dandy, and the earl wondered even more cynically if Evesham Abbey would be descended upon by dunning tradesmen.

"My dear boy," Lady Ann said, lightly tapping her fingertips on his buff sleeve. "It is nearly time for luncheon. Let me ring for a footman to take up your luggage. We can spend the afternoon getting better acquainted."

The comte bestowed upon her a boyish grin, calculated, Justin thought, to stir Lady Ann's maternal instincts. And when he murmured over her hand, "I am your slave, my dear lady," the earl thought he would puke again.

By evening's end, the earl had decided that the young man was no one's slave. Indeed, it seemed that all the women had quite fallen under his charm. Even his Arabella appeared to accept the comte's presence without question. She had smiled more in the young man's presence than she had since Justin's arrival. He didn't like it one bit.

During the next several days, the earl was left to wonder if he was still betrothed. He saw little of Arabella. If she wasn't in long fittings with the seamstress and Lady Ann for her bridal clothes, she was riding with the comte, fishing with the comte, exploring the countryside with the comte, visiting neighbors with the comte, all in all treating the earl—her own betrothed— with complete indifference. Even at his most infuriated, the earl would never fault her with flirting with Gervaise de Trécassis. No, what he saw was a young woman being pulled from her grief. He watched many times with amazement her exuberance and vitality. It was just a pity that he didn't appear to be able to bring this out of her. That Elsbeth accompanied Arabella and the comte on all their jaunts didn't help. He felt the weight of injustice. However, since he was an earl, a very important man, actually, he felt it important that he remain cool and in control. Thus he tended to treat the three of them like an amused and tolerant uncle. It made Lady Ann arch her fine brows at him, and, had he but known it, made Arabella grind her teeth.

The earl found his only ally to be Dr. Branyon. It was the doctor who said in a measured voice one evening as Lady Ann and the three younger members of the group were playing whist, Arabella partnered by the comte, "Undoubtedly the young comte is harmless enough, though I do find his sense of *timing* to be almost suspiciously flawless, shall we say. I ask myself why he did not make himself known years ago. After all, the late earl was his uncle by marriage. Why did he wait to come here after the earl, his uncle, had died? Yes, it bothers me, this timing of his."

The earl said slowly, watching the young man adroitly lose a hand to Lady Ann, which only made Arabella grin at him, "That is an excellent observation. Perhaps the comte's prior activities bear closer examination."

"He cannot have much prior experience for he is very young. I asked him his age and he told me he was twenty-three. That is only four years younger than you, Justin. He seems a mere boy to me."

"And I appear an old man?"

"No, but you are a man. You know who and what you are. As for the comte—" Dr. Branyon shrugged. "I find myself wondering what he is thinking. And he is thinking, mayhap even scheming. I don't like it."

"That inexhaustible charm of his, I begin to believe he was born with that. He is very good. Better than most men twice his age. Scheming? We will see."

The comte suddenly threw up his hands in mock despair at that moment and exclaimed, "Elsbeth, you have trumped my spade. I had not expected it. Arabella, forgive me for my lapse—but what can I expect when I am surrounded by three beautiful women? I am just relieved that I managed to win two hands."

"You were too careless, Gervaise," Arabella said. She was a fierce competitor, but she was still smiling. "Congratulations, Elsbeth, Mother. Well done."

"I wonder if you and I will be invited to join them in taking tea," the earl said. He rose slowly, his eyes on Arabella. "Ma'am," he called out, "we are powerfully thirsty. Have you a suggestion?"

"Yes," she said, walking straight up to him. She went up on her tiptoes. "Just wait until after we are wed. Then you will see the breadth of my suggestions."

"Ma'am, you shock me," he said, inordinately pleased.

"Not yet, sir."

"Why does he call her ma'am and not Arabella?" the comte asked Lady Ann.

"They aren't married yet," Lady Ann said, and winked at the earl.

The earl was pleasantly surprised the next morning to find himself sharing breakfast with only Arabella. "Ah, you're here. I hoped you would be. How are you this morning?"

"I slept well. I have had no visitations from the ghosts, thank God. Why did you hope I would be breakfasting early?" He sat down and allowed Crupper to serve him.

"I haven't seen much of you since the comte has come to Evesham Abbey. I see that you are fit, you are smiling, and you look reasonably content. It is good. Now I must hurry. It is pleasant to see you, sir." She quickly grabbed a slice of hot toast, downed a quick gulp of coffee, and jumped up from her chair, her eyes on the door.

"Ma'am! There are toast crumbs on your chin. You have lost your last ounce of dignity—if you ever had any—and above all, you don't want the comte to think you a messy eater."

Arabella touched her fingers to her chin, rubbed away the crumbs, and said, "Thank you for telling me. Now, I must hurry. We do not wish to be back too late this afternoon."

"And just where are you going today?" He sounded testy, and he hated it. He drew a long steadying breath.

Arabella drew up and smiled at him with affection. Yes, he was certain it was affection or something close enough to it. "Why, I am taking Gervaise, and Elsbeth of course, to see the Roman ruins at Bury Saint Edmunds."

"It didn't occur to you to invite me?" Now he sounded like a whining ass.

She cocked her head at him. "But, sir, you have already visited the ruins. Do you not remember? You told me that when you arrived in the area, you toured the countryside before coming to Evesham Abbey."

"Ma'am, we are to be married in two days' time." Good God, now he sounded like a wounded dog.

"Something I am not likely to forget," she said. "if you would like to join us, sir, I'm certain Elsbeth and Gervaise wouldn't mind. I just don't want you to be bored."

The earl rose from his chair, walked to his betrothed, and lightly placed his hands upon her shoulders. "It is just that I haven't had you to myself at all these past days." She felt his fingers lightly caressing her shoulders. She liked it. She wanted him to continue. She raised her head, hoping that perhaps he would feel like kissing her. He hadn't, not since that night over a week before. She said, looking intently at his mouth, "You can have me as much as you wish. Would you like me to remain home today?"

"No." He wanted to say yes. He wanted to take her down to the lily pond and make love to her. "No, go with the comte and Elsbeth. Just don't forget me, ma'am."

"Impossible." She sighed and nestled her face against his shoulder, her arms moving around his back. "You feel so very nice, sir, all hard and strong and capable." She started to say he felt just like her father had when she'd hugged him, but decided that perhaps that wouldn't be just the thing to say to the man she was going to marry.

"So do you, ma'am, all soft and strong and capable. I particularly like the way your breasts feel against my chest." There, he'd shocked her. Well, she deserved it.

Instead of acting remotely shocked, she rose on her tiptoes and kissed the cleft in his chin. She pressed against him, then giggled. "I like the way your chest presses against my bosom."

He was immediately harder than the chair leg. He gently pushed her away. "Go now or else I just might lay you atop the table, between the eggs and the kippers, and have my way with you."

Thank God that fewer than forty-eight hours remained before his lust would be magically proclaimed absolutely proper and he could rightfully claim his husbandly rights.

She hugged him again, kissed the cleft once again, then left the breakfast parlor.

The earl returned to his breakfast. He tried to concentrate on his rare sirloin instead of the exquisite pleasure he knew awaited him on their wedding night.

He planned a regimen designed to keep body and mind thoroughly occupied for the remainder of the day. He met with Blackwater in the morning, shared luncheon with Lady Ann and Dr. Branyon, whom, the earl observed, was now almost a daily visitor to Evesham Abbey, and made the rounds of several of his tenants throughout the afternoon. It was late in the day when he returned to the abbey and stabled his horse. Since there was still sufficient daylight, he decided to make a brief inspection of the farmyard. The cows had not yet been brought back for their evening milking, and only a few desultory chickens pecked lazily about their graveled pen. He neared the large two-story barn, and stopped for a moment to inhale the sweet smell of hay. To his surprise and delight, he saw Arabella come around the side of the barn, slowly pull open the front doors, and disappear inside.

He stood struggling with himself for several minutes, his body very much demanding to follow her, and his mind quickly reviewing all the pitfalls of such an action. "Oh, the devil," he said to a goat who was eyeing his boot. He could see Arabella on her back, lying on a thick pile of hay. He could see himself over her, stroking her, kissing every white inch of her. What did two days matter? She would be his wife.

He stepped toward the barn, only to stop dead in his tracks. He saw a movement from the corner of his eyes. He turned and saw the Comte de Trécassis striding toward the barn, his natty cloak billowing out behind him.

A deep foreboding, something he could not explain, swept over him. The earl did not call out to the comte. He didn't move forward to greet him. Instead he remained firmly planted where he was, his eyes fixed on the elegant young man whom he hadn't hated until this moment, only despised because he didn't trust him.

The comte paused a moment before the barn door, glanced quickly around him, tugged at the handle, and as Arabella had done, disappeared into the dim interior.

In a swift military motion the earl clapped his hand to his side where his deadly sword had hung for so many years. His hand balled into a fist at finding nothing more deadly than his pocket. He drew a deep breath and remained standing stiffly, his eyes never leaving the barn door. Arabella was in the barn. The comte had gone into the barn.

No, he wouldn't believe what he had seen. There was an explanation. One that would make him laugh at himself. But even as he sought for any explanation at all, he felt a black, numbing misery building in his belly. He felt he was losing a part of himself, a precious part, one not yet fully understood or explored. But no, that didn't have to be true.

Time passed, but he had no sense of it. From the meadow just beyond the farmyard came the insistent mooing of cows. The sun was fast fading, bathing the barn in gentle golden rays of dusk. The day was coming to a close much the same as any other day, yet he felt no part of it.

Even as his eyes probed the barn door, it opened and the comte quickly emerged. Again he looked about him with the air of one who does not wish to be discovered. In a gesture that left the earl shuddering with black rage, the comte swiftly adjusted the buttons of his breeches, brushed lingering straws from his legs and cloak, and strode with a swaggering gait back to Evesham Abbey.

Still the earl did not move, his eyes fastened to the closed barn door. He had not long to wait, for just as the last light of day flickered into darkness, the door opened, and Arabella, her hair disheveled and tumbling wildly about her shoulders, ventured out, stood for a moment executing a languorous stretch, then turned toward the abbey, humming softly to herself. Every few steps she leaned over and picked bits of straw from her gown.

He saw her wave gaily to the half-dozen farm boys who were busily herding the cows toward the barn for their evening milking.

A gruesome kaleidoscope of images whirled through the earl's mind. He saw clearly the first man he had killed in battle—a young French soldier, a bullet from the earl's gun spreading deadly crimson across his bright coat. He saw the leathery, grimacing face of an old sergeant, run through with his sword, the astonishment of imminent death written in his eyes. He wanted to retch now, as he had then.

The earl had no romantic illusions about killing; he had learned that life was too precious, too fragile a thing to be dispatched in the heat of passion.

He turned and walked back to his new home. His shoulders remained squared. His stride was steady, his expression controlled. But his eyes were empty.

12

"It is a joyous and sacred ceremony that brings us together today. In the presence of our Lord, we come to join two of his children, his lordship, Justin Morley Deverill, tenth Baron Lathe, ninth Viscount Silverbridge, seventh Earl of Strafford and Lady Arabella Elaine Deverill, daughter of the late esteemed Earl of Strafford, in the holiest of earthly bonds."

He saw the comte straightening his trousers when he'd come out of the barn.

But the day before she'd kissed him, spoken so boldly to him, pressing herself against him. Spoken so boldly, as if she knew exactly what a man did with a woman. Jesus, he couldn't bear it.

Arabella gazed up at the earl's finely chiseled profile. She silently willed him to look at her, but he did not, his gray eyes remaining fastened intently upon the vicar's face. He had seemed rather withdrawn, even cold toward her the previous evening, and now she suppressed a grin, deciding that either he was nervous about this whole marriage business, or he had been afraid to get close to her because he would want to seduce her. She wouldn't have minded another kiss or two. She wouldn't have minded him telling her again how he wanted to feel her breasts against him. She shivered at that memory. She knew that tonight she would get much more. Exactly what that much more was, she wasn't exactly certain, but she was eager to find out.

"If there is any man present in this chamber who can state objection to the joining of this man and woman, let him rise now and speak."

She'd met the comte in the barn and let him take her. She had coldly and freely betrayed him. He had wanted to kill both of them, but he hadn't. He knew what was at stake.

She'd had straw in her hair, her gown was askew, and she was whistling. She had obviously enjoyed herself thoroughly. He'd wanted to kill both of them. But just that day she had been so free with him, so giving. She'd wanted him, hadn't she?

Lady Ann felt a brief catch in her throat and swallowed quickly. She had always turned up her nose at mothers who wept with abandon at their daughters' weddings, usually after they had done everything in their power to bring the wedding about, including many times buying the bridegroom. But a tear or two was certainly all right. Besides, she couldn't help it. Arabella looked so very beautiful, so much like her father, so much like Justin. Ah, but she wasn't at all like her father. No, she was good and kind and strong-willed and obstinate as a mule. She was everything a mother could ask for in a daughter. Another tear fell.

The vicar said quietly, "Naturally there would be no one to come between the two of you. Now we will proceed. My lord, will you repeat after me: I, Justin Morley Deverill, take thee Arabella Elaine . . ."

He wanted to choke. No, he wanted to choke her. It was odd though. She hadn't looked even once in the comte's direction since she had come into the drawing room, looking so utterly beautiful in the soft gray silk wedding gown. Her hair was braided atop her head, several small diamond combs flashing in and out of the thick braids, several long ropes of hair lying gently on her white shoulder.

Why hadn't she looked at her lover? How quickly had she taken him as her lover? The first day he had arrived? No, that didn't seem right. Surely she had waited at least three days until she had let him have her in the barn. So she had given herself to him nearly a week now. A week.

Beginning after she had said she would become his wife. Her betrayal was bile in his throat. He should denounce her right here, tell everyone present that she was a slut with no more loyalty than a snake. He opened his mouth. No, he couldn't do it. He couldn't and wouldn't beggar Evesham Abbey, he wouldn't beggar the Deverill line.

"I, Justin Morely Deverill, take three Arabella Elaine to be my lawfully wedded wife . . ."

His voice was low, yet sounding strangely harsh to Arabella's sharp ear. She looked up at him as he spoke the words, wishing he would say them to her, but he didn't. He looked just beyond her, never directly at her. How odd. She thought she heard Elsbeth sigh. She smiled at him, but still, he didn't look down at her. He was taller than her father had been. It pleased her. Why wouldn't he look at her?

Lady Ann felt those tears swimming in her eyes. She didn't want them, but they had gotten there nonetheless. Her only daughter was getting married. She would be her own woman now. She looked beyond beautiful. She looked so much like her father, so much like her soon-to-be husband. Those gray eyes, that thick lustrous black hair. She didn't think she would ever be a grandmother to a blond-haired blue-eyed little boy or girl that looked more like her.

Justin was a man to admire, a strong man, a handsome well-formed man, surely a man Arabella could come easily to love. He was standing so straight, so controlled, repeating his vows. He had known he would marry Arabella for the past five years. He had never swerved, never backed away at least as far as Lady Ann knew. Her husband had never said anything about it if Justin had questioned his decision. She wondered if Justin had any doubts now that the day had come. No, she couldn't believe that he had. There was simply too much at stake. Besides, she had seen the two of them looking at each other. They were luckier than most couples. No, it was more than that. Lady Ann smiled behind her gloved hand. There had been stark desire in Justin's eyes that first night when she and Elsbeth had arrived unexpectedly early from Talgarth Hall. It would be all right.

"In the presence of God, and by his laws and commandments, I now ask you, Arabella Elaine Deverill, to repeat these words after me."

Elsbeth had strained to hear the earl repeat his vows, his voice deep, yet somehow sounding strangely hard to her ears. She saw Arabella gaze up at him while he spoke, a bemused smile on her lips. An eager smile. Elsbeth added her own smile.

She had betrayed him. Knowingly, she had deceived him with that miserable little French bastard. She had spoken to him so boldly, and he had believed it from her innocence, her candor, her guilelessness. But it hadn't been any of that. He wanted to howl his pain. It was near to unbearable.

Arabella spoke her vows in a loud, clear voice, "I, Arabella Elaine, take you, Justin Morley Deverill, to be my lawfully wedded husband, to love, honor and obey . . ."

Obey—Lady Ann's mind clutched at the simple word. That is quite a concession from my headstrong independent daughter, she thought. She heard herself repeating the same vow to another Earl of Strafford, as if it were only a moment of time ago, her voice unsteady and barely audible in the large cathedral. She had known that her powerful father, the Marquess of Otherton, would kill her if she didn't marry the man he had handpicked for her.

Obey.

He had hurled the word at her on their wedding night, when she had cringed away from his mauling hands. She had obeyed, had submitted, her fear and pain heightened by his harsh demands. She had always submitted, knowing she had no other choice, and when he did not curse her for lying passively beneath him, he avenged himself on her body in other ways, cruelly demanding ways that made her nights a conscious nightmare. It was a pity that her father hadn't died before the wedding he had forced upon her rather than being thrown from his hunter only two weeks after she had become the Countess of Strafford.

Life had seemed to be a series of pities. She had hated her husband more than she'd believed it possible to hate another human being. At least he had given her Arabella. If he'd hated Arabella—another girl child—as he'd hated Elsbeth, she imagined that she would have brought herself to the breaking point and killed him. But he'd adored Arabella, adored her more than life itself. How odd of him, this despot who had wanted a son more than anything.

Lady Ann brought her mind back to see Justin, after a peculiar brief hesitation, slip a gold band upon Arabella's third finger.

She had been humming. He could clearly hear her voice, soft and pleased with herself, humming as she'd come out of the barn. Humming even as she had pulled straw from her hair. Humming even as she had straightened her clothing. He saw her clearly leaning down and pulling a straw out of her slipper. The betraying bitch.

"By the authority vested in me by the Church of England, I now pronounce you man and wife."

The curate beamed at the young couple and whispered to the earl, "You are a very lucky man, my lord. Lady Arabella is beyond lovely. You may now kiss your bride."

The earl's jaw tightened. He had to look at her. She was his wife, forever. He forced himself to lean down and brush his lips against her mouth. God, she was soft, moist, eager, the slut. The radiant glow on her face sickened him. She tried to keep his mouth just a moment longer on hers, and just grinned wickedly up at him when he jerked away from her. He turned quickly away and gazed with hopeless intensity at the golden cross behind the curate's left shoulder.

Lady Ann found herself praying silently that Justin would be gentle with Arabella. But that wish brought a wry smile to her lips. Only that afternoon, as she had bustled about Arabella, showing her each new article of clothing that she had paid little or no attention to, scolding her for her inattention as her maid toweled her damp hair, she had thought it time to do her duty as a mother. Nervously she had dismissed the maid and faced her daughter. "My love," she began slowly, "tonight you will be a married lady. I think you ought to know that there will be certain changes. That is, Justin will be your *husband,* and that means many things. For example—"

Arabella interrupted her with a shout of delighted laughter. "Mama, are you by any chance referring to the imminent loss of my virginity?"

Oh goodness. "Arabella!"

"Now, Mama, I am sorry to shock you, but you must know that Father most superbly detailed the entire, well, let's call it a process, though, to be honest, Papa called it mating. I am not afraid, Mama, indeed, I can think of nothing more pleasurable than making love

with Justin. I think he will be very good at it. Don't
you think so? A gentleman should gain experience and,
well, skill, before he weds. You don't doubt that I will
disappoint him, do you? Oh dear, I know little of nothing when it comes to the actual doing of things. Perhaps there are a few things you could tell me to make
him, well, know that I believe him to be beautiful and
not at all terrifying?"

Lady Ann didn't know a single thing. A man, beautiful? Perhaps he had been beautiful, but she'd been so
afraid, hated him so very much, that she'd kept her
eyes closed as much as possible. A man, beautiful? She
had never even considered such a thing. Perhaps . . .
She just stared at her grown daughter, helpless, totally
beyond her ken. Her father had told her everything?
Had he told her that men were savage and brutal and
cared nothing for the woman's pain? No, evidently not.
He'd only told her the process. The bastard. That was
disgusting enough in itself. No, perhaps she should
think about this more. She pictured Dr. Branyon in her
mind and blushed a red as a stormy sunset.

"Mama, are you all right? Oh, I see, you think I
shouldn't know all that I happen to know. I promise
I'm not a fallen woman, but I do think it utterly ridiculous that ladies should not enjoy lovemaking. And
when I think that many girls are taught to regard it as a
most disagreeable duty—well, I think they deserve
whatever boring toad they get in their bed. I know you
and Papa must have been different. Justin and I will be
different as well. We will be good together. Now, don't
worry. I love you. Don't worry about me, Mama."

"You're certain there's nothing I can tell you?" Lady
Ann wanted to faint. But instead she had to act normally, she had to continue the deception. God, she had
hated him, hated him to her bones, to her very soul.
Arabella truly believed that her father had loved her
mother? Had given her pleasure in bed? Dear God,

what a travesty their marriage had been. She'd hated being a victim.

"No, Mama. You're looking quite white. At least you're not blushing anymore. Don't worry yourself any more about it. You know, I do love you dearly for your concern." Again, as Arabella scooped her mother into her arms and gave her a fond, reassuring hug, Lady Ann had the inescapable feeling that she should have been the daughter.

Later that evening, as Lady Ann tied the ribbons on Arabella's lovely white satin nightgown, she felt nearly overwhelmed by her daughter's excitement, her anticipation, the lust she knew she saw in her daughter's eyes. Her eyes sparkled. There was no fear in them. It was lust, there was no other way to describe it.

She forced Arabella to sit down and began to brush her hair. "No more, please, Mama," Arabella said, jumping up. "Will he come soon? Oh, Mama, I don't want you to be here when he comes to me."

"Very well." Lady Ann stepped back and placed the hairbrush on the dresser.

"Justin will be delighted. You look beautiful. I don't believe he has ever seen you with your hair loose down your back. Oh yes, he has, I remember. That night the both of you agreed to marry. Ah, Arabella, do leave the buttons on your nightgown alone."

"I know," Arabella said, doing a small dance around her bedchamber. "I must keep the silly thing on for just a while longer."

Lady Ann gulped. "Justin will be here soon. I will leave you now." She turned, then whipped about to hug her daughter. "Be happy, Arabella. Be happy. If something goes wrong, well, I don't know that it will, but . . . no, don't worry." Oh God, what could she say? How could she warn her? What if Justin was like her husband had been?

Arabella said very quietly, gently, "In matters regarding me, Mama, Father never erred in his judgment. Never."

At her daughter's words, Lady Ann looked up quickly. Perhaps it was her imagination, but she thought she detected a fleeting sad awareness in her daughter's voice. No, that wasn't possible. She gave her head a tiny shake and turned abruptly away. "I hope you are right, Arabella. Good night, my love. I hope to see a smile on your face tomorrow."

"A very big smile, Mama."

After her mother had left her, Arabella paced the bedroom with the eagerness of pleasurable anticipation. She delighted in discoveries, and tonight, well, tonight—She hugged herself with excited impatience. She chanced to look at *The Dance of Death* panel, stuck out her tongue at it, for she hated uncertainty, fear of the unknown, and let her eyes rove to the large bed. She was beginning to wonder, an impish smile on her mouth, if her mother hadn't trapped Justin and was telling him out to go along, when the door opened suddenly and her husband appeared. How magnificent he looked in the dark blue brocade dressing gown. Her heart quickened at the sight of him. His feet were bare. She doubted very much that he was wearing anything beneath that dressing gown. She hoped not. She couldn't wait to set that dressing gown off him. She wanted, finally, to see him naked. He was hers.

The earl closed the door, fastened his fingers over the key, and clicked it into place.

"I'm glad you did not leave me waiting too long, Justin. Do you know that I have never before spent the night in this bedchamber? I would not like to if I were alone. But since you're here, I doubt I will even notice that miserable *Dance of Death* panel. Do you like my hair? My nightgown? Mama made me keep it on." She was babbling, she knew it, but certainly it was all right.

She was a new bride, and she was a bit nervous after all. She was so nervous she even gave him a curtsy.

He stood by the door, unmoving, just looking at her, his arms crossed over his chest. "Your hair is beautiful. The nightgown is beautiful. You look very virginal. I'm pleased, but a bit surprised."

"Indeed, I hope you are pleased. Why should you be surprised?" She was so filled with excitement she didn't hear anything strange in his voice.

Still the earl did not move toward her nor did he answer her question. Arabella, with a light, dancing step, skipped to him, her bare feet soundless on the thick carpet. She laid her hands on his shoulders, felt the smooth flesh beneath her fingers, rose to her tiptoes, and kissed him.

His hands moved to her arms, and suddenly, with no warning, he shoved her away from him. She staggered back, clutched the back of a chair, and stared at him, mouth agape, stunned with confusion. "Justin? What is wrong? What happened? Didn't you want me to kiss you?"

He wanted to kill her. No, he couldn't do that. But he would make her suffer. He would hurt her as she had hurt him. He said in a very precise voice that was colder than the winter frost of the previous winter, "You will take off your nightgown. You will do it now and you will do it quickly."

Now she understood. Men were men, her father had told her that men got foxed at the oddest times. "Justin, if you have been drinking, I would just as soon that we did not—" Her voice fell like a stone from a cliff as he strode toward her. She saw the taut, angry cords standing out in his neck. She saw the fury in his gray eyes.

Fury?

At her? What was going on here? He should be as excited as she was. He had loved kissing her, pressing her close. He had told her that he wanted her breasts against his chest. Now was his chance. It was his wedding night as well as hers. Why was he angry?

"Do as I tell you, you damned slut, or I will rip it off you."

Slut? He had just called her a slut. She could but stare at him. "I don't understand," she said slowly, eyeing him as she backed away from him, and stood behind a very large winged chair. "Please, what is the matter? Why did you call me that? How could I be a slut? I'm eighteen and married for only five hours. I'm a virgin. More than that, I'm your wife."

There was no mistaking the raw fury in his eyes, in the way he held himself. He said nothing. He stalked her. She didn't understand what was wrong, but she wasn't stupid. She ran to the other side of the chair. Soon he had cornered her behind a dressing table set close to the wall. She held out her hands in front of her. "Justin, stop this, please. If this is a game, I do not understand the rules. I don't like this game. My father never told me that it could be like this."

He laughed, a raw harsh laugh that brought fear hard and deep into her. Something was very wrong. He was furious with her and she had no idea why.

He grabbed her suddenly, but she jerked her arm free, whirled about and raced to the door. She was very fast. Fear did that. Oh God, the door wouldn't open. She turned it wildly first one way, then the other, but it wouldn't move. Damn, what was wrong? The key. He'd locked the door. Her palms were sweaty. She grabbed that key and wrenched at it. She felt him standing behind her, watching her. Suddenly, he grabbed a handful of hair and began to wind it about his hand, pulling slowly, inexorably, until she cried out in pain and stumbled back against his chest. He jerked her about with his other hand to face him.

For a very long time, he simply stared down at her. Then, very quietly, he said, "You will do what I told you to do and you will do it this instant. You really don't want to know what I will do if you refuse me."

Instinctively she realized that she could not reason with him, that he was beyond reason, he was beyond her and who and what she was to him. She could only try to save herself. She gritted her teeth against the stabbing pain in her scalp and brought her knee up and forward with all her strength. She connected with his hard thigh. He'd been too fast for her.

His eyes were nearly black with fury. He would strike her now. She tensed, awaiting the blow. Instead, he drew a deep breath and jerked at her hair, bringing her face to within inches of his own. He looked down at her, looked directly into her eyes, eyes so much like his, and said quietly, "I presume your esteemed father taught you that trick to bring a man low. It would have been the worse for you had you succeeded, you know. You would have made me very angry then. You would have invited me to wring your treacherous neck."

"Justin." She felt numb, her mind empty and blank of other words.

In a swift, violent motion he released her hair, dug his fingers into the ruffled lace about her throat, and ripped downward with a force that doubled her forward. The sharp rending of satin filled the silence of the room, and Arabella looked down stupidly at her gown, torn from her throat to her ankles. Before she could react, he jerked the gown from her shoulders, tearing apart the small buttons from her wrists. She saw the satin-covered buttons bounce and roll about the carpet near the remnants of her nightgown. She felt his eyes sweep over her, staring first at her breasts, then lower, at her belly. She was finally shocked into action at the awareness of her impotence. Without thought, she balled her hand into a fist and with all her might struck at his face.

He blocked her arm before it reached his jaw. He

said in a very calm, low voice, "You wish to fight me, do you, madam?" Yesterday, he had spoken to her with barely banked excitement, his voice tender and yet wonderfully demanding. She'd responded fully to him, yesterday. But not now. His voice sounded calm, yes, but dead as well. So dead it made her die inside. He grasped her about the waist and flung her hard over his shoulder.

Arabella pounded at his back, knowing it did little good. He was a man, strong and fit and she had no chance against him. He hurled her away from him, and she fell sprawled on her back on the bed, her breath knocked out of her. Even as she gasped painfully, she thought only to escape him, and clutched at the covers to scramble to the far side of the bed. She cried out as his hand grasped her ankle and gave it a wrench, flipping her again upon her back.

"Damn you, lie still. Yes, that is much better. Now, I think it only fair that I examine my purchase."

Dear God, he was mad, quite mad. There was no other reason for him to do this. Surely her father would have known if the man he'd chosen for her was perverted, crazed, a man who enjoyed a woman's pain. No, surely not.

She yelled up at him, "Stop this, Justin. It's madness, do you hear me? Why are you doing this? I won't allow it. Let me go, damn you!"

He said nothing, merely stared down at her breasts. She knew he was studying her, and he looked bored, only the rage was still burning deep and constant in his eyes. She was afraid, suddenly, very afraid.

13

"**D**amn you, stop it!"

"You have the language of a tavern wench. I should have guessed that it meant something more vile in you that anyone could see. Something vile and deep."

"Vile? What the devil is vile about me? I know I have a temper. So do you. There is nothing vile about a temper. Are you mad?"

"Shut up," he roared at her, not even looking at her face.

Appalled, she again tried to jerk away from him, but quickly, he clamped his hands around her ankles.

"Move again and I shall tie you down," he said in a cold voice that froze her to her soul. "I have paid dearly for my inheritance and that includes having you in my bed, though I doubt there will be much pleasure for me. There will certainly be none for you."

She had to try again, she had to. She reached her hand up to touch him, but he slapped it away. "Why are you doing this, Justin? What have I done to you? Why did you call me vile? Why did you call me a slut? Please, tell me what is wrong. Surely you must know that it must be a mistake."

He was looking at her breasts, saying quietly, more to himself than to her, "I knew you would be beautiful. I knew your flesh would be as white as virgin snow. I pictured you so many times lying on your back like this with all that white flesh and your incredible black hair falling in tangles over your shoulders. I knew I wouldn't be disappointed in your body and I'm not. I don't want to desire you, indeed my own lust sickens me, but I will take you. God forgive me, I want to take you, now. I must do it. This damnable marriage must be consummated."

He was looking at her breasts again. She couldn't stop their deep up and down motion. Dear God, this could not be happening to her.

"You asked me why I call you a slut, why I am treating you like this? You want to know why I'm not treating you like my sweet little virgin bride? I detest your damned lies, your protestations of innocence. Damn you, Arabella, you betrayed me. You took that damnable little French bastard as your lover, and for that, you bitch, you will pay dearly." His hand touched her breast. She bowed off the bed, screaming. He slammed his palm over her mouth. "Surely that does not surprise you or shock you." He lifted his hand off her. "No, I don't believe I could bear seeing you play the whore. If I continued touching you, caressing you, you would begin to moan and cry out, would you not? No, I will get it done. As I said, there will be little enough pleasure for me and none at all for you. At least with me there will be no pleasure for you, damn you."

Abruptly he stood back from the bed and untied his dressing gown. He shrugged it from his shoulders. He stood naked before her, carefully watching her face. There was an ugly sneer on his mouth.

Arabella stared at him. She had never before seen a naked man. By God, he was beautiful, all hard planes and hollows and corded muscles. There was no fat on him, just lean hardness. She realized she was staring, and sucked in her breath. He'd called her a whore, he'd accused her of taking the comte for her lover? That was mad, simply mad. He had talked about not touching her

and had told her that he wouldn't. She looked at the
thick black hair at his groin, at his sex, hard and ready.
Oh yes, she'd seen horses mate and knew very well
what that meant. Surely he was too big for her. Surely
he wouldn't force her. Oh God, she hated herself, her
own weakness, her fear, but still, she said, "Justin,
please, what do you intend to do? You are very big. I
don't think this will work." He looked like he would
spit on her. Her rage became whole and full. "Damn
you, I am a virgin! I took no lover, not even that miserable little French bastard! Who lied to you? Did Gervaise? Tell me, damn you, who told you this?" She
frantically pressed her legs tightly together and brought
her hands up to cover her breasts.

"Dear God, what an actress you would have made."
He stretched, and again, she stared at him. He laughed,
an ugly hoarse laugh that scared her to her toes. "You
may believe me that your body will easily take my sex.
Oh yes, I would wish that you cease your fiction, your
damnable lies. You want to know who lied about you?
I will tell you. No one told me lies about you. I saw
him, I saw you, the both of you coming out of the barn,
just moments apart. It was obvious what you had
done."

His breathing was so harsh now she could barely
make out his words. "Perhaps I should give you pleasure. The only thing is that you might not shout out my
name when you take your release. That would be a
blow to me, wouldn't it? No, I will simply get it over
with. Yell and scream and curse as you like. It will
make no difference."

She could only stare at him and mutely shake her
head back and forth. He'd seen her with the comte?
Coming out of the barn? But it was impossible.

He leaned over her, wrenched her legs apart, and
straddled her. She began a silent struggle, scratching at
his face, kicking up at his groin with her knees. He

simply flattened her hands over her belly and held down her legs under his own. She felt his hand move between her thighs, and froze.

He realized at that moment that he couldn't force her—no, he couldn't rape her and that's what it would be—rape. He strode over to his dressing table, dipped his fingers into a pot of cream and returned to her. She was lying there on her back, her eyes disbelieving and shocked.

"Don't move." To make sure, he held his palm flat on her belly. She struggled a moment, then stilled.

She watched his finger, coated with cream, come down toward her. Then she felt that finger, coated with that cream pushing against her. Even as she struggled, trying to break his hold on her hands, she felt his finger shove inside her, moving deeper and deeper still. God, she hated it. He was alien to her, his finger a punishment. The barn? What was this about the barn?

"Justin, please, stop this, please. Don't hurt me. None of what you believe is true. There was no barn. I barely tolerate the comte. Why—" She screamed, a pitiful sound really, high and thin. His finger was gone. Now, his sex was inside her, shoving deeper and deeper. He paused an instant, grasped her hands, and jerked them over her head. With an almost tender motion he pulled the tangled strands of hair from her eyes.

"God, I cannot believe that you have done this to me." He pushed deep, the cream easing his way, but it wasn't enough. The pain ripped through her. She was sobbing, feeling herself choke on her own tears, and when he paused just a moment in his mad thrusting, arrested by her maidenhead, he stared at her, sudden shock and uncertainty in his eyes.

"Justin," she whispered, "no." Her body bowed with pain, her soul empty of anything she knew or understood.

He growled deep in his throat, released her hands

and dug his fingers into her hips, jerking her upward. He tore through her maidenhead and drove hard to her womb.

It was over quickly. He was panting hard over her until suddenly he froze and she felt his seed deep inside her. A man's release. He was over her, his head bowed, his strong arms trembling as he held himself above her. A man was inside her. Justin was inside her. Her husband had forced her, had hurt her, because he believed she and the comte were lovers.

Arabella was drained of fight, of courage. She'd told him it wasn't true, but he hadn't believed her. The pain lessened a bit as he pulled slowly out of her, for his seed eased his way. Still, it hurt and she moaned, hating herself for it, but unable to hold it close in her throat.

He wondered if he could stand, but he managed to. His fury was exhausted. She was staring up at him. She looked devastated. No, surely that wasn't right. Had she expected to fool him? Well, she had, damn her. She'd been a virgin. He'd not expected that. He met her eyes, saw the pain in them, the awful awareness of what he'd done to her, and for an instant, he doubted.

She had been a virgin. She'd told him she and the comte weren't lovers.

But then, clearly in his mind's eye, he saw the comte coming out of the barn, his swaggering stride as meaningful as a man's crow of victory. And then she had come out of the barn, disheveled, tumbled, yes, tumbled, the look of a woman who had been made love to, thoroughly and with great enjoyment. It hardened his soul against her. She was perfidious. She had betrayed him, then lied to him. He began to turn away from her, still not saying a word, but then looked down at her. Her legs were sprawled. Her virgin's blood and his seed mixed with the white cream were on her thighs and on the bedcovers. He didn't like himself at that moment. He had never hurt a woman in his life, never. He'd been an animal. But no, no. He'd been justified. He hadn't hurt her overly, he'd merely taken her as a man had to take a woman to consummate the marriage. He'd been fast, gotten it over with quickly. He'd used cream. He hadn't raped her. He would have been justified had he raped her, but he hadn't, no, he'd merely gotten it done with.

She'd lied to him.

He grabbed a towel from the washbasin and tossed it to her. She made no move to catch it. It fell over her belly. "Clean yourself. You are a mess."

Arabella still didn't move. She only stared at him, not really seeing him, not wanting to see him, for that would burn into her soul what he had done. He believed her capable of such deceit. It made no sense to her, but he believed it. It had made him cruel, brutal.

He said to her with empty bitterness, "Don't look at me like that. It isn't any of my doing. I merely did what I had to do to secure my inheritance. I did not rape you. I used cream." He plowed his fingers through his hair, standing it on end. "Damnation, so I was wrong about your virginity. That came as a big surprise. How very nobel of the damned comte to leave you intact for your wedding night, to grant me the honor of deflowering you. Did you convince him to leave you intact? Did you tell him that I wasn't that big a fool? Or perhaps he was the one who didn't want me to guess that I wasn't your first man? He was afraid I'd kill him outright?"

His gray eyes narrowed. His voice continued bleak. "I want to kill the little bastard. I am thinking hard about what I shall to do him. Of course, there are certainly other ways. You have fooled me yet again, but now I understand. There are so many other ways, are there not? Did he sodomize you? Yes, very probably. And, of course you pleased him with your lovely mouth. A man—a Frenchman in particular—enjoys that as much as coming inside a woman."

What was he talking about? What did sodomize mean? What did he mean about her mouth? She was shaking her head. Words still seemed beyond her. She felt so very cold, so very empty.

He laughed. A raw laugh that turned back on himself. "Well, now that your husband has claimed your maidenhead, you can take your lover in more conventional ways. My thanks, *dear* Arabella, for this mockery of a marriage."

She felt his deadly fury, winced at his damning words. Yet, they were meaningless sounds to her. How could he believe that she had a lover? She'd made her decision to wed him; with that decision, she'd given herself to him, only him. This made no sense. Nothing made sense, nothing except the pulling soreness inside her body. She felt curiously numb, blessedly detached from the pitiful woman who lay there, naked, legs sprawled, listening to this man who hated her.

Her silence was a confession of guilt to him. Infuriated he grabbed up his dressing gown, flung it on. "That you betrayed me makes me want to kill both you and him. But I can't kill you, can I? If I did, I would lose everything. You have made me pay dearly for my inheritance, an inheritance that you wanted for yourself. I only ask, dear wife, that in future you conduct your affairs with more discretion. I filled you with my seed this time. I will not do it in the future. You will have no child by me. If you do become pregnant, I will not claim the child. I will announce to the world that you carry another man's babe—a Frenchman's wretched get—that you are filled with another man's seed. Believe me on this."

He turned on his heel, and without looking back, strode into the small adjoining dressing room and very quietly closed the door behind him.

The gilt-edged ormolu clock on the mantelpiece ticked away its minutes with time-honored accuracy. The orange embers in the fireplace crackled and hissed in their final death glow, eventually succumbing to the invading chill of the room. The hideous grinning skeleton, mouth agape, eternally suspended on *The Dance of Death* panel, silently taunted the motionless figure on the bed.

Lady Ann broke her habit and took Mrs. Tucker quite by surprise by appearing at the inordinately early hour of eight o'clock at the breakfast parlor door. It was really rather a foolish thing to do, for in all likelihood the newlywedded couple would not emerge for hours. Yet Lady Ann had awakened with a vague sense that something was not quite right, and in spite of the comforting warmth that tempted her to snuggle down in her bed, she had swung her feet to the floor, rung for her maid, and dressed with more speed than was her usual habit.

"Good morning, Mrs. Tucker," Lady Ann said with a smile. "I suppose I am the only one to demand breakfast this early in the morning."

"Oh, no, my lady. His lordship has been in the breakfast parlor for a good half hour, though I can't say that he has quite done justice to Cook's kidneys and eggs. Indeed, I don't believe he has touched his breakfast.

Lady Ann experienced a sudden sinking in the pit of her stomach. This surely wasn't right. But what could possibly be wrong? She said, "If that is the case, Mrs. Tucker, Cook won't have to prepare more kidneys for me."

The door to the breakfast parlor was slightly ajar. As Lady Ann stepped into the room, she was able to observe the earl before he was aware of her presence. His plate was indeed untouched. He lounged sideways in his chair, one leather-breeched leg thrown negligently over the brocade arm. His firm chin rested lightly upon his hand, and he appeared to be gazing out onto the south lawn at nothing in particular.

Lady Ann straightened her shoulders and walked into the breakfast room. "Good morning, Justin. Mrs. Tucker tells me you are sadly neglecting Cook's breakfast. Are you feeling all right this morning?"

He turned quickly to face her, and she saw the tense line of his jaw, the shadows beneath his gray eyes, the haggard lines about his mouth. The lines smoothed out in a trice. He looked remote and quite calm, but she knew she hadn't been mistaken. Something was very wrong.

"Good morning, Ann. You are certainly up and about early. Do join me. I am simply not hungry this morning. There was enough food served yesterday to fatten up a battalion."

Lady Ann sat in the chair to his right. She wanted desperately to question him, but she found herself at a loss as to how to proceed. His face grew rather forbidding, as if he guessed her thoughts. She began to methodically butter a slice of warm toast, and without raising her eyes again to his face, she said, "It seems odd that you are now my son-in-law. Dr. Branyon obligingly pointed out that I can no longer escape my new title of Dowager Countess of Strafford. How very ancient it makes me feel."

"Give yourself another twenty years before you consider assuming that title, Ann. Ah, by the way, are you planning to marry Paul Branyon?"

"Justin, what a question, why I—" She was totally taken off her guard. Her toast slipped from her fingers and fell atop her marmalade. She gulped. "That is quite a question to be hit with this early in the morning."

"Yes, and a very important one that I'm sure you have no wish to answer. Do forgive me, Ann. Questions such as that tend to place the person being asked in a rather difficult position, do you not agree?"

"Yes," she said slowly, "naturally you are right. That was very well done. I don't believe I've ever before received such an elegant poke in the nose."

He rose, tossing his napkin beside his full plate. "If you will excuse me, Ann, I have many matters to attend to this morning." She watched him walk from the room. She said nothing more to him. What was there to say?

She stared down at the array of dishes Cook had happily prepared for the newlyweds. Dear God, whatever could have happened? Arabella had been so very happy and excited the night before—not at all a nervous young bride.

Arabella. Oh God, she must go to her. Her concern made her feet fly up the stairs to the earl's bedchamber, the chamber she hated more than any other in this great mansion.

The door stood partially ajar, and she tapped on it lightly as she entered.

"Oh," she said in surprise at the sight of Grace, Arabella's maid, standing alone in the room, the tattered remnants of a nightgown held in her hands.

Grace quickly dropped a curtsy, her brown eyes darting quickly away from Lady Ann's face.

"Where is my daughter?" She walked forward, her eyes on that torn nightgown in Grace's hands.

Grace gulped uncomfortably. Lady Arabella had given her strict orders to straighten the room before anyone was about. Here she was standing in the middle of the room with the evidence of the earl's brutality in her hands. "Ah, my lady, her ladyship is in her own room."

"I see," Lady Ann said slowly, her eyes taking in the dried bloodstains on top of the bedcover, the red-tinged water and the blood-flecked towel on the washbasin. She felt sick with apprehension. No use in putting more questions to Grace. She would protect Arabella. She was out of the bedchamber before Grace could offer her a curtsy.

Lady Ann walked more and more slowly as she neared her daughter's bedchamber. She could not help remembering her own wedding night, filled with pain and humiliation. She shook her head even as her steps slowed further. No, it could not have been like that. Justin was so very different from her late husband.

Still, her hands were damp when she knocked lightly on Arabella's door. There was no answer. Not that she expected one. She knocked again. Would Arabella refuse to let her come in? Then she heard, "Enter."

Lady Ann was not certain what she expected to find, but when she walked into the bedchamber, she looked at her very normal daughter of yesterday. Arabella calmly rose to greet her, dressed in her black riding habit, her velvet hat set high above smoothly arranged curls, the black ostrich feather curving over the brim, nearly brushing her cheek.

"Good morning, Mother. Whatever has you up and about so very early? Is Dr. Branyon coming?"

She sounded calm. Laced with that calm was centuries of arrogance that dared Lady Ann to say anything. Had she not seen Justin, not visited the earl's bedchamber, she would have felt the complete fool.

"You ride as usual?"

"Of course, Mother. Is there any reason why I should not? I always ride early in the morning. Is there something you would like me to do?"

There was more arrogance, so much Lady Ann felt she would drown in it. Lady Ann found that she could not rise to the challenge. If Arabella did not wish to confide in her, she could not press her. She realized then that Arabella had rarely taken her into her confidence over the years. Only her father had shared her thoughts, her dreams, her fears, if, that is, she'd ever had any.

"No, my dear, if you wish to ride, it is certainly your affair. I simply could not sleep and thought to bid you good morning. That is all. Well, I did see Justin in the breakfast parlor. He did not look quite well rested. He looked a bit tense, even, perhaps despondent for some very odd reason, well—"

An arched black brow shot up in suspicious inquiry. "I suggest that if you are concerned for Justin, you simply ask him how he fares. Now, I fear you will grow overtired if you do not get your rest, Mother. If you will excuse me—" Arabella drew on her gloves, tipped her hat to a more jaunty angle, and walked to where her mother stood. She kissed her lightly on the cheek, her expression softening almost imperceptibly, and walked quickly out of the room.

Lady Ann stood staring after her daughter. Damnation, what had happened?

As Arabella guided Lucifer past the old abbey ruins to the country lane that led to Bury St. Edmunds, her eyes were clear and straight, her gloved hands steady on Lucifer's reins, her chin raised high.

Poor Mother, she thought, feeling suddenly guilty. She hadn't treated her well. How had her mother known that something was wrong? And she had known. It was a mystery. So Justin hadn't looked well rested, had he? He had looked despondent? Damn him to hell! Arabella rather hoped that he would rot, in addition to hell. He deserved to rot. He deserved every bad thing that could happen to him did happen.

Still, how had her mother guessed that something was wrong? Oh dear, had she seen the shambles in the master's bedchamber? Had Grace not had enough time to burn her nightgown and the sheets? She would ask her when she returned to the abbey.

She flicked Lucifer lightly with the reins on the neck, urging him into a gallop. If only she could leave

behind her all the ugliness, the pain, the hatred of
the night before. And that horrible cream that had
eased her, but still, it hadn't mattered. Nothing had
mattered to him. She felt sick with disappointment,
with despair. She wanted to cry. But even as the wish
flashed through her mind, she saw her father's face
filled with contempt. It was weakness, cowardice, to
deny any experience that touched one's life. It was utterly unacceptable to cry. Her shoulders straightened
from long habit, however difficult, but she managed it,
and her firm chin thrust forward.

Touch her life? God, Justin had ripped through her
life, doing his utmost to destroy her. The nagging soreness between her thighs was bitter proof that he had
violated her body. She would not let him ravage her
mind and spirit as well.

His words were clear in her mind, yet they were so
absurd that she had difficulty crediting them. She tried
to remember his words, to give them some meaning
she hadn't yet comprehended, not to excuse him for
what he had done to her, but to allow her to understand.
Absurdly, he believed that the comte was her lover.
And he'd spoken of seeing them at the barn. It made no
sense at all. She could not fathom how Justin had
drawn such a damning conclusion. Someone must have
lied to him, convinced him that she had betrayed him.

But who could have done that and, for God's
sake, why?

She frowned between Lucifer's ears. It was beyond
obvious that he had believed the lie. Then why had he
gone through with their marriage? Ah, but she was being stupid. If he hadn't gone through with the wedding,
he would have lost the greater portion of his inheritance. And he'd said it himself. He'd been quite clear.
She had betrayed him but he couldn't kill her else he
would lose everything. But he was thinking about
killing Gervaise. She wondered dispassionately if he

would kill the comte. She found that she didn't care a great deal, except, of course, that the comte was innocent of bedding the earl's bride.

She pulled Lucifer to a halt. He was breathing hard. She looked about her and realized with a start that she had ridden past the Roman ruins without even noticing. She drew up and patted her horse's neck. She suddenly remembered a phrase she had overheard her father say to one of his friends: "I rode the wench until she would have thrown me off, if she could." She thought ironically that at least the meaning of his crude remark was now clear to her.

Almost unwilling she turned Lucifer about and headed at a slow trot back to Evesham Abbey. She must have ridden for hours, for the sun was reaching its zenith in the sky.

She could feel her bitter calm begin to crumble the nearer she drew to *his* home. Justin would be there, waiting. She would have to face him, not just today, but tomorrow, a lifetime of tomorrows. For a fleeting moment she considered confronting him, to plead her innocence again, to demand to know who had told him such a damning lie. She pictured such a scene in her mind and saw herself pleading and him rejecting her pleas, as he had the night before. Instinctively, after his rage of last night, she knew that he would still disbelieve her. She pictured renewed fury and savage reprisal. In that instant she hated that she was female and thus weaker, hated his superior strength that could allow him to dominate her through sheer physical power.

Arabella shivered despite the hot sun that beat down upon her black riding habit. Surely he would not force her to submit to him again. Hadn't he said he wouldn't spill his seed in her again? Hadn't he said that he wanted no child from her? His revenge upon her had been thorough and merciless. But it was over now, or at least for as long as he kept to his vow.

She guided Lucifer into the stable yard, pulled up before her sweating groom, and slid to the ground. She hated the feeling of wariness, of dread that washed over her as she neared the front doors of Evesham Abbey. God, if she did not have her pride, she would have nothing. He must not know how he had hurt her, disillusioned her. She would not allow that. She thought again of his words of the night before, spoken so calmly at her and yet there was such deadly fury in his voice. She had played his words over and over in her mind, yet there was one word he had said to her that she did not understand. Strangely, it seemed vitally important to her that she know the meaning of that word.

She glanced up at the sun, guessed that it neared luncheon, then let herself quietly into a side entrance. She thought only to avoid seeing Justin before it was absolutely necessary. She trod through her home to the library, slipped through the door, and shut it quietly behind her. Arabella was not an enthusiastic scholar, certainly not much addicted to the use of the dictionary. Thus she spent several minutes perusing the book-lined shelves to locate it. She had always assumed that any words her father did not use were not worth knowing about. She was beginning to think that in this instance she was wrong. She pulled the leather-bound volume from the shelf, wet her fingertips on her tongue, and began to riffle through the stiff pages.

Her fingers sped down the columns until she found the word she sought. *"Sodomy,"* she read. *"Middle English and Old French 'sodomie'."* There were biblical references, but nothing to tell her what it meant. "Well, damnation. What could he have meant? What?"

14

Arabella suddenly felt movement behind her and whirled about, nearly dropping the dictionary, so thick and heavy that it would have broken her foot. She looked up at the earl, who stood with negligent ease, his hand resting flat on the top of the desk. Her mouth went dry. She felt guilty even though there was no reason to. She'd even been speaking out loud. Had he heard her? Of course he had.

"Well, my dear wife, what word could be of such interest to bring you to the dictionary?"

He sounded colder than he had the night before. Utterly apart from her. Contemptuous of her. Would he hurt her again? Rip off her clothes again? She shook her head even as she looked down at the word, so very damning by itself, and she tried to slam the dictionary closed. He moved quickly, wresting it from her arms.

"Surely we could have no secrets? Aren't we married? Come, Arabella, if you wish to know the meaning of a word, you have but to ask me."

For a brief instant, she wanted to demand that he call her ma'am, but she couldn't. Everything had changed. It was now too grave, too perilous. She said nothing. There was no hope for it. He would find the word. She hadn't done anything wrong. She'd be damned if she would act guilty. She said with a tone she prayed was as cold as his, "I was looking up a word you screamed at me last night. I had never heard it before. I wanted to know what it meant."

"What was this word I screamed at you?"

"Sodomy."

His black eyebrows went up a good inch. She had no shame, the damned slut. She was shoving it right into his face, rubbing it in his nose. So be it. He turned slowly to place the dictionary onto the desk. Then he looked at her. She was standing tall, her shoulders squared. He looked at her, stripping her naked as he had the night before, and it was all there in his eyes, all the condemnation, the contempt, the rage. "Poor Arabella, did not the comte give you a term to describe your activities? I understand it can be painful, this way a man can take a woman. I have never done it. But perhaps now, that he has breached you, I will do it. Was he gentle with you? But you are an intelligent woman. I cannot understand why he did not tell you what he was doing to you is called. How very remiss of him."

"I have no lover," she said in the calmest voice she had ever heard from herself. It was flat, no emotion scrambling about to humiliate her further. "The comte is not my lover. I have no idea what this sodomy means. Either you will tell me or you will get out of my way. I will repeat it once more: the comte is not my lover. I have no lover or any sort. Tell me or move."

She actually shoved at him. He grabbed her arms and forced them against her sides. "Sodomy," he said slowly, looking down at her. "Very well. I will tell you what it is. You will recognize it quickly enough and I will see the knowledge of it in your eyes. When he took you, you were on your hands and knees, that, or on your belly. Damn you, stop looking so blank. He took you from behind. Is that plain enough for you? He took you as he would take a boy were he a pederast."

This hadn't occurred to her. She felt utterly stripped of anything that she knew. "But surely that is impossible. Horses don't do that, and I have watched horses mate. My God, it would be horrible. It isn't what is proper, for man nor beast. What is a pederast? What do you mean?"

"Shut up, damn you. Very well, so he didn't use you in that way then. Then it was your mouth." He jerked her forward, leaned down and kissed her hard. "Open your mouth," he said against her lips. "Open your lips so I can taste you. Did that miserable little bastard spill his seed in your mouth?"

She didn't open her mouth, despite the force he used. Finally, he let her go. He raised his head. Lightly, he touched his fingertips to her lips. "Yes," he said slowly, "he let you take him in your mouth. You have a beautiful mouth—soft and giving, even though you refuse to give it to me, I can imagine what it was like for him to caress his sex with those lips of yours."

She saw him in her mind's eye, his sex, swelled and long, thrust into her mouth. No, it wasn't possible. She ran her tongue over her lips. He laughed. She wanted to kill him. He believed the comte had put his sex into her mouth? That he had found his release in her mouth? She shuddered with disgust. She didn't try to escape him again. She wouldn't allow him to destroy her.

She smiled up at him, her voice as calm as her mother's. "You are lying. No one would do what you have described. It is absurd, unbelievable. I will tell you one last time that the comte is not my lover.

"Ah, but look at you, you believe it so completely. Thus you must trust the person who told you. Who was it, Justin? Who told you this lie?"

It was he who stepped away from her. He had sworn that he would not again allow his bitter anger and disillusionment to get the better of him. Ah, but she enraged him with that calm of hers, trying to turn the tables on him, to put him in the wrong. He managed to smile at her, but it was difficult. He wanted to strangle her, to throw her on the Axminster carpet, jerk up her riding skirt, and plunge deep inside her. He drew a deep breath. "No one told lies of you, Arabella. You have only yourself to blame for my knowing the truth. *I saw you. I saw him.*"

"You saw me? You saw the comte? Who cares? What bloody truth? That makes not one whit of sense. What in the devil are you talking about? Damn you, don't just stand there like a preacher searching out witches, tell me!"

"Perhaps when you meet again at the barn or wherever, you can show him your newfound knowledge. You can tell him that you want him to sodomize you. Yes, but caution him to go slowly, Arabella. Tell him that he must be gentle, that he—"

She thought she would vomit. Instead, she struck him with her fist in his jaw. His head snapped back she had hit him so hard.

She picked up her skirts and ran to the door.

He called after her, even as he rubbed his jaw, "You will pay for that, Arabella."

"I have already paid," she whispered as she pulled open the door and slipped through it.

"Another macaroon, I think, my dear." Dr. Branyon smiled at Lady Ann as he slipped another cookie onto his plate.

"Elsbeth, more tea?"

"No, thank you, Lady Ann," Elsbeth said, turning her wandering attention to her stepmother.

"I suppose it is not so very odd that the earl and Arabella do not join us." The comte spread his hands expressively, a knowing gleam in his dark eyes.

Lady Ann gave him a look that she had until today used only with Sir Arthur Bennington, a local baron who had tried to kiss her once behind the stairs. The gleam disappeared quickly. Good. Even a Frenchman understood that gleam. She nodded, raising her chin, then turned to Dr. Branyon. "Paul, I trust you will join us for dinner this evening. It is Thursday, you know, and Cook will prepare Arabella's roast pork."

"Pork, hmm? Perhaps I can force myself," Dr. Branyon said. He looked at the clock on the mantelpiece and quickly rose. "If I am to have a chance at snabbling any dinner, I must leave now and see to my patients. Six o'clock?"

Lady Ann nodded and walked from the drawing room to the great double doors with him. He turned, saying quietly, "Ann, something is troubling you. Ah, it's the marriage, is it? You know that you must become used to the fact that Arabella is a married lady."

Lady Ann didn't know what to do. She looked up into his face, a face she had known since she was seventeen years old, a face so beloved that all she wanted to do was touch him and kiss him and hold him so tightly he would never let her go. The truth then, she thought, at least about Arabella. About her own feelings, they had to wait. She had no idea what he felt about her. Oh yes, he was fond of her, that much was obvious, but for anything more—

She said, "I promise that isn't the problem. I believe Arabella was born being grown up. A married lady? I neither had nor have any difficulty accepting that." She drew a deep breath. "There is something wrong between them. Something very wrong."

Dr. Branyon frowned into her clouded blue eyes. It was on the tip of his tongue to make light of her concern, but he had found over the years that her perceptions about people were usually appallingly accurate. He said, "Since I haven't seen them today, I can't say anything to the point. This evening, well, I will watch them. I hope you are wrong, Ann. I really do."

"So do I. But I'm not." She wondered if she should

tell him about Arabella's ripped nightgown. No, that was going too far. It was far too intimate.

God, how he hated to see her upset. Without thought he lifted her hand. As his mouth brushed her palm, he felt a slight tremor in her hand. Her fingers closed over his. He forgot everything except his need for her. He looked hungrily at her mouth, then into her eyes. He didn't at first believe what he saw there even though it was so clear a blind man couldn't be mistaken.

"Ann, my dearest love." There was such longing, such complete commitment in his voice that Lady Ann didn't notice the groom approaching with his horse.

But he did. He tried to smile, difficult when all he wanted to do was kiss her until neither of them could breathe. He wanted badly to touch her, just lightly touch her, it was all he asked, but it wasn't to be. He drew a deep breath and swallowed a lurid curse. "We have no privacy here. I would speak with you further, Ann."

She stared up at him, at his mouth, and said without hesitation, "When?"

He chuckled and released her hand. "I want nothing more than to have you all to myself right at this moment. Damnation. I have patients."

"Tomorrow then," she said.

He took the plunge. "You know, Ann, the fishpond is lovely this time of year. Do you think you would enjoy a stroll around its perimeter tomorrow afternoon, say at one o'clock?" Actually he was seeing her on her back, her beautiful hair spread out about her face, lying in the midst of daffodils. He swallowed. He was losing his mind.

Again, she said without hesitation, "I think I should like it above all things."

Dr. Branyon forgot the years he had spent without her, thinking now to the future. Actually, he was thinking about tomorrow at the fishpond. "Just maybe life is perfect." He rested his hand lightly against her cheek and smiled at her tenderly.

"Tonight for dinner and I swear I will observe. Then, tomorrow at one o'clock, dearest Ann." He turned and strode down the front steps to his waiting horse, his step light and confident. He waved to her before he wheeled his horse about and cantered down the graveled drive.

"Yes, Paul, just maybe life will be perfect." She felt so full of happiness that, absurdly, she wanted to run after the retreating stable lad and fling her arms around him. She hugged herself instead.

By the time she returned to the drawing room, she had dimmed the outrageous sparkle in her eyes. She thought that only Justin would notice a change in her. But then, in all likelihood, Justin would not be there.

She was surprised to find only the comte in the drawing room. She smiled at him, a blond brow arched upward.

"*Ma petite cousine* wished to retire to her room to compose herself for dinner. I believe she is fatigued." He gave her a charming shrug, all French and meaningless.

"I see," she said. How she wished now he had gone away to compose himself as well, or that she had gone directly to her room, or perhaps to the parterre. She wanted to be alone, to turn over each of Paul's words in her mind, to savor the implications, just to picture him in her mind and smile with what might come, what might happen.

"Lady Ann, I am delighted that at last I can speak with you alone," the comte said suddenly, sitting forward in his chair, his voice intense. "You see, *chère madame,* only you can tell me about my aunt Magdalaine."

"Magdalaine? But, Gervaise, I hardly know anything about her. She died before I met the former earl. Surely

Magdalaine's brother, your father, would know far more than I and—"

He shook his head. "It is of the most unfortunate, but he could only tell me of her girlhood in France. Even on that, his brain was muddled. He knew nothing of her life in England. Please, tell me what you know of her. Surely you must know something."

"Very well, but let me think a moment." Goodness, she knew so little, she wasn't lying about that. She jostled her memory, piecing together bits of information about her husband's first wife. "I believe the earl met your aunt while on a visit to the French court in 1788. I do not know the sequence of events, only that they were wed quite soon at the Trécassis château and returned to England shortly thereafter. Elsbeth, as you know, was born in 1789, but a year after their marriage." She paused and smiled at the very beautiful young man. "Of course, Gervaise, you cannot be much older than Elsbeth yourself. I imagine that you were born near to the same time."

The comte shrugged in vague agreement and waved his elegant hands for her to continue.

"Now I come to the point where I am not certain of my facts. I believe Magdalaine returned to France shortly after the revolution broke out. I do not know her reason for traveling at such a dangerous time." She shook her head. "You, I am certain, know the rest. Unfortunately, she became ill soon after her return to Evesham Abbey and died here in 1790."

"You know nothing more, *madame*?"

"No, I'm sorry, Gervaise." It was nice that he wanted to know more about his aunt, but surely this disappointment of his at how little she knew was a bit much. She thought about Paul. What a lovely name.

The comte sat back in his chair and drummed his slender fingertips together. He said slowly, his eyes intent on Lady Ann's face, "It would seem that I can add to your store of knowledge. I do not wish to wound you, Lady Ann, but it seems that when your late husband came to France in 1787, his fortune was—what do you English say?—ah yes, his fortune was sadly in need of repairs. My father, Magdalaine's elder brother, told me that the Comte de Trécassis offered the earl a huge sum of money upon the marriage. There was an additional portion of her *dot* that was to be paid later, upon fulfilling certain conditions."

Lady Ann was silent for a moment, her thoughts drawn back to her own huge dowry and the earl's none-too-subtle haste in wishing to marry her. She remembered her bitter disillusion as a shy, self-conscious girl who had inadvertently overheard her betrothed blithely tell one of his friends that her dowry hadn't been quite as plump as his mistress, but she was the daughter of a marquess, and surely that must mean something. He'd added that he hoped her virgin's blood would not be a boring red.

It occurred to her now to wonder why the Comte de Trécassis would offer such a huge dowry for Magdalaine's hand. After all, Magdalaine's lineage was impeccable, the Trécassis being mixed in bloodline to the Capets. It was almost as if her dowry were some sort of bribe. Now that was odd. Why?

The comte rose and straightened his yellow-patterned waistcoat. He really was quite a handsome young man, and those dark eyes of his, well— "Do forgive me, *chère madame,* for taking so much of your time."

Lady Ann shook away eighteen-year-old memories and smiled. "I'm sorry, Gervaise, that I could not tell you more. But, you see"—she splayed her white hands—"Magdalaine and your family were hardly ever mentioned in my presence." She knew it wasn't because her husband had dearly loved his first wife. No, just look what he had done to poor Elsbeth. No, there had been no more love, no more caring for poor Magdalaine than he'd had for her.

"How true. What man would want to speak of his first wife to his current wife? Oh, Lady Ann, I neglected to tell you that I find the pearls you are wearing most elegant. As the Countess of Strafford, your jewel box must be under guard. It must be gratifying, *non*?"

"Thank you, Gervaise," she said, not even hearing him for she was thinking again of Paul. She would see him in but three hours. Surely that was too long a time without him.

"Oh, the Strafford jewels," she said, bringing her attention back to him. "I assure you they are so paltry that the Prince Regent would not even deign to give them to Princess Caroline, whom, I understand, he holds in great dislike."

"That is must curious, I think," the comte said. "Most curious indeed."

"Yes, if you say so. One wonders how such an alliance could be formed with the mutual distaste apparent in both parties."

"Eh? Oh, yes, certainly. It is the royal way, *chère madame*." He bowed over her hand, then strolled from the drawing room.

Lady Ann shook out her skirts and walked to the door. Perhaps she would wear the pink silk gown tomorrow, with its rows of tiny satin rosebuds. Surely it was not so very bad to break the monotony of her black mourning just one time. As she mounted the stairs to her room, she thought of the rather daring expanse of white bosom revealed by the gown, and smiled wickedly. It was an Arabella smile, she thought, or at least it was an Arabella smile before she had married Justin.

Oh, dear.

15

Dinner that evening was set back because the smithy had been trying to shoe Squire Jamison's black beast of a stallion and the brute had bitten his shoulder. "Poor fellow," Dr. Branyon said with a sympathetic shake of his head, "he was furious at himself and he wanted to kill the horse. He said that damned horse would never wear a shoe again for all he cared."

Certainly his story was not all that amusing, Dr. Branyon thought as he led Lady Ann in to dinner, but nevertheless it deserved better than the strained smiles it received from the earl and Arabella. The comte had laughed in that French way of his that Dr. Branyon didn't really appreciate. Elsbeth smiled demurely, as one would have expected her to, but not quite in her usual way.

Dr. Branyon found his eyes drawn to Elsbeth again as they entered the dining room. He had carelessly described her to Lady Ann just last week as a 'diffident little girl, afraid at any moment that an adult would send her to her bedchamber with a slice of moldy bread and water.' Now he was not quite so sure. There seemed to be a new self-assurance about her, her quietness borne of a kind of confidence rather than her fear of putting herself forward. It must be her inheritance from her father. She finally realized that she had value. That she'd had value to her father, a man she had undoubtedly worshiped all her life. It was a pity that it had taken a good deal of money to make her reach that conclusion.

"Come, Arabella," Lady Ann said, "you are now the Countess of Strafford and it is now your duty to sit in the countess's chair."

Arabella stared blankly at her mother for a moment, her hand already on her own chair. Oh God, her mother was right. She was the Countess of Strafford. No, it didn't matter. She didn't want to do anything that would make her feel more bound to the earl than she already was. She shook her head. "Oh, no, Mother, I have no wish to take your place. It is altogether ridiculous. I will keep my usual seat."

Arabella's knuckles showed white on the back of her chair as the earl said in a calm, bored voice, "Lady Ann is quite correct, Arabella. As the Countess of Strafford, it is only proper that you take your place at the foot of the table. This way, every time you look up, you will see your husband. Does that not gratify you?"

Yes, indeed, she thought. It was bloody wonderful. Eating and then looking at him would surely make her stomach hurt. She meant to speak lightly, but her voice came out thin and shrill. "Father always called it the bottom of the table. Come, let us cease this nonsense, my roast pork grows more leathery by the moment. Mother, please, keep your place."

"You will sit yourself where appropriate, madam. Giles, will you kindly assist her ladyship into her place?"

The second footman, never having rubbed Lady Arabella against her grain in all her eighteen years, turned beseeching eyes to Lady Ann.

"Come, my dear," Lady Ann said very quietly, "do allow Giles to seat you." Oh drat, she should never have raised the matter in the first place. It had given Justin more ammunition. But why did he want to use it? Arabella looked white with strain. She also hadn't moved.

Lady Ann waited with held breath to see if Arabella would turn the dining room into a battleground.

Arabella wanted to hurl the chair at her husband. She wanted to hurl all the knives at him as well. But she knew she couldn't. If she continued to resist, everyone would quite clearly see that all was not right between them. She cursed beneath her breath. Only Giles heard her. She thought he would faint when she turned to tell him she would take the bloody chair. She managed to smile.

Following a very silent first course of turtle soup, Dr. Branyon asked the earl, "Have you made the acquaintance of old Hamsworth, Justin?"

A slight smile indented the corners of the earl's mouth. "A testy old curmudgeon and a tenant who has well served the land. He provided me with quite a long list of the improvements he wished to see made on the estate. He told me I was probably too young to step into the old earl's boots, but he would try to help me stay on the proper course. He even provided me with hours he would be available to me."

"He was forever doing the same with Father," Arabella said without thinking. "Always telling him he should do this and not that. Father ground his teeth. But he never lost his temper with Hamsworth."

"And what was the outcome?" the earl asked, his eyes meeting hers down the long expanse of table.

"Father never listened to him, so Hamsworth was forever trying to bribe me."

Justin thought of the leering old man and his vulgar observations on one of the milkmaids, and felt his hand tighten about his fork. "Oh? What were his bribes?" His tone was so very harsh that Elsbeth's almond eyes flew from her sautéed mushrooms to his face in confusion. Even the comte laid down his fork and stared at the earl.

Arabella felt an uncontrollable demon burgeon

inside her. Why not? She allowed a knowing smiling to flit over her face and raised her brows. "How very odd that you should ask, my lord. When I was five years old, his bribes took the form of apples from his orchard. Of course, as I grew older, old Hamsworth became more creative. Goodness, some of the things he offered to show me still make me blush. Of course, then he wasn't all that *old*."

Her reward for so outlandish a tale was a dull flush of anger that spread over her husband's tanned face. She returned to her dinner, finding that if her pork was not actually leather, it tasted so in her mouth. She was only dimly aware throughout the remainder of the meal that her mother and Dr. Branyon conversed almost solely with Elsbeth and the comte.

"Arabella."

She raised her head at the sound of her name. Lady Ann continued softly, "Whenever you would like the ladies to withdraw, you have but to rise."

What an awesome power, to be sure, and she had not even thought of it. Swiftly she pushed back her chair, leaving poor Giles in the lurch, and rose. "If you gentlemen will excuse us, we will leave you to your port." How very simple it was. She was free. She looked the earl straight in the face, then turned on her heel and strode so quickly from the dining room that Lady Ann and Elsbeth were taking double steps to keep pace with her.

"Whatever is wrong with Arabella?" Elsbeth whispered to Lady Ann as they trailed after her into the Velvet Room. "And his lordship? He spoke to her so very coldly. Indeed, I thought he looked angry, but surely that cannot be right. They are newly married. It can't be right."

"Sometimes, my dear," Lady Ann said finally, "married people, when they are first wed, do not always agree. It is a lovers' quarrel, nothing more. Don't worry about it. These things pass quickly." If only she could believe that. Dear Elsbeth, she thought, how very innocent she was. It seemed that Elsbeth had accepted her simple explanation, her attention already elsewhere, perhaps to her future Season in London. Yet, Lady Ann was puzzled, for it had been days since Elsbeth had made any reference either to her ten thousand pounds or to their trip. Nothing was quite right.

Lady Ann eyed Arabella, who was restlessly pacing in front of the long French windows. She turned to her stepdaughter. "Do play for us, Elsbeth. Perhaps some of your French ballads, the happier ones, not the ones that make me cry."

Elsbeth complied willingly, sat gracefully at the pianoforte, and soon heartbreaking chords filled the room. These were the crying ballads.

Lady Ann walked to her daughter and laid her hand on her sleeve. "Why did you tell such a lie about poor old Hamsworth? You know perfectly well that your father never allowed you within a mile of his cottage. I even remember that he threatened to keep you off a horse for an entire week if you disobeyed him. You never did."

Arabella felt incredibly weary. She wanted to cry. She also wanted to shriek. She tried for some spirit but couldn't find any. She could only shrug and say, "It was only a jest, Mother, nothing more."

"A jest that made Justin very very angry. You did it on purpose. You wanted to anger him. Why did you do such a thing, my dear?"

"It was what the earl expected, no, it was what he *wished* to hear. I but fulfilled his expectation."

"Arabella, whatever are you talking about? How can you say that such a story as you concocted is what he wished to hear? Surely you can't be right. He is your husband, not some jealous lover for you to taunt."

Arabella raised fine gray eyes to her mother's face.

Her dinner began to churn uncomfortably in her stomach. She had very nearly given herself away. If only she were gazing into her father's world-wise eyes rather than her mother's so very innocent blue ones. She took a tight hold on her disillusionment, shrugged her shoulders, and said, "Please, Mother, don't take what I say seriously. I'm sure you have guessed that the earl and I have had a slight misunderstanding."

Before Lady Ann could even open her mouth, there was a swirl of black satin and Arabella called over her shoulder, "I shall set up the table for lottery tickets."

To Arabella's relief, the earl and Dr. Branyon did not join in the game of lottery tickets. She found, though, that the excitement of winning and losing her fish did nothing to enliven her spirits. Because the earl believed the comte to be her lover, her most innocently spoken phrases took on a guilty meaning to her. She tried vainly to ignore the comte and found to her horror that a dull flush crept over her cheeks when his beautiful dark eyes rested upon her. If she were not certain herself of her own innocence, she would have pronounced herself to be guilty. She would have announced that she was a slut.

The friendly word and glance of yesterday seemed today fraught with betraying dual meaning. She fell as quiet as the burning logs in the great fireplace.

When Crupper entered with the tea tray, she was near to the breaking point. She dispensed the tea without her mother having to tell her to and luckily she didn't spill any. As soon as she had filled the last cup, she rose quickly from her chair. She yawned rudely. "It has been a long day. I wish all of you a good night."

She nodded to the group in general, avoiding the earl's eyes, and made for the door.

"Do wait a moment, my dear," the earl said, stopping her. "I myself am also ready to retire."

Arabella wanted to run, but knew she could not. He

had adroitly cornered her, and to protest would announce her fear to everyone. She stood in tense silence
until the earl, with his customary grace, had made his
round of good nights. She knew he was taking his time
on purpose.

Dr. Branyon didn't like any of it. He watched the
earl slip his arm about Arabella's waist and lead her
from the room. He hoped Ann would not ask him
to speak to the earl. He had no idea what he would
ask, or, for that matter, what the earl would say to
him. He imagined that Justin could be just as ruthless
as the former earl had been. Could he also be as
carelessly cruel? There was indeed trouble between
Justin and Arabella, but why? What the devil could
have happened?

Dr. Branyon had remarked to the earl that the comte
seemed to have a fair way with the ladies. The earl had
replied, "It perhaps serves his best interest to be all
things to all people." He had then said more to himself
than to Dr. Branyon, and in the most oblique manner,
"I shall shortly know if our young French relative has
the spirit of a dove, the fangs of a viper, or simply the
unprincipled instincts inherent in his French blood. I
believe you saw him very clearly when he first arrived,
Paul."

Dr. Branyon hadn't really seen a thing. He'd had just
instinctively disliked the young man. He'd said, "It you
do not like him, why not tell him to leave?"

The earl had been quiet for a long time. Finally, he'd
said, "I can't, not just yet. Besides, I do believe I would
rather kill him than allow him to leave Evesham
Abbey. I would very much enjoying killing him."

Good God, Dr. Branyon had thought. What was going on here?

Arabella maintained a wary silence until they reached
the top of the stairs. She tried to pull away from him

but could not. She said between her teeth, "Let me go. I want to go to my bedchamber now."

He tightened his arm around her waist. "Of course, you mean to say *our* bedchamber. That, my dear, was exactly where I was taking you."

"No, damn you, no." She managed to wrench away from him. She sped down the corridor to her room and flung the door wide. She stopped dead in her tracks. A sense of unreality seized her. All the furniture was swathed in ghostly holland covers. Her favorite pictures were gone, her personal belongings nowhere to be seen. The room was stripped of her presence. It was as if she had never spent a moment in this bedchamber, never existed. With a gulp of panic she raced to the armoire and pulled at the ivory knobs. All her gowns, cloaks, and bonnets were gone; even her slippers, lined in a colorful row, had vanished. She turned slowly and saw the earl standing in the doorway, his arms crossed over his chest.

"What have you done? Where are all my clothes, my pictures, my brushes? Damn you, answer me!"

The earl straightened and said matter-of-factly, "I decided your room was not big enough for both of us. Thus, during dinner I had your belongings removed to the earl's bedchamber. If Evesham Abbey's ghostly visitors return, we will simply have to accustom ourselves to them. Now, come, wife, your husband awaits his pleasure."

Arabella slipped her hand into the pocket of her gown, closing her fingers over the smooth ivory handle of her small pistol. When she had seen it next to her jewel box before dinner, she had wondered at herself for not remembering it earlier. Ironically, her father's gift would protect her now from the man he had so carefully chosen for her. There had to be irony in that somewhere. She drew up now to her full height. "Were you intending another rape tonight?"

He shrugged indifferently. "It was not rape. I used cream to ease you. It is not my fault you fought me. However, it will be as you wish it. I will use no cream on you tonight. If your lover is to enjoy you by day, I see no reason why I should not be equally indulged at night.

"Besides, I am not yet bored with you. Did you forget that I told you that your breasts were lovely? I didn't examine you all that closely last night. Tonight, I intend to explore every inch of you. Surely you would enjoy a man's attention focused entirely on you."

She flinched at his words, seeing him staring down at her last night. He believed he could do anything to her, order her to obey him in all things. He thought she was a slut. He thought she had betrayed him. Well, she wasn't and she hadn't. She also had a pistol. Never again would he force her.

She smiled at him and watched the surprise leap into his gray eyes. "I won't allow you to do anything more to me. Isn't it amazing that my father did not gain your measure before he gave you the greatest inheritance a man could ever wrangle?" Her smile fell away, but her voice was cold and confident. "To think that *I* must protest my innocence to one such as you. I will tell you once again, my lord, but I fear you are deaf to all truth: *I have no lover.*"

"It is true that your father made a mistake, but not, I assure you, in my character. It is fortunate that he is not here to witness the corruptness of his own daughter. Come, Arabella, I grow tried of this nonsense. I have told you what to do. You will obey me. You really have no choice in the matter." That she continued to lie to him made him want to throttle her. He hadn't intended to take her tonight, in spite of her taunting remarks at dinner about the lecherous old Hamsworth, but rather to force her to experience pleasure at his hands. He wanted to force her to passion, to make her surrender to him.

Just to him.

Though he would not admit it to himself, he wanted to win her, to make her forget the comte. He wanted her to beg his forgiveness, to plead with him to take her back.

What had he done to make her betray him? A question he had asked himself more times than he could count. There was no answer, not as long as she kept denying her betrayal.

He crooked his finger at her impatiently. Without another word, Arabella preceded him from the room. Though he did not again take her arm, she knew he was ready. If she attempted to break free of him, he would capture her in an instant.

When they reached the earl's bedchamber, he stepped back and waited until she entered the room. Even before she turned to face him, she heard the key grate in the lock.

"I will play your lady's maid, Arabella. I want you naked. I want to look my fill at you. I want to hold your breasts in my hands. I want to explore your woman's attributes. Come here and let me unfasten all those buttons."

"No," she said calmly, standing tall and straight. "You will not touch me, Justin."

His nostrils flared, just as she'd known they would. He was not used to being denied. But an instant later a smile of lazy confidence played about his mouth and his eyes glittered with the challenge she had flung at him. He said with slow emphasis, "As I said before, it will be as you wish it. Do you want your gown shredded, Arabella? For that is what your refusal will mean. But realize, my dear, after a week or two, you will have no more gowns. Not, of course, that I mind having you naked during the day as well." He strolled confidently toward her.

Arabella flew to the other side of the great bed, knowing that there was nothing she could say to dissuade him. Her eyes measured her distance from him, and her fingers curled about the butt of her pistol.

"Since you like games, it is just as well that we excused ourselves early." Still confident, he stalked her with maddening slowness, walking slowly around the side of the bed. She could retreat no further, her back finally touching the long velvet curtains.

"You will come no closer to me." As she spoke, she withdrew the pistol from her pocket, held it straight out in front of her, and leveled it at his chest.

He smiled at her grimly and took another step. "By God, where did you get that? Put the gun down, Arabella, I would not wish you to hurt yourself."

"You want that pleasure reserved only for yourself. Now you will listen to me. I am really quite well trained. Could you possibly not believe that my father wouldn't have had me shooting from the earliest age? And I do not actually wish to kill you, you know. But, Justin, come one step nearer and I shall put a bullet straight through your arm. I will let you select—your right arm or your left?"

He stared at her with a curious mixture of anger, frustration, and admiration. Damn it, he believed her. As a matter of course, he quickly calculated his chances of disarming her. He made no movement toward her. He could well imagine that the late earl had trained her well. Probably from the age of five. At this distance, she could and readily would, he believed, put a bullet through whatever part of his anatomy she chose. He saw that she was regarding him with a kind of cold detachment, her head and hand as calm and steady as his own would be before a battle.

He tasted defeat and hated it. "This is just one small

foray, Arabella. You have no chance, you know. Enjoy your brief victory for it will be your last." He turned on his heel and without a backward glance strode into the adjoining dressing room and slammed the door.

Arabella shifted the pistol to her other hand and wiped her sweaty palm on her skirt. She felt her bravado begin to crumble as she foresaw a succession of endless nights in similar conflict. She felt awash with bitter disillusionment. God, was she to hold her husband off at gunpoint for the remainder of her days? She shook her head, too drained to think rationally about what she should do.

She looked at the bed, but passed it by. She sank down into a large stuffed chair beside the fireplace, curled her legs beneath her gown, and wearily laid her face against her arm. Somehow, she wished she could cry, but she knew she would not. Crying solved nothing. How many times had her father told her that? She remembered him saying that in a contemptuous voice once when her mother was crying. She had agreed with him. She kept her fingers curled about the butt of her pistol.

Arabella awoke shivering early the next morning, her legs cramped from long hours in one position. A blanket was covering her. She jumped, realizing she didn't have her pistol. She saw it lying on a tabletop near her chair. Her heart pounded. Justin had come into the bedchamber while she had slept. He could have done as he wished with her. Yet he had merely covered her and removed the pistol from her fingers. She rose slowly and stretched.

She did not understand him.

At least, finally, she had a plan.

16

"The lilies grow in great profusion."

"The laws of nature make it so. There must be a lily pad for each frog."

Lady Ann stopped then and grinned up at him. "I believe that now I am through trying to distract you." She drew a deep breath. There was so much to say to him, so much to pour out to him from her very soul.

Dr. Branyon cupped her face in his palm. "Just looking at you distracts me. Truly, you don't wish to tell me now how thick the water reeds are?"

She kissed his palm. His flesh was warm. She felt him tremble. She could make him tremble? It was an awesome thought. Her late husband, well, she wouldn't think about him. But she did, she couldn't help it. She'd known that he had very likely felt only disgust with her, never had he trembled when she had kissed his hand. Actually, she couldn't remember ever willingly kissing any part of him. She kissed Paul's palm again, then raised her head. "The water reeds are rather thick, but not so thick that they are displeasing," she said.

"I am in complete agreement. Now, I shall volunteer my coat so you can settle yourself amongst the so very thick green reeds."

But she didn't move. She just wanted to stand here for the rest of her years and look up at him. She loved his face, smooth and lean, and the lines on either side of his mouth—his doctor's creases—she'd once teased him. His eyes were a pale green, as light a green as the oak leaves glistening beneath the strong afternoon sun. She realized that she wanted more than just a kiss, more than just a hug, perhaps. She wasn't certain, but she decided that she would like him to kiss her throat, perhaps even lower, her breasts. She blinked. Her breasts? It was apparent to her that she wasn't the same woman that she had been but ten minutes ago. No, it now appeared that she was a woman who wanted. For the first time in her life she wanted a man to touch her.

Dr. Branyon clasped her hand in his and led her to the other side of the pond. He found a likely spot, spread his coat upon the springy moss and grass, and bowed to her. "Allow me to assist you, Ann. I want you to be very comfortable."

She sank down gracefully onto his coat and smoothed the flounce of her pink gown over her ankles. Then she pulled up the gown to her calves. She wanted him to see her ankles. "These are new stockings," she said. "Do you like them?"

He swallowed hard. He stared at her feet, at her ankles, not really seeing the damned stockings.

"Perhaps I should have brought a picnic lunch," she said, for he was standing motionless as a tree, just staring down at her legs. It pleased her inordinately. She thought to pull her skirt higher, but there were too many years of rules and embarrassment holding her back.

He blinked. "I believe that after eighteen and some odd years, I want no piece of chicken to come between us. Your stockings are lovely."

"Oh, I thought you were looking at the ground."

He laughed. "No, you didn't. You know very well that those damned water reeds hold no interest at all for me." He sat down close to her. She felt suddenly warm, and with unsteady fingers untied the bow below her left ear and lifted off her bonnet.

Dr. Branyon picked up the bonnet and gently tossed it off to one side. Slowly he lifted his hand to her face, letting his fingers trace over her smooth cheek, her straight nose, and come to rest lightly against her pink lips. "Your ankles are lovely, your hair is lovely, but most of all, you are so utterly beautiful inside, it makes me wonder if I can ever come to deserve you."

"You deserve me? Oh goodness, Paul, it's the other way around. No, you are perfect. I haven't yet seen your ankles, but I know that I want to run my fingers through your hair and just stare at you. May I stare at you for the next fifty years?"

Now this was something utterly delightful he hadn't expected at all. He'd prayed for something like this, but he hadn't expected it. "Are you proposing to me?" He gently slipped his hand behind her neck, over the thick coil of heavy blond hair, and drew her to him. He thought she looked like a young girl readying for her first kiss. He had the good sense and patience to realize that her gesture was a tentative one, even though she had just proposed something to him. He prayed it was marriage. She was staring at his mouth and not answering. He kissed her gently, barely touching his lips to hers, savoring the taste of her, the softness of her mouth. He felt a fluttering response in her and lightly rested his hands on her shoulders and pushed her onto her back. Her eyes flew open and he read uncertainty, perhaps fear. Probably fear. He was moving too quickly. Immediately he released her and balanced himself on his elbow beside her. He had been certain for years that the earl had not treated her well. Yet, there was an air of fragile innocence about her that even her husband had failed to extinguish. Perhaps when they were married, she would speak of him.

"Did you mean to propose to me, Ann? If you want to stare at me for that long a time, surely marriage is the only solution, the only way to prevent our neighbors from gossiping about us."

She smiled up at him, a lazy, impish smile, now devoid of uncertainty, and said, "Indeed, I fear that I must, Paul. I would be a terribly loose woman were I to kiss a man I did not intend to wed."

"Then I must kiss you again to double ensure your compliance."

She was laughing when he kissed her, and his tongue entered her mouth. She could not help the shock of fear that made her grit her teeth suddenly against him. In that instant it was the earl, and not Paul, whose mouth was grinding against hers, bruising her, forcing her lips open. How she had hated his wet, probing tongue, not that he had ever wasted much of his time kissing her. No, he wanted her on her back, naked and silent, open and willing.

Dr. Branyon instantly drew back. There was no tenderness in his eyes or in his voice. "I'm not the damned earl," he said. "Look at me, Ann. I'm not that man who hurt you and humiliated you." She was shaking. He took her hand in his and kissed her fingers. "I would never hurt you. I would never humiliate you. I would never make you feel like less than nothing. You know that. You know me. You know I would protect you with my life."

"I know that you would. It won't happen again."

"It might and it doesn't matter. You will be free of him soon. Do you believe me?"

She did. "I hated him so very much, hated him as much as Arabella worshiped him."

He wanted to know what that bastard had done to her, yet he knew that it wasn't fair to push her. No, if she wanted to tell him, eventually she would. He had to remember that the bastard was dead and he wasn't. Her memories would fade and disappear. He would have her with him forever. He asked quietly, "Do you trust me, Ann?"

She raised her fingers to touch his mouth. "I trust you more than I feared him," she said simply.

He gathered her into his arms and pulled her gently to him. He pressed his hand against the small of her back and felt her snuggle close against him, her full breasts against his chest, her belly and thighs pressing against his. She slid her arms about his neck and buried her face against his neck. Just having him close to her, feeling his warm breath on her back, made her replete with happiness.

He hoped she couldn't feel his sex, hard and shoving against her belly. For one of the few times in his life he was thankful for the many layers of clothing women wore. He wanted to caress her hips, kiss every delightful curve of hers, but he forced his hands to remain on her back.

He wanted to take off her clothes, stroke her, kiss her, and come inside her. He wanted her to hold him against her. He wanted her to find her woman's pleasure. But it was too soon, despite her teasing, her bravado. He forced himself to calm, but it was difficult. They lay in each other's arms until the sun began its rapid downward descent.

He awoke to light soft kisses against his chin, his cheek, his nose. He'd fallen asleep. He couldn't believe it. "Damn," he said as he turned her face up with his thumb and kissed her mouth. "How long have you been taking advantage of me?" he said into her mouth. She jumped, then grinned. Then, quite suddenly, she was on top of him, her hands around his face, her lips parted, kissing him with a good deal of enthusiasm. Her hair had come free of its rolls and was a thick curtain on both sides of his face. The smell of her made him wild. He didn't want to frighten her, but he groaned, and it was deep and hoarse.

She wasn't frightened. If anything she was more enthusiastic. He wanted to come inside her this very instant, but he was wise enough to let her keep control. He had to be patient; he had to keep on a steady course. He was a physician, for God's sake, not some randy, ignorant boy. He groaned instead, his hips lifting.

"Ann, it's going to be a close thing for me. Eighteen years is a very long time to wait to have you."

She raised her head and looked down into his eyes. "It's a ridiculously long time," she said. "It's too long a time. If you wait for another minute, then I will have to rhapsodize about the lily pads again."

She was laughing even as she jumped to her feet and began unfastening the buttons on her gown. He stared at her. There was no hesitation in her, no fear, only her beautiful face flushed with excitement, with anticipation. They were both laughing by the time they were on his coat again, naked, in each other's arms. And when he finally came to her, she welcomed him with a soft moan. And when she cried out, he took her cries into his mouth, and gave himself to her completely.

He believed she was asleep, when she said, "Paul, that is the first time I have ever felt pleasure. It is something I couldn't have imagined. Will it always be like that with you, with us?"

"If it isn't, I'll cut my wrists."

"I didn't know—"

He kissed her ear. "No, I never thought you did. Now you do. Forget all the rest of it, Ann. There's just us now. I will give you pleasure until we both cock up our respective toes and pass to the hereafter."

"And I gave you pleasure?"

She sounded so uncertain, perhaps even frightened. He kissed the tip of her nose. "You give me any more pleasure and I'll need to have a doctor." He yawned.

She bit his shoulder, tasted the warm muskiness of his flesh, and kissed him again. "This pleasure—no, don't tease me—it's quite extraordinary. I knew something was going to happen to me but I had no idea that it would shake me to my toes and lift the hair off my head."

He stroked her hair. "There are all sorts of ways to bring you to pleasure, Ann."

She came up over him, balancing on her elbow, chewing on her bottom lip. "How many?"

He groaned. "I'll be a dead man before the year is out. Enough, Ann, you are too sore for us to come together again today. No, don't go all maidenly on me, it's true. You are still unused to a man and I have no intention of hurting you. Now, I want you to distract me. No more talk of pleasure. But I want you to know something. It's something that's very important. I love you. Only you. It's always been only you."

He loved her. Only her. "And I love you," she whispered against his shoulder. She realized she was aching between her legs. But it didn't hurt. It felt wonderful and strange and she wanted to feel it every moment for the rest of her life. She sighed, kissed his closed mouth.

"Distract me, Ann. I mean it."

She said, frowning, "Whatever shall we do about Arabella and Justin?"

"That was mighty fast. I expected a smoother, slower transition between passion and the damnable problems of the world. Here I am, just a poor man whose woman has used my man's body for her pleasure, wrung me out so that I'm now only a husk, and is now unaware of the fact that I still have my hand on her beautiful bottom."

She moved and he moaned. "Stop that else I'll never have another intelligent thing to say. No, distract me. I won't complain again, I swear it. At least for ten minutes. Now, you're worried about Bella and the earl."

He knew that he wouldn't think long about them unless he removed himself from her. As much as he hated it, he pulled away from her, rose, and began to dress. She followed suit. Soon he was helping her fasten the buttons on her gown. He leaned down and kissed her throat. She was damp with her sweat. Her flesh tasted wonderful. "You know, Ann," he said slowly, thoughtfully, "I believe that their difficulties involve the comte."

Lady Ann looked startled. "Gervaise? But how could they? I can't imagine how Gervaise could have anything to do with their problems."

"I have seen Justin look at him. It is clear to me that he despises him. I would wager that he would challenge him to a duel if it weren't against the law. Justin has enough brains to realize that he would have to flee the country were he to kill the comte, and if it came down to a duel, he would most certainly kill him.

"But he wants to. It's eating at him. Nor does he trust that young man. Not as far as he can spit. I believe he's even made inquiries about him in London. But surely it's too soon for him to have received any answer. I've tried to figure out why and the only thing I can come up with is that Justin is jealous of him."

"Jealous," she repeated slowly. She tucked errant wisps of hair back into the smooth coil of hair at her neck. "Jealous? And that is why he despises him? How could Justin be jealous of any other man? He is handsome, well-spoken, a peer. It makes no sense to me." It was her turn to sigh. "Perhaps you are right, but it seems improbable. Arabella doesn't even know that Gervaise is alive. I would swear to that. I believe she even feels a dab of contempt for him. For his French blood? I don't know, but that is possible. After all, she patterned herself after her father in so many ways, and he never kept his opinions about foreigners to himself." She fell silent a moment, then said, "But you know, Paul, Justin hurt her very badly on their wedding night."

"Well, she was a virgin. Some pain was unavoidable."

"No, it was much more than that." She told him about the shredded nightgown, the blood all over the bed. "When I spoke to Justin, I could tell that he was not only unhappy, he was angry. He was furious, but there was this iron control in him. Why? He wasn't about to tell me. As for Arabella, she tried to act as though nothing was wrong. But you've seen for yourself that nothing is right."

"I had no idea," he said as he gave her his arm and began to guide her away from the fishpond. "I would have thought that our confident little Bella would have most charmingly seduced her bridegroom without a by-your-leave. As to Justin, I cannot believe that he would be so green as to frighten her. So it's more than that. Damn, this is difficult, Ann. You believe he forced her?"

"Yes, I do. She's afraid of him. My daughter, afraid! But I've watched her. She doesn't want him to know it, she doesn't want anyone to know it, but she is. We must do something, Paul. I know, I will simply tell the comte to leave. If he's gone, then Justin will get over his anger, surely."

"No, it is not your decision, Ann. If Justin, for some strange reason, really believes that Arabella wants Gervaise rather than him, then it is his decision on what must be done. Since he hasn't killed the young man and since he hasn't ordered him to leave Evesham Abbey, well, then, he has something else in mind. Justin plays deeply. I believe he is known as a military man of clever stratagems. I would trust him. Besides, we have no choice at all."

"You know, now that I think about it, it was strange of him to speak to me at such length about Magdalaine."

"Good God, Gervaise wanted to know about Magdalaine? Why? What did he ask you?"

"He wished me to tell him all about her life in England. Of course, I know very little of her. She was dead long before I came into the picture. Gervaise, mind you, then proceeded to tell me about her family's rather unusual dowry settlement with the earl. It seemed that not all of her dowry was given to the earl upon their marriage. I really do not know why he told me all that, for Magdalaine died so very quickly after her return from France, indeed less than two years after her marriage to the earl." She paused for a moment and then looked up with a sudden smile. "How very stupid of me, to be sure. Paul, you were attending her when she died, were you not? Gervaise should speak to you if he wishes to know more about his aunt."

Dr. Branyon looked away from her. When he finally spoke, his voice was uncommonly grim. "Yes, I was with Magdalaine when she died. As to Magdalaine's dowry, I know nothing of her family's arrangement with the earl. But why, I wonder, did our little French cock tell you all that? He gave no reason, no explanation for it?"

"No, not really."

As they wended their way through the geometric patterns of the parterre, he asked, "Did the comte wish to know anything else from you, Ann?"

"Nothing of importance, really, but he did nearly make me laugh aloud. He wondered about the Strafford jewels. He thought that as the countess, I must have a jewel box worth a king's ransom. I told him it wasn't at all the case."

"Hmm," was all that Dr. Branyon replied until they reached the front steps of Evesham Abbey. He took Lady Ann's hand to his and squeezed it. He looked deeply into those beautiful eyes of hers. "Listen to me. You're now mine, Ann, all of you. I will love you until I pass to the hereafter, then if my soul is hovering about, it will continue to love you. Let's not wait eight more months. Marry me, Ann. Soon. Very soon."

She was staring up at his mouth. "Soon," he said again, and his voice wasn't steady. "You know, people can tell when a woman is well-loved. Already there is a wicked sparkle in your eyes and that smile of yours would take the skin off an orange it's so brilliant."

"Is tomorrow too late?"

He laughed, hugged her, uncaring if every servant in Evesham Abbey was watching. "Let's wait only until we can solve this matter between Justin and Arabella. Then we won't have to think of a single thing other than ourselves."

"I will speak to Justin right now."

He kissed the tip of her nose. "No, let's think about this a bit more. Let me speak to Arabella."

"All right, but do it quickly. Perhaps we will solve all their problems by Friday?"

"I'll try my damndest. Ann?"

"Yes?" She was sliding her palms over his chest. He grabbed them and held them tightly in his own.

"Will you mind being married to a simple doctor?"

He was deadly serious and she knew it. She said calmly, her spirit radiant in her words, "I've always believed your intelligence of the highest order. Never have I believed you at all simple. That was a foolish question."

He threw his head back and laughed deeply.

Her voice was low now, so serious, he felt a catch in his throat as she said, "I would marry you if you were but a simple farmer. It matters nothing to me. This is Arabella's home, not mine. It never was my home. My home is with you, Paul. I want only to be with you. Forever."

"I am very glad that you came into my life," he said, then he kissed her, lightly touching his fingertips to her lips as he took his leave. He doubted he could speak another sensible word if his life depended on it.

17

Why can I not feel anything? Please, God, let me feel something. Is it your punishment for my sin? Oh, please, let me feel my love for him. Just once.

His lips roamed hungrily over her small uptilted breasts, and she wound her fingers in his short black curling hair to press him harder against her. He thought her gesture borne of a desire that matched his own and suckled hard at her breast. He was young, enthusiastic, and his confidence in himself was profound.

She gritted her teeth at the pain, willing herself not to cry out. She brought her hands up to cup his smooth chin and eased his mouth away from her breast to her lips. His beautiful dark eyes were nearly black with his lust, and she saw a gleam of impatience, she knew it. It was impatience. She wasn't as other women. She was slow. She wasn't enough of a woman for him. Oh, God, she had to do something. She was afraid he would guess that all his caresses, his kisses, the stroking of his hands, did not bring her pleasure, indeed, froze all feeling inside her. Instinctively she moaned softly into his mouth and arched up against him. She felt a quickening in him, and for an instant knew an overwhelming desire to push him off her, to beg him not to drive his man's sex into her. She hated it beyond anything. She held her breath, ashamed at such unnatural thoughts, and suffered his grinding mouth and probing tongue. She must remember that he loved her, that, above all things, she did not want to lose him, to give him a disgust of her.

She tried to relax, to inhale the sweet smell of hay. But all she could smell was him, the musky scent of him, the scent of sex. *It is you who are the lucky one, the chosen one. He does not want Arabella or any other woman. To give him your body is proof of your love for him, it's proof of your worth.*

Suddenly he reared back on his knees, clutched her knees, and pulled them apart. She closed her eyes as his fingers fumbled to part her. She heard him growl with frustration, and a red veil of shame clouded her mind. She felt his fingers, wet with his own spittle, rubbing at her, pushing inside her. She winced as his fingers went deeper, widening her, and in a haze of misery she wondered yet again how she would bear that thick shaft shoving inside her.

He poised himself over her, unable to contain himself, and shoved hard inside her, feeling as he did so the eruption of all his senses, a moment's suspension of thought and time. His seed flooded the small taut passage, easing his way, and he pushed into the depths of her. He felt an ecstatic instant of animal victory, an affirmation of his maleness, his superiority over this female. Her small hands clutched at his shoulders, and he believed yet again that he had conquered her as a man must a woman, possessed her entirely, and by his own passion given her a woman's fulfillment.

He eased his weight off her, kissed her moist lips lightly, and rolled on his side next to her. The smell of him filled her nostrils. She thought she'd gag. She felt leaden, her body wet and prickly as the cool air settled upon the thin sheen of sweat left by his body.

"I adore you, *ma petite cousine,*" her said, knowing it his duty as her conqueror, as her lover, as the man she worshiped, to reassure her with binding words that cost him so very little. Certainly it had heightened

his vanity to seduce his shy cousin, yet, too, he had
guessed that to ensure her absolute compliance, he
had also to possess her body. Her furtive virginity had
pleased him.

"And I you, Gervaise," Elsbeth whispered, her body
already stilled to its outrage, her memory already hazy
from the pain and humiliation of it. She thought how
very blessed among women she was, to be loved by one
so very handsome as he, with his dark eyes, almond-
shaped as were hers, and his flashing white teeth. He
was more handsome than the earl, whose very size terrified her, particularly now that she knew what men demanded of women. Her soaring spirit dimmed. If only
she could feel her own pleasure, glory in but a moment's passion. Surely it wasn't too much to ask. But
perhaps it was. Perhaps it was only men who grunted
and heaved and yelled when their lust overtook them.
She tried to turn her mind away from her selfishness.
If there was a lack, it was in her. She must believe that
to have him, to let him delight in her body, was enough
for her.

"You know, Elsbeth," he said after a moment, "I
spoke to Lady Ann about your mother, Magdalaine.
She knew far less than I had expected her to about your
mother's circumstances and her life here in England."

Elsbeth pulled the edge of his cloak over her and
turned on her side to face him. "What do you mean, her
circumstances?" Why was he speaking of her long-
dead mother? Why didn't he want to talk about their
future together?

He quickly patted her cheek and let his fingers rove
over her breast. He had moved too quickly, caught her
unawares. Women were strange little creatures. They
had to have constant reassurance. He shrugged indifferently and yawned. "Oh, it's nothing, really," he said.
She smiled, lulled, again satisfied that his attention was
focused upon her.

But he couldn't let it go, not now. Time was growing short. He sensed that the earl wanted him gone, no, the damned earl wanted to kill him. How could he have found out about Elsbeth? Why hadn't he said anything to him? Why, in God's name did he even care? But he did; Gervaise saw the anger, the banked rage in his eyes.

He had to hurry. "Perhaps I shouldn't have said circumstances. My father merely told me some rather unusual stories about your mother. Are you not interested in your mother, Elsbeth?" There was gentle reproach in his voice. Like a trained dog, she heeded it immediately.

"Certainly, it is just that she died so very long ago, when I was but a baby. I have no memory of her at all. As to any stories about her, I should, naturally, be delighted to hear them."

"Perhaps then sometime soon." How very easily he could divert her thoughts, to call forth the insecure lonely child, striving so desperately to please. Though he was certain that he had bound her to him, he wondered if her loyalties to Lady Ann and to Arabella might render her incapable of doing what he wished.

He appeared to grow bored with the subject. It was enough for the moment that he had planted seeds of curiosity in her mind. He let his gaze wander up and down her body. He said nothing. In his experience, the woman believed he was thinking only of her body and praying that he believed her beautiful. He could not know that she was frantically searching her mind for something of interest to distract him, to keep him from thrusting into her body again. With sudden inspiration she said, "Gervaise, I do think it wonderful that you care to know more about my mother. Did you know that my maid, Josette, was also my mother's nurse? She knew my mother from a baby, and indeed, accompanied her here to Evesham Abbey after her marriage to my father. She would know everything about my mother."

He was looking vaguely at her white belly. God, how stupid he'd been. Josette, of course. Now he would not need to count upon Elsbeth. Would not Josette feel loyalty to the de Trécassis family, to him? He felt a surge of confidence. Thinking to reward Elsbeth for providing him the answer, he spurred the cold embers of his passion and swept his hand between her thighs, glorying in the dampness of his own seed that clung to her. He jerked away his cloak and pulled her possessively against him. For an instant he thought she pushed against his chest, but then she moaned softly against his neck, her lips soft and wet, and wrapped her arms about his shoulders.

"Yes," he said, kissing her throat. "Oh, yes."

She wanted to cry, but she didn't.

Elsbeth glanced at the small gilt clock on the table beside the copper bathtub, sighed contentedly, and lowered herself deeper into the warm, scented water. She felt supremely happy, even as she had scrubbed herself until the soft flesh between her thighs hurt. She stayed for a long time in the warm water, the violent, embarrassing man's side of love all but forgotten, her mind soaring with unbounded pleasure into a romantic image of Gervaise as her dashing, gallant lover, the man she adored, more importantly, the man who adored her above all other women. Arabella included. He did not even know that Arabella was alive. Surely that had to mean something.

"Come, my lamb, it grows late. You would not wish to be late for dinner."

Elsbeth turned toward her rheumy-eyed maid, Josette, vaguely aware that there was an unusual sharpness in her withered voice.

"Come, mistress," Josette repeated, waving a large towel toward Elsbeth.

"Ah, very well," Elsbeth said, her voice all soft and vague, and rose, her arms outstretched.

"Really, my baby, you are a lady, not a *grisette* to flaunt her naked body." She quickly bundled Elsbeth into the towel, averting her eyes as she did so.

Elsbeth eyed her faithful old maidservant with a secret woman's smile. How very old-fashioned she was, she thought, forgetting that but a short time before, she would never have emerged from her bath until Josette had positioned her towel before she'd stood up.

"Oh, do not scold me, Josette, for I'm much too happy. Finally, I'm alive. Finally, I know what I should know."

Josette grunted, pulled Elsbeth's chemise over her head, and forced her arthritic fingers to tie the dainty ribbons. The pain in her fingers made her say crossly, "Just because you are now a rich young lady, with ten thousand pounds, it's no reason for you to go bounding about screeching like a scullery maid."

"I'm not screeching. Oh, I may as well tell you, you sharp-eyed old eagle, for you will know soon enough." She whirled about and clasped Josette's gnarled hands, pulling her wispy gray head close to her. "I am in love!"

Josette felt a bizarre moment of muddled confusion. No, it was not Magdalaine who was in love. Elsbeth? Surely that wasn't possible. She grasped at the vague realities that filed in lopsided order through her mind and drew back with a gasp of shock. "Oh, no, my little pet. You cannot love the earl. He has wedded with Arabella." She groped to remember. "He did marry Arabella, did he not?"

Elsbeth gave a trill of laughter and hugged the familiar stoop-shouldered old woman. "Yes, indeed, the earl has married Arabella. It's not the earl, no."

"But there is no one else," Josette said slowly, her mind squirreling about, finding nothing but more confusion. She wished that the dainty, smiling girl in front of her were not so very like Magdalaine. Such transports, such gaiety, when Magdalaine was in love.

"My cousin, of course. The comte. Gervaise. Is he not handsome and altogether wonderful?"

"The comte," Josette repeated, her voice slower still, so vague she could have said anything at all.

"Dear Josette, is it not marvelous? Am I not the luckiest of women? He loves me, and now that I am independent, I may wed him without the shame of being penniless. My father did love me, Josette. He did."

The old woman became suddenly rigid in Elsbeth's arms. She shoved the girl away and dashed her stiffened fingers across her forehead.

"Josette, whatever is the matter?" Josette's face seemed to crumble, as if some great unknown force were collapsing her inward upon herself. The old woman whipped back her head and shrieked, "By all the Gods, no!"

Elsbeth recoiled, staring dumbfounded at the old woman. Her mind had finally snapped, she thought, revulsion holding her silent. Then compassion filled her. "Now, Josette, you must speak to me. Tell me what is wrong."

The old woman's anguished cry sent Elsbeth staggering back. "No, you cannot wed him, Magdalaine, no. It is against God. It is against everything that is holy."

"I am not Magdalaine, Josette. Come, look at me. See, I am Elsbeth, her daughter."

Josette stared at her young mistress and began to shake her head back and forth, wisps of gray hair escaping from her mobcap and whipping across her thin mouth. She whispered in a singsong voice, "It is God in his final retribution. All is finished now. It is over. I should have seen it coming, but I did not." She could no longer bear to see the eager, concerned young face, and turned away, shuffling from the bedchamber.

"Josette, wait," Elsbeth whispered, not really wanting the old woman to come back to her. No, not yet. She felt gooseflesh rising on her arms and a knot of fear growing. The door closed and she was alone. Clumsily she dressed herself and coiled her black hair into a thick roll at the back of her neck. She shook her head sadly. Josette was quite mad, her mind slipped irrevocably back into the past. *But why, Josette, your muttering about God and His retribution? Of course, you thought I was Magdalaine, but still, why would you say such a thing about my mother?*

Elsbeth forgot her questions when she was told by Lady Ann that Lady Talgarth and Miss Suzanne Talgarth were expected momentarily for dinner. Elsbeth silently bemoaned Josette's strange mood that had left her to clumsily knot her own hair. Upon the arrival of Lady Talgarth and Suzanne in a flurry of sparkling jewels and clinging satin and lavender gauze, she patted her own black gown, aware that a small lump of jealousy had risen in her throat. She felt awkward and tongue-tied, as she usually did in the presence of the voluptuous and laughing Suzanne. She gazed at Lady Ann and Arabella and decided that all the Deverill women faded into insignificance in their unrelenting black.

She was cheered when, as they filed into the dining room, Gervaise whispered in her ear, "How very fragile and delicate you are, *ma petite,* not like that pink-and-white English cow. She quite offends me."

She wanted to yell that she loved him, but of course she couldn't. She lightly slapped his sleeve. She heard the earl chuckle, and looked up to see his dark head bent close to Miss Talgarth's golden curls. Her eyes flew to Arabella, and she saw with confusion that her half-sister was smiling openly at the couple. Why was she smiling? Why wasn't she furious at Suzanne Talgarth? Elsbeth thought she would kill any woman who flirted with the comte the way Suzanne was doing with the earl.

It made no sense.

18

Excellent, Suzanne, Arabella was thinking. *I could not have planned for a more effective diversion. Father was really quite wrong about you, Suzanne. Witless, missish little fool indeed. If he could but see you now, I would wager that he would be vying with Justin for your attention.*

"I declare, Ann, what am I to do with my little girl?" Lady Talgarth was saying, the weary shake of her crimped sandy curls belied by the ringing pride in her strident voice. "All smiles she is, and happiness. Such a beauty, isn't she? Those incredible dimples of hers, those eyes so blue the summer skies cannot compete. Two offers of marriage in her first Season, Ann, and my little girl keeps both gentlemen languishing." She bent her penetrating stare down the table. "Arabella, surely you met young Viscount Graybourn? Such an eligible young man, to be sure. Why, his father is the Earl of Sanbridge, and quite rich, not that it matters, of course since her father and I just want our little girl to be happy. And their houses—I was told that Lord Graybourn's father owns five fine estates, scattered throughout England. My darling could live any place that pleased her at the moment. Is she not blessed?"

Arabella blinked, sent Suzanne a quick look, and said, "Lady Talgarth, surely you are not speaking about that dear clumsy young man with no chin to speak of?"

Suzanne laughed, full and deep, not a young lady's

trained laugh, but a very real one that brought smiles to nearly every face at the table. "You see, Mama, Arabella quite agrees with me. You forgot to add, Bella, that at but twenty-and-five, he is already paunchy. I had it on the best of sources that the only reason Lord Graybourn rises before noon is that he is afraid that he will miss his breakfast. I'm told he adores kidneys. It is enough to make me flee to France in naught but my petticoats."

"Suzanne! Well, now, not exactly that, I trust. That is hardly kind, my little darling. Really, now, just think of all those delicious gowns and jewels you would own. Just think about all those houses, five of them. Spread all over our fair country. Five, Suzanne."

"But I already own all the delicious gowns I could ever want, Mama. As for jewels—" Suzanne shrugged. "I don't think I could bear to have to be nice to Lord Graybourn just to have a rope of diamonds around my neck."

Suzanne laughed toward Arabella, then raised coquettish wide eyes to the earl, pursed her pink lips, and said with all the wickedness of a born actress, "I think that I would prefer a gentleman with more worldly experience. Perhaps a gentleman with military training— like you, my lord. A gentleman who is decisive, yet a gentleman who knows exactly how to treat a lady. How very protected and secure you must feel, Bella."

"I am only two years older than poor Lord Graybourn," the earl said, smiling into his wineglass. Suzanne Talgarth was a baggage.

As for Arabella, her fingers tightened about the stem of her wineglass. She noted with a passing glance that the earl's eyes had narrowed ever so slightly. She forced a smile at Suzanne. "I think it wise to look to oneself first for such things as protection. It is many times difficult, I think, to determine beforehand the actions of another."

"Good grief, whatever that means," Suzanne said. "But I don't doubt that you have again defended my opinion." She turned to the earl. "Bella always agrees with me. Those few times that she didn't, why I talked and talked until she fell in a faint at my feet, finally nodding her head."

"I feel some small amount of pity for your future husband," the earl said.

"Dear Miss Talgarth," the comte said, his accent heavy and obscure, "surely it cannot be so very important, these years of worldly experience you speak of. My dear mademoiselle, a French gentleman comes into the world with such gifts."

"In my opinion, it is all one and the same," Lady Talgarth said, confusing everyone. She harked back to her grievance. "I'm certain that neither Arabella nor you, Suzanne, can accuse Lord Hartland of being paunchy of or having no chin. I have it on the best authority that he never gets up early to eat kidneys. No, he doesn't even arouse himself before two o'clock in the afternoon. So, you see, all is fine in that quarter."

To Arabella's surprise, Suzanne faltered. Arabella said quickly, "Indeed, you must be right, ma'am. And as to *experience,* why, he is at least fifty years old, has already buried two wives, not to mention supporting his several quite expensive aspiring offspring. Yes, Lord Hartland would appear quite unexceptionable. I imagine he wants a mother for the younger four children, and a housekeeper. I trust he doesn't also expect a brood mare as well. But you know," she added, perfectly serious, "I heard that he didn't rise before two o'clock because of his gout. Does not your father suffer also from the gout, Suzanne?"

Lady Talgarth wanted to smack Arabella. It was a very close thing. Her fingers itched.

Justin barely stopped the laugh. Goodness, she was good. Well, sometimes she was good. With him, she was—He stopped the thought. There was nothing to be gained.

"Has the prince gone to Brighton for the summer?" Lady Ann asked in a loud voice.

"How odd Arabella looks sitting in your chair, Ann," Lady Talgarth said.

"I think she looks positively matronly," Suzanne said, and laughed aloud when Arabella choked on a bite of peas.

"About the prince and Brighton," Lady Ann continued, her voice even stronger.

Suzanne turned to Lady Ann and said, "Oh yes, and although Papa is complaining sorely from his own gout, Mama has persuaded him that I, at least, should pay a long-overdue visit to my aunt Seraphina. Her house faces Marine Parade, you know, and one can observe simply *everyone* going to and from the pavilion."

"I wonder," Arabella said, "if Lord Hartland and Viscount Graybourn plan to set up in Brighton?"

"I can only pray that breakfast kidneys will stop the one and the gout brought on by excessive numbers of offspring and brandy will stop the other," Suzanne said. "Besides, there will be more fish swimming about. Unhooked fish. At least I hope it will be so."

"I shall, of course, accompany Suzanne to my sister's," Lady Talgarth said pointedly to Lady Ann, ignoring her daughter, whom she would deal with later.

Justin tapped the stem of his wineglass with his fork to gain everyone's attention. "Let us drink to your visit to Brighton, Miss Talgarth, and to the gentleman who will be so lucky as to pluck such a lovely rose."

As Arabella drained her glass—it was a delicious Bordeaux—she thought how very adept Suzanne had become in her handling of gentlemen. She was certain that the lovely rose could show her thorns most effectively, if crossed the wrong way. Lady Ann cleared her throat and stared at Arabella.

Arabella rose and nodded to the earl and the comte. "If you gentlemen will excuse us, the ladies will now repair to the Velvet Room."

Justin rose also and said pleasantly, "I don't think we need to linger over our port this evening, my dear. If you ladies do not mind, we would join you now."

Lady Talgarth said to Lady Ann in a whisper calculated to penetrate even Crupper's ears, who stood at the far end of the dining room, "It still seems very strange for Arabella to be in *your* place, my dear Ann."

Arabella pretended not to hear and looked back only when Suzanne tugged on her sleeve. "Goodness, you walk so very quickly. Come, Bella, don't mind Mama. You must know that she is jealous because you have contracted such an eligible alliance before I have managed even an ineligible one."

"As if you would ever care." Arabella gave one blond curl an affectionate pull. "You make it sound like I've caught some vile disease, like measles."

Other blond curls fluttered and bobbed over small shapely ears. "Certainly not. I think your groom very handsome, not at all like measles. And if *you* caught an earl, no doubt I shall become a duchess. Mayhap this wondrous duke will have seven houses scattered all over England. He will throw at least three ropes of diamonds around my white neck."

Arabella looked at the dimpled laughing face and found herself smiling. "You will make a perfect duchess, Suz. I just hope you can find a young one."

"Well, old dukes have to have sons, don't they? Surely they can't all be snapped up. You know, it would serve Mama right were I to marry our chinless paunchy viscount. All the money that has been lavished on clothing for my back for the Season—why Papa was livid when the only result he saw was one visit from a gentleman who could not play at whist and the other visit from a gentleman who could talk only of his mistress." She paused, then turned. "Yes, Mama, it's true. Don't look so shocked. No, no one said that in front of me. I, er, was standing just outside Papa's library and overheard it." She paused a moment and sat daintily beside Arabella, arranging her lavender skirt in becoming folds about her. "Oh, my, Elsbeth is going to play. I do hope Mama will not insist that I follow such a performance. She is so very talented. It is depressing. It is difficult to keep up pretenses."

"I know. It's as if she puts all her passion into her music. If she would speak as she plays, I think she would be an excellent orator."

After a third Bach prelude, Suzanne began to fidget. She put her blond head next to Arabella's ear and whispered behind her lavender-gloved hand, "How very lucky you are, Bella. The earl is so very handsome and, well, handsome as the devil actually. If I were not a properly brought-up young lady, I should long to be wicked and ask you all about your wedding night. So, how was it?"

The stark memory of pain and bitter humiliation sent bile into Arabella's throat. She finally said, "I will forget what you asked. Just know that wedding nights aren't—no, forget that. Be quiet. Listen to Elsbeth."

"Such a spoilsport you are."

After Elsbeth's performance had received its usual loud applause, and Suzanne had complained convincingly to her mama of a sore finger that would render her in horrible pain if she had to strike a single pianoforte key with it, Arabella found herself paired with the comte against the earl and Suzanne in a game of whist.

She soon discovered that the comte's skill was nearly on a par with hers. She began to play with the daring and skill that her father had taught her. Without intending it to be so, she found herself engaging in silent battle against her husband, the comte and Suzanne fading out of her thoughts, out of her sight. When Lady

Ann halted their game for tea, Arabella and the comte had soundly thrashed their opponents. Suzanne, who was in reality as competitive as Arabella, merely laughed gaily and fanned the deck of cards in colorful profusion about the tabletop.

"You were just like Jeanne d'Arc, strewing her enemy in her path," the comte said, admiration and something else in his voice. He clasped Arabella's hand and kissed her wrist.

The earl's eyes were narrow. He looked ready to kill. She grabbed her hand back and said, "That is nonsense, and you know it. I dislike flattery. We had excellent cards, nothing more. Suzanne is the killer."

"No, I'm only a killer occasionally. The comte is quite right, Bella," Suzanne said. "You're a veritable dragon. Don't you remember when we were children and you were always trying to drum the strategy of the game into my head?"

"You have far too lovely a head for nonsensical games, Miss Talgarth," the earl said as he helped her to rise and drew her arm through his.

"I had believed you a man of truth, my lord," Suzanne said. "Come, admit it, you could most willingly have wrung my neck when I trumped your winning spade in the third game."

"Very well, I will admit it. Truth is sometimes the very devil, isn't it, Miss Talgarth?"

"His lordship finds the lovely Miss Talgarth most amusing, is it not so, cousin?"

Arabella raised gray eyes to the comte's too-handsome face and said, "I daresay, monsieur, but then again, I myself find Suzanne most amusing. She enlivens any conversation, brightens any party."

When, amid wraps and bonnets, Lady Talgarth and Miss Talgarth took their leave, Arabella quickly excused herself, not meeting the earl's eyes, and hurried up the stairs. She locked the door to the earl's bedchamber, and heaved a sigh of relief, only to gasp with surprise as the door to the adjoining dressing room slowly opened. She stood frozen in the middle of the room, as the earl strode toward her.

He saw her eyes fly to the small nightstand, guessed her pistol lay in the drawer, and drew to a halt. He watched her closely as her hands balled into fists and her face paled in the dim candlelight. A picture of Arabella, dancing toward him in her nightgown, smiling confidently and unafraid, darted through his mind. Their wedding night seemed an eternity ago.

He said to her in an even voice, "You will not need your gun tonight, Arabella. I merely came to wish you a good night. You were an excellent hostess. I was pleased. I believe the evening was successful."

"Thank you. I agree," she said, nothing more. She stood there unmoving until he had strode from the bed-chamber and into the adjoining room, closing the door behind him.

Rain slashed against the windows and cascaded in thick sheets onto the rows of rosebushes, flattening them against the outside wall of the library. Arabella sighed in frustration at her enforced inactivity and hurriedly scanned the dark-paneled shelves for a suitable book to while away the afternoon hours. How very strange it was that she, the Earl of Strafford's favorite daughter should be roaming furtively about the abbey, purposely avoiding nearly all of its occupants. Even Dr. Branyon, who was expected later in the afternoon for tea, had joined the ranks of those whose penetrating stares made her feel like a guilty intruder in her own home.

"Oh, damn, how absurd it is." She grabbed the first colorfully bound book that caught her eye. Once in the earl's bedchamber she realized she had selected a book of plays by the French writer Mirabeau. As her French was as deplorable as her efforts at the pianoforte, deciphering the lines word by word was about as pleasurable as having a splinter in her finger. After a while she looked up from her shadowed corner and rubbed her eyes. She was struck again by her desire to be alone, be hidden away from everyone. Had she not unconsciously selected the darkest corner of the room to pass the afternoon?

By the time she had forced herself to translate the supposedly witty lines in the first act, the book lay open on her lap and her head fell against her arm.

Arabella was not certain what awakened her, perhaps her fear that the earl had come into the room to find her, but in an instant she was alert, her muscles tensed for action.

She gazed across to the more lighted portion of the room and saw with some confusion the stooped figure of Josette, Elsbeth's maid. The old woman moved to *The Dance of Death* panel, looked quickly about her, and began to run her gnarled hands over the carved, uneven figures on the surface.

Arabella rose from her chair and walked from her shadowed corner, a question already framed on her lips. "Josette, whatever are you doing here?"

The old woman jumped back from the panel, her arms flopping to her sides. She gazed in consternation at the young countess, her throat so dry with fear that only jumbled incoherent sounds erupted from her mouth.

"Come, Josette, whatever is so very interesting about *The Dance of Death* panel? If you wanted to examine it, you had but to ask me. Surely it is no excuse for you to be sneaking about." Arabella frowned at Josette, her mind suddenly alert to the trapped, confused look on her face.

"Forgive me, my lady," Josette finally managed to say in a strangled whisper, "it is just that I . . . that I . . ."

"You what?" Arabella said, her head cocked to one side. Goodness, the old woman looked as if she expected the grim laughing skeleton to reach out from the panel and grab her by the throat. This was all very odd.

The old woman wrung her hands, clasping them over her thin chest. "Oh, my lady, I had no choice. I was forced to do it, forced." She broke off suddenly, her eyes rolling upward. Before Arabella could question her further, she ran from the bedchamber in a frenzied, loping gait.

Arabella made no move to stop her. She stared at the closed door, wondering what the devil the old woman had meant. After a few moments she walked to *The Dance of Death* and stood for a long while looking at the bizarre panorama of grotesque carved figures. She moved her fingers lightly over the surface. The skeleton screamed his soundless commands to his demonic hosts. The panel was as it always was. Arabella stood there before the panel a moment longer, then turned with a shrug and returned to her darkened corner.

19

Arabella quietly slipped through the door of the adjoining dressing room, her wrapper knotted loosely about her waist, her black hair streaming down her back. She ran noiselessly to the earl's bed. "Justin, Justin, wake up." She leaned over him and shook his shoulder.

His eyes flew open and he struggled up to a sitting position. "What? Arabella?" He was at once startled and alert. He could barely make out her pale features in the dim early light of dawn.

Arabella drew a deep breath. "It is Josette, Elsbeth's maid. She is dead, Justin. I found her but a moment ago at the foot of the main staircase. I think her neck is broken."

"Good God." He threw back the bedcovers, insensible to the fact that he was quite naked, and added impatiently, "Come, Bella, hand me my dressing gown."

As she handed him the rich brocade dressing gown, she looked at him, she couldn't help it. He was utterly beautiful, all lean muscle, and big, his chest covered with black hair and his groin as well. She stepped back, appalled at herself, wondering if he had seen her staring at him.

The earl appeared quite oblivious of her panic, and said brusquely over his shoulder as he strode toward the door, "Well, don't just stand there, come along, Bella. You did come to me first, did you not?"

"Of course," she said simply. "Who else would I have gone to?" And it was the truth. She took a double step to catch up with him. "I couldn't sleep and I was going to the library to fetch a bit of brandy."

"Thank the good Lord the servants are not up and about yet."

She stood back as he leaned over the twisted form of the old woman and made a brief examination. He rose after a moment and nodded. "You're right. Her neck is broken. Also she feels cold and very stiff. She'd been dead for some time." He was silent then, looking back up the stairs, then back to the shapeless body. A slow frown spread over his smooth brow, drawing his black brows together.

"What are you thinking, Justin?" Arabella asked, her eyes following his up the winding staircase.

"I am really not certain at this moment what I am thinking," he said slowly. Suddenly efficient, he added briskly, "We must do first things first. Fetch a blanket to cover her while I carry her to the back parlor. I will send for Dr. Branyon."

Dr. Branyon arrived within the hour, his face drawn with concern. He had imagined any number of frightful accidents, for the stable boy could tell him nothing.

As he gratefully accepted a cup of steaming coffee from Arabella later in the Velvet Room, he said, "There are several broken bones, but she died, as both of you supposed, from a broken neck in the fall down the stairs. It's a pity." He sighed. "Lord, it is hard to believe that she has been in England for more than twenty years. She was Magdalaine's maid, you know. She has taken care of Elsbeth all her life. Elsbeth will be quite upset over her death." He turned to Arabella. "You have waked your mother? I suggest that Ann inform your sister. I will remain and give her a drought to calm her, if necessary. Ah, poor Elsbeth."

Lady Ann remained with Elsbeth for most of the day, emerging only briefly for luncheon.

"I had no idea that my cousin would be so concerned over a servant's death," the comte said as he took a goodly bite of baked ham, a hint of incredulity in his voice.

"Josette was like another mother to Elsbeth," Lady Ann said quietly. "Elsbeth has been close to her all her life. I would be surprised were she not distraught. But she goes a bit better now, poor child."

Arabella stared at the comte, wondering if he was totally without sensitivity. As if he felt the condemnation of everyone at the luncheon table, the comte spread his hands before him in apology and hastened to say, "Do forgive such an impertinent observation, Lady Ann. It must be that the English take such matters to heart more than we French do. Of course, you are correct. I applaud my cousin's feelings. An unfortunate accident, to be sure."

The earl rose abruptly and tossed his napkin over his plate. "Paul, if you would care to join me in the library to make final preparations? The coffin maker will be here shortly." He nodded to Lady Ann and Arabella and strode without a backward glance from the dining room.

It was late in the afternoon when the coffin maker left bearing Josette's body. Though Arabella could not explain it, she felt compelled to watch his departure. The earl emerged from the great front doors to stand quietly beside her on the steps.

"God, how I hate death," she said, her voice raw and hoarse. "But look—" she pointed after the lumbering black coach that carried Josette's body—"it's like the very harbinger of death, with those black plumes on the horses' bridles and the ghastly black-looped curtains in the windows." She added bitterly, "And look at me, all swathed in the trappings of death. I am a daily reminder that death's power is supreme. We are as nothing, all of us. Oh, God, why do those we love have to disappear from our lives?"

The earl brought his eyes to rest upon her pale wstrained face and said gently, "Your question is the plaything of our philosophers. Even they can only propose answers, all of them absurd. Unfortunately, it must always be the living who suffer, for those we loved are beyond pain." He paused a moment to gaze out at the immaculate perfection of nature's making. "It is a depressing thought that we are set in the midst of this enduring nature for but a moment in time, but it is true.

"Now it is I who am talking nonsense. Bella, why don't you donate all your black gowns to the curate? Your love and memories of your father are within you, after all. Why submit yourself to the ridiculous restrictions of society?"

"You know," she said slowly, "Father always hated black." As she turned to walk away, she remembered Josette's strange visit to the earl's bedchamber the day before, and looked back. "Justin, perhaps it is nonsense and means nothing at all, but Josette was sneaking about *The Dance of Death* panel yesterday afternoon. She did not see me, for I was dozing in that large chair in the corner of the room. She seemed frightfully upset when I spoke to her. She said nothing that made any sense. When I kept asking her what she wanted, she scampered out as if the devil himself were on her heels."

"What exactly did she say?"

"Only some vague phrase about her being *forced* to be in the room. She really made no sense at all, as I said. Her behavior has become quite strange, you know. Perhaps her wits were so addled she believed Magdalaine still to be alive and in the earl's bedchamber." She paused and shook her head.

"There is something else?"

"I was just wondering why Josette was wandering about in the middle of the night without a candle to guide her."

For an incredible moment Justin felt himself drawn to a long-ago sweltering night in Portugal. He and several other soldiers were scouting the perimeter of a scrubby wooded area on the outskirts of a small village in search of the elusive guerrillas. There was an almost discernible odor of danger that reached his nostrils. He jerked his companions to their bellies against the rocky ground just as shots rang out above their heads. Now, as then, he scented danger—certainly not in the form of cutthroats lurking about—but danger nonetheless. He felt he could say nothing of his vague feelings to Arabella, and thus turned to her and said lightly, without thought, "Perhaps old Josette was off to meet a secret lover. A candle would surely find her out."

She withdrew from him as if she had suddenly been whisked to another county. Guilt and shame filled her eyes. And bitterness. His belief that she had betrayed him reduced her to dull silence.

"Arabella, wait, I did not mean—Well, damnation." He stopped, angry with himself, but she was gone.

"Would you believe it, Bella? Our chinless viscount just happened, mind you, to be in the neighborhood on his way to Brighton. Mama cooed and made a great fuss over him. Bless Papa, for he treated him most vilely. Of course, it was his gout that made him so cross, but it sent Mama into a dither. How she scolded him about ruining my chances to get myself shackled."

Suzanne Talgarth drew up her mare and patted her neck. "Papa guffawed until he was positively purple in the face when I told him that if Arabella Deverill could catch an earl, then I was assured of a duke."

Arabella reined in Lucifer and looked thoughtfully at her friend. "You know, Suz, it is a great joke, but I do not think it wise that—"

"Lord, Bella, whatever is the matter with you? Ever since you got yourself married, you have changed. You're too quiet. You stare right through me when I'm being particularly witty. What are you talking about? What the devil isn't wise?"

"I haven't changed, not really. It's just that, no, that's none of your business. I will tell you what isn't wise and that is raising young girls to idolize the vision of some ridiculous man who will be their husband. That is ridiculous."

"You must take care, Bella, for that sounds like a woman disappointed. Mama indeed tried to raise me to believe such nonsense, but you know me. If a man is an ass, well, that's what he is. You know, sometimes I think it is you who are the great romantic, Bella, not me. I believe you thought to find the *grand amour*, didn't you?" At Arabella's silence, Suzanne laughed, flicking the reins on Bluebell's glossy brown neck. "Come," she called over her shoulder, "we are almost at Bury Saint Edmunds. Tell Lucifer that he must do a bit of work today. It's so lovely, let's explore the ruins."

But they didn't do any exploring. Suzanne dropped gracefully to a grassy mound in the shade of a large elm tree, patted the spot beside her, and continued her thoughts of many minutes before. "No, I would never believe in a *grand amour*. Indeed, such a notion is absurd, particularly after observing Mama and Papa all these years. In fact," she said with a tiny frown, "such a thing as love must indeed be for the common people, for I have seen none of it in couples of our class. I suppose it would be nice if someone had it. Do you think perhaps it is possible?"

"I had no idea you were such a snob, Suz," Arabella said. "But perhaps for girls like us, well, we marry as we're told to and that's that. Just like I did, just as my father ordered me even though he was dead." She smoothed the folds of her blue riding habit about her ankles. How marvelous it was to box away all those dismal black gowns.

Suzanne had just looked at her and nodded. "I like your gown. I hate black as well. My mama will have a fit when she sees you, but you never care. Now, am I a snob?" Suzanne shook her head. "No, not a snob, Bella, merely a realist. Undoubtedly my duke will be well over forty, running to fat, and a gamester in the Carlton House set. But, do you not see, I will be 'your grace,' have countless servants to carry out my every whim, and enjoy what one is supposed to enjoy. And that, I think, must be marvelous lobster patties and as much champagne as I can drink."

"You really do not believe in loving the man you are to wed?" Arabella asked slowly, so unhappy she thought she'd choke on it.

"Such a question coming from you, Arabella? Ah, here I was forgetting your handsome husband. He is beautiful, there is no question about that. He is also charming and well, dominating, but in a protective sort of way. Perhaps you are fond of each other. That would be nice. And I think you're lucky to wed such a man. He has a chin and he doesn't have gout. And he is very smart. There are not many like him that I have seen in London. To think, your father handpicked him just for you. Yes, you could definitely have done worse for yourself. And knowing you, if the poor fellow didn't ride like a champion, you would have ground him into the dirt."

"Yes, it was my father's idea, his order." Arabella said, looking off at the ruins in the distance. "I had no choice, not really. I could not leave Evesham Abbey, you see."

"How strange it is," Suzanne said after a few moments, "when we were children, I never quite imagined you as a married lady. You were always so very certain of yourself, so very forthright and strong. If you were not so pretty, you could probably pass quite well as a gentleman. My father was always telling me not to let you lead me into mischief. He said you should have been a damned boy because your father only encouraged you in sowing wild oats. He could never understand why Lady Ann didn't take charge of you. But, I usually saw a gleam of admiration in his eyes when he grumped and complained about you."

"I remember that you got me into trouble on more than one occasion," Arabella said. "As for your thinking I wouldn't marry, that is rather strange. What else is there for a woman to do? Be like that ridiculous Stanhope woman or my aunt Grenhilde? No, marriage is doled out to us. As to my being certain of myself and strong"—Arabella paused, carefully choosing her words—"perhaps it would be better for me now were I more bending, more submissive."

"Ah, your dominating husband. I begin to think that you and the earl are in a tug of wills, Bella. And it is obvious to me that despite all the bravado and wild exploits of our youth, you are simply not wise in the ways of women."

"Wise in the ways of women? That sounds like an old gypsy crone who makes up love potions. What on earth are you talking about?"

The twinkling laughter dropped from Suzanne's eyes and her voice became suddenly very serious. "I will tell you, Bella. You have a strong character, but it is simply not a *woman*'s strong character. No, now don't interrupt me, for I believe that I am getting to the kernel of the corn. I have never known you to shy away from something, even if it was unpleasant. You are always forthright, honest, and loyal—and those are the traits gentlemen are supposedly noted for.

"You see, that is exactly your problem. Gentlemen think that we are playing games, or lying, even when we are honest. And when we are forced to be less than honest, they do not know the difference anyway. Therefore, my dear friend, why disappoint them?"

"You have said a lot there, Suzanne, and I'm not certain that I have quite gleaned your meaning. I am honest, most women are, yet it makes no difference to gentlemen if we are or not. Is that what you said?"

"That is close enough."

Arabella sighed, pulled up a blade of grass and began chewing on it. "I invited you to ride with me to cheer me up. You must know that Elsbeth has sunk into total gloom since her maid, Josette, fell to her death. I expected gentleness from you. I expected tender wit and perhaps even soft pats on my shoulder. But here we are, and I find that all you wish to do is to dissect my character."

Suzanne sighed herself and pressed her lips together. She stretched out her legs and wiggled her toes inside her soft calf riding boots. "I see that all my wisdom will go unheeded. I will tell you, Bella, I think you almost as much a romantic ninny as dear Elsbeth."

Arabella turned startled eyes to her friend. "Come, Suz, stop twitching your toes and tell me what you mean. Elsbeth a romantic? Why, the thought is absurd. She is such an innocent child despite her twenty-one years. She would have no notion at all about romance."

"Poor Arabella. Even Elsbeth tries to dissemble although she isn't at all good at it yet. Haven't you noticed how she hangs on to the comte's every word? I swear she is much taken with the young Frenchman. He is her cousin?"

"Yes, of course he is her cousin. Her mother was his aunt. But really, Suz—"

Suzanne threw up her hands. "Oh, Bella, how can you be so blind? Your dear half-sister is not such an innocent child. I vow she has quite set her sights on her young cousin. Why last night I happened to look at her when the comte was playing whist with you. There was hatred in those pretty eyes of hers, Bella, hatred and jealousy of you, and all because the comte was just being his French self."

Elsbeth and Gervaise? It cannot be possible. But wait, Arabella, think back. Have there not been many times when Elsbeth and Gervaise have both been absent during the day? Has Elsbeth not seemed to become more confident, more sure of herself? And she seems to talk so freely with Gervaise.

"Oh my God." She surged to her feet. *Justin believes the comte to be my lover. I did not understand. I had no answers. All I could do was swear that I was innocent. Can it really be that Elsbeth, my shy, uncertain Elsbeth, is the comte's lover?*

Suzanne untangled her shapely legs and rose to stand beside Arabella. There was a blind glazed look in her friend's eyes that quite unnerved her. She grabbed her arm and shook her. "Bella, what has upset you so? I daresay that I could be in the wrong about Elsbeth and the comte. You know me, I'm always talking, and not necessarily thinking enough before I do speak."

Arabella turned to look at her friend. "No," she said slowly, "you are really quite right. I have been blind to what is going on about me. I have paid dearly for my blindness. As has Justin. But how did he know? Why did he believe it was me? And he was so very certain, as if he'd seen me, but that isn't possible, is it?" She added urgently, her riding crop tightening in her hand, "I must return to Evesham Abbey now, Suzanne. I have much to think about. Oh God, there is so much to say now, so much to learn. Listen to me, Suz. Please keep this to yourself. But I thank you for telling me. I thank you from the bottom of my heart."

Arabella swung upon Lucifer's back and dug in her heels before Suzanne could put two thoughts together.

20

The earl stared thoughtfully down at the single sheet of paper from his friend Lord Morton, of the war ministry. Jack certainly conducted an efficient operation despite French control on the Continent. He read the few lines once again, then shredded the letter and watched the fragments settle atop the logs in the grate. He lit a match and watched the small pieces of paper grow black about the edges and then crackle into orange flame.

He was on the point of leaving the library when the door opened and Lady Ann appeared. "My dear Justin, I am so glad that you have not yet gone out, for I wished particularly to speak with you."

The earl's thoughts flew to Arabella. He looked at Lady Ann's set face and grew instantly wary. He became instantly formal. "It is true that I was on the point of riding to Talgarth Hall, Ann, but of course I have still a few minutes. Would you care to sit down?"

Lady Ann sat down and patted the place beside her. She said quietly, "I have no intention of bringing up uncomfortable topics, Justin, so you may be at your ease. It is Elsbeth I wished to discuss."

"Elsbeth? Surely all decisions relating to her are in your domain, Ann." He crossed a booted leg over the other and waited none too patiently for her to speak.

Ann knew she couldn't carry off her fiction any longer. "Very well, Elsbeth is my domain and I frankly don't care what your opinions are concerning her." She drew a deep breath. "I know that you do not think highly of Gervaise de Trécassis. For that matter, neither do I and neither does Dr. Branyon. I don't trust him, it's that simple. I don't care for his attitudes in many areas. There is something wrong. He is not what he appears. I don't approve of the easy way he has with Elsbeth or Arabella. I do know that Arabella quite detests him. What I wonder is why he is still here. Why don't you simply ask him to leave Evesham Abbey? You don't need to kill him as Dr. Branyon thinks you would like to do."

He eyed her for a very long time, then said something that made her blink. "What makes you think Arabella detests him? That is a very strong word, Ann."

All that and he had thought only of Arabella. "I know it's true because I can see that not only does he repel her, she's also afraid of him. I think she's afraid that he will speak untruths about her to you. Has that happened?"

"No."

"Ah, well, he might, at least Arabella thinks so. But what I don't understand is what she believes he will say to you."

"Has she told you this?"

"No, not really. But I am her mother. I understand her very well. It's odd, but Elsbeth quite appreciates him. Several times when he has said something that is not quite the thing, she has defended him. Isn't that strange?"

"Elsbeth defending her cousin? Perhaps it isn't so very strange. They are first cousins. She's an impressionable young girl—"

"Perhaps, but she is still nearly three years older than Arabella."

"Well, but she is very innocent in the ways of the

world. Perhaps she has some hero worship for the comte?"

"Why do you hate him, Justin?"

He rose quickly and walked to the sideboard. He poured himself some brandy and drank it down. "Leave it be, Ann," he said at last. "Just leave it be. You don't understand and it is not something I can speak to you about."

"Oh, I quite understand. And I applaud your discretion, except in this case you are quite wrong. You have somehow come to believe that he and Arabella are lovers."

He'd known it was coming, he'd known. So Arabella had cried on her mother's shoulder to intervene. He should have expected it. There was an unpleasant sneer in his voice as he said, "Ah, has your daughter confided that to you, Ann? Has she told you that she hated marrying me so much that she took him as her lover even before we were married? Did she admit to you that ours is a mockery of a marriage? Did she beg you to use your influence with me?"

She could not believe the depth of the bitterness in his voice. She must go carefully here. There was so very much at stake. "Listen to me now, Justin. Arabella avoids me as much as she does you. She is bitterly unhappy. I also know that you hurt her on your wedding night. I saw her shredded nightgown and all the blood that following morning. She has said nothing to me, not a single word. You believe that she has begged me to intervene? Have you lost your wits? Arabella begging anyone?"

"I'm sorry. Of course that wouldn't be in her character, but others things are, Ann. You mustn't be blind to them just because she is your daughter."

"What are you sorry for? Are you sorry that I had to learn that you had hurt my daughter?"

"I'm simply sorry that everything has happened as it has." Jesus, he wanted to get out of here.

"Listen to me, you idiot, I am anything but blind when it comes to my daughter. What do you mean there are other things in her character? Tell me, Justin."

"Very well. She deserves whatever I mete out to her, Ann. Please, just leave it alone. There has been too much between us and yet not nearly enough. There is nothing you can do. Suffice it to say that Arabella is his lover. Now, as for Gervaise de Trécassis, well, we will see. I don't want him gone just yet. Paul is quite right. I would dearly love to kill him—not with a bullet and cleanly, but with my bare hands. No, he will remain a while longer. I have always believed that if there is a snake about, it is wise to keep your eye on him and not let him slither away only to sneak back and catch you unawares."

"With your bare hands?"

"Yes, that would be pleasurable, but I cannot, at least not yet."

"Why? And don't give me more imagery about a damned snake slithering about!"

"All right, Ann, plain speaking. I must know who and what he is before I act. You are quite right. He is not what he seems. I will not let my anger at Arabella interfere with my plans. Yes, Ann, I should very much like to kill the man who seduced my wife. I daresay Paul Branyon would like to kill any man who seduced you."

She just shook her head. "She didn't take the comte as a lover. Wait. Are you saying she wasn't a virgin on your wedding night?"

"Some discussion about Elsbeth," he said, his voice as acid as his belly at that moment, and he drank down some more brandy. It burned all the way to his belly. "I should have known."

"Yes, you should have."

"Are you quite through?"

"Not at all. Well? Was Arabella a virgin on your wedding night?"

He sighed. "She was a virgin."

"Then what the devil are you talking about? Are you a complete idiot? Ah, I believe I shall shoot you!" Lady Ann jumped to her feet. For an instant, he thought she would attack him, but she stopped just short of him and laid her hand on his sleeve. "What?" she said again. "She was a virgin. She told you that he wasn't her lover. What then?"

"Ann, you were a married lady. You know there are many ways to pleasure a man."

She looked at him as if she would heave up her lunch. "Oh, no, surely Arabella would never do that. It's horrible. No, not her mouth, no."

"Our conversation isn't all that is proper, Ann. I don't wish to speak of this further. Suffice it to say that I am completely positive that Arabella took the comte for her lover before we married. Positive, do you hear me? I am not a liar. I did not make this up, it is not speculation or guesswork. Is she still seeing him? I don't know. Of course she denied it. All of it. What would you expect her to do?"

"Arabella has never lied in her life."

"How little you know your daughter, Ann."

She slapped him as hard as she could. His head snapped back with the force of her blow. Her handprint was on his cheek. He said nothing, merely stared down at her.

"You are wrong. Completely wrong," she said, her back stiff as a board, her chin raised.

He touched his fingers to his cheek. It stung. She was stronger than she looked. What to do about Arabella? His new home had become a battleground. Even Lady Ann, his soft-spoken, charming mother-in-law, had hit him. Was he the only one who believed Arabella guilty? God, were his affairs being discussed in the kitchen?

Suddenly, the library door burst open and Arabella rushed into the room. She drew up short on the threshold, utter dismay flooding her face. She threw out her hands as if to ward them away from her. "Oh, I thought you were alone, my lord. But you're not, are you. Not alone at all. Why would I think that? How are you, Mother?"

"I am quite well, Arabella. Did you enjoy your ride with Suzanne? No, don't answer that silly question. No, dearest, do not rush away, for I was just on the point of leaving. Justin, please consider what I have said. Perhaps we can speak of it again later." This was something unexpected, Lady Ann thought, patting her daughter's hand as she passed her, Arabella wanting to be alone with her husband.

Suddenly Arabella grasped her mother's hand and held it fast. The look on the earl's face was forbidding. It struck her forcibly that Suzanne's observation about Elsbeth and the comte might only serve to make her appear the more guilty in his eyes. If she had not been aware of the closeness between her half-sister and the comte, then most assuredly Justin would not have noticed. She wanted to strike out. Even now she read mistrust and condemnation in his eyes. She drew back, positioning herself closer to the door, behind her mother.

"It wasn't important. I'm sorry for having disturbed you, my lord, Mother. I have nothing to say, really. Nothing of any importance. I think I shall go to my room now. Yes, that is a good place to go."

"Wait, Arabella," the earl said sharply as she turned to flee. Lady Ann was aware that Arabella was using her as s physical shield between her and her husband. She saw her daughter tense as the earl drew near to her.

He pulled a key from his waistcoat pocket. "If you wish to go to the earl's bedchamber, you will need this key."

Lady Ann had held her peace long enough. Her hand still burned from the blow she had struck on her son-in-law. "My dear child, first of all, I was just leaving. You did not interrupt us. Secondly, why ever, Justin, have you locked the earl's bedchamber?"

He shrugged. "I discovered loose floorboards about the room. I did not wish any of the servants to come to harm. Thus, until I have seen to repairs, I wish to keep the room locked. Here you are, Arabella."

Arabella grabbed the key from his outstretched hand, turned, and rushed from the room.

"You have much to answer for," Lady Ann said, looking at him straightly. "You have messed things up royally, Justin."

"Perhaps, but I don't think so. Now, if you will excuse me, I really must pay my visit to Lord Talgarth. I shall consider what you have said."

"I doubt it. You are a man, and in my experience, you accept one belief and die with it before you will consider that you were possibly wrong. God, I hate the lot of you." She turned, only to whirl about again, this time pointing her finger at him. "Arabella has never been afraid in her life. Yet I have seen her change since her marriage to you into a silent, withdrawn, even frightened girl. She has not tried to tell me what to do a single time since you've been married, and believe me, that is not like her at all. Oh yes, you wretched specimen, you have so much to answer for. Damn you."

This time she left the room. He stared after her for many minutes. Gentle, utterly guileless Lady Ann. She had become a tigress.

He left for Talgarth Hall and stayed there for the remainder of the day.

21

Elsbeth loved the sweet smell of fresh-cut hay. The smell filled the barn, making her breathe in deeply and smile. She walked quickly to the stall in the far darkened corner of the barn. It had been at least a week since she had slipped away from Evesham Abbey to meet him here. Far too long. He hadn't spoken to her of his masculine need for her since Josette's death. She honored him for such noble sentiments. His sensitivity to her grief after her old servant's tragic fall made him all the more precious to her.

Yet as she spread her cloak upon the straw, smoothing the edges with loving hands, she frowned. She had sensed that during the past several days there was much on his mind. She even imagined now, even though she didn't want to, that he had hesitated at her diffident offer to meet him here this afternoon. His slight pause before agreeing brought Suzanne Talgarth's face to her mind. How she hated Suzanne. She knew that Suzanne wanted the comte. What woman could not? He was everything a woman could possibly want. Oh yes, Elsbeth was acutely aware of everyone's feelings when they came close to him. Yes, Suzanne wanted him, the bitch. But he would not go to her, would he? Surely not, even though Suzanne was so gay and beautiful with her blond hair. No, he wouldn't betray her.

The week that she had not lain with the comte had

served to nurture her romantic belief that their physical union was an exquisite proof of his love for her. She had even prayed that she would feel delight at the touch of his hands, moan when his lips touched her.

She began to grow nervous as she waited in the dimly lit stall. Surely he must have been detained by a very pressing matter. She was on the point of rising to look out the front doors of the huge barn when she saw him slip silently into the stall.

"Oh, my love, I was growing worried." She threw her arms about him, pressing kisses to his throat, his shoulders, his chest. "Is there a problem? Did someone keep you overlong? It wasn't Suzanne Talgarth, was it? She was trying to make you come to her? Tell me everything is all right."

The comte kissed the top of her head, then gently pushed her down onto the cloak.

"What is this about Suzanne? If she tried, *ma petite,* to make me come to her, I would laugh in her face. I would tell her that I do not like the pink-and-white English girls with their bovine faces."

He dropped gracefully onto the cloak beside her, looking at her sweet face, at the besotted look in her almond-shaped eyes, eyes so like her mother's. "No, dear Elsbeth," he said, lightly stroking his fingers over her smooth cheek, "I was merely in conversation with Lady Ann. It would not have been polite to leave her abruptly."

She leaned forward and clasped her arms about his neck. She felt guilty at her doubts. She felt like a shrew because she had questioned him. She wasn't worthy of him. Yet here he was, he had chosen her. She felt a light kiss touch her hair and waited for him to pull her into his arms. But he didn't jerk her wildly against him. She waited. Nothing. She drew back, puzzled, her eyes growing darker in her worry. Surely after a week he should want her. Had Suzanne been at Evesham Abbey after all? Had he lied to her? No, she wouldn't think that, not for a minute. She also wouldn't think about the relief she felt that he wasn't taking her clothes off.

"What is wrong, my love?" she whispered against his neck. "What has happened to upset you?"

He sighed, coming down onto his side, balancing himself on his elbow. "You are perceptive, Elsbeth. You see a lot." He saw the pleasure his easy words gave her. She would be anything he wanted her to be, do anything he asked of her. At least he prayed it was so. He considered his next words carefully, saying at last, "You must know that the earl and I do not deal well together. His antipathy toward me grows daily. I believe if he could manage it, he would kill me. No, no, Elsbeth, it's all right. I can deal with the earl. You know, I wonder why he hasn't ordered me to leave, but he hasn't. It is strange. I do not understand him nor do I understand this hatred he has for me. I have done him no ill."

Elsbeth could not help herself. "Kill you, oh no! Surely that is going too far. Besides, you wouldn't allow it. You are brave and strong and smart. He is nothing compared to you. You wouldn't allow anyone to harm you. I hate him. What shall we do?"

She believed everything she had said. So passionate she was. He had found himself wondering about that passion of hers, if perhaps he'd not seen her as she really was, but listening to her now, the passion in her was real, very real. And he knew that passion was the same in all things. He smiled at her. He could be sure of her now.

She clutched at his sleeve. "He hates you because he is jealous of you, Gervaise, I know it. He sees that you are everything that he is not. He despises you for it. Oh God, what will we do?"

Completely satisfied, the comte smiled a tender, slightly bitter smile, and said softly, "You are always so sensitive to the feelings of those around you, Elsbeth. Perhaps you are correct about the earl, perhaps there is something in him that makes him feel less the man when I am around. But it doesn't matter. Evesham Abbey belongs to him. I am merely a guest. I can become uninvited anytime." He shook away the pain of it, and took her small hands between his. "In any case, just a while ago he more or less ordered me to leave Evesham Abbey by the end of the week. Our time together grows short, my love." The earl hadn't really ordered him, but it had amounted to the same thing. He had merely asked Gervaise to the library, closed the door, faced him, saying finally, "You will wish to leave Evesham Abbey by the end of the week." Nothing more, just that, for the longest time. And he had looked at Gervaise with that cold deadness in his eyes, his body perfectly still, and Gervaise had felt such an instant of fear, that he found he could not yet speak. "What? Not a word? You have nothing at all to say to me?"

Still, Gervaise had said nothing, merely shrugged his shoulders.

"There is a lot about you that offends me, comte. But I have allowed you to stay—for many reasons. But those reasons will resolve themselves very soon now. The end of the week. Now, leave me."

And that had been all that was said. Gervaise left the library, leaning against the wall when he was alone, hating himself because he had not told the earl that he was a coward, a bully, and not worthy to wear Gervaise's boots. No, he had said nothing.

"Yes," he said now to Elsbeth, "our time grows short. I must be gone by the end of the week."

Elsbeth started forward. "Oh no, it cannot be so. Gervaise, I cannot let you go away from me. I have just found you and I won't want to lose you. No, please." Tears filled her eyes. She gulped, trying to control herself, but she couldn't. Tears streamed down her cheeks. "It isn't fair. Arabella has everything—truly, even if she doesn't appear to enjoy what she has. Even Lady Ann is now her own mistress; she can do anything she wishes to. It's only I who have been the supplicant all my life, the one outside, the one nobody wants. I can't bear it. Please, I don't want to be alone again."

He couldn't bear it, this pain in her that colored everything she thought, everything she said. But he had no alternative. The comte gently flicked away the tears and said, "We must be brave, Elsbeth. This is, after all, the earl's territory, as I told you. His decisions, whatever his motives may be, must govern the actions of those about him. In short, I have no choice in the matter."

"Did you not tell him that you didn't wish to leave? Did you not tell him that you and I love each other and do not want to be separated?"

"I did," the comte said, without an instant of hesitation, "but he did not care. As I said, I believe he hates me."

Elsbeth sagged to her knees. She had lost Josette, and now she could lose Gervaise as well. "I know," she said, suddenly hope filling her, "I will speak to the earl. Perhaps he will listen to me. He has been very kind to me since he arrived here. Actually, he has been kinder to me than he has to Arabella, and she is his wife. No, I shall speak with Lady Ann, for she, I know, loves me. I will tell her of our love, that we wish to wed as soon as possible, that I shall die of unhappiness if you are forced to leave me."

He knew momentary panic at the thought of her speaking either to the earl or to Lady Ann. She could ruin everything through her stupidity and ignorance. He had to make her understand. He had to control her. "Listen to me, Elsbeth. As I said, I already told the earl of our feelings for each other. Doubtless he will tell

Lady Ann. But don't you see? It doesn't matter. He does not want you to be with me and thus, he will convince Lady Ann of his opinion. Ah, my little one, I forbid you to demean yourself in such a fashion." He grasped her slender arms and shook her. "No, that is not the way. Listen to me, Elsbeth, we will make other plans. You will accompany Lady Ann to London when her period of mourning is over. I will meet you there and we will flee together. It will be as nothing for us to do. I will take you to Bruxelles."

The misery fell from her face at his words. Her eyes filled with excitement. "Oh, my dearest love, it is a fine plan. I know that you can do anything. How romantic it will be. With my ten thousand pounds, we shall not have to worry about anything. You are so very clever, Gervaise, you will wisely invest it and make us terribly rich."

He was satisfied. Now, at least, he need have no further worries about Elsbeth.

Suddenly her eyes dimmed. "But, Gervaise, Lady Ann will not wish to go to London for another six months. Must we be parted for such a long time? No, I cannot bear it. Say there is another way."

The comte snapped his fingers. "We have spent years without knowing each other, what is a mere six months? You will see, little cousin, that the time will fly."

She sensed he was growing impatient with her. She said quickly, "I suppose you are right, but allow me to say that I will miss you terribly."

"And I you." He nodded, pleased.

He prepared to rise. She took him off his guard when she grabbed his hand and cried, "Please stay with me now. It has been so very long, since before Josette died. Stay with me. I want you, truly I do."

He was stunned. The thought of making love to her—no, it was impossible. It was beyond impossible. It made his stomach clench. But he couldn't tell her, no. He tried to find calm, to speak gently yet firmly, to cloak the bitterness that gnawed at his guts. "Elsbeth, listen to me. I don't think we should meet like this again. The earl knows about us since I told him. He might become even more vicious. He might order me to leave before the end of the week. I don't want to leave you until I am forced to. Thus, we must take care now. No more meetings here, Elsbeth. No, don't cry. You know that taking you gives me great pleasure, but it would be fatal to our plans were we to be discovered or even suspected. Surely you must realize that. We must think of the future."

Elsbeth was so caught up in the tragic vision of her and Gervaise being torn from each other that the gift of her body now seemed to be her ultimate pledge of her faith and love. Passion flowed through her. "Just one last time, then, Gervaise. Hold me and love me just this last time."

The urgency in her voice, the passion shining from her dark eyes stirred revulsion in him—not at her—but at himself. Yet he could not let her doubt him. He forced himself not to pull away from her. He clasped her slender shoulders, leaned forward, and pressed his lips against hers.

In her frantic desire to secure their final moments together, to lock them forever in her mind, Elsbeth forgot her fear and felt an exquisite tremor of desire sweep through her at his touch.

He felt cold, benumbed, and when her lips parted against his, he could bear it no longer. He jerked away from her and rose shakily to his feet. "Elsbeth, oh God, I cannot. No, don't be hurt, it's not that I don't want you." He tried to calm his voice, to reassure her. "I cannot, my little cousin. I have promised to ride with Arabella. Surely, you can see that if I am late, she might suspect. We must be brave, Elsbeth. The end to all this will come soon, I promise you. You must trust me. Can you do that?"

"But, Gervaise—yes, I trust you." He would not change his mind. She knew him well enough. She nodded slowly. Those wondrous feelings that had scored through her, they were gone now. She wondered if they had existed or if she had simply conjured them up in her pain.

Before he left the stall, he kissed her lightly, passionlessly, on the cheek. She read intense sadness in his gentle gesture. She held back her tears until he was gone from her.

Lady Ann lifted her booted foot and allowed the groom to toss her into the saddle. "Thank you, Tim," she said as she adjusted the folds of her riding skirt becomingly about her legs. "I do not need you to accompany me, I am riding to Dr. Branyon's house. Tulip, here, knows the way very well."

Tim tugged respectfully at the shock of chestnut hair at his forehead and stepped back as Lady Ann flicked the reins on her mare's neck. Tulip broke into a comfortable canter down the front drive.

The frown that Lady Ann had momentarily banished in the presence of the groom now returned to crease her forehead. She drew a deep breath of fresh country air and pulled Tulip in to a more sedate pace. The mare snorted her gratitude. "You are like me, you old lazy cob," she said half aloud. "You stay comfortably in your pleasant stall and regard with a jaundiced eye anyone who disturbs your pleasure."

Lady Ann had not ridden in months. She knew that her leg muscles would protest in the morning. But even aching muscles did not seem important at the moment. She felt so very helpless and frustrated, her anger at Justin from the day before turned to despair. Evesham Abbey was a cold, immense, and empty tomb, and she found she could not bear it another moment. Justin was gone off somewhere, Arabella was very probably also riding, but her destination would be any place that took her as far as possible from her husband. As for Elsbeth and the comte, Lady Ann had not seen either of them since lunch.

It occurred to her as she wheeled Tulip toward Paul's tidy Georgian home that stood at the edge of the small village of Strafford on Baird, that Paul might not be at home. After all, unlike herself and the rest of the gentry, he could not very well tell someone who was ill that he didn't feel like taking care of them.

They had not had much time together since Josette's death. Today she felt that she must see him, just look at those beautiful brown eyes of his, and let her frustration and despair flow away. Oh yes, he could make her forget her own name. She thought about the fishpond, how he had loved her, understood her fear of men, and given her finally a woman's pleasure. She had liked that very much. She thought it could easily become a craving. She wanted it again and again.

"Now, Tulip, you can rest your tired bones," she said, turning her mare into the small yew-tree-lined drive. "Even though I don't see how any bone in your big body can be at all tired."

"Afternoon, milady." She was hailed by a sturdy sandy-haired boy, tall and gangly framed, nearly of an age as Arabella. She'd known him all his life.

"It is good to see you again, Will," she said as the boy limped forward to take the reins of her horse. He'd broken his leg when he had been quite young. "You are looking quite fit. Is Dr. Branyon at home?" She realized after a moment that she wasn't breathing. He had to be here, he just had to be. She needed him. It was an alarming realization, but true nonetheless.

"Aye, milady. Just returned from Dalworthy's. Crotchety old bugger broke 'is arm."

"Excellent," she said, not caring if Dalworthy had broken his neck. "Please give Tulip some hay, Will, but not too much. She's been eating her head off."

She slid gracefully to the ground and very nearly ran to the three narrow front steps. To her surprise, Mrs. Muldoon, Dr. Branyon's fiery, fiercely loyal Irish housekeeper, did not answer the knock.

"Ann. What a surprise. Good heavens, my girl, whatever are you doing here?" Dr. Branyon stood in the open doorway, his frilled white shirt loose about his neck, the sleeves rolled up over his forearms, his face alight with astonished pleasure.

Lady Ann stared up at him, not a single word forming in her mouth. She ran her tongue over her lips. She realized he was staring at her mouth. "I wanted to surprise you, Paul," she finally said. Goodness, she sounded like a twit.

He smiled at her, still staring at her mouth. "Ah, I'm rude, Ann. Do come in." He wanted to carry her inside. He then didn't want to put her down except on his bed. He wanted to kiss that beautiful mouth of hers, touch his tongue to hers. He shuddered. "I'm sorry. But Mrs. Muldoon isn't here. I'll make tea for us if that is what you would like. Mrs. Muldoon's sister has the mumps. Isn't that distressing?"

"Very distressing," Lady Ann said, about as distressed as her mare, Tulip, who was probably neighing with pleasure over her oats. She followed Paul into the front parlor, a cozy, light-filled room that she quite liked. It wasn't an immense empty tomb like Evesham Abbey.

"I suppose I like your riding hat," he said. "May I remove it for you?" He wanted to kiss her and he didn't want to have to find his way around a pile of black velvet.

She nodded mutely, raising her face. He didn't kiss her, but it was close. He pulled the narrow ribbons apart and lifted the hat from her head. After all his care, he couldn't prevent tossing the hat on a nearby table. "Now, come sit down and tell me what new calamity brings you here." Something had to have happened, he knew it. He supposed the kisses would have to wait. He sighed. "I'm fortified. No, you wouldn't come here just to surprise me, would you?"

22

She gave him a delicious smile. "No, I am here just to see you. Well, I suppose I did have rather a loud argument with Justin over Arabella. I hadn't meant to, but it happened. Then she even came into the chamber. She was terrified of him, Paul, terrified. As for the earl, God knows what was in his mind. But you are right, you know, about all of it. He believes that she has betrayed him with the comte. But he wouldn't tell me why exactly he believed it and that is what I wanted from him. But he wouldn't tell me. However, I do know him well enough to realize that if he believes something so ridiculous then he must have a reason." She sighed. "I wish he had confided in me."

"I wonder if he has yet ordered that young man from Evesham Abbey. He should, you know. Then perhaps he and Arabella can get this wretched misunderstanding all straightened out."

"I hate Evesham Abbey. Now it is even more cold and empty than before. Even when people are walking around, it is still empty. God, I have hated that place forever."

"Then you will live here with me."

She looked startled, then laughed. She looked about the drawing room, loving every piece of furniture, each drapery, each small sculpture or drawing or painting that was here. "Would you really let me live here with you? You wouldn't make me live somewhere else, somewhere you thought was grand enough for me?"

"No, you will be here, with me, and Mrs. Muldoon will bully both of us and love you, but like a mother would, not like I, who would be your husband and your lover. I know you enjoy this house, Ann. I also know that if it didn't please you, you would tell me. Eventually, anyway."

She rose from the settee and skipped to where he sat. She eased herself down on his lap, wrapping her arms around his neck. "Yes," she whispered against his ear, "I would tell you eventually if something displeased me. However, right now, I cannot think of anything." She kissed him. Lady Ann, that very proper, very beautiful woman he had loved since he had met her when she had just married the Earl of Stafford, nineteen years before. God was beneficent. "Oh yes," he said into her mouth.

When she finally raised her head, she was breathing more quickly, her breasts were heaving a bit. He was so happy he thought he would burst with it. "I don't suppose you want that tea, do you, Ann?"

"I forgot. If you would take me to Mrs. Muldoon's kitchen and show me the tea, I will endeavor to make some for us. That is, if you would like some boring tea."

"As opposed to what?"

"As opposed to me," she said, and sank down against him again.

He didn't want to make love to her here in the drawing room. No, he wanted her in his bed, where she would sleep every night for the rest of her life. He wanted her very badly. "Will you come with me, Ann?"

"To that wretched kitchen?"

"No, to my bed."

She was stroking her soft palm over his cheek. "I believe I would even go to Talgarth Hall with you."

"It's love then," he said, and rose, holding her tightly against him.

She was laughing. It was the most beautiful sound he had ever heard.

He took the worn carpet stairs two at a time, reminded fleetingly of the interminable years of nights he had walked weary and alone up these same stairs to his bedchamber. Soon, he would never walk them alone again.

A very replete hour later Lady Ann whispered against his neck, "I'm a loose woman. If you don't marry me then I will have to cast myself into a ditch. All that guilt and remorse for my sins, you know."

He kissed her, but didn't laugh. He was as serious as a man could be when he said, "You are prepared for the malicious gossip of our neighbors?"

She hadn't thought of it, but she knew it would happen. She thought about it now for all the time it deserved—about five seconds. "They can all go to the devil," she said, and he was so startled that he did laugh then.

"And Arabella?" he said then.

"I'm not worried about her, at least with regard to us, Paul. Surely she's guessed. Even Justin has. She is very fond of you. Why should she care if her dear mama finally finds happiness?"

He wanted to tell her that it was very possible that she would hate him as much as she loved her father. But he didn't know. Everything was strange now, nothing as it should be, except for them, he thought, kissing the tip of her nose. No, this was a perfect strangeness.

He helped her to dress. He found it very enjoyable, working all those little buttons back into their holes. They left his house together.

* * *

Lady Ann arrived at Evesham Abbey in barely enough
time to change her clothes for dinner. "I shall join you
shortly, Paul," she whispered. Turning to the butler,
she said, "Crupper, do tell Cook that Dr. Branyon will
be joining us for dinner this evening."

"Yes, my lady." Crupper nodded. He wasn't a blind
man. His mistress looked more beautiful than he'd ever
seen, and it was all due to Dr. Branyon. Oh Lordie.
Well, who cared?

Crupper eyed Dr. Branyon as he presented him with
a glass of sherry. Though the doctor was not a lord, he
was nonetheless a fine gentleman. It was the first time,
he thought, ruminating on the situation as he descended
the flagstone steps into the kitchen, that he had ever
seen the Lady Ann so very, not just beautiful, but
sparkling, yes, that was it. True it was but a short time
since his lordship's death, but what matter? Lady Arabella was settled with the new earl, and life was too
short anyway to worry overly about such things. He
smoothed his sparse gray hair and wondered if the two
of them would live here at Evesham Abbey after they
married.

Had Lady Ann not felt so unbearably happy, she
would have felt the undercurrent of tension at the dinner table. She saw the participants at the large table
through a pleasant blur, their words and tones softened
by the time they penetrated through the haze of contentment. She wanted to leap up and shout hallelujahs
when Paul folded his napkin, cleared his throat, and
rose to his feet.

"Justin, comte," he said in a clear voice, "before the
ladies adjourn to the Velvet Room and leave us to our
port, I should like to make an announcement."

The earl looked up, searched Lady Ann's face, and
smiled. Not a full smile, for there was that coldness about him, but it was a smile and it was a pleased
smile. He nodded. Arabella looked up, not caring,

just wanting to leave the dining room, to get away from him.

Dr. Branyon cleared his throat. "Lady Ann has done me the honor of accepting my proposal of marriage. We shall wed as soon as possible and, of course, live very quietly until her nominal year of mourning has passed."

The earl rose quickly and raised his own glass. "My congratulations, Paul, Ann. It is no great surprise, to be sure, but still a welcome occasion. I propose a toast—to Dr. Branyon and Lady Ann. May you have a long lifetime of happiness."

Arabella sat frozen. No great surprise? Her mother and Dr. Branyon? No, it couldn't be true, it simply couldn't. Her father had just died. His body was rotting in some forgotten ruin of a village in Portugal and her mother was calmly planning to marry another man. She couldn't bear it.

Anger rose like bile in her throat. She gazed across the table at her mother and saw with barely contained fury the delicate pink of her cheeks, the new brilliance of her eyes. She was nothing more than a damned trollop.

"Arabella. The toast, my dear." She turned her head to stare at the earl. Her husband. The man who hated her, the man who would punish her the rest of her life for something she hadn't done. She heard the command in his voice. By God, he approved this travesty of a marriage. She turned her eyes to Elsbeth and Gervaise. With her newly acquired insight, she saw them almost as one being, Elsbeth's dark eyes and hair blending, as if with the same artist's brush, into a blurred mold of Gervaise. It was as if one pair of almond-shaped eyes regarded her, their focus as one, their thoughts as one—their bodies as one. No, surely not. Elsbeth and Gervaise? But who else? No, Suzanne was surely right. They were lovers.

She thought they showed mild surprise, nothing more. Was she the only one who had not guessed?

"Arabella, child, are you all right?" Her mother's gentle voice, so vibrant with concern. Was there a pleading note? Was she seeking approval from her daughter, seeking forgiveness for her betrayal? Her blindness had known no bounds. She realized she'd been so very locked into herself, into her own misery, that she had missed what everyone else had clearly seen. Yes, she been a wooden puppet unseeing, her very thoughts frozen inside herself. How very surprised Dr. Branyon appeared at her silence. Or was he? Surely he would know how she missed her father, how she loved him beyond life itself. He had betrayed her. Both of them had betrayed her. And her father. Had they been lovers for years? Had they merely waited for her father to leave before they went to his bed?

"Arabella."

The earl's voice again, condemning her now. But then he had condemned her since they had wed. How could she expect him to see the truth, to understand that they had done?

Arabella rose unsteadily from her chair, her fingers clutching white on the edges of the table. She felt crushed with the weight of her own unawareness, the weight of their betrayal. So much betrayal, she thought, only she was innocent. They were not.

Her voice sounded out as a fallen autumn leaf, its spine snapped and broken underfoot. "Yes, Mother, I am quite all right. Did you call for a toast, my lord? I'm sorry, but you see, I don't have one." She heard a shocked, sharp intake of breath—from whom, she did not know. Only vaguely did she see the earl move angrily from his chair. She whirled about and raced from the dining room.

Justin threw his napkin down upon the tabletop. "Paul, Ann, do not attend to her. Please, all of you, take your coffee in the Velvet Room. If you will excuse me now, I would speak to my wife."

Lady Ann's face was perfectly white, her lips drawn in a thin line, but she didn't cry. She saw the wild anger in the earl's eyes. Oh God, she had to protect Arabella from his anger. She had never seen him so near to the edge. She stumbled from her chair, her hand toward him.

"Justin, wait. There is no reason for you to be upset. It is a surprise to her. Surely you know how much she loved her father. No, please—" But he was gone from the dining room without a backward glance.

Dr. Branyon walked to her side and clasped her hand. He said very quietly, for only her ears, "I was afraid of this. You know that Arabella isn't happy. I believe that she held to her father's memory to help her during this time with Justin. Please, Ann, don't let her hurt you for she doesn't mean to. There is such rage in her, such pain. Come, let's go into the Velvet Room and try to act natural, at least around Elsbeth. As for the comte, I could wish him gone right this instant, but it is not to be. Come, love."

Lady Ann said sadly, "How very stupid of me not to have realized, even foretold Arabella's reaction. I suppose I didn't want to delve too deeply. I just wanted to hug my own happiness close."

The comte was so startled by Arabella's outburst that he acquiesced with a mere nod. He slid Elsbeth's arm through his. As they followed Lady Ann and Dr. Branyon past the wooden-faced footman who'd heard everything that had happened, Elsbeth suddenly tugged at his arm, holding back.

"Oh, Gervaise, whatever shall we do now?" She was close to tears. He couldn't allow her to fall apart in front of Lady Ann or Dr. Branyon. He clasped her hands in his, squeezing them nearly to pain. "Listen, Elsbeth, as I told you earlier, it is as nothing. I will

think of a plan. Do not worry. Here, straighten yourself. Don't cry. Do not enact an ill-bred scene like your
half-sister just did. You are above that. You are gentle
and kind and you will keep control of yourself."

"Yes, Gervaise, yes, all right, I will try." She sniffed,
wiping her hand across her eyes, as would a child.
He felt something deep and painful move within
him. "Yes, I thought Arabella's behavior was shock-
ing. Why did she do that? Our father wasn't a loving
man, you know that. He hated me. Oh, all right, he
loved Arabella, but still, how could she behave so horribly to her own mother?"

Justin strode into the main hall and made directly for
the staircase. He took the steps two and three at a time
and was midway to the first landing before Crupper realized his destination. He waved his hand at the earl's
back, shook his head when there was no response, and
turned back to his post by the front doors. He simply
refused to shout after his lordship. Such a thing wasn't
done, certainly not done at Evesham Abbey.

The earl's anger was evident even to Grace, Arabella's maid, who scurried from his path the moment
she saw his face. His nostrils flared and angry cords
stood out taut on his neck. His hands were shaking, he
couldn't help it. Damn her, how dared she serve her
mother such a devastating blow? Had she not eyes in
her head to see where Lady Ann's affections were so
obviously placed? He would strangle her.

Justin jerked at the handle on the bedchamber door.
It was locked, as of course he had expected it to be, but
his futile fumbling at his own bedroom door only
added to his anger. He flung into the adjoining room
and sent his valet, Grubbs, staggering back in surprise.

"My lord, what is wrong? What has happened?"

Justin paid him no heed, and but an instant later
stood in the middle of the earl's bedchamber. He
wanted to bellow out her name, but saw that the room

was quite empty. "Bedamned," he said quite softly as he turned on his heel and strode back downstairs.

"Crupper, have you seen her ladyship?"

"Why, yes, my lord," Crupper said, with complete composure.

"Well? Where the devil is she?"

"Her ladyship left the house, my lord. Very quickly, I might add."

"Damnation, man, why the hell did you not tell me that little bit of news before?"

Crupper drew to his full height. "If you will pardon my liberty, my lord, your lordship was near to the top of the stairs before I was even aware of your presence."

"This is damned ridiculous," the earl nearly shouted as he strode past his butler into the warm night.

It did not occur to the earl to simply let her return whenever she wished to. He mentally reviewed her favorite haunts—the old abbey ruins, the fishpond, perhaps even the Deverill graveyard. For some reason he could not define, he knew that she would not be bound for any of her usual places. No, he thought, he knew she was trying to escape—from Evesham Abbey, from her mother, but mainly she would want to escape from him.

Lucifer. He would bet every sou he had that she was riding madly away from here on her stallion.

He ran full tilt to the stables. He was just in time to see Arabella, her skirts billowing out about her, astride Lucifer, galloping away into the dark night.

"James," he yelled.

His spindly legged head groom emerged in the lighted doorway, his eyes widening at the sight of his master's furious face. He waited miserably for the earl to sack him. But that didn't even come to the earl's mind. He knew that Arabella's word was indisputable law with all the servants.

"Fetch my stallion, James, and be quick about it."

As the seconds crept by, the earl was mentally calculating the lead Arabella would have on him. His bay stallion was Marmaluke-trained and of Arab stock. But, Lucifer, damn, the beast was strong as ten horses and fast as the wind. She could be in the next county before he even managed to reach the end of the drive. "James, hurry!"

He wanted to strangle her.

He wanted to shout at her until he ground her down, until she finally admitted what she'd done to him. He wanted desperately for her to tell him she'd made a mistake, that she was sorry, that she regretted it, that she would spend her life making it up to him.

He also wanted to see her, just see her, perhaps even tell her that he understood. He shook his head at himself. He was changing. He was easing. He was ready to forgive her. He wanted to kill the comte, but not her, not Arabella. He didn't understand himself, but there it was.

Well, damnation.

23

The moon hung as a slim crescent, barely lighting the vague outlines of the country road. The earl rode, head down, nearly touching his horse's glossy neck, his body molding into the form of the animal. His intense demanding pace brought back memories of another ride in the night, so long ago in faraway Portugal the critical dispatch folded carefully in the lining of his boot. He felt the same sense of purpose and urgency. He had been elated with the success of his mission when horse and man had very nearly dropped from fatigue at the end of the eight endless hours.

Rickety turnstiles, unpainted wooden fences, small rutted paths—all flew past in a blur of semidarkness. The earl knew of a certainty that Arabella would stay to the main road. She would want nothing to slow her escape.

As he rode, he remembered again her outburst at Dr. Branyon's announcement. Yes, he understood, but it didn't lessen his anger, not really.

At first he couldn't believe his eyes. Were he not so very angry with her, he would have been sorely tempted to laugh aloud at the very undramatic scene before him. Arabella was walking in the middle of the road in full evening dress, leading a limping Lucifer.

She halted as he reined in beside her. She looked up at him with dull eyes. She said nothing, damn her. "Well, madam, I see that you have ended your own merry escape." He swung from the saddle and faced her, legs apart, his hands on his hips.

She seemed oblivious of his anger, of the ferocious irony of his words. "Yes," she said, still not looking at him, "Lucifer threw a shoe. I shall have to speak to James. It is quite ridiculous that he should throw a shoe. Don't you think that is ridiculous?"

"Yes, I shall speak to James as well." The earl stopped and frowned. This was not at all what he had expected. "Of course, such a tame ending to your thoughtless ride must be a letdown. Just look at you. Dressed for dinner and walking beside your damned horse. Didn't it occur to you that there are bad men out here? That they could have come upon you? You can wager that they would have licked their chops at the sight of you. Beautiful and rich, yes, they would have believed they'd died and gone to heaven."

"No," she said finally, her eyes still on the road directly in front of her next step, "I didn't think about robbers at all. You say there are bad men out here? I think there are bad men everywhere. What difference where they are? Why don't you ride back to Evesham Abbey, my lord. There is nothing for you here. Not a single thing."

He made no answer, just walked beside her, the look on his face so forbidding that surely she would be shaking in her evening slippers. Soldiers had quaked in their boots at that look. But she wasn't. It baffled him. He admired her greatly in that moment.

Finally, she stopped and looked up at him. "Ah, I see now. You wish to yell at me, to strike me, perhaps? Perhaps even kill me? Well there's not much I can do about it, is there? Have at it, my lord." She patted Lucifer's nose, spoke softly to him, then dropped his reins. She turned to face her husband. Lucifer neighed softly but didn't move.

He ground his teeth and advanced a measured step

toward her. She stood her ground and regarded him with at best casual interest. "Do you plan another rape scene, my lord, or perhaps a beating? If you will allow me a choice, I would far prefer the beating."

He had expected anger on her part, indeed rather looked forward to her termagant's tongue. But there seemed to be no passion left in her. Her voice and very stance seemed uncaring, remote.

It made him so angry he wanted to spit, he wanted to push her to anger. He said with contempt, "Despite what you may think, raping you would bring me no pleasure. I did not rape you before, but you will pretend I did, won't you? Aye, you'll claim I raped you on our wedding night and hold it in my face for the rest of our lives. Damn you, madam, I did not rape you; stop shaking your head at me. I wasn't as gentle as I could have been, but you didn't deserve anything gentle from me. You deserved to be raped, yet as a gentleman, I refrained.

"As to beating you, I would as soon waste my energies flailing a spiritless old horse. Just look at you, all flattened down and looking pathetic. Damn you, Arabella, say something, do something!"

Instead, she turned away from him indifferently, saying over her shoulder, "That was quite a speech. Now, if you have done with me, then, my lord, it is a long walk back to Evesham Abbey." She picked up Lucifer's reins.

It sent him right over the edge. He grabbed her arm and whirled her around to face him. "Oh no, I am by no means done with you, and what I have to say to you is best done far away from the ears of your family."

She dropped Lucifer's reins again, walked to the side of the road, and sat down on the grassy bank. She began pulling up blades of grass. She shrugged, enraging him. "Very well," she said, "be done with it. I told you to do it before but you didn't. I would have thought you would have yelled your head off. That you would have cursed me to hell and back. But you just tried to justify your violence on our wedding night. If that wasn't rape, my lord, then I wonder what one would call it." She raised her face then and stared up at him, her eyes so filled with pain that he flinched.

She watched him stride over to her. He stood over her, like a black silhouetted giant of a man, blocking the bright moonlight. She couldn't bear to look at him. It hurt, horribly. She turned and fastened her gaze on the bank beside her, and waited.

"Damn you, Arabella, look at me."

He was angry now, but she made no move to obey him. He dropped to his knees in front of her and grasped her shoulders, shaking her until she raised her eyes to his. "Now, you will listen to me, you rag-mannered shrew. How dared you serve your mother such a turn? Are you blind? Even the scullery maid doubtless knew that she and Dr. Branyon were in love. Indeed, I expect he has loved her for a very long time.

"I admit that I expected their announcement to come a bit later, but it is of no importance. Life is too uncertain to be governed by ridiculous strictures. God knows, your mother deserves happiness. God knows, a good deal of the nineteen years she spent with your father were far from pleasant. Why, Arabella, why were you so unthinkingly cruel to her?"

He saw flames of anger kindle slowly in her wintry eyes. "Why, damn you?"

It was enough. It was too much. She jumped to her feet, shaking her fist in his face. "How dare you approve such a match? Even publicly proclaim your approval? You had no right, my lord, just as she has no right to betray my father! No, I had no idea that she had that kind of feeling for Dr. Branyon. I think her actions, as well as his, to be despicable. I will never speak to her again. As for Dr. Branyon, he is no longer welcome at Evesham Abbey. If she wants to disgrace herself and our name, then let her wed him and leave me alone."

She was panting now, bitter words spewing from her mouth. "Should I perhaps congratulate my dear mother for at least waiting for my father's death? Just how long, my lord, do you think they have been lovers? Poor Father, cuckolded by a faithless wife and a man he trusted. God, were I a man I would kill him in a duel."

He looked at her beautiful pale face, at the bitter fire in her gray eyes. So much pain and anger. He sought to understand her. He didn't disbelieve what she had said, no, she had meant every word. She had spoken openly, bitterly of her mother cuckolding her father, and her rage at the belief that her mother had been unfaithful to her father could leave no doubt at the sincerity of her condemnation of such an act. Yet had she not herself taken a lover before they had married? Had not she cuckolded him? Had she some sort of strange morality that had allowed her to take a lover before she married? And, for that matter, had she willingly given up the comte after her marriage to him? He wanted to throw her own act in her face, demand that she explain to him. Yet he found that his anger was melting away at the misery of the woman behind the facade of destructive words.

No, he had to deal with her bitter despair over her mother first. He silenced his own questions, so many questions that rose in his throat. He masked his voice with calm authority, for he knew that she would despise any gentling emotion coming from him.

"That is enough now, Arabella. I want you to listen to me now. Will you do that?"

She stared at him as if he had two heads. He merely nodded as he said, "I find it extraordinary that I, who have known Lady Ann only in passing during the past several years, would swear upon my honor that she was never unfaithful to your father. Whereas you condemn her with a snap of your fingers. You see she is in love and you assume that she has bedded the good doctor for how many years? No, Arabella, do not turn away from me. Do you honestly believe that she would be capable of such a thing?"

She gazed at him, still as stone, unspeaking.

"Very well. Though you do not wish to answer me, I will assume that you are at least thinking about what I've said. Now, to your father." He paused. Should he tell her the truth? There was no choice, not now. Only if she knew the truth about her father could she be brought to find forgiveness for her mother. He said quietly, "Do you remember when we first met—by the fishpond the day your father's will was read? I see you remember all too well. You cannot deny that you thought me your father's bastard."

"That isn't at all the same and you know it. Don't you dare throw that up to me."

"Different? Are there different rules of conduct for a husband? He is free of the restraints that bind his wife? I will tell you, Arabella, your father's marriage to Lady Ann was a sham. He wed her only for the huge dowry she brought to him. He spoke openly of his 'bargain' and laughed at his good fortune. Also, he thought nothing of openly parading his mistresses in front of her nose."

"I don't believe that," she said, panting hard, her words coming out in short gasps. "Why, I should shoot my husband were he to do that to me. That isn't true. My father would never do that, never."

"He did and thought nothing of it. You are your father's daughter. Your mother is gentle, quiet, trusting. Ah, she knew exactly what he did, but she kept quiet. She never tried to turn you against your father."

She tried to clap her hands over her ears.

"No cowardice from you now." He pulled her hands to her sides.

"No, I won't listen to you. You're making this up to protect her." Yet she felt the coldness of doubt sweep through her.

He gentled. "No, Arabella, I have no need to invent stories. In fact, several times when I met with your father in London and in Lisbon, even once in Brussels, I was entertained most charmingly by his mistresses. I remember him joking about his little milksop of a wife, about her coldness, her bourgeois fear of him. He said to me once, admittedly when he was in his cups, 'You know, my boy, I have at least forced the little fool to see to my pleasure. She does not do it well, she gags and cries, but I am a tolerant man. One should be, of course, to one's wife.' "

"No! He could not—Please, Justin, he did not say those things."

"Yes, Bella, he did. He was a man of demanding, extreme passions. That Lady Ann suffered from his nature is to be regretted. But do you not see, his very nature also made him a great leader. His men trusted him implicitly, for he never showed fear or uncertainty. He launched offensives that would have left lesser men quaking in their boots." The earl softened his voice even more. "His character also gave you a father to admire, respect, and adore. He loved you above all things, Arabella. I do not wish you to condemn him or blindly exalt him, for he deserves neither. I remember he told me once, not above a year ago: 'Be damned, Justin, it is just as well that my Arabella had no brothers. After her, they would perforce have been disappointments to me.' "

She said not a single word, but he knew she was listening to everything now.

"I would that you now consider your mother. She was always completely loyal to your father. More than that, she loves you dearly. She always has, she always will. She deserves your understanding, Bella, your approval, else you have dimmed her chance for happiness. And she does deserve to have her own happiness now. She gave eighteen years to you and to a man who held her in contempt. Please, Arabella, try to look at all this straight on, without fear, without anger, without pain. Will you do that?"

Arabella rose slowly to her feet and shook loose blades of grass from her skirt. He stood beside her. His eyes searched her face for a clue to what she was thinking. He sensed a change in her, yet he could not be certain. He wondered if perhaps she was thinking of her own sham of a marriage, a marriage of convenience that she dreaded enough to seek comfort in the arms of another man. He remained silent, waiting for her to speak.

"It grows late," she said finally, her voice far away. "If you do not mind, I would ride pillion. Would you send James to fetch Lucifer?"

He looked down at her, wondering, always wondering, what was in her mind. Then he couldn't help himself. He cupped her face between his hands, leaned down, and kissed her. It had been far too long, since before they'd married. Her mouth was soft, just as he remembered. God, he wanted her. But he had to know, he had to. He raised his face, his thumbs lightly tracing over her lips. "Arabella, tell me the truth, just admit to me that you took the comte as your lover. I don't believe he is still your lover, but I know that he was before we were married. Just tell me the truth, tell me why you did it, and I will forgive you. Was it because you felt forced to wed me? Tell me the truth. Then we can go back and begin again. Tell me, Arabella." He leaned down and began kissing her again.

The sharp pain brought him to his senses faster than a bucket of ice water. He jumped back, rubbing his shin. She'd kicked him hard. She was backing away from him, breathing hard. Then she yelled at him, "Damn you, that miserable man was never my lover. You're the blind one." It nearly burst from her mouth that it was Elsbeth who was his lover, but she held it back in time. No, she couldn't take the chance of telling him. The pain he could cause Elsbeth was incalculable. "Hear me, damn you! I did not betray you!"

She turned on her heel and ran to Lucifer. She clumsily climbed onto his broad back.

"Arabella, wait. Wait. Why are you still lying to me? Why? There's no reason. I want to forgive you. I'm ready to forgive you."

"You idiot, you wretched blind fool!" It was then that she realized that Lucifer was lame. She just sat there for a long moment, staring into nothing, then she slipped off his back. She walked directly back to Justin, drew back her arm, and sent her fist into his jaw. She caught him off balance. He flailed the air, but lost, and fell backward into a shallow ditch.

She took his own horse and was off. He was left with Lucifer. Just as well, he thought, as he dusted himself off. Both of them were lame, he in his head and the damned horse in his hoof.

Damn, but that was a good shot she'd given him. He rubbed his jaw. A very good hit.

Why wouldn't she just tell him the truth?

24

The earl stood at the breakfast parlor window, sipping his second cup of coffee, staring out toward the colorful parterre. Arabella came into view, walking beside her mother. He felt something move deep inside him at the sight of her. He could still feel himself hardening as he had kissed her, wanting her more and more each instant, and then he'd asked for her to tell him the truth, just admit to him that she'd lied, that she'd taken the comte for her lover. He even told her he would forgive her, that they would begin again. She'd kicked him but good. And she'd withdrawn from him. Completely.

What else could he offer her? She had betrayed him, not the other way around. Had he betrayed her would she have offered to forgive him? He doubted it very much. She was more strong-willed than his commanding officer in Portugal, and in his eyes, in his soul, she was the perfect mate for him. Except for the comte. Surely the English authorities wouldn't toss him in gaol if he simply killed the little French bastard.

He watched as Arabella shortened her longer stride to match her mother's step. He prayed then, prayed hard, that Arabella was apologizing to Lady Ann. Though he couldn't hear a word, he fancied he saw Arabella smile. God, he wished he could make her smile at him like that. He shook his head as he turned from the window. He was mad, utterly mad. She had betrayed him. He would ask her again tonight. He would proceed more smoothly, no, he would kiss her again, go very slowly, but make her want him, then ask her. Yes, that was what he would do.

He still wanted very much to kill that bloody comte.

"Good morning, my lord," Crupper said as he sailed soundlessly into the breakfast parlor.

The earl nodded, then said as he passed the butler, "I shall be in the library. Ah, Crupper, if anyone cares to disturb me, they're welcome to."

He had not gotten beyond a second column of numbers for spring market prices when Crupper most obligingly entered the library.

"Lady Talgarth and Miss Suzanne are here to visit, my lord. There is also a gentleman accompanying them—a Lord Graybourn."

The spotty viscount, the earl thought, grinning, the spring market prices forgotten.

"They are in the Velvet Room, Crupper?" He rose and shook out the fine lawn ruffles at his sleeves.

"Yes, my lord. The family are there also." He sniffed, his left eyebrow twitching. "I might add, my lord, that the young French comte is still here. He appears to be everywhere. It is disconcerting. I cannot like it. Indeed, I would wish profoundly that he would be gone."

"We share that opinion. He is leaving on Friday. Contrive to control your ire until then." Arabella was there in the Velvet Room. He wanted very much to see her.

The earl heard Lady Ann say without guile to the turbaned Lady Talgarth, "Dear Aurelia, how very kind of you to pay us a visit this morning. I was just saying to Arabella that it is so very nice to have friends." Lady Ann tried to keep her eyes from straying to Lady Talgarth's purple satin bosom, an awesome sight, one that made her eyes twitch.

"Ah, here you are, my lord," Lady Talgarth said in a

girlish voice, turning to welcome the earl. "We were showing our dear Lord Graybourn about the countryside. We could not exclude a visit to Evesham Abbey."

The earl lifted her beringed hand and kissed her plump fingers.

A merry smile played about Suzanne Talgarth's pink lips as she observed the earl. She said softly to Arabella, who stood at her side, "If only poor Lord Graybourn had thought to kiss Mama's hand. Had he done so, Mama would have forced me to wed the little toad, although," she added, a small frown on her forehead, "he isn't as much of a toad as I'd believed he was in London. No, not at all."

"Here, I forget my manners, my lord, what with you distracting me so obligingly. Yes, I have always liked a gentleman who could distract so nicely." Lady Talgarth sighed as she finally withdrew her hand from the earl's, though, in reality, it was she who was holding his hand. "My dear Edmund, allow me to present to you the Earl of Strafford, Justin Deverill."

The earl saw that Lord Graybourn had not been particularly favored by nature, only by fortune and birth. He was not above medium height, and the extra weight he bore made him look shorter than his actual inches. In five years, he would be fat as a flawn. His eyes were a bit on the protuberant side, but of a pleasant light blue. There was a good deal of intelligence in those eyes, and kindness as well. He affected dandyism, unfortunately, for the heavy jewel-encrusted fobs and rings, the high-starched shirt points, and the fawn breeches that stretched over his ample stomach, did not suit him at all.

Surprisingly, Lord Graybourn had a quite firm, pleasant voice. "A pleasure, my lord. I trust we do not inconvenience you with our visit this morning."

"Not at all," the earl said and liked the young man

immediately. "It is always a pleasure to see our nearest neighbors."

The earl took the offered hand and pumped it. He drew the viscount forward for introductions to Arabella, Lady Ann, Elsbeth, and finally Gervaise. He found himself smiling as he watched his wife greet the viscount warmly, politely inquiring after his journey from London.

She would not meet his eyes, and he was staring hard at her, damn her stubborn hide. What was she thinking? Was she worried that he wouldn't still want to forgive her? He found himself looking at her hands—white and smooth, the fingernails short and buffed. Her thumbnail was slightly ragged. That made him smile, just a bit.

As for Gervaise, he appeared to undergo a pronounced foreign transformation. He lisped his greeting to the viscount, who did not understand a word he said, and proffered a deep, flourishing bow reminiscent of the French court of Louis XVI. The viscount, believing such a formal greeting was in deference to his own notable lineage, and not wanting to seem discourteous, endeavored to return a bow of similar style. His cumberland corset creaked in protest.

Gervaise preened, there was no other word for it. He looked about complacently. He was quite pleased that he'd made a fool of the viscount.

Even though he'd succeeded, no one was about to reward him. He saw an angry gleam in Arabella's eyes. To his further chagrin, Elsbeth, who had stood quietly at Lady Ann's elbow, stepped forward and said in a clear, sweet voice, "Lord Graybourn. I am most delighted to meet you, sir. We have heard many nice things about you." She extended her small hand, and the viscount, who in a flight of confident gallantry, brought her fingers to his lips. She blushed charmingly and dipped a curtsy.

"But look, Bella," Suzanne whispered behind her hand, "your French cousin has had his nose much put out of joint. And to think that I dreaded this visit. Oh, the enjoyment of it all."

"It's true," Arabella said, "that one can never tell what any one of us will say next."

She was angry. There was no doubt about it, she wanted to yell at the comte, tell him that he was a rude ass. The earl saw that she was keeping quiet with an effort. So she was displeased with her lover—no, surely the comte was her *former* lover—she certainly didn't appear to even like him now. He smiled at her, nodding. She met his eyes for a brief instant. Her face was very pale, but her eyes, the gray was so brilliant yet strangely soft, as if she were looking at him with something akin to affection. That was possible, wasn't it? Hell, his shin still hurt from the kick she'd given him. Probably not possible at all. But what was going on here? He wished he could tell the lot of them to disappear. He wanted to speak to her, badly. He wanted to kiss her even more badly. He wanted to make love to her—that the worst of all.

Arabella said, "Come, let us all be seated. I shall ring for tea and morning cakes."

Once they had taken their places, Arabella turned to Lord Graybourn, trying her best not to look toward her husband. "What news can you give us of the fighting in the Peninsula, sir? I hope you can tell us something positive."

Lord Graybourn sought frantically to piece together bits of news that came from time to time to his grudging ears. While always ready to denounce Napoleon with patriotic fervor, he found the details of battles and the precarious fates of the European countries to be tedious in the extreme. He was an Englishman, thus England would remain supreme for all time.

He cleared his throat, and replied with what he

hoped to be the voice of informed authority, "Most proper that your ladyship should inquire." He suddenly remembered that the former Earl of Strafford was a renowned military man, as was the current earl. Bedamned. He cleared his throat again, looked toward the earl, and gave him a big smile. He said quite honestly, "I know very little compared to his lordship. Why I have heard it said that he was a hero in more battles on the Peninsula than any other officer. What have you heard lately, my lord?"

"No," Gervaise said, sitting forward, "I want to hear what you have to say, Lord Graybourn. You have been in London, it is you who should know exactly what is happening."

He wasn't content to want everyone to smack him, the earl thought, frowning. What was his purpose then? Was he so obtuse that he didn't realize his rudeness would soon have even the gentle, most charming Lady Ann pounding his head? He started to tell the comte to shove his rudeness down his malicious throat when Lord Graybourn said easily, "Very well, but understand comte, that not much is given out in London. We are fighting a war, after all, and I would expect our leaders to keep some secrets." He looked over at Lady Elsbeth. Such a gentle creature she was. She was looking at him with her full attention. He found suddenly that he didn't want to disappoint her. "Of course, all of England still suffers from Napoleon's blockade," he said, praying the earl wouldn't leap up and call him a bloody fool. "I understand, too, that Percival is under continuous pressure from both at home and abroad. His is a very difficult undertaking, poor man, but he is doing splendidly."

"Exactly so," the earl said. "Not many folk in London understand the pressure that Percival is under. You are very wise, Lord Graybourn, to perceive the matter so clearly."

Had Lord Graybourn been a woman, he would have kissed the earl for his generosity and goodness. As it was, he would only nod and wish fervently that the earl would continue to find him wise.

"It is repulsive," Lady Talgarth announced in a very loud voice. She wanted some tea and some of Evesham Abbey's delicious lemon cakes. Where the devil were all the servants? Then again, with Arabella now in charge, what else could she expect? They were probably all dancing in the orchard. Ah, but the lemon seed cakes were delicious.

"Yes, but what *precise* news of the Peninsula?" the comte pressed on, his eyes battened on Lord Graybourn.

Arabella nearly leapt out of her chair at him. She sucked in her breath, preparing to fire cannon at him, but the earl, winking at her, said smoothly, "Did I not tell you, comte? Massena is now in Portugal with sixty thousand men under his command. From my information, I understand that Wellington will launch an offensive against him in the fall. With the experience and pluck of Wellington's men, I believe we will taste victory. Forgive me, Lord Graybourn, but there was no way for you to know this. It is just now being doled out in very small amounts to the public."

Lord Graybourn nodded, and thanked the heavens that the earl was here and thought him wise enough to assist out of this quagmire.

The comte sat back, furious, wondering what had happened. He'd had the stupid fat fellow on the floor, the boot of his heel on his neck, and yet the earl had rushed in to save him. He had always heard that military men hated the ignorance of their countrymen. Certainly the French military men were contemptuous of anyone who ever dared question them or pretended they knew anything that was going on.

And the new earl was a proud bastard, every inch of him. Of course Gervaise knew, deep in his belly, he

knew—it was the cursed loathsome English—they protected each other. Not to mention that the earl hated
him. He had realized that even though he didn't know
the reason for it. Well, he would take care of that soon
enough and he would very much enjoy himself doing
it. He looked over at Elsbeth and his eyes narrowed.
She was smiling toward Lord Graybourn. How could
she do this to him?

Damn her.

Damn all of them. He couldn't wait to wash the dirt
of England off his boots. Filthy cold heathen country.

Lady Ann added, "Let us also hope that Wellington
will not have to turn his eyes elsewhere. Do not forget
that with Napoleon's marriage to Marie Louise only
four months ago, Austria now owes no loyalty to England. The French emperor is very carefully scattering
England's friends to the four winds. Nothing good will
come of this, particularly if Marie Louise becomes
quickly with child."

The earl was impressed. Finally, Crupper directed
two footmen in with the tea and cakes. He watched
Lady Ann pour the tea. It seemed that everyone
watched her, took their tea, and sipped in pleasure. He
himself loved the lemon seed cakes. He nodded, accepting a cup of tea from her, as she said, "I feel so
very sorry for the young empress. The poor child had
no say in anything, I am certain."

"French emperor indeed," said Lady Talgarth as she
ate her second piece of lemon seed cake. She was eyeing the earl, for he had just taken a second slice also.
There was only one left. She cleared her throat, hoping
to distract him as her fingers inched toward that last
slice, "I have heard it said that the Corsican has deplorable manners. What is a man if he has no manners?
What do you think, Lord Graybourn?"

Lord Graybourn nearly choked on his tea. "Manners

do tend to civilize," he finally said, and took the last slice of lemon seed cake.

Arabella said with a twinkle in her eyes, "My dear ma'am, judging from the continuous string of mistresses, right under the nose of Josephine, it would seem that not everything about the man is deplorable."

The comte laughed immoderately.

The earl was on the point of picking the comte up by his high shirt points and hurling him through the French windows when Arabella jumped to her feet and said, "Oh dear, Justin, I fear I have spilled tea on my gown. Would you please see that it will not stain?"

It was well done of her. He watched her come toward him, holding the material of her sleeve, her eyes on his cravat. He felt a powerful kick in the gut. God, but she was beautiful. She was also a termagant, loyal, brave, and he would forgive her. He would tell her tonight and then he would make love to her and he would do it right. He would make her forget the comte. And she would tell him the truth, finally.

She reached him, looked up into his face, and said softly, "Do you believe it will stain?"

He did not know or care if anyone was looking at them. He leaned down, looked at the very small wet stain, then kissed the tip of her nose, then her chin, and finally her mouth, very lightly.

"Goodness," Lady Talgarth said. "Surely, my lord, this display is inappropriate for my innocent daughter's eyes, not to mention dear Elsbeth's."

Suzanne laughed. "No, Mama. Finally Bella will be good for something. I will watch her with her husband and learn important things. Husband and wife sorts of things."

"Suzanne, I will have to speak to your father about this. I am certain that he will agree with me. All you have to do is observe us, my dear, to learn all the important things."

Suzanne felt close to hysterical laughter.

Luckily, Lord Graybourn was saying to Elsbeth, "Have you ever visited London before?"

And the conversation chaos was avoided until Suzanne said, "Come, Bella, you cannot remain standing there with the earl's arms around you. My mother will expire from the shock. As for your mother, just look at her pink cheeks." And Elsbeth was all pink in the cheeks as well, but that was because of Lord Graybourn. Life, she thought suddenly, was indeed whimsical. She realized she was enjoying herself immensely.

The earl looked up, saw that everyone's eyes were fastened on them, and sighed. He lightly touched his fingertips to her mouth. "Later then." He added at the wariness he saw clearly on her face, "Trust me. We will work this out, you will see. Go now before I embarrass us further. Your gown won't be stained."

"I wasn't embarrassed."

He merely nodded. He didn't know what was happening to him. It didn't hurt but it was strange, this awkward mixture of tenderness, fury, and lust. So much, yet not enough.

"At last, you are with us both mind and body again," Suzanne said.

Elsbeth said, "How I grieve for the poor Austrian princess. She was torn from her family and her country all as a political bribe to that horrid man."

"Do not forget, my dear, that Napoleon ardently desires an heir," Lord Graybourn said, much struck by this shy young lady's sensibilities.

"We poor women," Suzanne said, then ruined it with a giggle. "Bartered and traded about so that we can be the carriers of your precious men's names."

The earl laughed. "Come, Miss Talgarth, you paint us as uncaring fellows. Surely we have our uses." His eyes were on his wife. He wanted desperately for her to look at him. He would prove to her that he could please her, that he could make her laugh, make her eyes twinkle. He wanted to hear her shout and yell at him. He wanted everything in her.

Arabella said quietly, not looking at him, "You do not agree, then, my lord, that most gentlemen prefer their wives to remain quietly in the background, bearing their offspring, and unobtrusively working at their embroidery?"

The earl could not begin to imagine Arabella in the background of anything. She would always be right in front, directing, bellowing orders, laughing, yelling at him as well. He said, "I know you must be speaking metaphorically. I cannot imagine you embroidering for five minutes. You would become bilious. No, no needlework for you, Arabella."

Suzanne lifted her saucer in mock toast to the earl. "Quite true. Admit, Bella, his lordship has scored a point. Just yesterday during our ride, I could not hold you in conversation for much longer than five minutes."

Arabella looked first at the comte, then at Elsbeth, who was in quiet conversation with Lord Graybourn. Why hadn't the dratted man come before the comte had? Damn his eyes. How could he have ever thought he could like Suzanne? But perhaps there was still a chance. Gervaise would be gone soon. Perhaps then Elsbeth would forget him. But she knew she couldn't tell the earl. He wouldn't believe her, but even if he did come to believe her, he would not treat Elsbeth well. She couldn't begin to imagine what he would do.

Lady Ann said with a smile, "I have always admired Arabella's energy, dear Aurelia. I have never known boredom. When I didn't want to spank her little bottom I was laughing. Surely I was blessed. As were you with Suzanne. Such a bright, laughing, amusing girl. You must be very proud of her."

Suzanne nearly dropped her teacup. She stared at

Lady Ann. She had wished, at errant moments throughout her entire eighteen years, that Lady Ann could have
been her mother. They would have dealt together so
much better . . . well, perhaps not, but Arabella was her
father's daughter. Just her father's. There was nothing
of Lady Ann in her.

"There is that," Aurelia said obscurely, staring at her
daughter as if she wanted to strangle her.

"You were blessed, Ann, with your offspring," the
earl said. "And now I will be blessed with my wife."
Arabella stared over at him wondering, *Must I lie so
you will come to admire me? Accept me?*

Lord Graybourn said again to Elsbeth, "Will you go
to London, my dear?"

"Not as yet, sir. I had thought to . . ." Elsbeth lapsed
into silent embarrassment, her eyes flying to Lady Ann.

Lady Ann said with composure, "Our plans are at
present rather uncertain, Lord Graybourn. But I do not
doubt that Elsbeth will accompany us for an extended
stay during the winter."

"Oh, Bella, you are going up to London? What great
sport. We will take the *ton* by storm. Ah, yes, there are
some noses I want to tweak, and you will help me and
we will laugh and scheme. That Lucia Applebaum is
one."

There was a hint of defiance in Lady Ann's calm
voice. "No, Suzanne, I do not speak of Arabella. Elsbeth will accompany me and my husband to London."

25

There was dead silence in the large chamber, until Lady Talgarth rocked back in her chair. Goodness, they'd come for a duty visit. She hadn't even had the last lemon seed cake. But now that didn't matter. She'd never expected anything so wonderfully juicy as this. "My dear Ann," she said very carefully, unwilling to immediately accept her good fortune, "whatever do you mean by that?"

The earl said, "Allow me, Ann, to give our happy news to Lady Talgarth. We will shortly welcome Dr. Branyon into the family, ma'am. He and Ann plan to marry."

"My congratulations, Lady Ann," Lord Graybourn said, quite unaware he had waded into dangerous waters.

"I thank you, Lord Graybourn," Lady Ann said, nodding to him. "Dr. Branyon has been a dear and loyal friend of the Deverill family for countless years. And now he will be more. He will be my husband and Arabella's step-papa."

Lady Talgarth puffed herself up. "My dear Ann, surely you cannot mean it. Why, how very *odd* of you. The man is a doctor, he is in trade, so to speak, even though it is sick people he trades in. It still isn't what one would expect. I suppose he is a gentleman since his father was a squire in one of our remote counties, but he is a second son."

Mother and daughter drew together. Arabella turned

to the incredulous Lady Talgarth and raised her black brows with the exact amount of arrogance her father would have used. "I daresay *some* might consider it *odd,* ma'am. I myself think that my mother is far too young and beautiful to remain a widow. Just look at her—everyone believes her to be my sister. As for Dr. Branyon, he is a gentleman, no matter what he chooses to do, and ever so handsome and kind. I will welcome him as my step-papa. He will not only love me but he will ensure that I live until I am ninety—the benefit of having a physician for a step-papa."

Ah, it was well done. The earl was so pleased with her that he wanted to lift her out of her chair, kiss her, and carry her immediately up to their bedchamber. He wanted all those miserable clothes off her. Damnation, he was forgetting, and he refused to do that. All right, so she had a reason for lying with the comte, but she had to tell him what it was. He realized that he was thinking the very same thoughts over and over again. He was boring even himself. And the last lemon seed cake was gone. Who had snagged it?

Lady Talgarth wanted to box Arabella's ears when Suzanne said, taking Lady Ann's hands in hers, "I think it's marvelous, Lady Ann. Dr. Branyon is a good man and besides, he cured me of some vile illness when I was a little girl. My father would have given him the moon if he could. Ah, and now Dr. Branyon is effectively treating my father's gout. Besides, you are used to being your own mistress. I, for one, would remove to a tent if I had to live in Bella's household. She is really quite frightening. I begin to feel sorry for the earl until I see how he reduces her to delightful silence."

"That is certainly more than enough," Arabella said. "You have torn up my character and consigned the pieces to the four winds. I thank you."

Lady Ann said calmly, "That is surely enough about

my affairs. Lord Graybourn, how long do you make your stay? I understand your destination is Brighton."

Lord Graybourn hastened to say, "I had intended to stay only a day or two, my lady. But the kindness of my hostess"—he looked hearteningly at Lady Talgarth—"as well as the hospitality you have extended to me, makes me hopeful that I shall be asked to remain for a few days longer." The viscount's eyes rested momentarily upon Elsbeth. The comte wanted to kill the man. So did Lady Talgarth. Suzanne grinned from ear to ear. As for the earl, he was looking at his wife, whose teacup was shaking a bit in her hand. Why was that?

Lady Talgarth rose from her chair amid yards of rustling lavender silk and tapped her fan against her hand until the gentlemen had also risen. She drew an audible breath and frowned, not at Lady Ann or Arabella, but at Elsbeth. She then cast a look fraught with meaning at Suzanne, one that promised full reckoning.

Suzanne, well used to her mother's touchy humors, just shook her head, smiled, rose, and gave Lady Ann a quick hug. "I see that our visit is ended, Lady Ann. Please accept my congratulations. I am very happy for you."

"Of course, my dear." Lady Ann gave a gracious smile to Lady Talgarth. "We most enjoyed making the acquaintance of Lord Graybourn, Aurelia. You are, needless to say, most welcome at Evesham Abbey at any time."

"Indeed, my dear Ann, I cannot recall when I spent a morning that was more *enlightening*. Surely not any time in the recent past. But there were not enough seed cakes." She gave her daughter a sour look. "I daresay we will, however, be far too occupied to bring Lord Graybourn to visit again. You will certainly understand."

Lady Ann merely nodded. One neighbor down, she thought, but she didn't care, not one whit.

"Come, dear Edmund," Lady Talgarth said with unnecessary force.

He managed to move with moderate speed to her side. He smiled at everyone, a rather nice smile, Elsbeth thought, and bid his good-byes.

No sooner had Crupper bowed their visitors from the Velvet Room than Arabella collapsed on the sofa and burst into laughter. "I would have wagered that the old bat would burst her seams. It was excellent, just excellent. I had not dreamed to be so amused."

Lady Ann sighed. "I suppose that she had to be told, sooner or later. The poor viscount, really a quite unexceptionable young man, it was a pity he had to be here when she was told."

The earl remarked from his post by the fireplace, "I wouldn't care to be in the viscount's boots. I doubt the rest of his visit will be very pleasant. In any case, the poor fellow is quite unsuited to the dashing Miss Talgarth." His gaze rested for a moment on Elsbeth. He then said to his wife, his voice soft as butter, "If you are over your giggles, would you like some luncheon?"

The earl's look had plummeted Elsbeth into a pit of guilt. How very fickle of her to think Lord Graybourn a charming man, to believe that his sensibilities were quite in tune with her own. She found that she tended to avoid her cousin's eyes at the dining table. She thought his unkindness to the viscount uncivil and not at all the way a proper gentleman should behave. Her displeasure at his behavior made her uneasy. The cold slices of ham did not sit well in her stomach.

As for Gervaise, he was of the cynical opinion that the damned English were all the same. He had merely joined in what he had thought to be an English game of showing up the fat viscount, for a fool that he was, and just look at what they had done—drawn their ranks together against him, the French outsider. Even Elsbeth had sided against him. He managed to hide his displeasure, for there was much he had to accomplish today. At the close of luncheon, he managed to place himself next to Arabella.

"My dear countess," he said with all the charm in his repertoire, which was considerable, "I feel you have not paid me the attention I deserve. I am bereft."

Both Elsbeth and the earl were staring at the both of them. Arabella wanted to send her fist into the comte's face. What was Justin thinking? She couldn't bring herself to look at him. She finally managed to say, "I am newly married, comte. Surely that gives me a good reason for not giving everyone all the attention they feel they deserve. If you are bereft, I am, of course, sorry for it."

"Perhaps," the comte said, "it is I who have not paid you enough attention. As you know, I must take my leave in but two days. If your husband could spare you, I should delight in having you show me more of your beautiful English countryside. Please do not deny me this."

"I can spare her, but I do not do it willingly," the earl said, and Arabella thought her jaw would drop to the floor in surprise. He continued, all good humor, "What man would? I ask only that you take good care of her. She is all that is precious to me."

What was going on here? Why was he smiling at her, calling her precious to him, giving her permission to go with the comte, the man he was certain she had betrayed him with? It made no sense, unless . . . She drew a deep breath. He must believe her innocent now. Had he guessed that it must have been Elsbeth? She wanted him just to believe her, and perhaps it was true.

She didn't want to go to the front doors with the damned comte. She wanted to shoot him. She wanted to kick him to the floor. It was denied to her, dammit.

She forced herself to smile, saying, "I shall be delighted to explore with you. Where do you wish to go?"

He paused before replying, as if uncertain. "A difficult decision, Arabella, but I think I should like to visit your old abbey ruins once again. The few minutes I have spent there were not enough. Such a romantic place, full of ghosts of your English ancestors. I wish to be drawn back into the past, to forget the cares of the present."

Arabella thought this overdone, but she merely nodded. They agreed to meet in thirty minutes.

When she came down to the entrance hall not long thereafter, dressed in an old blue muslin gown and stout walking shoes, she asked Crupper, "Have you seen his lordship?"

He gave her a tolerant smile. "Your husband had an errand to do. He said I was to tell you that he would miss you"—old Crupper's eyes softened and Arabella stared—"and that he hoped you would spare him some time this evening."

"Oh yes," she said, nearly dancing, "I will spare him any amount of time he wishes. Thank you, dear Crupper."

"A pity you must spend time with that Frenchman," Crupper said.

"I agree with you. It is a great pity."

"He will be gone soon."

"Yes, isn't that wonderful?"

She grinned at him and went out to stand on the front steps. Gervaise appeared not many minutes later, dressed beautifully, as was his habit, a smile of anticipation on his handsome face.

He didn't hesitate to flatter this girl whom he would never see again in two days. It cost him nothing, and hopefully, it would make her more cooperative. "How very lovely you are, Arabella. An afternoon in your company will fill my memories for many a lonely day to come."

His flowery compliments nauseated her, but she forced a smile. Soon he would be gone. She couldn't wait. She fell into step beside the comte, thinking about her husband, wondering what he was thinking now. Surely he wouldn't insult her again, would he?

"A lovely day, Arabella. Finely suited for our explorations."

"Hmm," she said. "How very true." She walked faster. Time moved very slowly on occasion.

The old abbey ruins were bathed in the rich golden light of the afternoon sun, the rays striking the three stone arches that still stood, casting circular shadows over the large area of fallen rubble. Arabella tried her best to capture a mood of adventure. "Well, Gervaise, here we are. As you can see, the original abbey was a huge structure, covering most of this hill. See how high those two remaining arches are? On this level, only they remain. Now, of course, the rest of the walls are very nearly tumbled about themselves.

"The time we visited here before, I neglected to tell you of the abbey's history, which was not a very happy one. My father told me that it was a sanctuary of learning for nearly four hundred years before it was pillaged and burned in the sixteenth century on the orders of King Henry." Gervaise appeared fascinated with the recital, and she warmed to her subject. It helped pass the time. "When I was a child, I explored some of the old chambers that still exist under this level. See"— she pointed to the far perimeter of the ruins—"where the fallen rocks have been cleared away? Just below are the chambers—monks' cells. I have been told that if you are very quiet you will hear the monks intoning their prayers."

"Ah, very romantic, that. Elsbeth was telling me of a subterranean passageway. There are chambers still intact down there?"

"At least four or five chambers stand as they did

seven hundred years ago. They are in a row off the only passage that remains uncollapsed."

His interest seemed to kindle, his eyes shining. "We must make haste, my dear Arabella. I must see these chambers. I will never have another chance."

Arabella hesitated. "It isn't safe, Gervaise. I have seen some of the stone crumble just in the past ten years. Indeed, some nearly fell on me."

He drew himself up. "I would not dare to ask you to submit your person to any hazard, dear Arabella. I insist that you remain here in safety. I shall explore the old rooms." Masculine authority rang in his voice.

Well, damn, she thought. She couldn't very well let him go down there alone, despite his peacock's preening. "Oh, all right, one last time then. Let's go."

He looked pleased. She didn't understand it. "I of course will do as you ask." He gave her a flourishing bow and stepped back.

"Follow me and stay close," she said over her shoulder, and hunched down.

Arabella skirted the massive stones to the far side of the ruins. Here all larger stones had been rolled away to preserve the passage below for as long as possible. In some places the ceiling was so thin that tiny shafts of light could be seen filtering down into the darkness below. She turned to where crooked slabs of stone still framed the stairway leading downward to the lower chambers. She peered inside.

"I forgot to bring candles. It is too dark for us to see well enough if we go down there. Sorry, comte." There, now she could get rid of him. She wanted to find Justin. She wanted to kiss him until they were both out of breath. She wanted to ask him when he had finally realized the truth, when he had finally realized she had not betrayed him, when . . .

The comte drew two candles and matches from his

waistcoat pockets. "*Voilà*, dear Arabella. As you see, I have come prepared to explore."

She couldn't believe it. She was surely cursed. She took a candle from his outstretched hand. They lit the candles, Arabella saying, "It is wretchedly dark down there at the bottom of the steps. Take care and go slowly."

They made their way carefully down the jagged rock steps into the subterranean passage. But for the flickering of their candles, the darkness was complete. Arabella stepped gingerly over fallen stones. She wished he would fall and break his neck, but she said, "Be careful where you step, Gervaise." Her voice sounded eerie. She paused a moment and lifted her candle above her head. "Look, it is always so." She pointed to the walls. "They are always clammy with moisture. Isn't that strange when the sun shines so brightly above us?"

Gervaise obediently stepped nearer to the wall and ran his fingers over the rough wet surface. "It is fascinating. Where are the monks' cells, Arabella?"

Odd, but he sounded abstracted, impatient. It had been his damned idea to explore the ruins. It was even his damned candles. Where had all his fervor fled to? "The passage forks to the left just ahead. The passage to the right crumbled many years ago. It is too bad that the chambers are empty. There is really not much to see."

"It doesn't matter," he said behind her. "It is the marvelous atmosphere, the menacing romance of it all. I wish to have it seep into my bones."

The passage ended abruptly, and Arabella raised her candle. "This is the only corridor that is still standing. The rooms are in a straight row along the left."

She slipped through the narrow doorway into the first cell. "Don't put any weight against the door frame. You can see that the stones are already working themselves loose from the oak beams."

They stood side by side in the small stone room, their candles casting shifting dark shapes on the damp walls. The air was musty and close. "I hope it was more pleasant seven hundred years ago." Arabella stooped and ran her fingers through the soft sand that covered the floor.

"I wish to see the other cells," Gervaise said, moving away from her as he spoke. "Stay here, Arabella, I shall be back soon."

She nodded, quite content to stay where she was. It was very peaceful, and she didn't mind at all being alone. She saw his candle flicker outside the cell, then disappear.

She looked about the chamber, thinking how large it had appeared to her as a small child. She pictured a rude wooden cot along one wall and perhaps a small table along the other. Certainly the room was too tiny for anything else.

Suddenly there was a loud thumping noise overhead, just above the oak-beamed doorway. She clutched her candle close to her and stepped forward, only to hurl herself back when stones above the doorway tumbled to the floor in front of her.

She wanted to scream, but didn't. Oh God, she was stupid to have brought him down here. She had known it wasn't safe.

"Gervaise! Where are you? Are you all right?"

There was dead silence.

26

The silence didn't last. More stones fell, very close now. Arabella watched in horror as larger and larger stones worked themselves free of their ancient molding and crashed to the floor, blocking the open doorway, spewing dust and dirt into the air.

She screamed, falling back, choking, her nostrils clogged and her eyes burning from gritty dust and sand that swirled about her. Her candle flickered. She whipped about, cupping her hand about the precious flame. A rock struck her shoulder, and she cried out more in surprise than in pain. She scurried to the corner of the cell and huddled down against the wall, her legs drawn up to her chest.

The walls began to tremble around her. She tensed her body for the inevitable pain. She knew it must be just moments away. She'd brought this on herself. She was a fool. But, Justin, she didn't want to leave Justin. Dear God, she was only eighteen years old. She didn't want to die. She sobbed aloud, tears burning her eyes. Then she shook herself. Fool, one hundred times a fool, and now she was crying like a ninny. She got herself together. She raised her candle. In the dim candlelight she saw the far wall of the cell gently collapse forward, strewing more stone and rubble toward her. She closed her eyes tightly, fighting the swirling dust, and buried her face against the wall.

The oak beams overhead gave a final groan and fell

silent. She raised her head and knew a moment of surprise that she was still alive. She raised her candle again. She swallowed another sob. Alive, yes, but buried amid a tomb of rubble.

She surged to her feet and screamed, "Gervaise? Gervaise, are you all right? Where are you?"

She waited many long agonizing moments before she heard his voice on the other side of the crumbled doorway, muffled by the thick pile of stone between them. "Arabella? Is that you? Thank God you are alive. Are you safe?"

Safe? Was he perfectly mad? Still, she felt better hearing his voice.

"Yes, I am all right. There is much fallen stone and dust is clogging the air, but I am as yet unharmed."

His voice came clearer now, confident and sure. "Do not worry, Arabella. The passage still seems safe. I am going to fetch help. I swear that I will not be long. You must be brave. I shall return soon."

He would get Justin. Thank God the passage had not caved in. She thought of her husband and calmed. She must be patient. She wiped her hands across her forehead and saw in the flickering candlelight traces of smeared blood. How odd, she thought, for she hadn't felt any pain at all. A falling stone had cut into her scalp, and now her hair was matted with blood. Better her hair than dripping off her nose. She laughed. That was better. Justin would come. Everything would be all right.

The silence was a heavy weight. The minutes stretched out endlessly. Slowly she crawled to the center of the small cell. The sand floor was strewn with jagged pieces of stone, each positioned, it seemed, to poke and cut her palms and knees. She gritted her teeth against the sharp jabs. Carefully she cleared a small space and sat up, lifting the candle to look about her. The doorway looked as if it had vomited stone, leaving only a small space at the very top. She remembered the sound of collapse from the wall beside her, and carefully brought the candle about.

The breath caught in her throat, then spurted free. She screamed, a piercing, horrified sound that echoed back to her. Amid the fallen stone, stretched out toward her like death beckoning from hell, was a skeleton's hand. The bony fingers nearly touched her skirt. She scrambled back on her heels and closed her eyes, fighting down another scream. The image of a cowled monk, his head and face covered in a rough woolen robe, filled her mind.

She forced her eyes open and gazed again at the grotesque curling fingers. Slowly she raised the candle and forced herself to look into the hollow created by the collapsing wall. The skeleton's outstretched arm was attached to a body. It lay on its side, facing away from her, yet the head was twisted nearly backward, its eye sockets staring at her, but there were no eyes to see her. Broken teeth hung loosely in the gaping mouth. A white peruke was askew atop its fleshless head.

Arabella shuddered, gooseflesh rising on her arms. The remains of a long-dead monk would have been less terrifying. She felt a ghastly chill, the formless cold sweep of death.

For several moments she fought silently to force her courage to the forefront. As if to prove to herself that she wasn't a coward, she reached out her fingers and touched the filthy worm-eaten velvet sleeve that covered the skeleton's arm. How strange, she thought, it was still soft to the touch. She looked more closely. It was the skeleton of a man, dressed in a dark green coat and velvet breeches that fitted below the knees. She remembered as a child that her father had worn such a style. The man could not have been buried more than twenty years in his ancient tomb. She leaned closer and saw a gaping hole over the man's chest. It gave witness to his manner of death. At least he'd been dead before he'd been entombed.

It required a great effort of will for Arabella to slip her fingers into the coat pockets. Perhaps the man must have had some paper, some document to tell who he was. The pockets were empty. She drew a deep breath and plunged her hand into his breeches pocket. Her fingers closed around a small square of folded paper. Slowly she drew it out and sat back on her heels.

She unfolded the paper and saw that it was a letter. The ink was so faded with age that she had to hold the candle dangerously close to its yellowed edges.

She managed to make out the date—1789. The month had become illegible over the years. She looked down at the body of the letter and wanted to cry out in vexation, for it was written in French. With frustrating slowness she translated the letter word by word. She read:

> My beloved Charles, even though he knows of the growing unrest, the now violent revolts of the rabble against us, he forces me to come. He keeps my baby here to ensure my return to England. You know he is furious over what he believes to be my family's treachery. He wants the remainder of my promised dowry. Listen, my love, do not worry, for I have a plan that will free us forever from him. Once in France, I shall travel to the château . . .

Try as she might, Arabella could not make out the next few lines. They blurred into shadowy shapes. Who was this Charles, anyway? And this woman? She shook her head and skipped the smudged lines.

> Though our little Gervaise cannot escape with us, I have learned to bear the pain of separation. At least he will know safety with my brother. Josette will post

this, my last letter to you. Soon, my love, we will be together again. I know that we can escape him and rescue Elsbeth. We shall be rich, my darling, rich from his greed. A new life. Freedom. I trust in God and in you. Magdalaine.

Arabella sat quietly with the letter laying loosely in her fingers. She felt as if Magdalaine had come to her and unraveled the tangled, poignant threads of her short life. This man, Charles, was Magdalaine's lover. Gervaise was their child. He was not the Comte de Trécassis, but a bastard. She reeled back then as it struck her. Magdalaine was also Elsbeth's mother. Dear God. Elsbeth was his half-sister. Oh God, did he know? Surely not, even he could not be so evil. Of course, she was aware of the likeness of their features. But now she no longer saw it as the mere resemblance of cousins, but the deep inherited traits of brother and sister.

Poor Elsbeth. Dear God, she had to protect her sister. She couldn't let her ever find out that she had made love with her own brother. It would destroy her.

Arabella jerked as the truth hit her. Her father's first wife had been unfaithful to him. Indeed, she had borne a child before her marriage to him. Had the Trécassis family bribed her father with some fantastic sum to marry Magdalaine to save themselves from scandal? She looked down again at the letter. If only she could make out those yellowed blurred lines. She read once again.

"We shall be rich, my darling, rich from his greed."

She sat silently for a long while, sorting through what she knew and what she could only guess at. She looked back at the skeleton, her eyes fastening on the bullet hole in his chest. She thought of the times her father had expressly forbidden her to explore the ruins. Was it simply because he had feared for her safety?

No.

Her father must have killed this man, Charles. A duel of honor—yes, it must have been a duel of honor. Her father was no murderer, no matter what, no.

She suddenly remembered that Magdalaine had died suddenly after her return from France. She felt her blood freeze in her veins. A hoarse sob broke from her throat. "No, God, please no. He did not kill her, too. He would not have. No, please."

Yet the faded passionate words from so long ago were damning. Hate, pain, and suffering clutched at her from every word. Her only thought now was to protect her father's name, to destroy this wretched letter. She jerked it up and with quivering fingers drew it near to the slender candle flame. She was not certain what stopped her, but she pulled the paper back, folded it again into a small square, and slipped it into the sole of her shoe.

The candle was burning low. It could not be much longer now. Gervaise said he would fetch help. Gervaise. An impostor, a liar. She remembered the strange thudding sound just before the stones over the doorway collapsed. Had he trapped her in here on purpose? Had he tried to kill her? If so, why? What in heaven's name did he want?

The candle sputtered and died. Her voice caught on a sob as she was plunged into darkness, her only companion a long-dead man who had betrayed her father.

As Gervaise jerked open the great front doors of Evesham Abbey and burst into the entrance hall, he yelled, "Crupper, quickly, fetch his lordship. Her ladyship is trapped by fallen rock in the old abbey ruins. Be quick, man, quick, before it is too late." He was panting hard from his run from the ruins, he could barely catch his breath.

What had the Frenchman said? "Her ladyship? Trapped?" he repeated slowly, staring at the foreigner he wanted so very much to leave.

"Damn it, man, we must be quick. The rocks may collapse on her at any moment. She could already be dead! Hurry, hurry, fetch the earl."

At that moment, the earl appeared at the top of the stairs. "What is this about Arabella being trapped? In the old abbey ruins, you say?" He bounded down the stairs.

"We were exploring the subterranean chambers in the old abbey ruins. One of the chambers caved in and she is trapped. It is all my fault. Oh please, my lord, we must hurry."

"She is still alive?" The earl's voice was as hard and cold as granite.

"Yes, yes, I called to her. She is unharmed, but I fear there will be more falling stone. It is all unstable."

The earl threw back his head, and bellowed, "Giles!"

When the second footman came running into the entrance hall, the earl said, "Go quickly, Giles, and fetch James and all the stable hands. Tell them to gather their shovels and picks. Her ladyship is trapped beneath the ruins of the old abbey. Go, man, I shall meet you there."

The earl turned to Crupper. "Inform Lady Ann and Elsbeth. I shall be at the ruins." He turned to follow Giles, then stopped abruptly and looked back to see Gervaise quickly mounting the staircase.

"*Monsieur.*" His voice was soft, yet it cut through the air with the sharpness of a rapier.

Gervaise spun on his heel and turned to face the cold set features of the earl.

"Do you not wish to assist in rescuing my wife? Did you not say it was your fault? Are you not concerned?"

Ah, the earl's voice was so soft, so quiet—it scared the comte to his toes. "I—certainly, my lord. I merely intended to go to my room for but an instant." Damnation, what was he to do now? "Please, my lord, you must hurry. I shall join you in a moment."

The earl said very quietly, "I do not think so, *monsieur*. You will not join me in a moment. You will not go to your bedchamber. You see, I require your presence at once. Now, not a minute from now."

What to do? Gervaise cursed with silent fluency. All this and he would gain nothing at all. It was very hard to clamp down on his rage, but he managed it, shrugging. "As you will, my lord."

The earl turned to the now astonished Crupper and said in a loud, clear voice, "You will remain here, Crupper, and, if you will, guard Evesham Abbey. No one—I repeat, no one—is allowed beyond the entrance hall until my return. Do you understand?"

The old man felt mired in confusion. He heard the earl's words and, of course, understood them, though their intent was quite lost on him. It was what his lordship required of him. It was enough that he could obey. "Yes, my lord. I will remain here. No one will enter."

"Excellent, Crupper. *Monsieur?* Let us go." The earl stepped back and waited for Gervaise to precede him through the front doors.

Arabella drew her legs up close to her chest and hugged herself for warmth. The dust and sand had settled and she could breathe more easily. She tried not to think of the skeleton but an arm's reach away, and of the terrible truth that she had discovered. Surely Justin must come to her soon, if, she thought grimly, Gervaise indeed wanted her to be rescued. But what had he to gain by leaving her here? What of Justin? Of course he would come for her. That, she could not doubt.

She felt tears sting her eyes. The wetness of her tears mixed with the grime about her eyes and burned. She lifted a corner of her skirt and rubbed it against her cheeks.

Suddenly she thought she heard movement from the other side of the fallen wall. She raised her head and peered into the blackness.

"Arabella? Can you hear me?"

"Justin!" She jumped to her feet, bruises and cuts forgotten. "I knew you would come. I'm trapped in here. Please, oh, please, get me out of here."

Again she heard his voice, calm and clear. "Listen to me, Bella. I want you to move to the far corner of the chamber and protect your head with your arms. This is a tricky business. The beams are unstable above the door. I want you far away from them in case there is more collapsing."

"But, Justin, I can start pulling rocks away from this side. I'm not hurt and I'm strong, you know that. I can help—"

She thought she heard a low chuckle. The voice that reached her but a moment later was irate. "Damn it, woman, do as I tell you. I am glad that you are quite unharmed, and I wish you to remain that way. Move to the far side of the chamber. Do it now. I want you out of there."

She groped her way back to the corner and slipped down to her knees and covered her head.

It seemed to Arabella that with each stone dislodged from its place, the walls and ceiling shuddered and groaned. She herself shuddered with their every movement. She felt it the most joyous sight imaginable when Justin pulled away enough rubble to ease his body through the opening.

Someone handed him a candle. The small cell was flooded with light. Light and life, she thought, and she was alive.

The earl called over his shoulder, "James, stay back. I shall bring her ladyship out."

Arabella rose slowly to her feet. She walked straight into her husband's arms. She pressed her face against his shoulder. "I am very glad you came to rescue me," she said simply. She raised her face. "You are the most beautiful man in the whole world. Before I believed you only the most beautiful man in England, but no longer. The world, my lord, the whole world."

"Am I now? Well, you never doubted, did you, that I would come and fetch you? Why, who would argue with me? Who would yell at me? Who would kiss me so sweetly?"

She buried her face again in his shoulder. "You believe me," she whispered. "You believe me now. You know he was never my lover."

He was silent for a moment. She felt the slight stiffening of his body, and she wanted to weep. "It doesn't matter." Ah, but it did. It stood between them as the collapsed door had stood between them.

"But you came for me. I thank you for that." He was rubbing his chin against her hair.

He drew back. "We have much to talk about, you and I. Come now, let's get out of here. I have no great desire to further test your charmed existence."

"A moment, Justin, I was not alone here." She took the candle from his fingers and carefully moved its light to shine upon the skeleton.

He couldn't believe his eyes. "Good God, I don't believe this." He looked at her and marveled at her steadiness. He dropped to his knees and briefly examined the skeleton. After a moment he rose and dusted off his breeches. "First let's get you out of this place, then I'll see that this poor fellow receives a proper burial. I don't suppose you know who he is? No, certainly not."

He held the light for her as she slipped from her prison into freedom. She thought of the letter now rubbing against the sole of her foot. She felt weighted down with unsought, damning knowledge. There was much to consider—her father's name, and of course, Elsbeth. She determined at that moment to hold her tongue; no one must know what she had discovered, even Justin, until she had time to think, to sort through all that she now knew.

When she emerged into the bright sunlight, she looked about her, realizing for the first time in her eighteen years how very precious life was. She savored the hot sun beating down upon her face.

Like a small child awakening from a nightmare, she walked to her mother and threw her arms about her shoulders.

"My sweet girl," Lady Ann said, stroking her daughter's filthy hair. "My dearest heart, it's all right, it's quite all right. You're safe now. You're with Mama. Goodness, you've cut your scalp, but no matter. We will take care of that."

But she wasn't safe, none of them were. Whether the threat was from the comte or from the letter in the sole of her shoe, she knew there would not be safety for a very long time.

27

"You're a mess," the earl said, his hands around his wife's upper arms. He realized he was afraid to let her go. "It was so damned close," he said, pulling her against him, holding her hard against him. "Too damned close. You won't do that to me again, will you, Arabella?"

She shook her head against his shoulder. "It was awful. I didn't think I'd ever see the sunlight again the way it slants over the house in the late afternoon." She paused a moment, rubbing her nose against the soft material of his jacket. "I was afraid I would never see you again."

"Ah," he said. He lifted her chin with his finger, stared down at her for a very long time, then kissed her, very gently. "We both need to bathe. Let me look at that cut in your hair."

It wasn't as bad as it looked, thank God. He let the matted hair fall back. It had just bled a lot, as did most scalp wounds.

"You'll do. Bathe now. Then, I would like to speak with you."

It was then that she made up her mind. He still didn't believe her, but he had come, nonetheless, to care for her. The very least she owed him was the truth.

"And I wish to speak to you."

Damn the consequences.

The earl just smiled down at her, wondering what

she would say, wondering if she would ask his forgiveness. He remembered her words against his shoulder in the small monk's cell. She'd thought he believed her. What was that all about? No, he wouldn't think about that. Surely she would admit everything to him. Hadn't she just said that she wanted to speak to him? He wanted it over and done with. And, he knew, there was more, so much more. There was Gervaise, and what the damned bastard had done.

"Grace is fetching your tub. I had best demand the same of poor Grubbs." he turned, reluctantly, not really wanting her out of his sight for a single moment, to leave the earl's bedchamber.

"Justin?"

"Yes?"

Her voice was softer than the butter Cook had served just that morning. "I thank you. You saved me. I knew you would come and you did."

"You would do the same for me, would you not?"

"Yes, I would, but you know, my lord, I imagine that I would have moved more quickly." She struck a pose. In her filthy gown, her matted hair, her scratched hands and face, she struck a wonderful pose, saying now, "I doubt though, upon serious reflection, that I would have left you entombed for quite so long."

He laughed, he couldn't help it. "That was very well done. Don't ever change," he said, and left her.

Unfortunately, they had no time to speak before the evening meal.

As to be expected, the dinner conversation soon turned to the mysterious skeleton uncovered in the wall of the chamber.

"There was no clue at all to the poor man's identity?" Lady Ann asked the earl.

"Unfortunately none whatsoever. From his manner of dress, I would estimate that he met his violent end some twenty years ago. As to how or why, or, for that matter, by whose hand—" The earl shrugged and forked down another bite of sautéed pork loin.

Arabella bit her cheek. She loved pork, but tonight she couldn't face it. Dear God, she held all the answers to their questions on a small square of faded paper. She could imagine the shock and horror on their faces were she to tell them that it was her father who had killed the man—Magdalaine's lover—a man named Charles. And Gervaise—how would he react, were he to know the truth? Or, perhaps, did Gervaise already know? She lowered her head and toyed with the few errant green beans in the middle of her plate. She wanted more than anything to be alone, away from everyone, to think. She had to decide what to do.

"Dear Arabella, how very awful for you to be shut in with the man's skeleton. You are so very brave. Goodness, I would have died of fright on the spot." Elsbeth shuddered, a pea dropping off her fork.

"No, you wouldn't have," Arabella said, focusing the full strength of her belief on her half-sister. "You would have found the skeleton and you would have turned perfectly white—at least that's what I did—but then you would have thought about it and been very practical about the whole matter."

"Would I?" Elsbeth was frowning down at her plate. She raised her head. "You believe I would have been as brave as you were?"

"There is no doubt in my mind. There should be no doubt in yours, only I pray that you will never have it tested in the abbey."

Dr. Branyon looked from one daughter to the other. If Arabella could have given Elsbeth all her strength, she would have done it, right here, right now, at the dinner table. What was going on? There were such changes in her. He shook his head. Ann would tell him what was going on later. He said to Arabella, "Both you and Elsbeth have the constitutions of horses, but you, my dear countess, you need a more thorough examination. I want to make very certain that you are quite all right."

Arabella managed a laugh. "What? And be victim to one of your vile potions? No, I thank you, sir. Mother, give him some of these stewed onions. It will focus his attention away from me."

Dr. Branyon turned to the earl. "Justin, cannot you persuade your wife to reason?"

Justin merely smiled and shook his head. "Let her bear her bumps and bruises in peace, Paul. I am persuaded that she has come to no ill. But you may be certain that I will keep a close watch on her tonight."

"It is I who must ask your apology, dear Arabella," the comte said, leaning toward her, waving his knife. These were the first words out of him. "I placed you unwittingly into such danger. It is unforgivable, it is beyond what a man's honor can tolerate. Tell me, what can I do to make retribution?"

Arabella raised her eyes to Gervaise. She wanted to tell him that he could damned well leave this minute and never come back. He could shoot himself. He could drown himself in the fishpond. She wanted to demand what he knew and why he had come here in the first place. She also realized that she'd heard a note of falseness in his lilting voice. It was now very clear to her. His concern didn't reach his dark eyes. Perhaps it was relief she saw, relief that she had not died? What was going on here? How could she find out?

She forced herself to smile brightly at him. "I accept your apology, comte. I most readily forgive you, for I also wished to explore the chambers. The fault is both of ours." Had her voice sounded as false as the comte's? She hoped it did, to him, the bastard. She didn't dare look toward Justin. She imagined he would tell her quite plainly exactly what he thought later.

Lady Ann said, "All that matters is that your are
safe. I now wish to give an order. No more exploring
those old ruins. I remember your father extracting such
a promise from you years ago. Come, promise me
again."

Yes, Arabella thought, Father wanted me to stay
away from the ruins. There is no doubt at all in my
mind. He was afraid of what I would discover. She felt
sick, sick to her very soul, but managed to say, "That is
the easiest promise I will ever have to keep, Mama."

Dr. Branyon shifted his attention to Gervaise. He
was beginning to detest the young man as much as the
earl did, but for different reasons. He was afraid that
he posed a threat to Ann. What kind of threat, he didn't
know, but it was a fear, deep in his gut. And he wondered yet again what Justin had found out about him
and what he was planning to do. Would he simply allow him to leave? He said smoothly, "I understand,
monsieur, that you will leave Evesham Abbey shortly."

Gervaise gazed between half-closed lids at the earl
before replying smoothly, "Yes, Doctor, there are
pressing matters that await my attention. I have enjoyed my leisure here in England, but I must return to
Bruxelles."

Dr. Branyon said, "Well, you have stayed here for a
long time, have you not? Perhaps it is best that you return to your home."

Gervaise looked about at all of them. He knew the
earl was aware of his goal when he'd come back to tell
of Arabella's accident. Ah, but he didn't know what it
was that Gervaise was after. And that was why the earl
hadn't kicked him out. He wanted to know. Then he
would want to kill him. Well, the damned earl would
learn about everything soon enough. And Gervaise
wouldn't be the one to die. It made him smile.

Arabella found herself closely studying Gervaise's
face. If only she could unravel why he had come to

Evesham Abbey in the first place. Surely he could not be so vile as to purposely set out to seduce his own half-sister. No, surely that would be beyond anyone. By chance her eyes roved to the head of the table. She caught her breath in surprise at the glint of anger in her husband's eyes. She quickly turned her attention back to the small square of pork on her plate. How very stupid of me, she thought. Justin observed me looking at Gervaise. He didn't believe her innocent. He would never believe her.

Arabella wished she could simply leave everyone right now, and take her husband with her. But there was an evening to be endured, unspoken lies in the air like layers of dust. How she hated the deception, the secrets.

Finally, at the close of one of Elsbeth's recitals, Arabella turned gratefully to Dr. Branyon as he rose and took her hand in his. He kissed her fingers, then said, "You will go to bed now, Arabella, no arguments."

She gave him a curtsy. "It would be unbecoming of me to disagree with my future new papa. I most readily do your bidding, sir." She rose on her toes and kissed him on the cheek.

He patted her hand fondly, then turned to Lady Ann. "I must go now, Ann, but I shall fetch you in the morning for our outing."

Arabella was on the verge of taking herself to bed when she chanced to see Elsbeth gaze with clouded confusion at Gervaise. She'd been blind not to see much sooner how her sister wore her heart on her sleeve. She determined then and there, despite the fatigue that was making her eyes droop, that she would not leave Elsbeth alone with Gervaise. The least she could do was to keep them separated until Gervaise left. She paced about the room for several moments, racking her brain for a solution. The earl watched her, wondering what the hell she was up to. He saw her

eyes rest upon Elsbeth, and then, more pointedly, on
Gervaise. Something was strange here.

He wanted her to himself. All to himself. He said in
a calm cool voice, "I agree with Paul. It's time for you
to fly off to your bed."

That was it. Arabella said, "Yes, I should indeed
go to my bed. Oh, Elsbeth, would you not accompany
me to my room? I should like it above all things if you
would tuck me up."

Elsbeth looked up, startled. She had thought to speak
to Gervaise, since he was to leave so shortly, to ask
him what he planned now that her stepmother was to
marry Dr. Branyon. But she could not think of refusing
her sister. She readily agreed and rose to walk to Arabella's side.

"We bid you good night, gentlemen," Arabella said.
She took Elsbeth's small hand firmly in hers and
tugged her in lockstep unceremoniously to the door.

Once in her nightgown, her black hair brushed loose
down her back, Elsbeth counting the one hundred
strokes, Arabella smiled at Elsbeth and kissed her
cheek. "Thank you. I'm glad you came with me. We
haven't spent enough time together. But soon we will.
Soon, you will see. Do go to bed now, Elsbeth. It is late
and I can see that you are tired."

She wondered if she should follow to make certain
that Elsbeth didn't join Gervaise. It made her blood run
cold to think of them together.

Elsbeth yawned and stretched like an innocent child
at peace with the world. "Yes, I shall go to my room
now. Thank you, Bella, for lending me Grace. I am
so very clumsy without Josette." Her piquant face
crumpled at the mention of her old servant's name.

Arabella didn't know what to say. She knew that
Elsbeth missed Josette. After all, Josette had been with
her all her life. She had been like a mother to her. She

simply patted her sister's hand and said gently, "I know, Elsbeth. I thank you for coming up with me."

Arabella slipped into her bed and blew out the candle beside her. She knew Justin would come to her soon. There was so much to be said. But for the moment she was alone, alone to think, to sort out the many facts and half-truths she had discovered.

She knew the contents of Magdalaine's letter almost by heart now. She had read it several times again before going down to dinner. As to the letter itself, she had slipped it into the toe of one of her evening slippers, a hiding place that she knew to be safe—even Grace never went poking about in her shoes, except to hover with the feather duster over them, and that surely no more than once a month.

She sat up suddenly. Lord, what a fool she was. Josette must have known everything. Did she not ensure the dispatching of Magdalaine's letters to her lover, Charles? Of course, Josette must have known that Gervaise was Magdalaine's son. Josette—the old woman was now dead. Gooseflesh rose on her arms. A tragic fall down the main staircase in the middle of the night with no candle to guide her.

Her mind leaped back to the afternoon. She was as certain as she could be that the collapse in the old abbey ruins was no accident. But then, if Gervaise had wished to harm her—or kill her, for that matter—why did he return so quickly with Justin to rescue her? What possible reason could he have had for any of his actions? Nothing made any sense.

She shook her head. Where was her husband? Her shoulders slumped. She felt as though she was wandering through the maze in Richmond Park without the key to show the way out. The key to this maze was the reason why Gervaise had come to Evesham Abbey in the first place.

It seemed obvious that her father must have known

of Gervaise's existence as the natural son of his first
wife. That must be the reason why Gervaise had not
come until after her father's death. But was there
something else her father had known about him, something else that had kept him away?

Suddenly, the door opened and the earl came into the
bedchamber. He was wearing an old dark blue brocade
dressing gown, the same one he had worn on their wedding night, its elbows grown thin over the years. His
feet were bare. She knew he was naked beneath the
dressing gown. Her fingers clenched. She felt heat
wash through her. Everything, suddenly, seemed so
simple.

She said to him as he neared the bed, "Gervaise was
never my lover. It was Elsbeth, not I."

The earl came to a dead stop. He saw that long-ago
moment in his mind as clear as if it had been but an
hour before. So clear it had been to him, all of it. He
said slowly, "I saw you humming as you walked out of
the barn the day before our wedding. It was just moments after Gervaise, looking as furtive as a pick-
pocket, slipped out."

"Because of that you believed I betrayed you?" The
pulse was pounding in her neck. It was nothing, and
yet he had turned on her? She wanted to leap up and attack him, but she didn't move, just waited. She swallowed hard.

"No, there was more. When you came out, your
gown was wrinkled, indeed, you were buttoning some
buttons and trying to straighten it. You even had to
lean down and tie the ribbons on your slipper. Your
hair was a mess, filled with straw. You looked very
pleased with yourself."

Still, she forced herself to keep silent. He sat down
on the end of the bed. "I didn't know what to think—
the comte came out. He had the look of a man who had
just made love to a woman. It is a look every man

knows well. There was no mistake. I was very certain, and I wanted to kill both myself and you for betraying me. Ah, and I wanted to wring his damned neck."

"You truly had no doubts then?"

"No, I was certain what had happened. I didn't want to believe it, but I did. There was no doubt at all in my mind. I wanted to die."

28

"You left immediately then?"

He nodded. "You are telling me that if I had remained but a few more minutes, I would have seen Elsbeth coming out of the barn?"

"Yes."

He ran his fingers through his black hair. "Why didn't you tell me?"

She could but stare at him.

He realized what he had said and shook his head. "No, you did tell me, didn't you? But not about Elsbeth."

"Yes, I did tell you once I realized what you believed, but you didn't want to hear anything I said. You believed me guilty with no trial at all."

"Yes," he said slowly, "I did. I believed what I had seen. There was no doubt in my mind. But then—" He shrugged. He looked over at her. "I came to believe that you weren't entirely to blame for what you had done. I came to believe that you felt trapped because of what your father had forced upon you. All I wanted was for you to tell me the truth—but of course you refused. When did you learn about Elsbeth?"

"When I was riding with Suzanne. She had seen the looks between them. She brought it up. At first I could just stare at her. At first I couldn't bring myself to believe her—shy Elsbeth, so diffident, so much a child."

"She is not a child if she gave herself to Gervaise."

"No, but she is still innocent."

"Now you defend her."

Arabella nodded. If she told him all of it then it would come out that her father was a murderer. She would take that to her grave. She knew that now. He must never know. "She is my half-sister," she said, and raised her chin.

Then he stood and was beside her, lifting her in his arms. "None of it is important right now. All that is important is that you forgive me. Dear God, I had prayed you would confess your betrayal to me, and like the magnanimous gentleman, I would have forgiven you. I deserve to be whipped."

"Yes," she said. "But not just this moment. Perhaps tomorrow I could take a whip to you. Or best, we wait until we have a roaring argument. What do you think?"

He kissed her, very lightly, very gently. She wanted to cry. "You truly believe me now?" she whispered against his mouth.

"Yes, I believe you. I will never disbelieve you again. I am a dog. I am a blind dog. If only I had told you exactly what I had seen, but I didn't. Please kick me."

"No, I'm sorry, but not now."

He held her face between his hands. "You are my wife and if you will forgive me, then we will begin anew."

"I would like that."

"You will forgive me?"

"Yes, I must. I really have no choice."

"That first night together, Arabella. You were a virgin, utterly innocent, so happy, so filled with anticipation and I violated you. I am more sorry about that than I can tell you. Will you give me another chance? Will you let me love you now? I swear to you that I can do it right."

She remembered that night, the humiliation, the pain, the helplessness. "It is difficult," she said, her breath warm against his lips. "Very difficult. But I love you, something I cannot seem to help. Yes, Justin, I would like you to love me now."

He kissed her again, and yet again, only this time he wasn't gentle at all.

And when she was on her back, her nightgown on the floor beside the bed, her husband over her, his hands lightly stroking over her breasts and belly, she said, "Our marriage did not begin so very well."

"No, but from this moment on, it will be as perfect as I can make it." His hand slipped lower to stroke her. Her hips arched and she stared up at him. He was smiling, and there was wickedness in those gray eyes of his. "Yes," he said, as he kissed her breasts, "you have the same look in your eyes when you're pleased with yourself."

He brought her to pleasure before he entered her. He wanted no fear in her, no hesitation. Her release was shattering, her astonishment clearly written on her face. She was staring up at him even as her heart pounded in the aftermath of a pleasure so wild, so intense, she could never have imagined such a thing. "That was very nice, Justin," she managed to say after a moment.

"There's more I hope you will enjoy." He eased into her, feeling her tense around him, her muscles tightening in shocks of pleasure. He went deep and deeper still. And she couldn't believe this, couldn't believe what it made her feel.

"You're part of me," she said against his neck, and then she bit him, and her hands were wild down his back and his hips. "I will never let you go."

"No," he said, "no." And he turned into a wild man, heaving and thrusting and then his own pleasure overtook him and he threw back his head and yelled with the power of it.

He was flattening her but she didn't care. She bit his

shoulder again, then kissed him, again and again. "That was nice," she said. "Perhaps we can do it again?"

He managed to raise himself on his elbows and stare down at her. "I cannot," he said. "I am just a man, Arabella, just a weak man and you have wrung me out."

"I don't know if I like the sound of that."

He leaned down and kissed the tip of her nose. "Give me a little while and then I will please you again." He paused, then said in a low gruff voice, "Do you forgive me for hurting you? Can you forgive me for all of it?"

He was deep inside her. She lifted her hips and he moaned. "Yes," she said. And he began moving deep inside her again and she loved it, no, craved it, and soon she was with him and it went on and on.

She snuggled into the warmth of the covers, held tightly against him, and soon fell asleep.

She was magically transported to the chamber beneath the old abbey ruins. Rock rumbled and fell about her, striking her head, her face, her shoulders. She tossed forward on her face, frantically trying to avoid the sharp, jagged stones, desperately flailing her arms about for protection. Her fingers clasped about brittle, spiderlike projections. She felt her hand squeezed with such force that she was jerked forward. Though she was struggling in darkness, she saw with terrifying clarity what held her so mercilessly. A skeleton's hand held her fast, its fleshless fingers digging into her wrist. She heard a low cry, a moan of hate and pain, the rattle of imminent death. The skeleton rocked up from its prone position, broken teeth falling from its rotted hollow mouth. Slowly, before her eyes, the bones of its hands began to turn to dust and trickle away. The head tottered backward and fell, crashing and crumbling to the ground. She heard hellish screams all about her. She felt death upon her, clogging her throat, enclosing her in a shroud of terror.

Arabella awoke, her hands tearing at the bedcovers,

a final cry dying on her own lips. "Arabella, dammit, wake up!"

The earl lit a candle and raised it above her head. She drew back with a gasp as the light fell upon the jeering face of the skeleton on *The Dance of Death.* Dream and reality mixed in her mind. Had the screaming come from the skeleton? Could it have been the wailing of an infant? The hopeless cries of a woman? Had she heard the ghosts of Evesham Abbey?

"Arabella, wake up. Come, love, come back to me. You had a nightmare. It's over now." He drew her to him and began to rub his large hands up and down her back.

She drew a shaking breath. "It was that horrible skeleton in the old abbey ruins. Then I thought I heard from our ghosts, but now I begin to doubt that their cries were not my own. Oh God, it was horrible."

"I have heard the ghosts." He looked over at *The Dance of Death* panel. "I do not like that thing. Should you like it if we removed it to the attic?"

She nodded slowly. "It was odd, Justin, but somehow that panel was part of the dream. I don't understand it. Yes, let's send it to the attic. It means nothing to anyone now." She snuggled against him again. "I came very close to dying this afternoon. I would have died without ever having known all of living. I would have died without knowing you as my husband. I thank you for saving me."

"You're shivering." He was kissing her temple, shoving her hair from her forehead. "Here I am trying to avoid speaking honestly to you. It is because I am a man, I suppose. We don't wish to speak of things so deeply felt. It makes no sense, but there it is. If you had died, I couldn't have borne it. It's that simple."

"Gervaise tried to kill me today. No, don't shake your head. I know that he must have. The collapse of all the rocks and dirt were only around the cell I was in.

He asked me to stay there. He said he wanted to go exploring. Why, Justin? Why did he want to kill me? I have thought and thought about it but I can't dredge up a reason. Why did he do it?"

The earl was silent for a long time, but he didn't loosen his hold on her. His fingers lightly caressed her shoulder, the softness of her upper arm. "He didn't want to kill you," he said finally. "What he wanted was to get me out of Evesham Abbey. He wanted to come here, to our bedchamber. There is something in this chamber that is hidden, something he wants, something probably poor old Josette knew about and that is why he killed her. Did you not wonder why I had this bedchamber locked? Why I gave that ridiculous excuse that some floorboards were loose and thus posed a danger? It was to keep him out until I found out what he was after.

"I risked your life because I wanted to trap the little bastard. It was all I could do not to wring his mangy neck today, Arabella. But the game is soon up. He will not leave here until he has made a last try to get into this room and retrieve what it is he is looking for."

"You know he killed Josette."

"It sounds like you had already guessed as much yourself. It makes sense. It was you who pointed out that she had no candle with her to guide her in the darkness. Yes, it only makes sense. Did she threaten to expose him? I don't know. I suppose I could simply beat him until he's either dead or he tells me the truth of why he came here.

"But before he leaves on Friday, he will try again. When he came running in here to tell us you were trapped in the old abbey ruins, I immediately began running to the front door. I turned to see him going quickly up the stairs. He trapped you so that he could get me out of the way, come to this room, so he could retrieve what it is he is after."

"Let's kill him. Now."

He was shocked into silence, his brain numb, but just for an instant. She was like no other woman he had ever known in his life. He laughed, even as he was kissing her ear. "You delight me. You're no fainting miss, and that pleases me. You will probably flay me with your tongue many times in the future. I shall relish each time. You are magnificent. Now, tell me. How shall we kill the bastard?"

"I would like to tie him up and leave him in the abbey ruins until he tells us why he came here."

"I like it," he said, nibbling now on her earlobe. "Will we give him water?"

"Water, but no food. He will be utterly alone. You will visit him but once a day to ask him one question. If he fails to answer, you will leave again. I predict he will break in three days, no longer."

"I'm sorry, Bella, but I don't believe we can do it. However, I do appreciate the way your mind works. Now, there is Elsbeth to consider. What will we do about Elsbeth?"

She swallowed. It was decision time. But she couldn't, not yet. She turned to face him. "Not yet, not yet. Love me again, Justin. Love me."

He did, and it was wild and frantic, and she still didn't know what to do when she listened to his breathing even into sleep.

Life wasn't simple. It was vastly irritating, particularly since she had her husband again and wanted nothing more than to have him love her until she was unconscious, which should require at least several years, by her reckoning. She had all of him now, finally, and it was beyond splendid. She wanted all of him forever.

But forever didn't seem to be measured in a very long stretch just now.

29

The earl flung back the heavy curtains that covered the long row of narrow mullioned windows in the family portrait gallery. He brushed a light layer of dust from his hands, mentally noting to bring this neglected room to Mrs. Tucker's attention. He would have liked to open the windows to air the room, but a fine gray drizzle had become an earnest downpour.

He was not certain why he had come to the family portrait gallery, save that he wanted to be alone. He gazed down the length of the long narrow room, scarcely wider than the second-floor corridors, his eyes resting briefly on the portrait of his great-uncle, haughtily staring at the world beneath the dark flaring Deverill brows, his dark hair covered by a white curling wig. What a proud, lecherous old man he must have been, the earl thought, his mouth twisting unwillingly into a grin.

Both he and Arabella had fallen asleep deep in the middle of the night. He had awakened first this morning, kissed her, then realized he shouldn't make love to her again so soon. She was certainly sore—she had to be after they had made love three times during that marvelously long night. He'd left her. God, but it had been difficult. If she had awakened in those moments, he would be willing to wager that he would still be in their bed.

Neither of them had again discussed how to kill

Gervaise, since he'd only seen her in the company of
Lady Ann and Elsbeth. A pity. Justin wanted to kill
him very badly. He had been trained all his adult life in
military strategy. He couldn't escape it now. Never kill
an enemy until you have what it is he wants. It was that
simple. Arabella had known that without a whit of
training.

What to do?

One thing he fully intended to do today was search
the comte's bedchamber. He doubted that the little bastard had left anything about, but search he would. If he
had to, he wouldn't let Arabella kill the comte until he
had tried to fetch what it was he had come for.

He looked up to see his wife standing beneath the
portrait of a long-dead Deverill of the sixteenth century, the ruff coming to her pearl-encrusted ears.

"My love," he said, his voice deep and low. It
sounded so very natural. He felt it to the very depths of
him. He'd never said that to another woman. He was at
her side in a moment, drawing her up against him. "I
have missed you."

"Why did you not awaken me?" Her hands were
stroking up and down his back, then lower. He held in
his breath. "I woke up and you were gone. I wanted to
kiss your mouth and throat. I wanted to kiss your belly,
the way I did last night. Remember? You told me you
would very much like it." She grinned wickedly at him.
"I seem to remember that you groaned until I drew
away, then you sighed in disappointment."

He was trembling. He shook his head, saying simply,
"It was difficult to leave you, but you had to be sore.
We came together too many times last night and you
are too new at this business not to be sore. Were I of a
crude disposition I might say that I rode you until you
collapsed beneath me."

"I wonder," she said thoughtfully, her finger in the

cleft in his chin, "could I perhaps ride you? Is it possible? Is it done? Would it give you pleasure?"

His eyes crossed. His breathing quickened. He looked at the wall. He wanted her desperately. She laughed suddenly. She knew what she had done to him, even though she wasn't all that certain of how she'd done it. He would teach her all about riding him this very night.

He managed to say, "Tonight. I give you until tonight. Now, before you make me forget my brains, this morning I didn't want to leave you but I knew that if I stayed with you, I would have come to you again. I didn't want to rut my wife. Rest today and perhaps tonight—very well, tonight and not a moment later. It's likely, though, that I will bite my fingers through wanting you so badly during the rest of today." From one moment to the next, he was deadly serious. He stroked his fingers over her face. Such a beloved face. "Do you still forgive me, Arabella?"

She leaned forward in his arms, looking up at him closely. This was as serious as life got and she knew it. She said slowly, her heart in her words, "You are my other half, so much a part of me that if I did not forgive you, then I would not forgive myself. Yes, I forgive you. I even realized that you and I are so much alike that if I had witnessed you coming out of the barn and another woman following, that I would have drawn the same conclusion. I would have made your wedding night a misery just as you made mine. But it is over now. We have begun again." She stood on her tiptoes and kissed him full on the mouth.

"Open your mouth."

She did. His tongue was sliding between her lips and she jumped with the newness of it, the excitement of it. "Justin," she whispered, kissing him deeply, touching her tongue to his, "You know, my lord, perhaps I'm not all that sore."

He laughed, then groaned. Slowly, he set her away from him. He was harder than a rock. Jesus, he couldn't believe how she affected him. He cleared his throat, but his voice was still a croak as he said, "Tonight, not before. I shall be in control here. I know what is best. You are still ignorant, though I pray that will not last long. Actually, I will promise you that it will not last long. Ignorance is not something to be desired when it comes to men and women.

"Now, obey me. Keep your hands to yourself, well, at least keep them above my waist. Shall we gaze at our ancestors together?"

The earl said to his wife as they strolled in the parterre late that morning, "I want you to take Gervaise away with you this afternoon. Elsbeth as well. Suzanne if you can get her. I want to search his bedchamber and I must know that he won't walk in on me. If he were to, then I would have to kill him and we wouldn't know why he came here to Evesham Abbey in the first place."

It burned in her throat, her knowledge of Gervaise and Elsbeth. Burned deep, but her loyalty to her father, to Elsbeth, burned even deeper. She held her tongue, but it was difficult. She owed this man all of her, and she was holding back. But what choice did she have?

"Yes," she said, "I will get Suzanne. She would doubtless be shamelessly delighted to get away from poor Lord Graybourn. I will send a messenger to her right now. She doesn't dare refuse me."

"You know, I believe, if we are lucky, that Lord Graybourn just might prefer Elsbeth to Suzanne. That would delight Suzanne and put her in my debt." She beamed a smile up at him. He wanted to have her atop him, bringing him deep inside her, her back arched, her head thrown back. He drew in a deep breath. "All right," he said. He raised his hand, his fingers lightly touching the tip of her nose. "You are beautiful and ruthless and loyal. You are the most splendid wife a man could have."

"If you ever forget it, I will hurt you badly," she said as she lightly punched her fist into his belly, quickly kissed his mouth, and stepped back, whistling like a boy. Once she knew how it would be when she was astride him, he wondered how she would whistle then. He grinned shamelessly after her.

There was no reason to send a messenger to Suzanne. Both Justin and Arabella heard the sound of carriage wheels in the drive. They turned to see the Talgarth carriage draw to a standstill in front of Evesham Abbey. He felt a moment of surprise to see Lady Talgarth follow her daughter out of the carriage. It had stopped raining, although Lady Talgarth was eyeing the sky with some disfavor. She obviously didn't trust the weather. Neither did he.

The earl said to his wife, "I wonder. Do you believe that Lady Talgarth has decided to forgive Ann for marrying Paul? I had rather hoped she would hold firm. I have always had an affinity for gossiping biddies. I dislike having to revise my opinions."

She laughed. Together they walked forward to greet their guests. He left his wife so that he could clasp the lovely Suzanne's gloved hand and give her a formal bow. "Why, Miss Talgarth, how very brave of you to venture forth in such bad weather. Although it has stopped raining—just for your visit—I do fear for the immediate future. You bring no ill news, I trust."

Suzanne dimpled, shot an amused glance at Arabella, and said, "No, my lord, Mama and I are here with a bit of grand news. Aren't we, Mama?"

Lady Talgarth looked like she'd swallowed a caterpillar. She managed to smile, but it fell away when Ann came into the room. Civil greetings were managed, just barely. "Ah," she said, "here is tea. However, I do not see any lemon seed cake."

"I will send Crupper to see if there is any left," Lady Ann said, smiling behind her hand.

Suzanne said, "Mama, I just told the earl that we bring no ill tidings. In fact," she added, now looking at Arabella, "we are here to issue an invitation."

Lady Talgarth choked on her tea. Ann gently thumped her broad back, which was covered with a bright purple brocade.

"Yes," Suzanne said, "an invitation."

"That sounds interesting, an invitation, you say, Miss Talgarth? Come, I am certain that neither Arabella nor I would think of disobliging you. Well, perhaps Arabella might. She wants only my company, you know, but perhaps if you are very kind and very persuasive, she might consent to this invitation of yours."

"So, it's like that, is it?"

The earl disliked that gleam in Suzanne Talgarth's lovely eyes. The minx wasn't a dolt, not at all. "Yes," he said, flicking a piece of lint from his sleeve, "it is. Behold a reformed man. As for my wife, who can possibly say? I daresay it will be a mystery that will tantalize me for the remainder of my days. Now, what is your invitation?"

"Such a pity that I did not meet you first, my lord."

"Suzanne," Arabella said, "I will cosh you into the carpet if you don't get to the point. Just look at your dear mama. She wants to issue an invitation yet you won't stop talking long enough to let her."

"I have always believed you were a baggage, Miss Talgarth," the earl said.

Lady Talgarth cleared her throat. Her massive bosom trembled. "We are here," she said in a ringing voice, "to invite you to a card party tonight, with dancing naturally for the young people. Even though you and Arabella are married, you must still be considered

young, so I imagine that you would enjoy dancing. As
for you, my dear Ann, I suppose that you must come
also. Dr. Branyon as well. He is my husband's physician, as you know. Hector thinks highly of him. Yes,
he must attend as well, there is no hope for it, no matter
what one would wish. However, there is no call for you
to dance, since you are a mother of a grown woman
and a fairly recent widow."

"No indeed," Lady Ann said without hesitation.
"What a wonderful idea. Why, I do believe, dear Aurelia, that you can give me advice on my wedding
trousseau."

"I would know nothing of such things."

"Mama, of course you would. Did you not wed Papa
before you birthed me?"

"Suzanne! Mind your tongue or I will tell your father!"

"Do tell him in front of Lord Graybourn, all right?
Please, Mama?"

When the earl led Lady Talgarth to the carriage, Arabella tugged at Suzanne's sleeve. "However did you
bring your mother around?"

"Well, it wasn't difficult at all, Bella. Papa and Dr.
Branyon have been friends for too many years to allow
such silliness to sour their acquaintance. Of course, I
slipped in that Dr. Branyon was, after all, *her* doctor as
well. 'Why, Mama,' I said, 'whatever would happen if
you became ill? Why, there would be no one about to
prescribe for you. After all, you could not expect Dr.
Branyon to want to see you fit and well if you insulted
his lady wife, now would you?' She quite came around
at that point. Am I not a veritable Socrates? Or do I
want to be a Solomon? It is difficult, these sorts of decisions. And these were men, after all. What could they
possibly know?"

Arabella just stared at her lifelong friend. "You terrify me, Suzanne. That was just excellent."

"Well, Mama doesn't want to be ostracized, you

know. She isn't stupid. She will come around completely once Lady Ann does the deed."

Then it struck her. A card party with dancing would be perfect. It was the comte's last evening here. What better way to keep him from Elsbeth?

Suzanne kissed Arabella quickly on the cheek, then turned to the earl. She smiled at him pertly, then held out her hand.

The earl looked faintly amused. He took her hand and carried it to his lips. He said, "Do not wed Lord Graybourn, Miss Talgarth. You would send the poor fellow stuttering off a cliff. No, you need a gentleman who will beat you daily and tell you jests. You must also remember that Arabella is as fierce as a tiger. If you continue with your outrageous remarks, she just might challenge you to a duel. She is very accomplished, Miss Talgarth. I am a caring fellow. I warn you for your own good."

Suzanne tossed her blond curls and smiled impishly at Arabella. "Oh, Bella is far too certain of her own accomplishments to ever be concerned about mine. She would never hurt me, she would see no need. She would just laugh and tell me to hie myself off to buy a new pair of gloves."

Suzanne gave a trill of laughter and moved with Arabella to the door. She confided in a carrying voice, "Do you know that Mama absolutely refused to allow poor Lord Graybourn to accompany us this morning? As I said, she isn't stupid. She knows that he is taken with Elsbeth." A look of rather morbid satisfaction crossed her face. "I daresay it would serve her right. First you catch an earl, and now Elsbeth seduces my eligible suitor from right under my nose."

"As if you cared," the earl said as he gave Miss Talgarth a salute, then turned away. It amused him to realize that Lady Talgarth was the one to provide him with the perfect solution, a final test of the comte's greed.

This was Gervaise's last chance and the earl knew he would take it. He met Arabella's eyes. She knew it as well.

It was over luncheon that the earl informed the others of the invitation.

"I was pleased," Lady Ann said, waving her fork at him. "I never believed she would come around. But it is pleasant, is it not, to have neighbors to care for you?"

"Ann," the earl said, "you are too gullible, too forgiving. It frightens me."

"No," she said easily, spearing a thin sliced piece of ham on her fork, "not at all. The old witch knows what is what. She has had to swallow her ridiculous antiquated notions, and it quite makes me want to laugh."

"Mama, you astound me. You really said that, didn't you? And you look so very sweet."

"Yes, dear, I know." She ate another piece of ham and smiled at all of them impartially.

Arabella saw a series of rather mixed emotions flit across Elsbeth's face and wondered what her sister was thinking. While Arabella was looking at Elsbeth, the earl's eyes were upon Gervaise's finely chiseled features. He was certain that he saw a momentary darkening in the young man's eyes, then a slight smile of satisfaction about his mouth.

Yes, you bastard, the earl was thinking. You make your plans for tonight. Then I'll have you. The expression was gone in the next instant, and Gervaise's face was wreathed in smiles of innocent anticipation for a simple evening's pleasure.

After the ladies discussed at some length the appropriate gowns to be worn for the evening, the earl sat back in his chair and said easily, his face filled with bonhomie, "We are now blessed with the sun. Since it is the comte's last day with us, why don't you ladies take him for a final outing around the countryside?"

Elsbeth felt a tug of surprise. Arabella patted her hand and said, "That is an excellent idea. Indeed, I believe we shall stop by Talgarth Hall and invite Suzanne and perhaps Lord Graybourn to accompany us. What do you think, Gervaise?"

"I only ask that you keep your distance from the old abbey ruins," Lady Ann said, waving her fork at her daughter.

"I have promised, Mama," Arabella said. "No more ruins for me." She smiled toward her husband.

Lady Ann blinked. Thank God, she thought, thank God. They had worked things out. Justin no longer believed that the comte was her lover. But who was? Or had he been utterly deluded? She chanced to look at Elsbeth. She very nearly dropped her fork. Her stepdaughter was looking at Gervaise with her heart in her eyes. Oh dear, Lady Ann thought. Oh dear. It couldn't be true, could it? But then she realized that it had to be true.

And both Arabella and Justin knew. What was she to do? She wished Paul was here right now, right at this very instant.

With only the slightest of hesitation Gervaise replied gallantly, "I would be most delighted to be in the company of three such lovely ladies. And you, my lord? Will you also accompany us?"

"Unfortunately," the earl said as he swirled the deep red wine about in its crystal glass, "I must remain here. The carpenters are here again to see to those loose floorboards in the master suite."

Without pause, Gervaise said, "It is I who will have the enjoyable afternoon, my lord."

"I trust so," the earl replied pleasantly. "Since you are leaving on the morrow."

The estate carpenter thought it rather odd to spend his afternoon pounding useless nails into the solid floor of the earl's bedchamber, but he said nothing.

When the earl entered his bedchamber near to teatime, ostensibly to inspect the carpenter's work, he cheerfully praised the now overly secure floorboards.

"Actually, my lord," Turpin said, scuffing the toe of his boot on one of the over-nailed boards, "there was very little to be done. Of course, what there was to be done, I did an excellent job, as you would expect, as I would expect from myself."

The earl smiled at him. "I agree, Turpin. Here is a guinea for your labor."

Turpin accepted the undeserved piece of gold, gathered his tools, and made his way after the earl from the grand suite. He would never understand the Quality, never.

Lady Ann tracked the earl down in the estate room. "Justin, I would speak to you, if you don't mind."

He set down the ledger, giving her a guilty grin. "Please, Ann, do come in and speak all you want. I admit that I have read this page three times now and still have not gathered together a correct total. I miss Arabella. I can see clearly that she will save my wits in the future."

"I just realized at luncheon that you and Arabella have come together. I am more pleased than I can say. It was also evident that both of you have guessed then that it is the comte and Elsbeth, not the comte and my daughter."

He gently laid his quill down on the desk. "I would have spoken to you, Ann. Your daughter has forgiven me my stupidity, my blindness. She has told me that since I am her other half that not to forgive me would be the same as not forgiving herself. It is a logic that isn't all that logical to me, but since I am the beneficiary of the logic, then I readily accept it.

"I love your daughter, Ann. I would give my life for her. I will spend the remainder of my days on this earth making up for my mistake." His smile widened. "I doubt not that Arabella will see that my nose is often rubbed in the dirt."

"Tell me how you came to believe that she deceived you in the first place."

And he did. All of it, not sparing himself. "I was a fool, yet I was so very certain because of what I had seen."

"Did Arabella tell you that she has what I called her private place in the barn? She would go there even when she was a young child when she was unhappy, when she was furious with her father or with me, when she was uncertain what to do. She obviously went there the day before your wedding because she wanted to think about how her life would change.

"It is a pity that you were there and saw her. It is more a pity, indeed it is a tragedy that Elsbeth is Gervaise's lover. I don't know what to do about that, Justin. Obviously you and Arabella have discussed it."

"Yes, but neither of us is really thinking about it until, well, until after the comte leaves."

"Why did Gervaise come here, Justin?"

"You know more than you are telling, don't you, Ann?"

"Oh no. It's just that there are so many mysteries, so many unanswered questions, indeed, so many questions that have never been asked. I don't trust Gervaise. I would like to know why you have allowed him to remain."

But the earl just shook his head. He wasn't about to tell Ann that he and Arabella wanted the comte to make his move tonight. He didn't want to worry her. Also, he didn't want her to take matters into her own small white hands. He didn't know if the mother was possibly as unpredictable as the daughter. No, he wouldn't take the chance. "You and I can discuss it perhaps tomorrow, Ann. When Paul is here. Is that all right?"

"You're lying to me," she said, sighing. She rose, shaking out her primrose skirts. "I am pleased that you and Arabella have mended your fences. As to the rest of it, well, I will speak to Paul, you may be certain of that. If he comes after you tonight at the Talgarths', you will know what he wants, Justin."

"Yes, I'll know," the earl said.

30

her face. In his arms, so warm. Smiling. She reached up, caressed his cheek, traced his mouth. Smiling, he whispered, "Now I want to see you singing. Actually I wish I only heard you, then I might be content..." That mouth closing over her mouth, caressing, caressing, tasting... "You will be here when I wake, won't you?"

"Yes, I will," he said.

When everyone arrived back late in the afternoon from their explorations, Arabella immediately excused herself and went to the earl's suite. She eyed the floorboards and grinned. While Grace was fetching her bath, Arabella restlessly paced her room. Where was her husband?

He strode into the huge bedchamber while she was singing a high G at the top of her lungs in her bathtub.

"If I weren't looking at you, I would believe that I had a screeching magpie in my bedchamber. Goodness, Arabella, did you not have voice lessons?"

"You're back! Where have you been?" She realized that he was staring pointedly at her breasts, and waved her hand at him. "Look at my face or you will make me blush like the maiden I was until just a short time ago. Yes, that's better. No, you're still staring at me. All right, my lord." She stood up, sending the water sloshing over the sides of the tub.

"Oh my God."

She grabbed the towel off the stool beside the tub and quickly held it in front of her.

"I wish you hadn't done that," he said, disappointment stark in his voice. He sounded almost as if he wanted to cry. "Perhaps you would consider dropping that towel? You're beautiful. Do we have time before we must dress for dinner? Ten minutes would suffice, maybe less. Indeed, much less."

She stared at him. "You want me? Now?"

"Yes."

"Well, actually, it is very likely that I could also be wanting you, very much, right at this very moment. You say less than ten minutes?"

She dropped the towel, looked at him and said, "Justin. The thought of ten minutes or less with you makes me shake. A full night would make me shake harder, but I shan't quibble. One takes what one can get when one can get it."

"I love your brain. Yes, let's do—"

There was a knock on the bedchamber door. "My lady?" It was Grace.

Arabella grabbed the towel from at her feet. "Damn," she said. "Oh damn. It's Grace." She wagged her finger at her husband. "You will come back very soon and tell me what you found this afternoon in the comte's room."

He gave her a small salute, his voice filled with a wealth of sorrow. "I would rather you dropped that towel for me again." He sighed deeply and laid his palm over his heart. He turned on his heel and disappeared through the adjoining door.

She was seated in front of her dressing table, Grace behind her arranging a dark blue ribbon through her black hair, when the earl reappeared, a black jewelry box in his hand.

"Ah," he said, "you haven't yet selected a necklace for that gown." The gown in question was a pale silvery gray, quite flattering, and Arabella hated it for what it represented. At least it wasn't black.

"No," she said, eyeing him in the mirror, "I haven't picked anything." She looked at that jewelry box in his hand. Slowly, very slowly, teasing her, he opened it, but held it away from her. "Your father told me to give this to you after we were married. He said it belonged to his grandmother, that he had never given it to either of his wives. He said that it was to be yours." The earl held it out to her.

Arabella sucked in her breath. It was a three-strand necklace of perfectly matched pale pink pearls. There were earrings and a bracelet to match. She had never seen anything so beautiful in her life. She fingered the pearls, pressing them into her palm. They felt warm to the touch. "Ah, Justin, put them on me."

He leaned down, kissed the nape of her neck, ignoring Grace who was quite interested in this connubial behavior, and fastened the pearls around her neck. Arabella looked at herself in the mirror. "I had hated the gray gown until just this moment," she said.

"And now?"

"The pearls—they make it seem to glisten. It's amazing. The pearls are nearly as beautiful as you, my lord. Thank you."

She heard Grace sigh, and added, "Naturally, the earrings are far more intriguing than you could ever be, but nonetheless, there is still the bracelet. Regardless of where you fall in the spectrum, you are still adequate."

She was laughing as she turned around. "Grace, thank you for your help. Please excuse his lordship and me. We are newly wedded and thus are quite silly. His lordship has convinced me it is a requirement of persons not married longer than twenty years."

"I believe I said forty years."

Grace didn't want to leave, that was obvious, but as Arabella just kept looking at her, she was forced to curtsy and quit the bedchamber, her footfall heavy.

The earl laughed, leaned down, and kissed Arabella's neck again. "Are you certain they are as beautiful as I am?" he whispered, then lightly bit her neck.

She leaned back against him. "I don't wear so many clothes. It would be simple, but—"

He eased his hands down her bodice. Her flesh was warm and soft and he thought he'd never survive the assault. "No," he said. "No, there isn't time. Actually two minutes would be enough, but then you would disdain me because I was a pig." Slowly, he lifted his hands out of her gown. His palms tingled. He managed to draw away from her, but it was difficult. It was late and he knew it, dammit. "Put on the bracelet and earrings. We must go downstairs, curse the lateness and the heavens."

She giggled, a perfectly delightful sound to her husband. He closed his eyes a moment, breathing in her particular woman scent, listening to that giggle. They were so much alike—two stubborn mules—and yet so wonderfully different from each other. Thank God.

It wasn't until they were all seated in the Deverill carriage that Arabella realized she didn't know if Justin had found anything of significance in Gervaise's bedchamber. Nor did she know if he had made any plans this evening.

It didn't matter. She wouldn't let the comte out of her sight this evening. Her eyes were slits as she gazed across the narrow space at him, seated next to Lady Ann, Elsbeth on her other side. It was well done of her mother to keep them separated. Obviously, Arabella thought, her mother now knew the lay of the land. She well imagined that her mother was as filled with questions as she was.

Talgarth Hall was a low, rambling mansion in the Georgian style, erected by the father of the present Lord Talgarth. A mere upstart mushroom, Arabella's father had once remarked as he gazed upon his own awesome mansion, Evesham Abbey. Still, to be fair, it was a lovely house, rendered more so on this moonlit night by the bright candlelight shining through its myriad sparkling windows, lighting the carriages of the local gentry in attendance. Roaring flambeaux were held by a score of footmen, most of which had been hired in for the occasion, Suzanne had told Arabella that afternoon behind her hand, giggling. "Mama," she had told Arabella, "had to instruct them first what flambeaux were—most of them thought it was some sort of dish to eat—and then what they were to do with them."

With a flourishing bow, the earl opened their carriage door and solicitously assisted each lady to alight. Arabella was the last, and as Justin took her hand, her fingers tightened about his.

"Come, love," he said quietly, "all will be well, you will see. Just stay close to your mother and Dr. Branyon. I will take care of everything."

She searched his face. There was no expression there save for the stark danger she read in his eyes. "The devil you will," she said just as quietly. "You cannot put me in a closet to keep me safe. I am part of this, Justin. If you forget again, I will have to do something perfectly outrageous." He felt her hand moving down the front of his britches. He grabbed her hand and drew it up to his mouth, kissing her palm.

"I won't forget," he said. "But heed me, I am your husband and I will take care of the comte. You will do exactly as I tell you. I will take no more chances with your safety. I mean it. Obey me, Arabella."

Her chin went into the air. She pulled her hand away from his and marched up the stairs of the Talgarth mansion, Lady Ann and Elsbeth following after her. As for the comte, he already awaited all of them at the top of the stairs.

Lady Talgarth swooped down upon them before the butler could announce them formally, her overly bright, toothy smile embracing them all, except possibly, Lady Ann. "Ah, my dears, how very delightful. My *dear* Ann, how very exquisite you are this evening. The gray is so much less black than it should be, don't you agree? Of course, I should never be seen wearing a color that did not show proper respect, but all of us are different, are we not?"

"Very different, thank the good Lord," Arabella said. "Come, Mother, let us mingle." She grabbed her mother's hand and dragged her into the vast ballroom of Talgarth Hall. Every neighbor in the entire area was present. Flocks of brightly colored peacocks, Arabella thought, a magnificent sight.

"Really, my darling," Lady Ann said, laughter lurking in her voice, "you show her no pity."

"She's a bitch," Arabella said, her voice indifferent. "But who cares? You certainly don't. I know Suzanne will be much better off when she is married and away from her. I just hope she can find someone as splendid as Justin for her husband. But I fear there is no other man to match him."

"Spoken like a girl blindly, madly, in love," Lady Ann said. "I am pleased, dearest. I spoke with Justin, as you have probably already guessed. He told me everything. Well, I don't know if that's true or not. At least he told me enough. You and I will discuss it later." She was already searching about her. "Has Paul arrived yet, I wonder? Unfortunately, I was unable to see him during the day, as you know. Or perhaps you don't, since you're so involved with your husband."

Now that, Arabella thought, keeping her mouth firmly closed, was an understatement. "Oh look, Mama, there's Suzanne. Isn't she lovely? I love that shade of pink on her."

Suzanne was soon whirling about them. She clasped Lady Ann's hands. "How beautiful you look, Lady Ann. And you, Bella. Goodness, just look at those pearls. They're exquisite. Where did you get them? Oh, don't tell me. Your handsome husband gave them to you, didn't he?"

Arabella actually blushed. It was amazing, Lady Ann

thought, staring at her. "I have never seen them before and they look to be quite old," she said slowly.

"Justin said that my father gave them to him to give to me after we were married. He did, this evening."

"Oh, my love," Lady Ann, "you are my precious and Justin's as well. Isn't life grand?"

"I think so," Arabella said slowly, for out of the corner of her eye, she saw Gervaise dancing with Elsbeth. She was not about to forget that she must keep him under view for the entire evening. Surely he would try something. She knew it as well as Justin did.

She also saw Suzanne curtsy to the earl, heard her laughing voice. "I vow a score of young ladies have been fluttering about the past hour or more waiting to meet you, my lord. You will not stick to Arabella's side all evening, will you? No, of course you won't, a gentleman has to flaunt himself, show the world that he doesn't wear his heart on his sleeve."

"I am yours to command," the earl said. Arabella watched him, her expression filled with hunger, had she but known it, when he asked a young lady to dance with him.

Arabella turned to find Gervaise at her elbow. *"Monsieur,"* she managed in a creditably calm voice, "Will you not join us? There are many people you must meet." *Yes, you bastard, let's just see what you will do this evening.*

There was an instant of hesitation in his dark eyes before he said easily, "But of course, Arabella, I am your servant, as always." Arabella introduced him to Miss Fleming and watched the two of them take their places in a country dance.

"Mama," Arabella whispered, "look over by the fireplace. Poor Dr. Branyon, held captive in conversation by the gouty Lord Talgarth. He looks desperate, Mama. His eyes are glazing. I believe you'd best go rescue him before he takes a fireplace poker to his host."

"By all that's wonderful, but you are a marvelous daughter." Lady Ann kissed her daughter's cheek and was off, her step as light and happy as a young girl's.

Arabella next introduced Gervaise to the quiet Miss Dauntry, the fourth daughter of a fondly doting mother. As he turned to lead the young lady to the dance floor, Arabella saw Lord Graybourn sweep by with Elsbeth on his arm. He was, surprisingly, a very graceful dancer. Elsbeth was laughing up at his face. This certainly looked promising.

Suzanne whirled by with Oliver Rollins firmly in tow. He was a chubby, well-meaning young man, whom Arabella had bullied mercilessly from their childhood. Suzanne called out to her, all gaiety, "Do not fret, Bella, I shall send one of *my* gallants to dance with you. But you must give up the earl, for we have an overabundance of young ladies tonight."

Oliver Rollins managed a stuttering hello before being borne away.

Arabella turned at a tap of a fan on her arm. Lady Crewe, a formidable dowager of indeterminate years and bright red hair that was still untouched by gray, stood at her side, two great purple ostrich plumes swinging about her angular face. "You are looking fit, Arabella. I see that marriage agrees with you. It's rare, you know, fine marriages, that is. Except when it involves money, of course. But you two young people— both of you looking as besotted as my peacock Larry and his peahen Blanche. A fine choice your papa made, and I would tell him so if he were here.

"Damn, I wish he weren't dead. I'm sorry to remind you, my dear, but I know you loved him very much." She patted Arabella's hand even as her brilliant hazel eyes swept across the room to rest a moment on the earl, creditably performing his part in the country dance with the very buxom Miss Eliza Eldridge. "Yes," Lady Crewe said more to herself than to Arabella, "the new earl is a fine figure of a man. How very like your papa he appears. And you as well. You look so alike, the two of you. You will have handsome children. Your father would have been mightily pleased."

"I hope," Arabella said, looking at her husband, "that we will have a score of children. And yes, they will be handsome, you are right about that. I just hope they all have clefts in their chins, like my father and Justin. My father made an excellent choice."

Lady Crewe paused a moment and turned a large ruby ring about her thin finger. "Perhaps your mama will be surprised, Arabella, but I do not fault her for marrying Dr. Paul Branyon, as does poor Aurelia Talgarth. Silly woman! All her nonsense about his not being a lord, not being of our class, why, it is really too absurd." Her eyes were shrewd. "You are open, Arabella. I like that. Your father never really was, but that's neither here nor there. I can see that you, my dear Arabella, have given your approval to your mama's marriage to Dr. Branyon. It's wise of you. It shows a maturity that is refreshing as it is pleasing."

"My mother is very beautiful and too young to spend her life alone. Also, I am very fond of Dr. Branyon. I have known him all my life. There is no kinder man. I'm pleased he will be my step-papa."

Lady Crewe was still looking toward Lady Ann. She said slowly, her voice meditative, "I will tell you, my dear, that for the first time in nearly twenty years I have found something admirable about your mother besides her immense sweetness and good looks. At last she has shown character and spirit that match her beauty. I do believe it came quite easily to her, proving it was there all the time." She added very quietly, "Your father was a very strong man, a very dominant man who wouldn't accept a female ever questioning him. Yes, your mother has come into her own now."

Arabella, who was still trying to keep the comte in

view, was a bit distracted. "Yes, ma'am," she said briefly.

Lady Crewe mistook her response. "Now, Arabella, you are a married lady. I have marveled at the fact that your mother survived these nineteen years and has still retained her youthful bloom. Perhaps God, in his infinite wisdom, does reward the innocent."

She caught Arabella's attention fully. She turned to Lady Crewe and in her eyes was an understanding that she would not have had, had Justin not spoken frankly to her about her father. She looked searchingly at Lady Crewe, noting the traces of beauty still evident on her proud face. She knew then that Lady Crewe and her father had been lovers. She felt no anger, only a mildly detached acceptance of the fact. She finally accepted that her father had been a man, an adult, and she had been a child, blindly believing him to be perfect. But she was no longer a child.

Lady Crewe had, of course, observed the new maturity on the young countess's face, seen the understanding then the acceptance in her eyes—her father's eyes. She said kindly, "Do come and call on me, Arabella. I believe that we would have many interesting things to discuss. I have stories to tell you about your papa, stories, perhaps, that you don't know. He was an amazing man."

"I shall, ma'am," Arabella said. She realized that she did indeed wish to further her acquaintance with Lady Crewe. She left the older woman's side to join the dancing with Sir Darien Snow, a long-time crony of her father's. He smelled faintly of musk and brandy, a pleasing combination. She saw somewhat sadly that the years were gaining inexorably upon Sir Darien, deep lines etched about his thin lips and eyes, knots of veins on the backs of his hands. He was as gentle and unassuming as her father had been loud and boisterous. Undemanding as always, he led her through the steps with the practiced grace of long years in society. He didn't speak, which relieved her. She had to keep her eye on the comte. She saw him dancing with Elsbeth. Damn, if only there were some way to get Elsbeth suddenly on the other side of the ballroom. She tugged on Sir Darien's arm, taking the lead from him, to draw closer to Elsbeth and Gervaise. At least she wanted to hear what they were saying. As they drew near, she heard Gervaise say in his lilting caressing voice, "How lovely you are this evening, *ma petite*. These English parties seem to agree with you."

Then they were swept away in the crush of other dancers, and she was unable to hear any more. If only she could have heard more.

At that moment, Elsbeth was saying to the comte, "Thank you, Gervaise. I do much enjoy dancing and parties. My aunt was rather retiring and did very little entertaining." Elsbeth paused a moment before continuing, a hint of guilt in her voice, "I really should write to my aunt Caroline. She has shown me only kindness, you know. She will of course wish to visit us after we are married." How odd that sounded to her ears, somehow unnatural, somehow forced.

He said nothing, but there was a quiver in his hands. "Yes," he managed to say finally. He gazed down at his half-sister, her dark eyes bright and almond-shaped, as were his. He knew her simple innocence, her unquestioned trust of those about her. If only that wretched old servant Josette had told him sooner that he was not the natural son of Thomas de Trécassis, indeed, that he and Elsbeth were born of the same mother. Thank God he hadn't made love to her that last time, after Josette had screamed at him that Elsbeth was his half-sister.

He would be gone soon, gone with what was rightfully his. Yet, somehow, he wanted to lessen the pain Elsbeth would feel upon his leaving. He missed a step in the dance and trod upon her foot. He was instantly contrite. "How very clumsy of me, Elsbeth, do forgive me, *petite*. You see, there are many things I do not do well."

She smiled up at him, but her smile faltered. She sensed a sadness in him, and replied quickly, "It is nothing, Gervaise. Do not speak like that, I beg you. You do yourself an injustice."

"No, Elsbeth, it is true. I—I am really quite unworthy of you." He paused, realizing they were dancing in the middle of the dance floor. "Come," he said, taking her hand. "I wish to speak to you. Let us go out on the balcony."

31

Elsbeth followed the comte without hesitation, unaware that every member of her family was watching them closely.

It was chilly outside this evening, but Elsbeth didn't feel it at all. She turned to look at him, lifting her face for a kiss, but he took a step away from her. "No, Elsbeth, you must listen to me. I have done much thinking, little cousin. Our plan to go away together, it is impossible. You must see that, Elsbeth. I would be the most dishonorable of men to take you from your family, to expose you to a life full of uncertainties and that would be all that I could offer you."

She could but stare at him, her mouth agape. "No," she whispered, "no. Why are you saying this? Gervaise, no, you cannot mean it. How can you say there will be uncertainties? There will be no uncertainties. Have you forgotten my ten thousand pounds? As my husband, the money would belong to you. You are very wise, Gervaise. We would have no uncertainties."

"Husband," he repeated, his voice low and harsh. "*Your* husband? Come, Elsbeth, it is time that you learned more of the realities of life. It is time you became a woman. You can no longer behave as a child."

"I don't know what you mean. What is this? What is in your mind? If there are any problems, I can help you. I am a woman now, you made me into a woman. Did

you not teach me what it was to be a grown woman?"
Without thinking, she took a step toward him.

He held up his hand. "You are such a romantic child.
Just listen to yourself." He managed a fine sneer and
forced his voice to mockery. "All I did, Elsbeth, was
take your virginity, caress your girl's breasts, and provide you with a romantic summer idyll, nothing more."

Her face paled with shock at his words. "But you
said you loved me," she whispered. She shivered, not
from the chill of the air, but from the burgeoning fear
deep inside her.

He shrugged, such a Gaelic gesture of indifference,
of contempt, she didn't know. "Of course I told you I
loved you. If you were a woman and not a child, you
would have known that passionate words of love make
an *affaire* all the more exciting and pleasurable."

There was such darkness, such emptiness, she couldn't
bear it. No, he couldn't be saying these things. She wet-
ted her lips. "But you told me you loved me and you
meant it, I know it, just as I know you."

"Of a certainty I love you," he said coldly, "as my . . .
cousin. It would be unnatural were I not to care for you
in that way."

"Then why did you tell me we would elope together?
Do you not recall your promises to me?"

He laughed unpleasantly, a sound that made her
shrivel, made something die deep inside her. She didn't
move. She didn't think she could move, no matter
what. He shrugged again, dismissing her as anyone
even deserving of love, "I said only those things you
wished to be told, Elsbeth. A wife will never be a part
of my plans. That you chose to believe otherwise
must show you that you are naught but a romantic
child. Come, my dear, it is time for you to emerge from
your sweet cocoon of innocence. Thank me for telling you the truth now. It's kinder than leaving you to

uncertainty. You would never have heard from me again, you know."

"Was I really such a child to give myself freely to you?"

He hated the tears brimming in her eyes, hated them, but he held firm, his voice as cool as the evening breeze that was making gooseflesh rise on her bare arm. "Yes, you were. Listen to me, you desired substance and reality when there was naught but dreams and phantoms. You must learn to face life, Elsbeth, not cower and weep like a helpless child. You will thank me one day. Hearts do not break—another piece of foolish nonsense. You will forget me, Elsbeth, you will forget me, and grow strong, become a woman. Do you begin to understand?" His eyes softened, yet she did not notice, for her head was bowed. He didn't need to pull his watch from his pocket to see that it was getting late. He must leave soon. He said now, quickly, "You are English, Elsbeth. Your future belongs in England, wedded to an English gentleman. You have tasted a brief *affaire de coeur*. It is over now. No, no more crying. Please, Elsbeth—" He lightly cupped her cheek with his palm. "Please, do not remember me with hatred."

"Yes," she said, looking at him now, "it is over." She swallowed her tears. Her back straightened. "Please take me back to Lady Ann."

After Gervaise left Elsbeth, he gazed about the crowded room, his eyes resting finally upon the earl. He didn't seem to be aware of anyone else in the room save the young lady he was speaking to. Soon Gervaise would never see him again, never have to feel his damning hatred of him, know that he wanted to kill him. Soon Gervaise would be the winner, the earl the loser, and it would be over and there would be nothing the earl could do about it. Indeed, the earl would never know. Damn, he wished he could know. He would leave him a sign, perhaps even a letter, so he would grind his teeth, knowing that he'd been beaten.

He watched him for a few minutes more, then turned to take the hand of Miss Rutherford. He saw Elsbeth being led onto the dance floor by Lord Graybourn, and his eyes darkened for an instant. No, he had to forget her. He whirled Miss Rutherford suddenly in his arms. She gasped and laughed in delight.

At the close of the dance, Arabella allowed Sir Darien to take her back to her mother. Lady Ann said complacently, "It appears that Elsbeth is quite popular tonight. I was worried when I saw her go onto the balcony with Gervaise, but he brought her back into the room soon enough so that I didn't have to interfere. I trust she will be all right. She is laughing with Lord Graybourn. That is a good sign."

Arabella didn't say a word, merely nodded.

"And as for you, my dear, I saw you speaking with Lady Crewe. That woman has always scared me witless. I remember once when she was visiting on a weekend, she told me that my gown was too girlish and that I was to go change it. I remember your father looking me over and then agreeing with her. As you can imagine, I fled to do her bidding. Whatever did you have to talk so long about with her?"

This could lead to a pit of snakes, Arabella thought. "She is charming and not at all scary, Mama. You should speak to her again. She was filled with your praise." Where was Gervaise? Oh there he was, dancing with Miss Rutherford. Arabella said, "Sir Darien grows so frail, Mama."

Dr. Branyon said, "Nothing wrong with him, to speak of. It's merely age, my dear, merely age."

"From the stories your papa told me, Sir Darien was a wild young man—a wild man even when he wasn't so young—and perhaps he deserves to be frail now."

Dr. Branyon was aware that his future daughter-in-law

wasn't really with them. She was looking at the dance floor. He said with a smile, "I believe Justin is fetching a glass of punch for Miss Eldridge, Bella. If Miss Talgarth has her way, I fear you will have very few chances to dance this evening with your husband."

"I promise I will survive without him tonight, sir." She turned around, her eyes again searching out the comte. She heard Suzanne's bright laughter from among the throng of young people. She didn't see the comte. Her heart speeded up. She looked again, searching, searching.

He was gone.

She didn't waste time. She knew the Talgarth stables were on the east side of the mansion. She looked around for Justin, but didn't see him either. Perhaps he was already following Gervaise, without telling her. It would be just like him, curse him.

It took her several minutes to reach the long, narrow windows, pull the latch, and slip into the moonlit night. She drew a deep breath, looking immediately toward the east side of the hall where Lady Talgarth had most adamantly insisted upon designing a parterre larger and more ornate than the one at Evesham Abbey. Her result had not been happy. Just beyond it were the stables. Her eyes strained into the darkness. She saw nothing.

Then, suddenly, she saw a cloaked gentleman walking quickly to the side of the hall toward the stables. It was the comte, she knew it. No other man walked with such a cocky gait.

As the comte neared the east side of Talgarth Hall, he turned abruptly to look behind him. The moonlight fell directly onto his face, and Arabella felt her heart jump. It was indeed Gervaise. In that moment he turned again and disappeared around the side of the hall.

She had to hurry. She turned and rushed back through the open window. She searched the dance floor but did not see the earl. Well, there was no longer any time to wait. Besides, she was certain he was already outside, already waiting for the comte to appear.

She quickly realized that it would take her too long to make her way through the throng of guests. She slipped back onto the balcony, leaned over the side, and eyed the distance to the ground. It was much too great a risk jumping. Her eyes fell upon a knotty old elm tree whose wispy branches touched the far edge of the balcony. Without a thought, she ran to the end of the balcony, bundled her skirts above her knees, and reached out for the branch. She clasped it firmly in her gloved hands and swung out away from the balcony, dangling for a moment in the air before her feet connected with a knobby outgrowth on its trunk. She felt the branch groan under her weight. She paid it no heed, easing her hands along the branch until, without too much risk, she was able to drop to a lower branch. Her skirts tangled about her legs and she nearly lost her balance. She flailed the air, then managed to catch herself. Damnation, if only God had meted out justice to females, she would be wearing britches.

She looked down at the smooth grass below, took a deep breath, and kicked free of the tree. She fell lightly on her feet, then set off at a run toward the stables, clutching her bothersome skirts high above her ankles. She heard from a distance, from the other side of the hall, the loud laughter of the servants who had accompanied their masters and mistresses. Suddenly she heard the steady pounding of horse's hooves.

She quickly lowered herself to her knees behind a yew bush and waited. But a moment later, horse and rider passed her, and she saw Gervaise's pale face in the moonlight.

She forced herself not to move, counting down long seconds, until he was out of her sight. She jumped to her feet and ran to the stables. When she drew up, winded, at the lighted stable door, she found herself facing a bewildered groom, who seemed unable to do anything but stare openmouthed at her.

"Ah, er, milady?"

Arabella drew two more panting breaths, took in the patent uncertainty on the groom's face, and said with all the arrogant haughtiness of her sire, "What is your name?"

"Allen, milady."

"Quickly, Allen, I want you to saddle Miss Talgarth's mare, Bluebell, this very instant." The groom faltered. Arabella said, still more haughty, "Do as I tell you or Lord Talgarth will see to you."

That did it. Allen moved probably more quickly than he had in many a long day.

She grinned at his back. She wanted to ask him if the earl had already come and gone, but she guessed the groom wouldn't tell her the truth. She had to admit that Justin could terrify a servant more effectively than she probably could.

Arabella eyed the gentle Bluebell, and wished she had Lucifer. Well, there was no hope for it. She ignored the groom, after he'd given her a foot up, and dug her heels into Bluebell's fat sides.

Her elegant hairstyle became tangles of flying hair even before Bluebell gained the main road. She pressed the mare to a steady gallop, promising her a large pail of oats when they reached Evesham Abbey. Yes, she thought, without a doubt Gervaise was riding to Evesham Abbey. It was about the only thing she was certain of at the moment.

She knew that what she was doing was perfectly outrageous. She also knew that Justin would be furious. So be it. She was very much a part of all this and it was only fair that she see it to the end. She really had no clear idea at the moment of what she was going to do after she found out what he was up to. She wanted to kill him. Yes, that was what she would do. That would save Elsbeth from ever learning the truth. She lowered her head and kept her eyes steady on the road in front of her. The wind was cold against her face.

As she turned Bluebell onto the graveled drive in front of Evesham Abbey, Arabella was not at all surprised to see Gervaise's horse tethered to a bush just to the side of the front steps. He must have taken his horse to Talgarth Hall earlier in the day and hidden it. She reined in the panting Bluebell and slid from the saddle. Everything was eerily quiet. Only a few candles were shining from the first-floor windows. There was but one light glowing from the second floor—it was from the earl's bedchamber.

She raced up the front steps and pushed the great doors open. The entrance hall was empty. She frowned. Where were the servants?

She thought of her small pistol, safely placed in the night table beside her bed. Well, it was simply impossible to think of fetching it, with Gervaise either in or near the earl's bedchamber. She ran silently through the entrance hall, past the Velvet Room, and quietly slipped into the library. Her father's favorite brace of pistols lay in their velvet case atop the mantelpiece. She gingerly grasped the butt of one of the pistols and drew it down. She felt again tingly with excitement as she probed the barrel with the loading rod. Finally the pistol was loaded and primed.

Slowly she mounted the staircase, the gun tucked in the folds of her skirt. It was Gervaise who had chosen the time and place where she would confront him. She wondered if she were not trying to prove something to Justin. Probably so. She devoutly prayed that Justin was close by. He had to be. He'd been watching Gervaise as closely as she had.

The door to the earl's bedchamber stood slightly ajar. She saw the flicker of a single candle weave itself into bizarre shapes and dancing patterns on the opposite wall. Slowly she pressed against the door.

The earl's eyes swept the crowded room as they had at regular short intervals throughout the evening. He soon spotted Lucinda Rutherford, standing quite alone, looking for the world like a homely friendless little pug. "Damn," he said under his breath. But a short time ago—just moments ago, it seemed—he had seen Gervaise leading Miss Rutherford into a quadrille. Satisfied, he had left the large ballroom with Lord Talgarth leaning heavily on his arm to help his gouty lordship into his library. "Thank you, lad. I've had quite enough of this nonsense."

He had been gone but a moment. He looked down distractedly into Miss Talgarth's upturned face. Where had she come from? "Do forgive me, Suzanne, but I must take you to your mama."

She wanted to know what was going on, but to her credit, she just pouted a bit, patted his arm, and let him lead her to her mother.

The earl offered Lady Talgarth and Suzanne a perfunctory bow before retreating quickly to the ballroom entrance. His eyes searched the room once again for Gervaise. He was not there. He had taken the bait, and Justin knew that if he did not hurry, he would lose all, through naught but his own carelessness. But he had only been with Lord Talgarth for no more than five minutes. Damnation.

"Justin." He whirled about at the sound of his name. He saw Dr. Branyon beckoning to him. He was loath to waste a precious minute. "Arabella was searching for you," Lady Ann called. "I thought she intended to go to the balcony, but now I cannot find her. Have you seen her, Justin?"

"No, I have not. You must excuse me—when you see Arabella, tell her that I will return shortly."

"But where are you going?"

He didn't turn at Dr. Branyon's question, just kept going through the crowd of chattering guests from the ballroom. It was only when he stepped out into the clear moonlight that the force of Lady Ann's words broke upon him. Arabella had left, followed the comte.

He would strangle her. He would thrash her. He would burn her ears until she was whimpering. His damned wife, she had gone after Gervaise. Oh God, it could be dangerous. Gervaise had absolutely nothing to lose. He would do anything to gain what he wanted. And now that Justin knew exactly what he was after, he knew Arabella would be in grave danger if she happened to confront him.

He gained the stables in a trice. The groom stood in the doorway, fidgeting nervously. He was not certain whether he should have sent a message to Lord Talgarth that the Countess of Strafford had taken Miss Talgarth's horse.

The earl bust in upon the groom. "My horse is the bay stallion already saddled in the far stall. Bring him to me at once."

The gentleman had brought his horse over early in the day. What was going on here? Was his wife running away with that young man who had first come to the stables? Oh goodness, but this was exciting. He couldn't wait to tell all the other lads.

Maybe his lordship didn't know, maybe—"My lord, her ladyship, your wife—" The words died in the still night, for the Earl of Strafford was already plunging down the drive astride his stallion. He did not look back.

When but a few moments later another young lady came to the stables and begged him to drive her to Evesham Abbey, Allen didn't hesitate. It was a drama worthy of London and he wanted to see every bit of it. Then he would tell the other lads.

* * *

Arabella stood motionless in the open doorway of the
earl's bedchamber, the heavy pistol held firmly at her
side, hidden in the folds of her skirt.

She watched Gervaise as he stood before *The Dance
of Death* panel, a candle raised high in his hand. The
image of Josette flashed through her mind. The old servant had stood just as Gervaise stood now, her eyes
searching the macabre carving.

She saw him carefully probe with his left hand into
the slight hollow recess just beneath the skeleton's
raised shield. She thought his fingers closed over
something, perhaps a small knob. As if by magic, the
lower edge of the skeleton's heavy dark wooden shield
suddenly slid away and exposed a hidden compartment, no wider than a hand's width.

So Justin had guessed something. This was why he'd
had the carpenter in here supposedly to fix loose floorboards. He didn't want Gervaise in here. She was smiling as she said, "It is a very clever hiding place,
monsieur. Perhaps Josette would have found it if I had
not interrupted her. But I'm not certain. As I remember,
she wasn't feeling close to the skeleton's shield. Perhaps her wits were clouded and she didn't remember."

She started to bring up the gun and level it at him,
but decided there was no reason to, not yet. She said
easily, "Do move aside, Gervaise."

He was staring at her, saying nothing, just staring.
"Oh yes, I watched you closely all evening. Both Justin
and I knew you would have to make your move. Did
you not wonder where all the servants were? Justin told
them to remain in the kitchen. He wanted you to be
able to come uninterrupted to this room. And you did.

"You are a despicable animal, comte."

Gervaise very slowly took a step away from the
panel. He looked surprised, then furious. Now there
was no expression at all on his too-handsome face. He
looked past her then. He thought Justin should be here,

not she. Well, he would be soon. There was no doubt in his mind that the damned earl would be here soon.

"You are looking for the earl. He will be here very soon now."

So she had no idea where the earl was. She was praying out loud, trying to convince him. He was more certain that she was, the little fool. No, she was quite alone. He smiled pleasantly at her. His hand relaxed away from the pistol at his belt and fell to his side. "Arabella, you have surprised me, I will admit it. Would it be foolish of me to ask why you are here?"

"I followed you. Like my husband, I have watched you all evening, Gervaise. I was on the balcony and saw you going to the stables. I followed you."

"A wild moonlight ride," he said, still smiling at her. "And in your ball gown. How very enterprising of you, *chère madame*. But now the time for games, the time for gallantry, is well over. I beg you won't faint. I won't hurt you."

Then he laughed.

32

Arabella looked down at her fingernails, a look of utter boredom on her face, until he stopped his laughter. "Ah, you're finished? Good. No, you're right. You won't hurt me this time, comte, but my incarceration at the abbey was a bit too close for my liking, but I believe you were by far the more enterprising. Do not let me disturb your search."

He paused a moment, then shrugged, that damned Gaelic shrug that meant everything and nothing, yet it was always insulting. "Very well. You can witness my legacy." He slipped his fingers into the small compartment. A bellow of fury erupted from his throat. "They are gone! No, it is not possible. No one knew, save Magdalaine, no one." He was feeling in the small compartment frantically now, but there was nothing there, nothing at all. He was gasping with rage and disbelief.

Arabella drew back from his sudden rage. "What is gone, *monsieur*? What did Magdalaine hide in the compartment?"

He seemed almost unaware of her presence. He was staring blankly at that empty compartment. "The Trécassis emeralds. Worth a king's ransom. Gone, gone."

For a fleeting instant Arabella pictured the smudged lines of Magdalaine's letter to her lover that she had not been able to decipher. She felt a sudden knot of anguish in her stomach. Her father had sent Magdalaine to France, in the midst of the dangerous revolution, to bring him back the emeralds. That was what Magdalaine must have meant in her letter to her lover about their becoming rich from her husband's greed. Magdalaine and her lover sought to escape Arabella's father. Had Magdalaine been fleeing from Evesham Abbey, with perhaps Elsbeth in her arms, to meet her lover at the old abbey ruins? Had her husband caught them? Murdered Magdalaine's lover? In his fury, had he also murdered Magdalaine?

She felt nauseous with the horror of what her father had done.

Gervaise had regained control of himself. He said in a more calm voice now, "My dear Arabella, I find it very curious that you are so superbly apprised of my affairs. Perhaps it is you who found the emeralds?" He took a step toward her.

"No, *monsieur,* I did not find your emeralds," she said quietly, her thoughts still on her father and the violent deaths of so long ago.

"Somehow I do not quite believe you." His hand shot out to grab her arm.

Arabella jumped back and drew the gun from the folds of her skirt. She looked at him with all the contempt she felt. "I am not such a fool, *monsieur,* as to face a murderer without protecting myself."

He eyed the gun, then stepped back. He splayed his fingers in front of him. He looked bewildered. "I promised you I wouldn't hurt you. What is this about murder? Murder, *madame?* I, a murderer? It is absurd. Come, you are weaving this all together in your girl's fantasies."

"Oh no, Gervaise, I know that you helped poor Josette to her death. It was obvious. Why should she be wandering about Evesham Abbey in the middle of the night without any light to guide her? It was careless of you not to have left a candle near her. Why did you kill her, Gervaise? Was it because I caught her in the earl's bedchamber, her hands roving over *The Dance of Death*? You were afraid she would tell me about the emeralds?"

He made no answer. She added in a still-cool, precise voice, "Or perhaps she threatened to expose you, *monsieur,* to tell everyone that you were a bastard, that you were Magdalaine's son? Did she tell you that your seduction of Elsbeth violated the very laws of nature? I only pray that Elsbeth does not ever discover that you are her half-brother. It would destroy her."

His face had gone chalk white in the dim candlelight, his dark eyes blind with bitterness and anger. His voice was harsh and grating. "No, damn you, Elsbeth does not know. I did not realize I was Magdalaine's son myself until that wretched old woman told me. Were it not for your damned interference, *madame,* and that of your wretched husband, I should be away now, free, with what is rightfully mine. None of it is my fault, none of it. I came here only to retrieve what is mine. Mine, do you hear?"

"What is rightfully yours, Gervaise? Most assuredly you're not a comte of anything. You are not even a Trécassis. You are a bastard, nothing more, nothing less. If the emeralds do exist, they would belong to Elsbeth, for she is legitimate. Nothing here belongs to you."

He stood staring at her, his mouth working, his pain and rage so deep that he could find no words.

"Damn you, where are my emeralds?"

"I have no idea. Did it not occur to you that the skeleton in the old abbey ruins was your father? I know it for a fact, for after you so obligingly entombed me in that chamber, I found a letter from Magdalaine to him in his breeches pocket. There is no doubt, Gervaise. His name was Charles. He was your father."

She saw it all come together in his dark eyes, saw the understanding, saw the string of events that had led to this day. He lunged at her. "Damn you to hell, your father killed him!" He was in a frenzy, taking her off her guard. His fingers tightened painfully about her wrist, and the pistol went spinning from her hand and thudded to the floor.

He flung her away from him, gasping, his breathing so harsh she imagined that he surely would collapse from it. She grabbed at the back of a chair to keep from falling. Arabella watched him pull the pistol from his belt. She watched him pick up her father's gun and lay it on a table beside him. His hands were shaking. Still she felt no fear of him, only anger at herself for being so foolish as to allow him to catch her unawares. If only she could get close enough, she would attack him.

"Now, my dear Arabella," he said in a soft lilting voice, as if nothing had happened, "now, I shall know the truth from you. Be quick about it for your husband must be near."

"I cannot help you, Gervaise. I don't know anything about the Trécassis emeralds."

She saw a sudden transformation in him. His dark eyes widened. He smiled at her unpleasantly. Now, for the first time, she was afraid. He said in that same soft lilting voice, "You know, my dear countess, you are really quite lovely. Perhaps it would not be a bad thing at all to have you for my companion, at least until your wealthy husband provides me with ample compensation. Of course, I would prefer the emeralds, but if you will not tell me where you have hidden them, I shall not repine. You will enjoy Bruxelles, Arabella. You will enjoy me as a lover. You will enjoy me until your husband pays for your release. Ah, but perhaps then you won't wish to return to him. What do you think?"

She laughed, actually laughed at him. She didn't know where that wonderful laughter came from, but she was thankful for it. It sounded nearly sincere to her own ears. "Do you really believe you could force me to

accompany you? Do you really believe I would allow
you to rape me? Do you really believe that my husband
wouldn't kill you with his bare hands if I hadn't managed to do it first? Do you believe in your wildest fantasies that I would prefer you to my husband? No, I can
see that you can't even dream that to your advantage.

"Now, I know nothing about your emeralds, Gervaise. Yes, now I can see that the thought of dragging
me screaming and kicking from here gives you pause.
It should because you would never know anything but
hatred from me and the threat of death. Doubt it not,
Gervaise."

She heard a man's deep voice behind her. "No, I
would kill you before my wife could, you pathetic little
bastard. And as she said, I would do it with my bare
hands."

Arabella whirled around to see the earl standing quietly in the open doorway. In his outstretched right hand
he held a pile of bright green stones, sprays of diamonds flashing around them. Huge green stones that
glittered in the dim candlelight. The de Trécassis emeralds. But Justin wasn't carrying a weapon. "Yes, *monsieur,* I have your bloody emeralds."

Her heart leapt at the sight of him, so calm, so in
control as he always was. "Justin, oh, you're here. I
knew you would come quickly. I am sorry that I lost
my gun, so very sorry. If I hadn't, surely I could have
killed him by now. Please forgive me."

"No," he said. He smiled at her, not a gentle smile,
but one that held great love and rage, an odd combination, but she understood it and accepted it. It would always be so between them, she realized in that instant.
They were so alike that they would fight like demons
from hell itself, but then there was such a deep bond
between them that it could never be severed. It would
but become stronger. She knew that as surely as she
knew that both of them would survive this night.

The earl said finally to Gervaise, "We knew you would come back tonight. There was no other choice since I had ordered you to be gone from Evesham Abbey tomorrow. Would you have left, I wonder, if you hadn't found the emeralds? Or would you have lurked about in the woods somewhere, hoping to try again?"

"No," the comte said. "I would have taken one of the women and held them captive until you returned to me what was mine. The emeralds are mine. Give them to me."

The earl only shook his head, though his hand, filled to overflowing with those emeralds, was still out-stretched toward Gervaise. "Yes, that would be a better plan. But it won't happen. Did you think me a fool, Gervaise? I knew weeks ago that you were not the Comte de Trécassis. Although my informant was uncertain as to your true heritage, I ordered him to keep looking. Yes, *monsieur,* I sought more knowledge of you. I didn't want to order you out of my house until I knew what you were about. I guessed you were a bloody little fraud, I knew you were dangerous, I just didn't realize how dangerous until after Arabella and I found Josette's body, until after I realized you had caused the collapse in the old abbey, endangering Arabella. It was then I knew it was something in the earl's bedchamber. What other room was there that you could not enter with impunity? How you must have gnashed your teeth when I kept the door locked.

"But enough. I searched your room, you know, just this afternoon while Arabella kept you out of Evesham Abbey. Without the exact instructions Magdalaine wrote to Thomas de Trécassis of the hiding place of the emeralds, I knew I should never know what it was you sought. With the instructions, it was all quite simple. The frustration you must have known all these weeks. I could almost feel pity for you if you weren't such a villainous little sod."

"Damn you, the emeralds are mine!"

The earl shook his head. He turned to Arabella. "I really wish you had remained safe at the ball."

Gervaise looked at the earl. It was all so very easy. There, the earl, all his attention riveted on his wife. The stupid man had no gun. Gervaise pointed the pistol at him. "I will have them now, my lord. Give me those damned emeralds."

The earl, to Arabella's shock, merely stared at Gervaise, his look one of boredom. Bored? "As you will, *monsieur*," the earl said. "They are really not all that important, you see."

"I don't trust you. Why didn't you bring a weapon? You are planning something, I know it. What is it?"

The earl merely shrugged. Then he tossed the necklace to Gervaise. He said nothing, merely watched as Gervaise slipped it into his pocket. He now pointed the weapon directly at the earl. "You know, my lord," Gervaise said easily, "it should have been so very simple for me to fetch the emeralds. But no, you had to meddle. You had to tell the world that there are loose floorboards, thus the locked door.

"And, Arabella, yes, she had to meddle as well. You forced me to go to desperate lengths, my lord, to retrieve what was by all rights mine. The old servant Josette was an encumbrance, with all her righteous rantings about conscience and duty. It was a pity, her death. It really does not matter now if you believe me, but I will tell you. I sought only to speak to the old woman that night, but she fled from me—afraid, she was, so afraid that she ran down the dark corridor, tripped, and fell down the stairs. As to causing the rocks to collapse in the old abbey ruins, I had no wish to harm you, Arabella, merely to empty Evesham Abbey of his lordship's interfering presence. Well, the game has taken a complicated turn, my lord, but I shall contrive. I know that you would not face me without a weapon unless you had an army of men waiting just outside this room. That is true, isn't it?"

"Perhaps. You will not know until you try to leave."

Gervaise paused, then continued in a meditative voice, "You know, my lord, I have never liked you. Arrogantly proud you are, just like the old earl, that filthy old man. Of course, I could not come for my birthright while he lived. Thomas de Trécassis cautioned me to wait, to be patient."

"No! Gervaise, no! It cannot be true! You are a thief? You are stealing from Justin?"

All of them stared blankly at Elsbeth, who stood just inside the bedchamber, breathing hard, for she had run as fast as she could up the stairs. "No, Gervaise, stop it now. You love me, don't you? At least you love me as you would a cousin? Don't do this. I cannot bear that you are doing this."

It was Gervaise who recovered first. He stared at Elsbeth, as emotionless as he would regard a stranger. "Elsbeth, you should not have come. I was just on the point of leaving. I have stolen nothing at all. I have what is mine."

"You came here just to seduce me, didn't you? It was some sort of twisted revenge?"

"No, my dear," he said, his voice oddly gentle, "I came here to find the de Trécassis emeralds. You were like a ripe plum to fall into my hands. I have always enjoyed virgins, Elsbeth, their anticipation, their fright, their little whimpers of pain. But even as a virgin you were of little interest to me. Forgive me, Elsbeth, but that wasn't what a gentleman should say to a lady, is it?"

Elsbeth drew herself up. She said very slowly, "I believe that you are no gentleman, sir. You seduced me,

you professed to love me, and you cared not a whit for
me. What did you want?"

He drew the emerald necklace from his pocket.
"This," he said. "The emeralds are mine. I came only to
get them. Now that I have them, I will leave you. I
don't wish you ill, Elsbeth. But you won't interfere
now. Stand very still, my dear girl, or you will not like
what I will do to your sister."

Arabella laughed. "I thought you told me twice, Gervaise, that you wouldn't hurt me. Why, you made me
feel like a helpless little maiden who should twitter behind her hand."

"Shut up, damn you."

"Gervaise," Elsbeth said, not moving an inch, "this is
all a mistake. Do you swear to me that you will simply
leave? Do you swear that you will not harm anyone?"

"No, my dearest cousin, I cannot swear to that. If
you weren't so utterly credulous, so completely simple,
you would realize that there are a score of men waiting
for me to emerge from Evesham Abbey. Indeed, I can't
imagine why they let you pass. Did you not see them?
You're shaking your head. Well, perhaps they were
told to remain hidden until I appeared. They also
doubtless have orders from the damned earl to kill me.
That is why he looks so calm, so arrogant.

"Though I am not by nature a murderer, unlike *your*
father, *madame,*" he said, staring at Arabella, "I do not
think, my lord earl, that I shall be overly troubled at
your unfortunate demise. It is an eye for an eye, as you
English say. Then I shall take your lovely Arabella.
She will be my hostage. I won't take Elsbeth. Ah, but
the countess is another matter. She is *his* daughter, that
dirty bastard. None of the men you have waiting for me
will dare to touch me as long as I have her. Yes, I think
this the wisest course to follow."

The earl swiftly measured the distance between him
and the comte, saw the pistol had yet to be cocked, and

dived his hand into the pocket of his cloak for Arabella's small gun that he'd taken from the bedside table.

"I hope you rot in hell with her father," Gervaise yelled as he whipped back the hammer and stepped forward even as he fired.

"Damn you, no!" Arabella threw herself in front of her husband.

33

A deafening roar rent the silence of the room. Arabella felt a great force hit dead on into her body, its impact flinging her backward. She was vaguely aware that Justin's arm was about her waist, keeping her upright. She saw Gervaise frantically leaping for her pistol on the table, his face distorted with frustrated rage. She felt Justin's arm jerk up, saw her own small pistol in his hand, and heard its staccato report. How odd Gervaise suddenly appeared. He clapped his hand to his arm and sank forward to the carpet on his knees. She heard Justin cursing.

She heard Elsbeth scream. The scream sounded so very far away. She felt a strange lassitude.

It was as if through a darkening mist that she saw her husband's face above her, and said only, "Justin, are you all right? My love, are you all right?"

Suddenly, she felt weightless, only dimly aware that the earl had lifted her into his arms. She thought she heard him speaking to her, but she could not be certain. She heard Elsbeth sobbing now and wanted to go to her sister, but she couldn't. He was holding her. She felt strangely without substance. She felt very close to nothingness.

"I am fine," she heard him say. "I'm so sorry, Arabella. I came with the pistol hidden because I knew you were here with him and I was afraid you would get hurt. Damnation, look at what my stupidity has brought. I should have walked in and shot the bastard—no words, nothing."

"No," she whispered, just a flutter of a sound. "Not your fault, none of it." She tried to focus her eyes on her husband's face, but saw instead a movement from the corner of her eye. Deep cold fear brought her momentarily back to her senses. Gervaise was staggering to his feet and moving, swiftly now, across the room to the open door. She saw him shove Elsbeth aside. She saw her sister tumble to the floor, crying out as she hit her head against a table leg.

"He is escaping."

"Don't worry, Arabella. He won't go very far at all. The little bastard was right about that. I've more than a dozen men waiting for him to appear."

She managed to focus for an instant on his beloved face above hers. "But, Justin," she said, "I wanted to kill him. He should die for what he did to Elsbeth." Then it was too much. Pain ripped through her, crushing her, dragging her into darkness so profound that she knew there would be no escape. But she didn't want to die, she didn't want to leave her husband after they had finally come together, she didn't want—

She felt the bed under her and saw her husband's face above her—naught but a pale blur. "It's all right, Arabella. Let Gervaise go. It's not important. Only you are important. Only you."

She accepted his words and was silent. Yet there was something else that was important, something she had to tell him. She struggled to keep the blackness from pulling her away, mayhap away from him forever. "Justin, you must listen to me."

"No, love, be quiet, please." She felt his hands on her gown, ripping it open.

She tried with her last ounce of strength. "I don't want to die, but I might, and you know it. You must know the truth in case I do. Justin, please, listen." Her voice was only a whisper now, raw and harsh, and he leaned very close to hear her. "Elsbeth is Gervaise's half-sister. Magdalaine is their mother. I found a letter on the skeleton in the abbey ruins. The skeleton was Gervaise's father and Magdalaine was his lover. My father, oh God, Justin, he must have killed them both."

His voice was as calm as night. "I understand, Arabella. You can trust me. You are not to worry about anything now." It was all right then. She let the darkness close over her mind and take her away from the pain.

The earl had ripped away her bodice and the silk chemise below, to bare the wound in her shoulder. The ball had entered high above her left breast. If she had not thrown herself in front of him, he thought grimly, the bullet would have gone straight through his heart. He worked with the efficiency that the years in the army had taught him, all of his energy focused on stanching the flow of blood. He wadded his handkerchief into a thick pad and pressed it over the wound. The blood welled up over his fingers. Even as he heard the servants' hurried footsteps up the stairs, pounding loudly down the corridor, he did not look up or lessen the steady pressure.

He did not even care when a man named Potter, whom the earl had hired to oversee the other ten or so men, appeared at his side, panting hard, saying at last, "We've got him, my lord. I'm sorry, but we had to shoot him."

He heard Elsbeth cry out.

"He is dead then?"

"Not yet, my lord, but I don't hold out much hope for him."

Even though he had ordered all the staff belowstairs for the evening, the sound of gunfire had, thankfully, made them disobey his orders. Giles stood panting in the doorway. "Oh my God, my lord! Oh, Jesus, what should I do?"

The earl said quickly, "Giles, ride to Talgarth Hall and fetch Dr. Branyon. Tell him that the countess has been shot and he is needed urgently. Go, quickly. Tell him, too, that it is all over."

He heard Crupper's familiar wheezing behind Giles. "Giles is bringing Dr. Branyon. Crupper, have Mrs. Tucker tear up clean linen and bring hot water. Quickly, man."

Crupper was weaving where he stood. "Yes, my lord," he finally managed. "But, my lord, let me kill the damned blighter first!"

"You can consider that later, Crupper. But first get me the cloths and the hot water."

"Yes, my lord. First things first. Of course her ladyship is more important than that piece of slime from a foreign swamp."

The earl could only shake his head. He kept the pressure on the wound. He prayed. He looked up to see Elsbeth weaving where she stood, her face white. As he looked at her, he now saw the tremendous resemblance between her and Gervaise. Never would she know, for he would never tell her, nor would Arabella. "It is all right now, Elsbeth. I am sorry that you were betrayed by Gervaise. But it is over now. You are all right. He will pay for what he has done. No, don't cry, Elsbeth, don't cry. I don't want him dead. But listen to me, sweetheart, he deserves whatever he gets."

Elsbeth fell to her knees on the floor. She began to cry, then shook her head, and dashed the tears away. "No," she said. "No, I won't cry. You're right, Justin, he's not worth it. But I wasn't crying for him. Please tell me that Arabella will be all right. Please, Justin, don't let her die. Please. It is all my fault if she dies."

"No, Elsbeth, she won't die. And none of this is your fault. I will strangle you if you ever say anything so stupid again. Now, I swear to you again that Arabella won't die. She is my life, you see. I cannot let her die or else I am nothing at all."

He turned from Elsbeth then and pressed harder on the wound. He searched his wife's pale face. She was deeply unconscious, thank God. He prayed that she would continue unconscious. There was pain to be borne. He knew the bullet hadn't gone through her shoulder. It would have to be dug out.

He wished that Gervaise was dead.

When Crupper came into the room, carrying both a basin of hot water and towels piled over his right arm, he said, "I don't believe anyone else should be allowed in here, my lord. I understand that Dr. Branyon will arrive soon. As for Miss Elsbeth, I have told Grace that she is to assist the young lady to her bedchamber. Oh, Mrs. Tucker, you're standing right at my elbow. Well, my lord, I could hardly tell Mrs. Tucker not to come in now."

"I know," the earl said.

Mrs. Tucker looked ready to faint and join Elsbeth on the floor. He said very gently, "Please, Mrs. Tucker, see Miss Elsbeth to her bedchamber. Then Grace will attend her. Thank you. I know I can trust you to keep everyone else away."

"But, my lord, what of the Frenchman?"

"Does he still live, Crupper?"

"I don't know, my lord. I will go ascertain his condition. Hopefully it is not a good condition."

"Thank you, Crupper." Justin pressed down harder. The cloth beneath his fingers was soaked with Arabella's blood. He began his prayers again. After he was certain that the bleeding was sluggish, he placed his hand on Arabella's breast to feel her heartbeat. It was rapid, but, he thought, steady. He looked down at her pale face, the heavy black lashes laying still against her cheeks. It was the plan of his own face. Except for the cleft in the chin. She didn't have it. He remembered that long ago day when he had first met her, how she had told him she didn't have the cleft. He remembered her bitterness, her anguish, her deadening grief for her father.

But now she was his. Now everything had been resolved. He wouldn't let her die. He wouldn't.

Finally, he slowly lifted the pad from the wound. He breathed a sigh of relief, for the bleeding had slowed to a trickle.

The earl did not again look up until Dr. Branyon hurried into the room. "Good God, Justin, what the devil has happened here? Giles told me that Bella had been shot by the comte. What the hell—"

The earl gently lifted the wadded pad from Arabella's shoulder, his eyes meeting Dr. Branyon's.

Dr. Branyon abruptly turned and held up his hand for Lady Ann to stop. He said curtly, "Ann, I do not want you in here. Go downstairs or go to Elsbeth and keep her with you. We will find out exactly what has happened later. I will come to you as soon as I can."

"No, damn you, Paul, no! She is my daughter!"

The earl said calmly, "Please, Ann, if Paul wants you gone, please go. Gervaise shot her thorough the shoulder. He himself is very likely dead now. Please, do as Paul says."

"Please, my darling. You would distract me. Please let me tend to your daughter as I should, Ann. Send Giles up when he arrives with my instruments."

The earl didn't say another word. He watched as Lady Ann turned slowly, grief and fear clear in every movement she made, and walked to the open door.

Paul called out, "She will survive, Ann, I promise you."

Lady Ann nodded, then thought: Elsbeth was already here? She had witnessed some of this? She would speak to her. Lady Ann picked up her skirts and ran full-tilt down the corridor.

As Dr. Branyon cleaned the wound and probed the area to determine the depth of the ball, the earl told him all that had happened. His voice was low, his choice of words placing entire blame upon himself, which Paul said, even though he never raised his face to look at the earl, was utter nonsense. "No, it's true. I was an idiot not to carry a gun with me."

"No, you feared for Arabella's safety. Now, is that all?" Dr. Branyon asked, his eyes hard upon the earl's face.

The earl thought about it. "No, there are other things, but it is not for me to tell you. I think it only fair for Arabella to tell you the rest of it and that only if she wants to. All right?"

Dr. Branyon nodded. Then he straightened. "You know that I must remove the ball when Giles arrives with my instruments. You have had experience with wounded men in battle, Justin. You must assist me."

"Yes, I will assist you. She will live, won't she, Paul? She must, you know. She is my other half."

"I know," Dr. Branyon said, looking at the young earl's face, a face he had come to know and like during the past weeks, weeks veiled in mystery and danger. And now, his Bella was lying here, close to death. But he wouldn't say that to her husband.

The earl realized that he was clasping Arabella's hand. He did not release it.

Arabella moaned.

Both men stiffened at the sound, their eyes meeting over Arabella's still figure.

"It isn't fair, Paul," the earl said, his voice harsh, raw with anger. "It isn't. It is too much for her to suffer you removing the ball from her shoulder."

For an instant Arabella felt only a great weight upon her chest. With an effort she forced her eyes to open and focus upon the faces above her. She felt bewildered. "Justin—Paul? You are both here? How very odd. Oh dear, I cannot bear this." She gasped, her back arcing. "I'm so sorry to be such a coward."

The pain was unbearable, deep and rending. She pressed her head back against the pillow as hard as she could, again arcing her back upward, trying vainly to escape. She felt a damp cloth being daubed against her forehead, strong hands clasping her shoulders, holding her steady.

Slowly she began to gain control over the dizzying, scorching pain. She bit down on her lower lip until her mind focused itself where she wished.

"My dearest, can you understand me?"

Justin's voice. He sounded so worried. She hated to hear him sound so very worried. She forced her eyes open. "Yes, my lord, what can I do for you? Just tell me and I will fix anything you require."

"Do for me? Bella, you must be brave now. Do you understand me? The ball in your shoulder must be removed. Dr. Branyon is here. He is quite perfect, you know. He will shortly be your step-papa. He loves you a great deal. He will do a good job of it. He will keep you safe."

"Gervaise distracted me, Justin. Otherwise I would have killed him. I bungled the job. I am sorry." Did she hear a laugh? Then suddenly, she was no longer aware of him, only of the vast blackness of the pain that engulfed her.

The earl did not look up from her face until Giles entered on tiptoe bearing Dr. Branyon's surgical case. He gazed at the sharp, slender scalpel and the array of other equally unpleasant instruments and said in a shaking voice, "God, how I wish we could spare her this." He had seen so many men in battle, crying out their pain until their voices were but raw sounds in their throats.

Dr. Branyon's voice was curt. "Justin, you must hold her firmly. I shall remove the ball as quickly as possible. You cannot allow her to move or I might kill her. Hold her very still." He added more gently as the earl hesitated, "Your pity cannot help her, only your strength."

The earl balanced himself over her, placing his hands upon her shoulders, unwilling at first to bear his weight upon her. He thought perhaps that she had fallen again into unconsciousness until Dr. Branyon, in a sudden sure movement, dug the scalpel into the wound.

She writhed suddenly beneath his hands, a choking cry torn from her throat.

"Damn it, hold her!" Dr. Branyon shouted.

Suddenly, Arabella saw herself whirled away, back into time, years ago. Her father stood above her, his lips curled derisively, his voice mocking. "A simple fall and you shed tears and cry out your foolish pain. I am disappointed in you, Arabella." And he had boxed her ears. "You will not act the girl again. I will not put up with it."

Gradually, her father's face because Justin's. And he was here and she knew he wouldn't leave her. She was biting fiercely down on her lower lip, tasting her own tears, trying to swallow her screams. She licked her dry lips and tasted a drop of her own blood. She gulped convulsively and gritted her teeth. She whispered to the face above her, "I will not be a coward."

The earl looked down at her helplessly. She was staring up at him. Yet she made no sound.

"Thank God, there, I've found it. Hold her firm, Justin, I must draw out the ball."

As the curved knife closed under the ball, Arabella felt a shattering explosion in her head. It was pain that was beyond anything she could possibly understand. She tried desperately to jerk away from the excruciating pain, to somehow escape it, yet she could not move. She gazed hopelessly into the blurred face above her, choked back a sob, and slid away into merciful blackness.

"Arabella!"

"She's not dead, Justin, merely unconscious. It is amazing that she bore the pain for so long."

The earl forced his eyes from his wife's pale face and gazed at the bloody ball. "It did not splinter?"

"No, thank God. My little Bella is very lucky." Dr. Branyon placed the blood-covered ball and his knife upon the table beside the bed. He straightened and ran his hand over his perspiring brow.

The earl wet a strip of linen and gently bathed away the blood from around the wound, and then with a grimace, washed away the purple rivulets from between her breasts.

"Hand me the basilicum powder, Justin. Then we will bandage her and fashion a sling for her arm."

The earl did as he was bid, surprised that his hands went so calmly about their tasks. Soon the bandage was in place around her shoulder and her arm supported in a sling of white linen. Dr. Branyon rose and placed his hand upon the earl's arm. "Well done, Justin. The bleeding is nearly stopped. With luck all we have to fear now is a fever."

The earl suddenly became aware that Arabella was still naked to the waist, her gown in shreds around her. "Her nightgown, Paul. I must dress her. I don't want Lady Ann to see her like this."

"No, not yet. Help me remove the rest of her clothing, then we will place only a light coverlet over her. I don't want to take any chances that the bleeding could begin again. No nightgown as yet."

After stripping Arabella, who lay as still as a statue, a white coverlet to her throat, the earl straightened.

"I'll stay with her, Paul. Perhaps you should go speak with Lady Ann and Elsbeth."

"Yes. Then I will bring Ann up to see her presently. Ann's solid. She won't break over this."

The earl nodded and turned his attention to his wife.

34

The earl took a deep drink of the strong black coffee Lady Ann handed to him. He set the cup in the saucer, never looking away from Arabella's face. He said finally, forcing himself to look away from her, "You look very tired, Ann. Why don't you go rest for a while? I'll be here. I'll fetch you if there is any change at all."

"No, Justin, I can't leave her, not yet. Just look at her—so utterly still. I don't believe I've ever seen Arabella still in her life. Even sleeping, she is so brimming with life, that you can practically see her moving even though she's really not. Her father once said that if she were a military man—and she would have been a general—soldiers would follow her even in her sleep. But now—oh God, I can't bear it." She broke off and lowered her face to her hands.

"Paul said she would survive, Ann. Both of us must believe him. Go rest." She got control of herself. She was not a woman to collapse. She wiped the tears off her cheeks. "I'm all right now. It's just that I love her so very much." She rose and walked to the windows. She flung open the long dark blue velvet curtains, tying them back with the thick golden cords. Sunlight flooded into the earl's bedchamber.

She turned to let the warm sunlight shine upon her face. "You know, Justin, Elsbeth has surprised me. I had thought that she would be quite upset, distraught really, for she is very sensitive, so delicate, yet she has been strangely calm. Until Paul came down, she sat in front of the fireplace gazing silently into the flames. It was Grace who was twitching about behind her. I thought the poor girl would weep when I came into the room, she was so relieved. It was Elsbeth who told me what happened, that Gervaise had come to Evesham Abbey to steal the emeralds, and for no other reason. She also told me that he had been her lover, but that he had told her she was merely a diversion for him, that she should just consider this summer as a brief *affaire de coeur,* nothing more. She said he told her that she must grow up now. She finished by saying that he'd been right. Now she was well on her way. I couldn't tell her that I'd already known, but it was difficult. I hated the pain in her, Justin. But it wasn't pain for herself, or for the mistake she'd made, no, it was something deeper, involving Arabella.

"And that's because she still believes it's all her fault that Gervaise shot her sister. That gave me something to sink my teeth into, let me tell you." Lady Ann told him the rest of it, thinking as she spoke back to the previous night, with just her and Elsbeth alone together. "I am proud of you, Elsbeth. You're strong, much stronger than I had ever imagined. You will live your life now a much wiser woman. You will accompany Dr. Branyon and me to London. There is life awaiting you, Elsbeth. You will do whatever you wish to do. Now you will look at people differently. You will judge them according to your new insights. But you mustn't be afraid or feel guilty, or any other destructive emotion. No, you must ready yourself to embrace life, only now you will perhaps see things a bit differently than you would have before."

"And do you think she will, Ann? Do you think she will recover from this and move ahead? Heal?"

"Yes, I do. As I said, Elsbeth seems stronger to me.

She also told me she wasn't pregnant, thank God. That would have posed a problem even for me."

He smiled at that until he realized he was smiling and it fell from his lips.

Lady Ann just shook her head at him and took a turn about the room to stretch her stiff muscles. She poured herself a cup of tea, disliking the black coffee, and walked to the bedside to look down upon her daughter. She placed her hand lightly on Arabella's brow. "Thank God, there is still no fever. I would dread Paul bleeding her, for she has lost so much blood already." She laughed, an actual laugh. "Do you know that Paul must have reminded me at least three times last night that Arabella has the constitution of a horse—a Lucifer-type horse?"

The earl said more to himself than to Lady Ann, "She was braver than most men I have seen wounded in battle. The pain was dreadful but she held herself in control. She was remarkable, Ann. I'm a very lucky man. And you are a very lucky mother."

Lady Ann said slowly, a reminiscent smile in her eyes, "She was always brave. I shall never forget the last time she was seriously hurt. Her father was in a black rage, ranting at her for falling like a clumsy idiot from her perch in the barn, yelling at her that it was unsafe and she wasn't ever to go there again."

The earl, who she had thought was not paying any particular attention, suddenly looked up. "The barn, Ann? You mean that private place of hers?"

"Ah, has she taken you there yet, Justin?"

He shook his head. "Not as yet, but she will. She has told me a little bit about it."

"It's one of her favorite haunts, as I'm sure you know. She never took her father seriously in his order and she was right, it was his fear that had made him try to protect her.

"It's this special hideaway in the very top of the

barn. There is this ladder just inside the front barn door
that leads up to the crawl way. She used to say it was
the most perfect spot for being alone—even better than
the old abbey ruins—for no one could hear her or see
her, and the stable hands could be milking cows below,
chattering away, but she wouldn't hear them. Yes, as a
child she would climb up the narrow crawlway whenever she wanted to be by herself. I shall never forget
that day—she could not have been more than ten years
old—when one of the boards gave way and she fell
some twenty feet to the ground, breaking her leg and
cracking two ribs. She was very lucky, for a broken
limb can result even in the best of circumstances in a
horrible limp."

"Is that when you fell in love with Paul Branyon?
When he managed to keep her leg straight and strong?"

"No, actually, I fell in love with him when I was in
labor with Arabella. It was a very long labor, but Paul
never left me. I do not believe I would have survived it
if not for him. He convinced me to fight, you see. He
has done so much for us over the years."

"Yes," the earl said. He set down his empty coffee
cup and sat close to Arabella again. "I believe he is at
this minute trying to save the comte. No, he isn't a
comte, he isn't an anything, but a damnable bastard—"

"What is this, Justin? What do you mean that Gervaise isn't the Comte de Trécassis?"

He cursed under his breath. He was so tired he was
no longer in control of his brains. He had simply forgotten that there were still several facts not known yet
to everyone. It was difficult to keep them all straight.
Well, now it was too late.

"Justin."

He gave it up. "Very well. When Arabella was
trapped in the old abbey ruins, she found a very old letter in the skeleton's pocket. His name was Charles. He

was Gervaise's father. Magdalaine was his mother and this man's lover."

She stared at him stunned for some moments before she realized what it meant. "Oh, no," Lady Ann said. "Oh, no. Elsbeth must never know, Justin, never."

"No, she won't. Indeed I hadn't intended to tell you. Arabella only told me because she was afraid she would die and she knew she could trust me. I suppose it really doesn't matter. Tell Paul, if you wish. I don't know what she did with the letter she found. There is one other thing. That man Charles and Magdalaine both died. Arabella didn't tell me sooner because of her loyalty to her father. If Gervaise hadn't shot her, I wonder if she would have ever said anything, even to me. She believes him a murderer, Ann, and bonds of loyalty are strong."

Lady Ann was pacing back and forth, pausing every step or so to look over at her daughter, still deeply asleep, held there by a large dose of laudanum.

"Do you know anything about this, Ann?"

"No. But if the earl believed himself to be betrayed, he wouldn't hesitate to act. Murder? No, that wouldn't be past him. I think now that it wouldn't be past me either. I think, though, that with another man, he would be more likely to fight a duel. He had complete confidence in himself. Utter complete confidence. What man could ever compete with him in the field of honor? Hopefully Arabella will be able to tell us more when she awakens."

If she awakens. In that moment, he couldn't bear it. He had to feel something of her that held her vibrancy, the echo of her spirit.

"I must go, Ann, for just a few minutes."

He left her staring after him.

The barnyard was bustling with early-morning activity as the Earl of Strafford, dressed only in breeches and

open, rumpled white linen shirt, made his way with
single purpose to the barn. Stable hands were busily
forking clumps of fresh hay into the wide wooden bins,
while the farm hands led out the fat, sleek cattle to pasture. His presence in the doorway called an abrupt, uncomfortable halt to all talk. Even the head stable lad,
Corey, said not a word.

He did not even notice that he was being eyed with
nervous skepticism. He slipped inside the barn and saw
immediately the small spindly ladder just to the left of
the door. He set his foot upon the first rung. He wasn't
even aware that the ladder creaked beneath his weight.
He climbed swiftly to the top, and stepped carefully
onto the narrow ledge that wound around to the far corner of the loft. He came presently to a tiny closed-off
area, almost a small room, that looked out over the
rolling hills behind the north pasture. It was a private
place, a place for thinking private thoughts, a place for
dreaming. Arabella came here when she wanted to be
alone. He breathed in deeply. Yes, he could feel her
here, but it was only the shadow of her, none of her intensity, none of what made her unique. This was where
she had been when he'd believed she had betrayed him
with Gervaise. He hated the ironies of Fate at that moment. If only he had never seen her, if only . . .

He stood silently for a moment longer. He could
faintly hear the sounds of the cows and the racket of
the stable hands.

Slowly he made his way back down the ladder and
out of the barn. He looked bleakly at the giant gnarled
oak tree where he had stood so long ago, witness to
what he had been certain was Arabella's betrayal. He
felt again his anger, his bitterness, and the overwhelming emptiness. He saw Arabella on their wedding night,
her face alight with anticipation until she had recognized his rage, until he had forced her, humiliated her.

He turned slowly and walked back to Evesham Abbey. He heard conversation from the Velvet Room and paused a moment. There were Lord Graybourn and Elsbeth. He was sitting next to her on the settee, holding her hand. He was speaking quietly to her and she was nodding.

Lord Graybourn took in the earl's disheveled appearance and the suffering in his eyes as he rose hurriedly from his seat beside Elsbeth. "Do forgive my intrusion, my lord. I had thought to stay with Lady Elsbeth for a brief while—to lighten her anxiety."

The earl did not have to force a smile. He was delighted the man was here. He was a good man, one who was caring. "You are very welcome, sir. I think it kind of you to take Elsbeth's mind off her sister." He turned as he spoke and gazed at Elsbeth with new vision, the vision Lady Ann had given him. She was right—there was none of the child left. There was a contained young woman seated on that settee, looking calmly at him. He wondered if he would miss the innocence of her, the childish gaiety she had displayed on occasion. If so, it was a pity, but life had a way of balancing the scales. Only time would tell. And perhaps Lord Graybourn.

He crossed to her and took her hands in his. "Arabella is sleeping soundly. She is made of stern stuff, you know, Elsbeth. She will come around."

She nodded, only a moment of pained dullness showing on her face. She said calmly, "Did you know that Dr. Branyon is upstairs with Arabella and Lady Ann?"

"No, I didn't know."

"He stepped in to tell me that Gervaise had died. Dr. Branyon said there hadn't been much hope, that he had lost too much blood."

"It is over then." The earl felt a moment of sadness for the waste of a young man's life. Greed was the very devil.

"Yes, it is over. I am sorry that he is dead, but perhaps he deserved to die for shooting Arabella."

"The shot was aimed for me, Elsbeth. Arabella saved my life."

"Elsbeth," Lord Graybourn said, moving swiftly to seat himself beside her. "I don't wish you to tire yourself. Should you care for some more tea, perhaps?"

The earl did not wait to hear Elsbeth's reply. Gervaise had died. He couldn't find another moment of pain, not really. the man had nearly destroyed their lives. He quickly strode from the Velvet Room and back to the earl's bedchamber.

"Ah, Justin, you are here." Paul Branyon straightened beside Arabella. "She has no fever. She is breathing slowly and smoothly. If there continues to be no fever, she will recover quickly."

The earl sagged where he stood. "I was scared to death. For the first time though, I believe you."

"Good. Oh, incidentally, Gervaise is dead."

"Yes, Elsbeth told me."

"There is something else." Dr. Branyon reached into his coat pocket and pulled out the emerald necklace. "I removed these from the comte's jacket pocket." He tossed them to Justin, who just stood looking down at them overflowing the palm of his hand.

"Bloody damned things," he said. "If only I had said something sooner, perhaps it would have made the difference, but I didn't tell Gervaise the truth. No, I strung him along, mocked him, and look what happened."

"What truth, Justin?" Lady Ann asked. "What are you talking about?"

Before the earl could answer, there was a gentle, almost childlike moan from Arabella.

35

"She never got the fever," Dr. Branyon said with a good deal of satisfaction. He wasn't about to tell her that he also was so relieved he'd sworn good deeds for the remainder of his days. "Yes, it is just as I told you, Ann, she has the constitution of a horse."

He had just changed the bandage, nodded his approval, and straightened to wash his hands in the basin that the earl held out for him.

"A horse, you say, sir? You don't even allow me to be a mare? A pretty filly?"

"Not you, Bella, and be grateful for it. Now, of course, don't mistake. It was I who brought you through it, not all by myself, for Justin was here occasionally, wringing his hands, and your mother sometimes stuck her head in and asked me how you were."

Arabella actually managed to laugh. "You are too outrageous to be my step-papa," she said, and took Justin's hand. She pulled him down to sit beside her on the bed. "Did you really just visit me occasionally? Did you really wring your hands? Just a bit?"

"At least once a day for a good five minutes," he said as he leaned down and kissed her mouth. "The same with the hand wringing." She raised her hand to touch his face, remembered that her mother and soon-to-be stepfather were standing just beyond Justin, and let her hand drop back to the cover. "It's good to be alive. Thank all of you very much. How is Elsbeth?"

"She is doing very well now that she is convinced you're on the mend," Lady Ann said. "Don't worry about her, Arabella. Everything that should have been said to her has been and anything that didn't have to be said, wasn't."

The earl whistled. "That was very convoluted, Ann. It says a great deal for my intelligence that I gleaned your meaning."

"I'm relieved," Arabella said. In the next minute, she was asleep.

"So relieved," the earl said, "that she dropped off to sleep on us."

"Justin, really. You are being quite ridiculous. I am certainly strong enough to walk across the bedroom." Arabella's protest didn't appear to have any result at all. He just grinned down at her and kept walking to the comfortable settee that he had moved to beside the window. It was a sunny afternoon, thank the beneficent God.

"There, madam," he said, gently easing her down. He plumped her pillow. He drew a light afghan over her legs to her waist. She was wearing a seductive peach silk peignoir that he had very carefully eased her into. She had no idea how it made her look. He took a very deep steadying breath and said, "Did I tell you yet today that you are incredibly beautiful?"

"Yes, this morning, first thing when I opened my eyes. But I thought you were overdoing it. As I recall, my hair was falling across my face."

"Did I tell you that you are more precious to me than my gun collection?"

"Not yet. However, I do not want you to feel coerced. If you don't wish to say that just yet, I will understand. Perhaps you should work up to that, my lord, for it is a big step."

"All right then," he said as he pulled a chair up next to her and sat down. "I will take your advice and not rush things." He leaned forward then, kissed her, lightly ran his fingertips over her nose, her cheeks, the line of her jaw. "If you are truly worthy, I will even wash your hair for you."

He saw the excitement in her gray eyes. Her hair was on the edge, a thick braid laying limp over her shoulder. "I should like that more than anything. Tell me how to be worthy enough."

That was a kick right to his groin. "Ah, I cannot have that expectation of you just yet. Like my gun collection, it must wait a while."

She didn't understand and he hadn't really expected her to. He gave her a shameless grin and patted her cheek. "All right, perhaps this evening. No, don't argue. I want you to rest here for a good long time, then we will dine together. If you still look as kissable tonight as you do right now, I will allow you to have your way."

She smiled at him, very possibly the most beautiful smile he had ever been granted in his life. He drew a deep breath, kissed her again and once more, then straightened at the sound of a throat clearing in the doorway.

"Ah, Paul, you are here to annoy us?"

Arabella tried to pull the afghan higher. The pain from the simple movement made her wince.

The earl gently raised her hand and laid it beside her again. "I told you I expect you to rest. Any strain on your shoulder isn't on the list. Obey me, Arabella, or I will let Paul do something vile to you."

"At least you have finally allowed me a nightgown."

"I didn't particularly want to," the earl said, kissing her yet again, "but Paul insisted. He told me that he didn't want me distracted in that manner, not for another good two weeks."

"Did I really say that?" Dr. Branyon said, coming to them. "My dear," he said, and immediately laid his palm on her forehead. Then he leaned down to listen to her heart. Finally, he lifted her wrist. "Ah," he said finally. "I am such a good physician that I have even surprised myself. It's been only a week and just look at you, Bella. Looking beautiful and soft as butter. Here's your even more beautiful mother. Ann, come here and treat your daughter to your presence."

Arabella laughed. Another laugh, the earl thought, so pleased he wanted to shout with it.

Dr. Branyon briefly examined her shoulder, then straightened again, nodding. "Excellent, just excellent."

Lady Ann patted her daughter's hand. "I would have brought Elsbeth with me, but she is riding with Lord Graybourn. Naturally he is no longer staying at Talgarth Hall. That would be pushing Aurelia's good nature far too far. No, he is currently residing at The Traitor's Crown, in the very best room Mrs. Current could manage. Now, my darling, tell me. Have these two gentlemen been provoking you?"

"Oh no, Mama, even Dr. Branyon hasn't prodded me too much. As for my lord here, why, he has promised to wash my hair for me tonight."

"That's true," the earl said, "but only if she obeys me. In all things."

Lady Ann blinked at this, then chuckled. "This besotted peace between the two of you is beginning to alarm me. It isn't natural somehow. Arabella, please regain your strength soon. I want you to stand toe to toe to Justin again. I want to hear the two of you yelling at each other."

"Never," said the earl.

"Oh no, Mama," said Arabella. "He is a saint. He is perfect."

Lady Ann began counting off fingers.

"What are you doing, Mama?"

"I am deciding how many days from now my wish will be granted. I even will make a wager on it. I think eight days and then the two of you will be ready for a good shouting match. I do look forward to it. It will be time to make Evesham Abbey a home again."

"That is one way of looking at things," the earl said.

"Eight days, Mama? That's all you give us?"

"It just might be sufficient," the earl said, and clasped her fingers.

"I just remembered something," Dr. Branyon said suddenly to the earl. "Justin, you were on the point of telling Ann and me something when Arabella woke. What was that? Yes, I know it was five days ago. Do you remember if it was important? I remember you said something about if only you hadn't strung the comte along, then perhaps things would have happened differently."

The earl released Arabella's fingers. "I had completely forgotten about them. Just a moment, please." He rose and walked to the small desk that was in the far corner of the huge bedchamber. He came back carrying the emerald and diamond necklace. The green stones glittered in the bright sunlight.

"The necklace?" Arabella said. "What does that have to do with anything?"

"That night when we faced down Gervaise I was holding out the emeralds in my hand, taunting him with them. Then I tossed them to him as if they meant nothing at all. Well, the truth is that the emeralds are worthless. They're paste, as are the diamonds. That is what I should have told him. If he had known that, perhaps he wouldn't have chosen the path he did."

"Actually," Arabella said after a moment, "I don't think it would have made much difference. I think it would have served only to enrage him all the more, that is, if he had even believed you."

"You're right," the earl said after a moment, his gray eyes brilliant. "He wouldn't have believed me, not for an instant. Had I been here I wouldn't have believed me either."

"Paste," Lady Ann said. She took the emeralds from him and held them up in the sunlight. "Paste. All this misery over a paste necklace of next to no value at all. Obviously Magdalaine's parents knew they were paste when they gave them to her to bring back to your father, Arabella. Remember, they were supposedly part of her dowry? And they gave their daughter a worthless necklace to give to her husband. Surely they couldn't have believed the late earl wouldn't have noticed. Ah, but the violence was escalating in France." Lady Ann shook her head as she stared at the emeralds. "*Paste*. It boggles the mind."

"And that damned necklace has stayed snug in the *Dance of Death* panel all these years," Dr. Branyon said. "Waiting to be found. I wish the damned thing had never existed in the first place."

Suddenly a tear rolled down Arabella's cheek. "Don't, love," the earl said, and gently drew her into his arms. "Don't cry. Will you trust me?"

She nodded, gulping back the tears, but still they fell, one after the other.

"Good, I want all of you to hear this. You know that I searched Gervaise's room that afternoon of the Talgarth ball. I found a letter to Gervaise from his uncle, Thomas de Trécassis, Magdalaine's brother. Obviously he had no idea that the necklace was worthless. It was in that letter that I learned exactly where the necklace was. But that's not what's really important. What's really important is another letter, one that fell out of Arabella's slipper when I was undressing her after she'd been shot."

"No, Justin, no."

"Please, trust me. There's nothing for you to fear. Trust me." She didn't want to, but he was holding her hand, he was looking at her intently, willing her to believe in him. Finally, she nodded.

"Paul," the earl said, "please read this letter. It is from Magdalaine to her lover, Charles, the skeleton Arabella found in the old abbey ruins."

Dr. Branyon took the creased and yellowed piece of foolscap. He smoothed it out as best he could. He walked to the window so that the sunlight poured in on it. He was silent for a goodly amount of time, sometimes frowning, sometimes puzzling over words he couldn't make out. Finally, he raised his head. "This is incredible, really incredible. Bella, my dear, you have been terrified to tell anyone of what you had found?"

"He was my father. I loved him. I told Justin because I thought I might die. But this paints him as a vicious murderer. Please, promise me that it will not go beyond this room."

"It won't," the earl said. "But it is time, Arabella, for us all to know the truth. Paul, can you tell us?"

"Yes, I can see that it is time. Magdalaine returned from France only to fetch Elsbeth. Then she and her lover would have probably fled to the Colonies. She must have brought the emerald necklace with her.

"Your father must have caught them. His wife had betrayed him, had stolen their child, and was fleeing with her lover. He would have been enraged. Yes, it would appear likely that he did shoot this Charles. But there is no dishonor in that.

"But listen to me, Bella, your father did not murder Magdalaine. She killed herself. I was here. I was with her all during her final hours. I won't lie to you and tell you that your father loved her and was devastated that she had tried to leave him, for at the end he didn't. She had betrayed him. He did not kill Magdalaine, although from reading this letter I can imagine how you drew such a conclusion. No, she killed herself. I swear it to you. She must have hidden the emeralds and written their hiding place to her brother before your father knew her intentions. She believed they would be her birthright to her son, Gervaise." He paused, then drew a deep breath. "No, he bore no love for her but he did not kill her."

Her tears stopped, though she still didn't look up. Justin saw the flash of pain in her eyes and knew her shoulder was hurting her. He said nothing. He would let her gain her own control.

She said then, "I have had this incredible burden of doubt and uncertainty lifted from my heart. All along you knew, sir, yet it never occurred to me to ask you."

"Had you asked, Bella, I am not certain I would have told you the truth. It was a long time ago. She was my patient. But now, to clear all this mystery away, well, I am certain she wouldn't have minded."

Lady Ann said, "But how did you know, Justin? No, don't try to deny it. Never would you have taken such a chance without knowing the answer first. Tell us, how could you be so certain that the earl did not kill her?"

He shrugged, saying simply, "He told me several years ago, not any of the details, of course, merely that his first wife had taken her own life. I could not be certain that you would believe me, so I asked Dr. Branyon to tell you."

Dr. Branyon said, "I think it time you destroyed this letter, Justin. No one need know anything. As for all our neighbors, I have already begun spreading it about that Gervaise was a desperate young man who had somehow discovered the existence of the emeralds. Indeed, to further dampen rumors and gossip, Ann and I have both told certain people that the gun went off by accident. As for Gervaise, we have simply said that he was shot trying to escape with the necklace."

"I had not even thought of doing that," the earl said. "Thank you both."

Dr. Branyon smiled down at Arabella. "Now, young

lady, you need to rest. No, do not gainsay me, for I have a formidable ally in your husband. Also he tells me that he will wash your hair for you if you are obedient." He passed the palm of his hand over her cool forehead. "Yes indeed, there can be no finer physician in the county."

Dr. Branyon and Lady Ann left the earl's bedchamber, arm in arm.

"Now, do you swear you will always trust me?"

She gave him a long assessing look. Slowly, she pulled him down to her and whispered in his ear, "Did I tell you about the second letter, Justin?"

He could but stare at her. "You little tease, by God but that was well done. My heart had plummeted to my toes. Promise me, Arabella. There is no second anything, is there?"

"No," she said and laughed. Her shoulder had been paining her, but her laughter had made it feel better.

He kissed the tip of her nose. "When we are not yelling at each other, do you think we could laugh together?"

"I should like that very much," she said. "It hurts my shoulder to pull you down to me. Could you come to me willingly now?"

He did, kissing her until she was breathing rapidly and her eyes were vague. He lightly laid his palm over her breast. Her heartbeat was quite fast. He grinned down at her. Between small nipping kisses, he said, "Life is really very nice, isn't it?"

COMING IN NOVEMBER

One

A night of intermittent rain showers had served to freshen the morning that burst on London one summer day in the year of our Lord, 1817. Dawn spread her banners across an amethyst sky as the sun rose to touch first the city's church spires with golden fire, then the humbler dwellings of mortals. At last a single beam of radiance stole through the curtains of an elegant Mayfair town house to bathe the admirable figure of Charles Trent, fifth Earl of Bythorne, Viscount Spring, Baron Trent of Grantham, of Creed and Whitlow—who sat on the edge of his bed with his head in his hands.

He was getting too old for this sort of thing, by God. He had arrived home only minutes before. When he had gone to Vivienne's dinner party the night before, he had only a few hours of dalliance in mind, but the beautiful widow had been desirous of much more. Lord, her demands—on his time, his energy, and his purse—were growing untenable.

Perhaps it was time to end that particular liaison. The Earl of Tenby's sadly neglected wife had been sending out some interesting lures lately.

Thorne sighed. On the other hand, the young countess, though undoubtedly a diamond of the first water, was also young and very silly. Perhaps he should reestablish his connection with Maria Stafford. She

Copyright © Barbara Yirka, 1996

was a bit on the hard side, and selfish as she could hold
together, but, in her favor—besides a complaisant husband—she was thirtyish—near to his own age, in fact,
and an excellent conversationalist and a comfortable
companion.

Good God, he thought in dismay. Had it come to
this? Was he actually weighing his potential mistresses
on a comfort scale? Had the thrill of the chase and the
sensuous delights of victory given way to the desire
for—for what? Friendship? He snorted. He had enough
friends.

Thorne bent his thoughts once more to the delectable
Countess of Tenby, she of the ripe, thrusting bosom
and swinging hips. He thought of the little pink tongue
that slid out to moisten full pink lips and felt a gratifying tightening of his loins. Comfortable, hell. He still
knew what he wanted from a woman, and it wasn't
conversation.

With this conviction turning reassuringly in his
brain, he prepared to sink into the softness of his bed,
only to be deterred by a scratching at his door, followed almost immediately by the entrance of a soberly
clad gentleman whose anxious demeanor seemed at
odds with features that seemed almost cherubic in their
insouciance. In a hand that fairly shook with agitation,
he carried what appeared to be a note.

"My lord?" whispered this apparition.

"What is it, Williams?" asked Thorne wearily.

"It's Miss Chloe, my lord. Her maid just brought this
to me."

He waved the paper before him as though it had suddenly caught fire, and advanced into the room. Hastily,
he thrust the note at his employer.

"Now what?" Thorne distastefully eyed the wrinkled
missive, noting the blotches and the tearstains with
which it was liberally embellished.

" *'My lord,'* " he read aloud. " *'I can no longer bear*

your unfeeling interference in my life.' " Thorne cast his eyes heavenward. "Good Lord, more histrionics," he muttered. " *'Now, you have committed the cruelest transgression of all. I tell you again, my lord, I will not be shackled at your whim to a man I do not even know. Your complete disregard for my feelings, as well as your contempt for everything I hold sacred has driven me to flee your tyranny.' "* The earl glanced at his valet with foreboding. "My God, don't tell me . . ." He trailed off, his eyes once more on the note. " *'I have, therefore, left your dubious protection to seek sanctuary with One Who Will Understand. Do not attempt to pursue me, for my mind is made up. You won't find me, anyway,' "* read the last sentence, somewhat smugly. " *'Yours truly, Chloe Venable.' "*

Rising, Thorne swore long and fluently. "The little twit! I might have known she'd try something like this. How long has she been gone?"

"I could not say, my lord. Pinkham seems to feel that she departed the house late last night after all of us— er, that is," he added with a sidelong glance at his master, "most of us—were asleep, for the young lady's bed has not been slept in."

Thorne sighed heavily. "Well, there's nothing for it. I'll have to go after her. Does Chloe's maid—what's her name—Pinkham?—have any idea where she might have scarpered to?"

"No, my lord. She has any number of friends here in London, but surely the parents of these young ladies would not act as accomplices. And, of course, she has no close relatives."

The earl, removing his lace-trimmed cravat, nodded grimly. "The devil take it, Williams, the chit has brought me nothing but grief since her arrival here. It's only been a few months, but it seems like a lifetime."

"Indeed, my lord," replied the valet, divesting the earl of his rumpled evening clothes so that he might garb himself in more appropriate daywear. "Being saddled with a ward of—of so nubile an age has proved an onerous responsibility."

Williams offered a discreet sigh.

"I suppose you'd better roust Aunt Lavinia," said Thorne, winding a fresh cravat about his neck. "She will no doubt expire from the vapors when she hears the news, but perhaps she will have some clue as to where Chloe has loped off to."

The valet bowed himself from the room and Thorne repaired to Chloe's bedchamber, where he began flinging open drawers and cupboard doors. All to no avail. She had left nothing behind to tell him of her whereabouts. A search of the little rosewood desk that stood near her bed was more fruitful, however. Thrust in a far corner of the uppermost drawer was a faintly drawn, hurriedly sketched map. Perusing it carefully, Thorne exclaimed in disgust. Why, it depicted the area around his country seat, Bythorne Park near Guildford, not twenty miles from here. Chloe must have drawn the map last month, when they had spent a week there. Thorne peered more closely at the names of nearby villages laboriously marked on the paper. The road wound past them all, coming to an end near the top of the map at a village called—what was it—Overby? Oddsbeck? He tossed the paper aside impatiently and for several moments stood in the center of the room running his fingers through soft dark hair that already looked as though it had been churned by a baker's whisk. He moved to the fireplace, but realized after a moment's stirring of the ashes that everything that had been placed there in the recent past had been thoroughly burned. Except . . . A single, charred piece of paper fluttered in the draft created by the flue.

Ah, good, he could read the date—only a week previous. And it had been written to Chloe. The rest of the missive, unfortunately, had been almost wholly consumed by the fire.

" '—how very pleased I was—' " he muttered, searching for readable fragments. " '—heartened by your—please do come—understand your—' Wait a minute. 'Please do come?' " His gaze swept to the bottom of the letter, but the signature was unreadable. Underneath, however, the writer had scribbled, "Rosemere Cottage," and the name of a village, which was also virtually indecipherable. The first letter, he was almost sure, was O—or D—or possibly C, and then an "m," perhaps or a "w" or a "v." Overcross! The name fairly leaped into his mind.

"Overcross." He tasted the name on his lips. Where had he heard it before? Turning, he scooped up the map from where he had tossed it on the floor. Yes, he was sure the name at the top of the map was Overcross, as well, but where had he heard it before? The village was not a great distance from the Park, but far enough so that it was unfamiliar to him. Yet—he was sure he had heard of it, and not too long ago.

He paced the floor, the map clutched in one hand, the letter in the other. His desperate ruminations were cut short a moment later as the bedchamber door opened to admit a short, plump woman whose feathery gray hair escaped in tufts from a cap tied sadly askew.

"Bythorne! What has happened? Williams told me—" Her gaze swept about the room. "Oh, merciful heavens. It's true! She has flown! Oh, the ungrateful little wretch! I believe I'm going to have a spasm! Beddoes, my vinaigrette!"

Holding a hand to her pillowy breast, she sank down on the bed, gesturing wildly to the maid who had hurried into the room behind her. Thorne crossed the room to seat himself beside her.

"Aunt Lavinia, you must not excite yourself so. I will find her. There, there," he said soothingly, patting his aunt's hand as she continued to bemoan her charge's perfidy. Lady Lavinia St. John, his mother's sister and a spinster of some fifty years, had acted as his chatelaine ever since the death of his parents, some years previously. She was a master of domestic arrangements and had kept Bythorne Park running smoothly for years. When he'd requested that she come to live with him in London to act as chaperone for his newly acquired ward, she had acceded without demur. Unfortunately, she was not a disciplinarian, and young Chloe had run virtually roughshod over all her well-intentioned precepts. Poor Aunt Lavinia, mused Thorne fleetingly. She did not merit this sort of chaos in her declining years. He augmented the hand-patting with a few more, "There, there."

When, at last, the lady's bosom began to heave less spasmodically, he asked, "Do you have any idea where Chloe might have gone?"

At her woeful shake of her head, he continued. "Does the name Overcross mean anything to you? I believe it's a village some distance to the north of Bythorne Park."

"Overcross? Overcross." She repeated the word several times, until at last enlightenment spread across her comfortable features. "Yes. Chloe traveled there last spring when we visited the Park. There is some woman living there whom she—just a moment."

She rose and moved to a shelf of books hung above the desk. Removing a volume, she returned to the bed. "Yes," she continued, reading from the cover. "It was this female—this Hester Blayne."

She handed the book to Thorne, who read aloud. " *'Women's Rights: An Apologia.'* Good God!" He dropped the book as though it had bitten him.

"You are familiar with the name?" asked his aunt.

"Of course. Good God," he said again. "Hester

Blayne is one of the most vocal of that incomprehensible breed, English feminists."

"Yes." Lady Lavinia nodded bemusedly. "Besides this book, Miss Blayne has written several others, all espousing the betterment of women—and two or three novels, as well, on the same theme. Chloe is a great admirer of Miss Blayne's. She has attended several of her lectures here in Town, and in April, while we were at the Park, it was all I could do to prevent her from haring up to see the female at her home—which apparently is in Overcross."

"I remember now." Thorne clenched his fingers. "Chloe nattered on at me for days to allow her to visit the Blayne woman—although I didn't pay much attention to her name at the time." He rose from his seat on the bed. "It's obvious that's where she's gone, but— Good Lord, how did she get there?"

"Well," snapped his aunt, "I wouldn't put it past the little wretch to simply hire a hackney to take her to White Horse Cellars, where all the coaches depart for Surrey. Oh, dear, Bythorne, she did not take her maid, so she must have set out on her own. Oh, merciful heavens, what if something has happened to her—a young girl traveling by herself . . . At the very least, she will be ruined."

"Not if I can help it," replied Thorne grimly. "If I set off now, I shall be in Overcross by this afternoon, and I shall have her back home before anyone is the wiser."

Thus, it was only a very short time later that vehicles and passersby on the Portsmouth Road were treated to the sight of the Earl of Bythorne's famous red and black racing curricle flashing southward from London.

It was some hours later in the same day that England's premier feminist, Miss Hester Blayne, knelt in the front garden of her cottage just outside the village of Overcross. She presented a rather unprepossessing figure, or she was of less than average height and slender of 'orm. Tendrils of brown hair, escaping from under a neat linen cap, drifted about absurdly youthful features, 'or her upturned nose and rounded chin belied her eight and twenty years. At the moment, she presented an even more nondescript appearance than usual. Garbed in sturdy boots and a serviceable muslin gown, she was engaged in a vigorous program of weed removal from her front garden.

She had been hard at this task for most of the afternoon and she felt almost drugged by the sun and the sweet summer scents of the afternoon. She lifted her head at a sound from the cottage.

"Hester!" An elderly woman stood at the doorway, peering nearsightedly into the blazing warmth.

"Here, Larkie. Come see what I've accomplished."

"Good heavens, child. You've been out here for hours. Why didn't you let the new servant girl attend to this? You said you planned to work all day on your book."

Hester stood and stretched muscles pleasantly tired from her exertions.

"Perkins has been busy all day in the kitchen with Cook, I think, and I simply had to get out into this glorious day. I'm well ahead of my deadline for once, so I decided to play truant."

The older woman smiled fondly. "Well, you'd best come in. The vicar's wife will probably be dropping by sometime soon. She said she would stop on her way back from the village with the embroidery floss she promised she'd pick up for me."

"I'll stop in a minute, Larkie. I just want to finish this border."

Miss Larkin made no response, but smiled and returned to the cottage.

Hester experienced a wave of contentment as she bent once more to her task. Her life, she thought with

pardonable satisfaction, had never progressed s
smoothly. The leap from her early days as an underpai
governess with a burning hunger to redress the outra
geous treatment of women in England to her presen
position as the foremost proponent of feminism in th
country had been made in giant strides. Such was he
success as a writer and speaker that she was at last f
nancially independent of her family.

Her mouth twisted as she recalled the words he
brother had spoken to her not a month earlier.

"Really, Hezzie, I wash my hands of you. If you per
sist in making us all a laughingstock, I have no choic
but to cut the connection. You can't know what it'
like to have people point at you, saying 'There goe
Sir Barnaby Blayne. Pleasant fellow, but his sister i
demented.' "

She had replied wearily, "Barney, do what you mus
I haven't accepted a penny from you in ten years, no
do I plan to avail myself of your dubious largesse
any time in the future. If you are so concerned abou
what people are saying, why don't you just leave m
alone?"

Indignation had sparked in her brother's pale gra
eyes as he spoke. "Because—well, demmit, Hezzi
you're still m'sister. I don't like to see you making
public quiz of yourself—even if you don't seem t
mind it."

Hester had been forced to laugh. "No, I don't mind
at all. You will be surprised to learn, Barney, that ther
are a number of people in this country who applaud m
work."

"Nobody who counts for anything," replied Barne
promptly, thus destroying the brief moment of amit
that had flickered between them. Since that momen
she had seen nothing of him, or his wife, the officiou
Belinda, nor her own two sisters, both of whom wer
firmly planted beneath Sir Barnaby's thumb.

Well, so be it, thought Hester. She was happy here in her snug cottage, with her books and her friends, of whom she numbered some of the foremost intellectuals of the day. And there was Larkie. God bless the day she had accrued enough money to rescue her former nurse from her dismal flat in one of London's seamier neighborhoods.

Hester smiled, but almost immediately afterward her lip turned downward. There was one minor cloud on her horizon. Well, perhaps not so minor. Her bequest from an indulgent aunt and the money she earned from her writings and lectures paid for most of the necessities of her life but there were other expenses that were a constant worry. The cottage mortgage, for example. The payments were not heavy, but every month she found that in order to meet them, other problems were ignored. The roof had been extensively patched and now it had become evident that a new one was needed. The chimney was in desperate need of cleaning—and Larkie needed new spectacles.

She sighed. Perhaps she should have embarked on another novel instead of a work of pure philosophy. The novels, of which she had published three, had proved unexpectedly successful, and, while yet another tome on the plight of women in England would garner a substantial readership, it would not be nearly so profitable. It was not too late to abandon the heavier work, entitled *Women as an Underclass,* in favor of another novel, but Hester felt compelled to produce something more serious at this point.

Hester leaned back on her heels, brushing the earth from her stained fingers. She remained so for a moment, her thoughts still on her financial difficulties. She had promised her publisher to finish *Women as an Underclass* in record time so that she could start on another novel, one that was to be much more gothic in nature and would, he assured her, make them both a

staggering amount of money. As a rule, she abhorre
the gothic genre, but—

"You, there! Girl! Run inside and fetch your mistress!

In her abstraction, Hester had not heard the rattle of
horse and carriage, but she jumped at the peremptor
insistence of the masculine voice. Good God, was h
speaking to her?

"I said, you there! I wish to speak to the mistress of
the house."

Fire building in her eyes, Hester turned to behold
very large, extremely angry man bearing down on her

A Rake's Reform by Anne Barbour

Have you read a Signet Regency lately?

Available at your local bookstore or call
1-800-253-6476 to order directly with
Visa or Mastercard

MORE FASCINATING ROMANCES BY CATHERINE COULTER

from **TOPAZ**

Rebel Bride   (404327—$4.99)
Lord Harry   (405919—$5.99)
The Duke   (406176—$6.99)
The Heir   (188616—$6.99)

CONTEMPORARY ROMANCES from **ONYX**

Beyond Eden   (403398—$5.99)
False Pretenses   (401271—$5.99)
Impulse   (402502—$5.99)

Buy them at your local bookstore or use this convenient coupon for ordering.

PENGUIN USA
P.O. Box 999 — Dept. #17109
Bergenfield, New Jersey 07621

Please send me the books I have checked above.
I am enclosing $_____ (please add $2.00 to cover postage and handling). Send check or money order (no cash or C.O.D.'s) or charge by Mastercard or VISA (with a $15.00 minimum). Prices and numbers are subject to change without notice.

Card #_____ Exp. Date _____
Signature_____
Name_____
Address_____
City _____ State _____ Zip Code _____

For faster service when ordering by credit card call **1-800-253-6476**

Allow a minimum of 4-6 weeks for delivery. This offer is subject to change without notice.

SWEEPING ROMANCE by Catherine Coulter

☐ **EARTH SONG.** Spirited Philippa de Beauchamp fled her ancestra manor rather than wed the old and odious lord that her domineerin father had picked for her. But she found peril of a different kind whe she fell into the hands of a rogue lord, handsome, cynical Dienwald c Fortenberry. . . . (402065—$4.9

☐ **FIRE SONG.** Marriage had made Graelam the master of Kassia's bo but now a rising fire-hot need demanded more than submission. I must claim her complete surrender with the dark ecstasy of love. . . . (402383—$4.9

☐ **SECRET SONG.** Stunning Daria de Fortesque was the prize in a strugg between two ruthless earls, one wanting her for barter, the other f pleasure. But there was another man who wanted Daria, too, for a entirely different reason. . . . (402340—$4.9

☐ **CHANDRA.** Lovely golden-haired Chandra, raised to handle weapons a well as any man, was prepared to defend herself against anything . until the sweet touch of Jerval de Veron sent the scarlet fires of lo raging through her blood. . . . (158814—$4.9

☐ **DEVIL'S EMBRACE.** The seething city of Genoa seemed a world away fro the great 18th-century estate where Cassandra was raised. But here sl met Anthony, and became addicted to a feverish ecstasy that would gui their hearts forever. . . . (141989—$4.9

☐ **DEVIL'S DAUGHTER.** Arabella had never imagined that Kamal, the savag sultan who dared make her a harem slave, would look so like a blor Nordic god. She had never dreamed that his savage love could make h passion's slave. . . . (158636—$4.9

Prices slightly higher in Canada

Buy them at your local bookstore or use this convenient coupon for ordering.

PENGUIN USA
P.O. Box 999 — Dept. #17109
Bergenfield, New Jersey 07621

Please send me the books I have checked above.
I am enclosing $_____ (please add $2.00 to cover postage and handling Send check or money order (no cash or C.O.D.'s) or charge by Mastercard VISA (with a $15.00 minimum). Prices and numbers are subject to change witho notice.

Card # _____ Exp. Date _____
Signature_____
Name_____
Address_____
City _____ State _____ Zip Code _____
For faster service when ordering by credit card call **1-800-253-6476**
Allow a minimum of 4-6 weeks for delivery. This offer is subject to change without notic

WE NEED YOUR HELP

To continue to bring you quality romance
that meets your personal expectations,
we at TOPAZ books want to hear from you.
Help us by filling out this questionnaire, and in exchange
we will give you a **free gift** as a token of our gratitude.

Is this the first TOPAZ book you've purchased? (circle one)

     YES   NO

The title and author of this book is: _____

If this was not the first TOPAZ book you've purchased, how many have
you bought in the past year?

     a: 0 - 5   b 6 - 10   c: more than 10   d: more than 20

How many romances in total did you buy in the past year?

     a: 0 - 5   b: 6 - 10   c: more than 10   d: more than 20 _____

How would you rate your overall satisfaction with this book?

     a: Excellent   b: Good   c: Fair   d: Poor

What was the main reason you bought this book?

     a: It is a TOPAZ novel, and I know that TOPAZ stands
        for quality romance fiction
     b: I liked the cover
     c: The story-line intrigued me
     d: I love this author
     e: I really liked the setting
     f: I love the cover models
     g: Other: _____

Where did you buy this TOPAZ novel?

     a: Bookstore   b: Airport   c: Warehouse Club
     d: Department Store   e: Supermarket   f: Drugstore
     g: Other: _____

Did you pay the full cover price for this TOPAZ novel? (circle one)

     YES   NO

If you did not, what price did you pay? _____

Who are your favorite TOPAZ authors? (Please list)

How did you first hear about TOPAZ books?

     a: I saw the books in a bookstore
     b: I saw the TOPAZ Man on TV or at a signing
     c: A friend told me about TOPAZ
     d: I saw an advertisement in_____magazine
     e: Other: _____

What type of romance do you generally prefer?

     a: Historical   b: Contemporary
     c: Romantic Suspense   d: Paranormal (time travel,
        futuristic, vampires, ghosts, warlocks, etc.)
     d: Regency   e: Other: _____

What historical settings do you prefer?

     a: England   b: Regency England   c: Scotland
     e: Ireland   f: America   g: Western Americana
     h: American Indian   i: Other: _____

- What type of story do you prefer?

    a: Very sexy   b: Sweet, less explicit
    c: Light and humorous   d: More emotionally intense
    e: Dealing with darker issues   f: Other

- What kind of covers do you prefer?

    a: Illustrating both hero and heroine   b: Hero alone
    c: No people (art only)   d: Other_____

- What other genres do you like to read (circle all that apply)

    Mystery   Medical Thrillers   Science Fiction
    Suspense   Fantasy   Self-help
    Classics   General Fiction   Legal Thrillers
    Historical Fiction

- Who is your favorite author, and why?_____
  _____

- What magazines do you like to read? (circle all that apply)

    a: *People*   b: *Time/Newsweek*
    c: *Entertainment Weekly*   d: *Romantic Times*
    e: *Star*   f: *National Enquirer*
    g: *Cosmopolitan*   h: *Woman's Day*
    i: *Ladies' Home Journal*   j: *Redbook*
    k: Other:_____

- In which region of the United States do you reside?

    a: Northeast   b: Midatlantic   c: South
    d: Midwest   e: Mountain   f: Southwest
    g: Pacific Coast

- What is your age group/sex?   a: Female   b: Male

    a: under 18   b: 19-25   c: 26-30   d: 31-35   e: 36-40
    f: 41-45   g: 46-50   h: 51-55   i: 56-60   j: Over 60

- What is your marital status?

    a: Married   b: Single   c: No longer married

- What is your current level of education?

    a: High school   b: College Degree
    c: Graduate Degree   d: Other: _____

- Do you receive the TOPAZ *Romantic Liaisons* newsletter, a quarterly
  newsletter with the latest information on Topaz books and authors?

    YES   NO

  If not, would you like to?   YES   NO

  Fill in the address where you would like your free gift to be sent:

  Name: _____
  Address: _____
  City:_____ Zip Code: _____

  You should receive your free gift in 6 to 8 weeks.
  Please send the completed survey to:

Penguin USA•Mass Market
Dept. TS
375 Hudson St.
New York, NY 10014